THE MOONLIGHT CHILD

KAREN MCQUESTION

PRAISE FOR THE BOOKS OF KAREN MCQUESTION

"*Good Man, Dalton* is a sweet confection you'll savor as Midwesterner Greta Hansen arrives in New York City for a job that doesn't exist—and discovers something better than money or fame." —Christine Nolfi, author of *The Road She Left Behind*

"I was riveted to the page and on occasion brought to tears. A book you don't want to miss."—Barbara Taylor Sissel, bestselling author of *Faultlines* and *The Truth We Bury* on *Half a Heart*

"Karen McQuestion just keeps getting better! *Hello Love* is an enchanting, impossible-to-put-down novel about big hearts and second chances."—Claire Cook, *USA Today* bestselling author of *Must Love Dogs*

"An emotional and engaging novel about family . . ."—Delia Ephron on *A Scattered Life*

"McQuestion writes with a sharp eye and a sure voice, and as a reader, I was willing to go wherever she wanted to take me. After I finished the book, I thought about how I might describe it to a friend, and I settled on . . . 'You should read this. It's good.'"—Carolyn Parkhurst on *A Scattered Life*

"The plot is fast paced and easy to dive into, making this a quick and exciting read."—*School Library Journal* on *From a Distant Star*

"I devoured it in one sitting!"—*New York Times* bestselling author Lesley Kagen on *Edgewood*

"At first glance *Favorite* is a story of a girl and her family learning to cope with loss. But at some point it morphs into a psychological thriller. It's an unexpected but welcome turn that will leave readers on the edge of their seats."—Jessica Harrison, *Cracking the Cover*

"This story featuring a strong protagonist who has mastered the art of being the new girl will appeal to girls who are fans of this genre."—*School Library Journal* on *Life on Hold*

"This is an adventure that is sure to appeal to both boys and girls, and I can't wait to read it to my students."—Stacy Romanjuk, fourth-grade teacher at Hart Ransom School in Modesto, California, on *Secrets of the Magic Ring*

"An imaginative fable about two witches that should excite young readers."—*Kirkus Reviews* on *Grimm House*

OTHER TITLES BY KAREN MCQUESTION

FOR ADULTS

A Scattered Life

Easily Amused

The Long Way Home

Hello Love

Half a Heart

Good Man, Dalton

Missing Her More

Dovetail

FOR YOUNG ADULTS

Favorite

Life on Hold

From a Distant Star

The Edgewood Series

Edgewood (Book One)

Wanderlust (Book Two)

Absolution (Book Three)

Revelation (Book Four)

FOR CHILDREN

Celia and the Fairies

Secrets of the Magic Ring

Grimm House

Prince and Popper

FOR WRITERS

Write That Novel! You Know You Want To . . .

For Jessica Fogleman, editor extraordinaire

CHAPTER ONE

Today was Morgan's birthday. Three years had passed, but in Wendy's mind, her daughter was still eighteen, the age she'd been when she'd had an argument with her mother and stormed out of the house with a backpack full of her belongings. Her parting words to her mother had been, "I am so done with you. You can just go to hell!"

Edwin had predicted she'd be back, but even on that day Wendy had a bad feeling. For several months prior to that, she and Morgan had gotten into a lot of fights, mostly about her daughter's much older boyfriend, Keith, and her new set of friends, all of them druggies, as far as Wendy could tell. Morgan had been a difficult teenager, and she'd gotten worse after she'd fallen in with this new crowd, the ones she'd met working as a barback in a sleazy place downtown. An eighteen-year-old working nights at a bar was undoubtedly a recipe for trouble. The news that she'd gotten a job there hadn't gone over well with her parents. Wendy had argued that it couldn't even be legal. "You're under twenty-one," she'd pointed out. "You're not even supposed to be on the premises, much less employed there."

Morgan had shot back, "With tips, I make three times as much as working in retail. You said that if I wasn't going to college, I needed to make enough money to support myself. Then when I go and do it, all you do is find fault." Morgan had a way of turning Wendy's words against her, something that made Wendy crazy. By nature, she was a peacemaker, but Morgan was determined to be contentious.

Edwin had said to take a hands-off approach. "Let her get it out of her system. She'll get tired of it. She'll see that those people aren't going anywhere in life. We raised her right. She'll come back to us."

"And if she doesn't get tired of it?" Wendy asked. "If she doesn't come back to us?"

"Wendy, we really don't have much choice. She's an adult. The more you push, the more she'll push back. If we're calm and keep touching base with her, she'll come to us when she's ready. Believe me, this is just a phase."

Every fiber of her being disagreed with him, but she'd deferred, thinking he was the more levelheaded, unbiased of the two of them. Besides, as a college professor, he dealt with kids Morgan's age every day. He was sort of the expert when it came to eighteen-year-olds. In her heart she felt he was wrong, but he seemed so sure that she doubted herself. She regretted it later. Mother's intuition was the one thing she had going for her, and she'd ignored it.

Drinking and drugs had become the monsters driving her daughter. She couldn't prove Morgan was using drugs, but her instincts told her it was true. Morgan's personality had changed. She was moody and had lost weight, something she'd attributed to the physicality of the work. To illustrate, she'd flexed her biceps and said, "I got this from carrying cases of beer up from the basement." Like it was a point of pride. When her new best friend, a woman named Star, came to the door looking for Morgan, all Wendy could think was that she looked like a drug addict out of a TV movie, right down to the stringy hair, bloodshot eyes, and twitchy movements. She'd come to borrow money, of course, something Wendy had picked up on even though the two young women's conversation had been whispered in the front hall.

All of this conflict and worry, and then she was just gone.

At first they thought she'd stayed over at a friend's house. After she'd been missing two days, Wendy had filed a police report. The police were sympathetic, but not too helpful. Morgan, they pointed out, wasn't technically missing. Morgan's parting words were a clear message that she was leaving of her own accord. The police were nice, though. They questioned all the sketchy people who frequented Morgan's workplace. They asked about the boyfriend, Keith, but no one knew much about him, much less where he was or how to reach him. To her utter shame, Wendy realized she didn't even know his last name. She'd asked Morgan for his full name and had been accused of interrogating her, so she'd let it drop. Now she knew that letting it go had been a big mistake.

The police quickly hit a dead end, but Wendy gave them credit for trying.

For her own sanity, Wendy got through the first year by staying busy. In addition to her full-time job as an accountant for a law firm, she put up posters, made phone calls, and created a website. She called Morgan's cell continuously, until it no longer connected with voice mail. The phone company said the account had been canceled, but they couldn't give her any other information. She still checked the website every morning for comments, even though they never led to anything concrete. The web page had a heading that said, *Have you seen our daughter, Morgan Duran?* Below she'd posted a collage of photos of Morgan, along with her physical description. Five-foot-six, slender build. Brown eyes, dark-brown hair, medium-tan skin. There was so much more to her than that, though, so Wendy had added, *Morgan, if you're reading this, please come home. We miss you so much.*

So many memories. From early on, her daughter had a smile that could light up the world and a laugh that was infectious. Her older brother, Dylan, had adored her—still adored her.

As time passed, she and Edwin would only talk about Morgan in bed, the darkness making it easier for her to spill out her grief and worries. Although Edwin denied it, Wendy got the impression that he thought Morgan was dead. He never said as much, probably because saying the words aloud would tear them both in half, but she got the message all the same. What he'd said was, "I'm just as devastated as you are, but I think we should be prepared for the worst."

She would never be prepared for the worst, but this in-between state, the not knowing, was just as bad, eating her up from the inside out. During her busy days at the law firm, she sometimes went hours without thinking of Morgan, but she never made it through a whole day without the agony of knowing her daughter was gone.

Dylan had suggested that all three of them send in a vial of saliva to both 23andMe and Ancestry.com so that their DNA was on file. Just in case. She did it, but her "just in case" included a scenario in which Morgan was in a coma in a hospital somewhere, unable to be identified, and when the DNA was matched and they rushed to her side, the sound of her mother's voice would bring her back to consciousness and lead to a full recovery.

After the first two years, friends and relatives had stopped asking, knowing that if there was any news, they'd be notified. Occasionally there would be an article or video segment online about a missing person, someone who turned up after having been missing for years and then subsequently reunited with their family. None of these were gentle stories. The subjects were never the victim of amnesia. None of them had been out of touch with their families due to a misunderstanding. Usually horrific things had happened to them, things Wendy wouldn't wish on her worst enemy, but for some reason, people felt the need to forward these news stories to her, as if to say, *See, it's not hopeless. It still might happen.*

Giving up wasn't an option, so she kept on searching online, checking in with the police, and reading the comments on the website. As if her efforts alone would lead to a happy ending.

Today, she stayed home from work on Morgan's birthday because someone needed to commemorate the day, to remember that there once was a girl named Morgan, who'd started off as a precious newborn, six pounds four ounces at birth, the sweetest baby she'd ever laid eyes on. Wendy recalled Morgan's childhood, how she loved to dress up as a princess, how she followed her older brother around the house like a little duckling, and how proud she was of making it all the way through middle school without taking a sick day, not even once. It was in high school when the trouble started—the defiance, the sneaking out of the house—but even then, Wendy saw signs of her beautiful, smart, funny daughter underneath it all. It was a phase, she'd told herself, a phase Wendy had prayed would pass quickly. Even with all the grief Morgan had caused, Wendy wouldn't have traded her for the world. And that was how it was until, unthinkably, the world took her away from them.

That day, after checking the website one more time, Wendy went to the pantry closet and pulled out a cellophane-wrapped two-pack of Hostess CupCakes. She'd bought them just for this occasion. They'd been Morgan's favorite. Wendy placed one cupcake in the middle of a small plate and stuck a candle in it. She got the box of kitchen matches from the junk drawer, and with shaking hands, she struck a match against the dark strip on the side of the box. It flared up nicely, and she lit the candle, then blew out the match and threw it into the kitchen sink.

Carrying the cupcake to the table, she sat down in front of it and began to sing in a quavering voice. "Happy birthday to you. Happy birthday to you. Happy birthday, dear Morgan, happy birthday to you."

Blowing out the candle, Wendy made a wish.

CHAPTER TWO

B efore that night, Sharon had never given them much thought. Even though their backyards shared a lot line, Sharon had never met the family. From the name on the mailbox, she knew their last name was Fleming. Occasionally during drives down their street, she got glimpses of them: the woman, a willowy redhead with a short, expensive-looking haircut; the husband, a grim-faced businessman; their son, an overweight, frowning teenager; and a small yappy dog. From googling she knew that the parents' names were Suzette and Matthew. No amount of online searching brought up the son's name, which was just as well.

Sometimes she saw the teenage son walking the dog, the dog pulling at the leash, the boy wearing an oversize hoodie, his shoulders hunched as if he carried some enormous burden. Her sightings of Mr. and Mrs. Fleming were more fleeting. Sometimes she spotted Matthew doing yard work, but most of the time it was brief views of them coming or going, Suzette backing down the driveway in her silver Audi, her husband getting his briefcase out of the trunk of his black midsize Toyota after having pulled into the attached garage.

Nothing about them seemed out of the ordinary.

A tall wooden fence at the back of the house kept them out of sight from the other side. As a single retiree, she had nothing in common with any of them, but she was curious by nature. Lately, most of her social interactions were comprised of friendly waves to the neighbors, going to lunches and movies with old friends, Sunday church services, and frequent phone conversations with her daughter, Amy, who had relocated to Boston.

That particular night, she planned to see the super blood moon lunar eclipse that everyone had been talking about. Even the cashier at the grocery store had mentioned it, saying it was going to be a clear night, perfect for viewing.

At eleven o'clock, Sharon pulled on her boots, gloves, and down coat, ready to go outside to get a better view. It seemed a little foolish to get all bundled up just to step onto her back deck—and even then, only for a few minutes—but there was no getting around it. January in Wisconsin could be brutal, and tonight the temperature was in the teens. Better to be bundled up than risk frostbite.

Once properly clad, she slid open the patio door and stepped out, closing the door behind her so that the cat wouldn't wander out. The night sky domed above her, the cold air showcasing the stars and a big bright moon hanging like a peach ripe for the picking. The shadow of the eclipse had already started to creep over the edge of the moon. The cast of light was a slight orange-red rather than the promised blood-red, but that didn't matter. It was really something. Awestruck, she gazed at the remarkable beauty.

Pulling off her gloves, she reached into her pocket for her phone. Once she had the moon centered in the frame, she enlarged the image and snapped. The resulting photo was unlikely to do it justice, she thought ruefully. Some things were best viewed in real time, not pixels.

As Sharon lowered her phone, an illuminated window at the neighbors' house caught her attention. Someone was in the kitchen.

She narrowed her eyes, trying to get a better look. A girl washing dishes by hand. A young child—maybe five or six? It was hard to say from this distance, but it definitely wasn't an adult or even a teenager. The proportions of the girl made it look like she might be standing on a step stool. Sharon had been certain the Flemings had only one kid, the teenage boy. Was it possible they had another child she didn't know about? Unlikely, she thought. Maybe a visitor? Possibly, but why would a girl that young be washing dishes at eleven o'clock at night?

From her spot on the deck, Sharon took a few pictures of the girl and then stepped down to cross the backyard. The powdery snow kicked up with each step, the chill of the air making her aware of every breath. Close to the fence was a raised planting bed, edged by railroad ties. Sharon stepped up onto the ties and carefully stood on her tiptoes, holding the phone up until the window was in view. After waiting for it to auto adjust, she clicked.

As she watched, another person became visible in the window: the lady of the house. Suzette hovered over the child in a way that didn't seem friendly. The woman's lips moved rapidly, causing the child to shrink away from her. Sharon gasped as Mrs. Fleming yanked on the girl's arm and pointed to something inside the house that wasn't visible to Sharon. A second later, they both moved out of sight.

What was that all about? So weird.

Sharon went back into the house, shook off her winter gear, and settled onto the couch to look at the pictures she'd taken. Just as she'd thought, the moon didn't look nearly as impressive in the photo. The picture of the girl she'd snapped from the deck was barely a silhouette. A person-shaped blob. The photo she'd taken at the fence was better, but still not great. The lack of clarity was probably user error, she thought. Even though she tried to keep up with technology, she fell short in so many ways. She couldn't count the times Amy had said, "It's not that difficult, Mom. You're overthinking it."

Easy for her to say. She'd grown up with the technology and had learned as it evolved. Sharon didn't have that advantage. She still remembered when microwave ovens had come on the scene and everyone had marveled at how quickly you could bake a potato. Which wasn't actually a baked potato since it was microwaved, but that wasn't the point. Cooking a potato that quickly was akin to something miraculous. Around the same time, the idea of videotaping a show and watching it at one's leisure had been something new. Now that was old hat. With the online streaming they had now, the idea of videotaping was as dated as a buggy whip.

One of these days she'd have to figure out how to do that streaming. It sounded darn convenient, being able to choose movies and TV shows and see them right that very minute. Like having a jukebox in her house, but instead of music she could pick what she wanted to watch.

She could have listed a hundred things like that—miraculous technologies and devices that didn't exist when she was young and now were such a part of the landscape that no one made much of them at all.

Life changed so quickly nowadays. It was hard to keep up sometimes.

Later, when she was in bed, she thought again about the little girl. There had to be a good reason, or at least a *plausible* reason, why a child was standing at the Flemings' kitchen sink at eleven o'clock at night washing dishes. Had to be. Puzzling over it was just a waste of time. Clearly, Sharon had been watching too many crime shows and reading too many thrillers. Still, her mind wouldn't let it go. She sighed and then made herself a promise, a compromise to put her worries at ease. If she could come up with one reasonable scenario, she'd allow herself the option of forgetting the whole thing. Her mind ran over multiple ideas until it settled on one. Perhaps, she thought, the girl was a relative visiting from out of town. And maybe, just maybe, the girl had gotten up out of bed to get a drink of water, then lingered to play in the water. Mrs. Fleming had appeared irritated because she was chiding the child for messing around in the sink when she should have been sleeping.

Put that way, it made perfect sense. Clearly, something like that was at play here. Feeling better, Sharon drifted off to sleep.

CHAPTER THREE

Sharon planned to talk to her daughter about the little girl in the window during their next conversation. The best approach would be to send the image through her phone so that Amy would have it for reference. She knew she wouldn't be able to do it, though, until Amy walked her through the process of texting an image, and that would be starting something. Sharon dreaded asking for help. Amy was apt to be impatient at having to explain it *again*, something that made Sharon feel like an idiot. "It's not that hard," she'd say, and Sharon had to admit she was right. It wasn't that hard. So why didn't it stick in her brain?

She was pretty sure the icon used for sharing photos was the little *V* with the circles on each end, the one that reminded her of *Star Trek* for some reason, but she was afraid to try it without double-checking first. "Why can't they just put the word *share* there?" she'd wondered aloud the first time they'd discussed it. "That would be so much easier."

"No, this is easier, and *better*," Amy had firmly stated, proceeding to make her case. "Because this way anyone can tell at a glance. The same way you instinctively know which symbol is the on button for all your devices." Sharon didn't have the heart to tell her that for the longest time the only way she could remember which one was the on button was by reminding herself that it looked like the outline of a teeny breast.

Amy was a real go-getter, an attorney who worked in corporate law. Her new job on the East Coast involved something with contracts for the shipping industry. It all sounded very dry and uninteresting to Sharon, but Amy thrived on the art of negotiation and studying the fine print. She was good at it, judging by her very large salary. Sharon was proud of her, even if she didn't always understand her.

Before Sharon retired, she'd envisioned her golden years as a chance for her and her daughter to spend more time together, but after Amy moved, Sharon had revised the dream and thought it would be an opportunity for her to take classes and do volunteer work. In theory it was a good idea, but soon after leaving the world of employment, she had discovered the joy of having a wide-open schedule, and she'd never looked back. Sweet freedom was doing what she wanted, when she wanted, and not having to account to anyone. Sharon liked her life, even if it was a little lonely at times.

She wasn't looking for trouble with the neighbors, but the little girl she'd glimpsed the previous night was on her mind first thing when she woke. Amy's insight into the matter could only help.

But when Amy unexpectedly called later that morning, the topic of the mystery child flew out of her head. Sharon was eating breakfast at the time, but she set her spoon aside to answer.

After exchanging greetings, Amy got straight to the point. "Mom, I hate to ask this of you, but I need a favor."

Sharon sucked in a breath. Amy never asked for anything. Even as a small child she'd shaken off Sharon's efforts to help, determined to figure everything out on her own. If she was asking her mother for a favor, it was only because she hadn't figured out any other way around it. "Sure, baby girl. What do you need?"

She could hear Amy's relief coming through the line. "I knew I could count on you," she said.

"Of course. Anything for you."

"Well, it's not for me, exactly," Amy said. "It's Nikita."

Nikita? Sharon had a sinking feeling. Nikita Ramos was a foster child Amy had been connected with in her volunteer work as a CASA—court-appointed special advocate. At the time, Amy hadn't said too much about Nikita—only that she'd been in foster care since she was twelve and that life was a constant struggle for her.

Sharon had only met Nikita once, and that had been before Amy moved to Boston, when Sharon had accidentally run into Amy and the girl shopping at the mall. Amy introduced them, and Sharon noticed how Nikita sized her up with one long look. Of course, Sharon did the same thing right back. Nikita struck her as one of those tough girls, both in body language and appearance. Her long hair was dyed raven black with one purple strip, and her T-shirt was black as well, with a large skull on the front, a snake dripping out of one eye socket. It was like she wanted to be stereotyped as someone not to be messed with. She seemed antsy, too, like she was overdue for a cigarette or something worse. Nikita had said hello and that it was nice to meet her, but the girl had never met her gaze, something that had struck Sharon as being suspicious.

"What about Nikita?" Sharon asked now.

"She needs a place to stay, and I thought, well, you're all alone there with the empty bedroom upstairs." Amy had a habit of making a statement and just letting it sit there, waiting for the other person to react. It wasn't from reticence, Sharon knew. Her daughter could be shockingly bold when it was necessary. This pause was a strategy, an opportunity for Sharon to come around to Amy's way of thinking.

"So you want her to live here?" Sharon said. Objections flooded her brain. She hadn't been upstairs in ages and had no idea what condition the room was in. And having a teenager come and live with her? She'd barely known how to raise her own daughter, and Amy had been so easy. A model child, by most people's standards. What did teenagers even eat nowadays? And who knew what kind of emotional baggage a former foster child would have. What if Nikita did damage to the house or was violent? What if she hurt the cat? Sharon shuddered at the thought. There were so many reasons to say no, but she knew Amy wouldn't ask if it weren't important. And she certainly wouldn't deliberately put her own mother in danger.

Amy said, "Just for a little while. She called and sounded desperate, said she couldn't stay there another night. She was frantic, ready to leave right that minute, but I talked her into staying until I could figure something out. Honestly, I don't know what the hell's going on. She wouldn't tell me, but I know she needs to get out of there right away."

"Wait a minute," Sharon said. "Back up. I thought she aged out of foster care." She was certain of this, remembering how Amy had taken a role in helping Nikita find housing after her high school graduation. By that point Amy had moved to Boston, but she'd flown back to Wisconsin to make the arrangements. Amy had a good heart.

"Yeah, she did, and she's lived in several places since then. I know what you're thinking, Mom. You're thinking that all this moving around makes her sound like she's a problem."

That was exactly what Sharon had been thinking, embarrassingly enough.

"That's not true. Nikita's gone through hell. All she needs is a room and a little support. Just someone to be in her corner, to let her know she matters." Amy's voice was firm. "I have friends I could have called, but I thought of you right away. I think you two would be good together."

"How long would she be staying with me?"

"Thank you, Mom, thank you! You're the best. I knew you would come through for me." Amy's gratitude burst through the phone in a rush, the words coming out so rapidly that Sharon's question got lost in the whirlwind. "I'll text you the address and Nikita's number. How quickly can you get there to pick her up?"

"Anytime, really," Sharon said, looking at her half-eaten bowl of oatmeal. She could finish it in a minute. As for the rest of her plans, well, the dishes could wait, as could the load of towels she needed to fold. This was the advantage of being retired and living alone. Her time was hers and hers alone. At least it had been, up until now.

"I'll call and let her know you're on your way. Thanks again, Mom. You're awesome!" In that moment Amy sounded more four-teen than her actual age of forty, making Sharon smile.

After they said their goodbyes, Sharon hung up the phone and hoped she wasn't making a big mistake.

CHAPTER FOUR

The GPS directed Sharon to a run-down neighborhood, an area she knew to have a high crime rate. The houses were a mix—some were maintained well, as evidenced by their tidy yards and neatly shoveled driveways, while others looked neglected, their facades showing peeling paint, their property littered with junk. Sharon shook her head. How did people come to have a refrigerator on the front porch or a car on cinder blocks in the driveway? People lived such different lives.

When she got to the correct address, she turned off the engine and got out of the car, then made her way up the snowy walkway to the front door. She pressed the doorbell and heard voices inside, first a woman angrily yelling something she couldn't make out, followed by a man responding just as loudly. She stamped the snow off her boots and waited until finally, a minute or so later, the door was pulled open.

A woman with a pinched face stood in the narrow opening. "Yes?"

"I'm here to pick up Nikita?" The woman gave Sharon a blank stare. *Darn it, I shouldn't have phrased it as a question.* Clearing her throat first, she tried again, this time more definitively. "I'm here for Nikita." No response, making her wonder if she was at the wrong house. "Is she here?"

"She's here," the woman said in disgust, then motioned Sharon inside. The woman turned angrily and walked away, the door still ajar.

Sharon let herself in and watched as the woman disappeared down a hallway. To her left, a staircase went to the second floor. On her right, in the living room, a bald man in his late thirties sat in a worn recliner, looking at something on a tablet. He had earbuds in and didn't seem aware of Sharon's presence.

"Nikita?" Sharon called out. "It's Sharon Lemke, Amy's mom. I'm here to pick you up!"

"Just a minute!" The voice came from upstairs, and a minute later, Nikita came into view pulling a large suitcase alongside her, a backpack slung over one shoulder. She was wearing ripped jeans and an oversize sweatshirt. The suitcase must have been heavy, based on the way it clunked on each step. Nikita looked different than she had that day at the mall, wearier and with dark circles under her eyes. Her hair was missing the purple stripe as well.

The woman came charging back down the hall, an angry expression on her face. She stopped just short of running into Sharon. For a second, she thought the woman might hit her, but instead she directed her fury at Nikita. "So that's it, then? You're just headin' out of here without even a day's notice?" She crossed her arms in front of her.

Nikita didn't answer; she only looked at Sharon. "Let's go." She tilted her head toward the door.

"What about your job? You aren't gonna be able to keep working there anymore if you're moving out of the neighborhood. How you gonna get there without a car? Bet you didn't think of that."

Nikita shrugged. "It wasn't that great of a job anyway." She toted the suitcase toward the door. "I'll get another one."

Sharon held the door open, and Nikita lifted the suitcase over the threshold.

Behind them the woman said, "You're just gonna walk out of here? We give you a room, treat you like family. Without your rent money, I'm gonna be short this month. What am I supposed to do about that? You don't even care, do you? You're just trash, that's what you are."

"Wait a minute!" Sharon said, but no one took note of her.

Nikita didn't look back. "I can't stay."

The woman let forth a string of profanities, which carried across the yard as they approached the car. Wordlessly, Sharon popped the trunk, and Nikita put her suitcase inside. Just as silently, they got into the car. As Sharon started the engine, she glanced back at the house, noticing the man staring at them through the front window.

They'd gone a few blocks before Sharon spoke. "Well, she was a real treat."

"Yeah." Nikita tucked her hair behind her ear and sighed.

"Are you hungry? We could stop somewhere and get some food."

Nikita shook her head. "No, thanks."

When they got closer to home, Sharon filled the silence. "We're almost there. I live right down this next block."

"Nice neighborhood." Nikita put her hand to the glass and peered out like a child.

The houses were deceptively modest in size, considering that most of the occupants lived privileged lives. Vacations in Hawaii. Tutors for their children. Summer homes on northern lakes. Financially, Sharon was an outlier by comparison. Not that she minded. She said, "Don't be too impressed. My house is one of the smaller ones. In fact, it's the smallest. By a lot." The real estate agent had told her that the house had originally been the guest cottage of a neighboring house, a notion that amused her.

Sharon remembered her daughter's reaction upon seeing the house for the first time. They'd been able to afford the house only because Sharon had gotten a lump-sum settlement from a car accident in which she'd been badly injured. Even after the bones had healed, her leg and hip had never been the same, but the $60,000 had helped with physical therapy and had even given her enough left over for a down payment on a house. Amy was a freshman in high school at the time, and Sharon was thrilled to find a house she could afford, right in Amy's school district. She excitedly showed Amy through the house right after the sellers accepted her offer, making a point to stress that her daughter wouldn't have to switch schools and would also have, for the first time ever, her own bathroom. She knew the house was tiny, worn, and shabby, but she hadn't expected Amy's lack of enthusiasm. Trying to put a positive spin on things, Sharon added, "You know what they say: the worst house on the block is the best investment!"

To which Amy had responded, "Yeah, but did you have to get the worst house in the whole *state*?" Sharon had burst out laughing then.

Thinking about it even now made her smile. The house had been a disaster, but it had served them well, and she wasn't planning on moving anytime soon, especially given all the improvements she'd made over the years: remodeling both bathrooms and the kitchen, switching out light fixtures, painting every wall, and replacing flooring in every room. Looking at old photos, it was hard to believe it was the same house.

Pulling into the driveway, Sharon pushed the button for the garage door opener, then paused as the door lifted. "Nikita, I want—"

"Niki."

"What?"

"Please call me Niki. Amy is the only one who gets to call me Nikita."

"Okay." A simple request, easy to do. She could certainly call her Niki if that's what she preferred, but it would have been nice of Amy to fill her in on this particular detail. She pulled into the garage and shut off the engine. "As I was saying, *Niki*, I want you to feel welcome here. I've lived alone a long time, so if you need something, please ask. I'm not used to having someone else around."

"I won't be here long, if that's what you're getting at."

"No, that's not what I meant." But Niki was already opening the car door now, so Sharon followed suit, getting out of the car and releasing the trunk latch. "That's the opposite of what I meant, in fact."

Niki pulled out her suitcase. "Okay."

Sharon led the way into the house, chattering nervously as she went. She found this girl unnerving, hard to read. Why would Amy have ever thought they'd be good together? She narrated as they went through the house. "In the back hall here there are hooks to hang up your coat and a boot mat, if your feet are wet." She slipped off her own boots and hung up her coat, but Niki just nodded and didn't make a move to take off her sweatshirt or her shoes. Moving on, Sharon said, "As you can see, this is the kitchen. The laundry room is behind that door. Feel free to use the washer and dryer. If you need help with them, let me know. They're fairly new and very high tech. They took me the longest time to figure out," she admitted. "I had to go on YouTube and watch a tutorial three times before I got it down pat."

Through all this, Niki pulled her suitcase along and kept her backpack looped over her arm. She looked around as if scoping out the exits, seemingly ready to bolt at any minute.

After walking through the living room, Sharon gestured to her ginger cat, who lay stretched out along the top edge of the couch. "That's Sarge. He's very lazy and probably won't bother you." Niki leaned over to pet Sarge's head, and the cat appreciatively bumped his head into the palm of her hand.

"He's a sweetie," Niki said, rubbing under his chin. "His name is Sarge?"

"Short for Sargent Snuggles."

"Perfect." Niki nodded in approval.

They continued on, Sharon pointing out the front entrance and circling around until they ended up in her bedroom with its adjacent bathroom. She walked through, opening the door to the bathroom.

Sharon had a well-practiced routine that she usually did when giving guests the tour, a sort of apology for the size of the rooms, and out of habit, she began to explain. "Not very big, but it's just me and—"

Niki let go of her suitcase for the first time and looked around the room, spellbound. "I think this is the most beautiful bathroom I've ever seen." She leaned over and peered at the honeycomb tile floor.

"Really?"

Niki stood up and nodded. "So pretty. And you have it all to yourself." She ran a finger over the granite countertops and looked up at the tulip-shaped pendant lights, an antique fixture that Sharon loved as much for its appearance as for the rosy glow it cast over the room. "You must love living here."

"I do. A lot of people my age are looking at assisted living apartments. I guess there are advantages to that kind of thing, but I'd rather stay here as long as I can."

"If I had this house, I'd never move."

Sharon smiled. "That's how I feel."

Niki nodded and then turned to face her. "So if I'm going to be on the couch, where should I put my stuff? In the laundry room?"

It took Sharon a moment to realize what Niki was saying. "Oh no, you're not sleeping on the couch. You can have Amy's old room upstairs. Come along. I'll take you up." She led the way, opening a door that was the entrance to the narrow wooden staircase. At one time this had led to a walk-up attic, but the previous owners had converted it into two bedrooms and a bathroom. The bigger room had been Amy's; the other they used for storage. The *junk room* was what they called it. Sharon explained all this as they climbed the stairs. When they got to Amy's room, she was relieved to find it tidy and dust free, the bed made and nothing cluttering the floor or the top of the dresser. Amy must have cleaned the last time she stayed over. "Just make yourself at home. The dresser should be empty."

Niki left her suitcase next to the bed and walked over to the window.

"You have a view of the backyard," Sharon said, joining her and pointing. "Nothing too exciting."

"Who lives in that house?" Niki asked. From this height, they could see into the backyard and look directly into one of the upstairs windows. Sharon hadn't been up here in ages and had forgotten that the second story afforded so much of a view.

"The Flemings. A couple with a teenage son and a little dog."

"You know them?"

"No, we've never met. I just see them sometimes, and I've driven past their house."

"Oh."

"I did notice something kind of weird about them just last night." Sharon had not planned on bringing this up, but the words just popped out.

"Weird how?"

She shrugged. "It might be nothing, but I was in the yard last night around eleven to see the lunar eclipse." Sharon paused, and when Niki didn't respond, she plowed forward. "And I saw a little girl washing dishes at the kitchen sink. A really little girl, like five or six? Looked to me like she was standing on a step stool. It struck me as odd because they don't have a daughter, at least not that I've seen." She found it difficult to read Niki's face. Did she just think she was an old busybody with nothing better to do than spy on the neighbors?

"And even if they did have a daughter, why would she be washing dishes at eleven at night?" Niki said, finishing her thoughts.

"Exactly," Sharon said. "I was thinking maybe they had house-guests, but even then why would she be doing dishes?"

Niki nodded, weighing her words.

Sharon added, "And then I saw Mrs. Fleming come in, and it was just for a split second, but she looked furious. She yanked on the little girl's arm, and then I couldn't see them anymore."

"Sounds like a foster child to me," Niki said.

"I don't think they have a foster child," Sharon said, then realized she didn't really know much about the family at all.

"They could have one and you might not know it," Niki said. "It fits what you saw. A little kid washing dishes late at night. She was probably being punished, and then she got in more trouble for not doing it right."

"No . . . ," Sharon said, shocked. "I can't believe someone would treat a child that way."

Niki laughed, a bark of derision. "Believe it. Happens all the time."

"But one that small? I mean, she looked like a little tiny girl."

"Absolutely." Niki's eyes narrowed. "I could tell you stories."

Sharon could hear Amy's words echoing in her head. *Nikita's gone through hell. All she needs is a room and a little support. Just someone to be in her corner, to let her know she matters.*

Such a simple thing and not much to ask for. Not much at all.

Sharon said, "I took pictures on my phone. Would you mind taking a look and telling me what you think?" Without waiting for a response, she got out her phone and scrolled to the clearest image.

Niki took the phone from her outstretched hand. She stared at the screen for a moment and then swiped to see the other images, finally landing back on the one Sharon had first offered. Her face colored with sympathy. "Poor little thing." She looked up and met Sharon's eyes. "Someone needs to help her."

"You think so?" Hearing someone else say what she'd been thinking was unnerving. "I had the same thought, but I didn't know what to do. I didn't witness anything abusive, just odd. And I don't know the family."

"It's a hard call," Niki said.

"Do you think I should call someone?"

"You mean like child protective services?"

"Yeah, like that."

Niki twisted her mouth in thought and then shook her head. "There's no abuse that you can prove. And you don't even know who this kid is. It might turn out to be nothing."

"But it seems like something," Sharon said.

"I think so too."

"So what to do?"

"Get to know them and watch. Trust me, if it seems odd, there's probably something wrong. When you know more, when you have more actual information, then you can report them. If you do it too soon, you give them a chance to cover it up." Niki sounded like she spoke from personal experience, making Sharon wonder yet again what she had gone through.

"Good advice." Sharon peered through the window, but there was no one in sight and nothing to point to a problem in the Fleming household. She felt better having told Niki. Two sets of eyes were better than one.

CHAPTER FIVE

"Mia! Mia, where are you?" Coming from the direction of the front door, Ma'am's voice sliced through the room. Mia, who'd crawled into the space between the couch and the wall, scrambled out. So far, no one knew about her hiding spot, and she wanted to keep it that way. When Mister was traveling, and Jacob was in his room or at school, and Ma'am was gone or busy, the spot behind the couch had become her place to just be, undisturbed. Of course there was her room in the basement, but she wasn't allowed to go down there until the end of the day, the reason being that she had to stay within calling distance. Sometimes seeing her idle reminded the family of something that needed doing, so if she stayed out of sight she could have a few moments of peace. Ma'am didn't like her on the furniture, and sitting on the stairs all the time was tiring. Being able to hide behind the couch helped, as long as she stayed alert. She still had to come when her name was called or there would be trouble.

And if Ma'am discovered she hid back there, punishment was sure to follow.

"Here, Ma'am." Mia came out of the living room, meeting her in the front hall. Griswold, Mia's faithful canine companion, trotted at her heels. Mia took Ma'am's purse and keys, then turned to put them away: the keys on a hook in the kitchen, and the purse in the linen closet, a place Ma'am believed burglars would never think to look.

Behind her, Mia heard the thunk of Ma'am kicking off her high heels. She knew her next chore would be to retrieve them and put them on the shoe rack in Ma'am and Mister's closet. First, though, they'd have to be inspected. If the soles were dirty, Mia would be expected to clean them, and if they were scuffed, she would need to polish them. Ma'am was very fussy about her things.

"Oh, what a day I've had, Mia!" Ma'am's voice had a weary air. "I had to wait for an hour at the doctor's office, and then he wouldn't even listen to me. After that, I had to stop and look at fabric samples at the upholsterer's, and that was your basic nightmare. Traffic was terrible, so I nearly missed my nail appointment. And then my friend was late meeting me at the restaurant for dinner. I'm completely frazzled. Believe me, I'll never schedule so much in one day again. You're lucky to be able to stay home all the time."

Mia answered from the kitchen. "Yes, Ma'am." She stood on tiptoe to put the keys on the hook. She had been proud when she'd first realized that she'd grown tall enough to do it without using the stool. That's how she knew she'd changed since arriving at the Flemings' house three Christmases ago. She could look at herself in the mirror, of course, but she didn't like the way she looked. Ma'am cut her hair short in what Jacob called a Dora the Explorer hairstyle. So often she wished for longer hair, but every time it grew even a little bit, Ma'am got out the shears and chopped it all off.

It hadn't always been so short. Once Ma'am had gotten impatient when combing it out after it was washed and said that Mia's long hair was too much trouble. After that, the regular haircuts began. If only she had pictures, she could see exactly how it had looked back then and how much she'd changed in the meantime, but Ma'am had made it clear that photos of Mia were forbidden. Once Jacob had taken a photo of her with his phone and added bunny ears and a nose, which made her look so cute and funny too.

He'd warned her not to tell his mother, saying, "If you do, you'll be sorry."

Sometimes Jacob said he would crush her, or throw her out in the yard face-first. He never did either of these things, but sometimes, when Ma'am berated him, she saw a change in Jacob, an anger simmering under the surface. To her, he was mostly nice, letting her have snacks when his mom wasn't around since she often did his chore of picking up the dog poop in the yard. She didn't mind. Griswold usually came with her and led the way, proudly showing her just what she needed to pick up. Silly little dog.

Mia went to put Ma'am's handbag in the linen closet, tucking it next to the hand towels, then straightened the towels to keep them orderly. Next she went to retrieve Ma'am's shoes. She was relieved to see that the bottoms were clean and they didn't need polishing. That was one advantage to winter. Walking through snow kept Ma'am's soles from getting dusty or splattered with mud.

In the kitchen, Ma'am yelled, "Mia, come here right now!"

Mia hurried to the doorway, a shoe in each hand. "Yes, Ma'am." As usual, Griswold trotted at her heels. Jacob always said that he was Mia's shadow.

"Did you finish the laundry and put it away?"

"Yes, Ma'am."

"Clean the upstairs bathroom and wash the kitchen floor?"

"Yes, Ma'am."

"Refill the soap dispensers and empty the wastebaskets?"

"Yes, Ma'am." Mia was proud to have gotten all of it done, and in record time, too, not that Ma'am cared how long it took.

"Where is Jacob?" Ma'am glanced over Mia's head as if her son might come around the corner at any second. This was unlikely to happen, especially if Jacob knew she was home. Mia had once overheard him talking on the phone to a friend, saying that he hoped his parents would get a divorce, and if that happened, he'd go live with his father.

Mia pointed upward, indicating that Jacob was in his room. Jacob was a senior in high school this year. When he was in his room, his parents always assumed he was studying. She knew better.

"Did he make dinner for the two of you?"

Mia nodded. "Yes, Ma'am." To Mia's delight, he'd served chicken nuggets, french fries, and applesauce. Not only had Jacob served this feast, he'd also let her sit at the dining room table with him and had allowed her to use as much ketchup as she wanted. He'd been looking at his phone the whole time, so he hadn't even noticed that she'd dropped a few choice bits of chicken to Griswold. If only dinner could be like that every night.

"Very good. I'll let you off early, then. You can put my shoes away and head downstairs."

"Yes, Ma'am." Trying to hide her glee, Mia walked up the stairs and carefully set the shoes in the rack in Ma'am's walk-in closet. Once downstairs, she passed by the kitchen, where Ma'am was pouring herself a glass of wine.

"Goodnight, Mia."

"Goodnight, Ma'am."

"Remember that tomorrow morning you can come up for breakfast, but then you'll have to go back down to your room. Not a peep from you." Ma'am inserted the cork back into the opening of the bottle and opened the refrigerator door. "The man is coming to install new blinds in the kitchen, and I'll need you to be quiet as a mouse. Understand?"

Mia nodded. The blinds had been lowered over the window as long as she could remember, blocking the sunlight and her view of the backyard. When the blinds broke—the top piece falling out of the bracket—Ma'am had blamed her, but it wasn't her fault. Mister had come to her defense. "The girl can't even reach the lever. There's no way she broke it." He winked at Mia, something she wasn't sure about. It made her think they were getting away with something, but what that could be she didn't know. She had no idea what had happened with the blinds. One day they were mounted over the window, and the next the blinds were laid neatly on the counter. Jacob, probably.

Ma'am stared at her over the rim of her wineglass. "The dog stays here. I'll be down in a minute to tuck you in."

"Yes, Ma'am." Mia held out a hand for Griswold to stay, and then she went down the stairs, happy at this turn of events. She had the rest of the evening to herself and part of tomorrow morning too. At the bottom of the stairs, she crossed the basement, going straight for the back corner to what Jacob called her *secret compartment*. "It's super cool," he'd told her. "I don't know anyone else who has a hidden room."

She was lucky that way.

The basement walls had been covered with light-colored wood paneling; the floors looked like hardwood but actually had a plastic-like grooved surface. When she'd first come to live with the Flemings, Ma'am had let her sleep in the extra bedroom upstairs.

The problem had begun when Ma'am had realized they needed a safe place to put her when company came over. After a few months, Ma'am had had a clever idea. She'd had a man come and build a wall on the far side, and behind the wall he'd made a room. Mia's room. A bookcase on wheels disguised the door. All the books were attached, and there was a small lock on one side of the middle shelf to secure the door from the outside. If the bookcase was in place, it looked like that wall was where the room ended. No one would ever be able to tell that Mia's room was back there.

Best yet, the bathroom was nearby. Mia's room and the bathroom combined made an *L* shape on that end of the basement. She was the only one who used that bathroom, really, so it was like it was her own space.

Mia had heard Ma'am talking to the man, telling him that the room was a place to store something valuable. *Something valuable.* She'd turned this phrase over in her mind, pleased to be considered this way. The notion had been dashed when she'd repeated the story to Jacob. "She wasn't talking about you," he'd said. "That's just something she told the guy."

Jacob knew things because he was close to being a grown-up, while Mia was still little. She had recently asked Jacob why she didn't have birthdays like everyone else, and he had explained that it was because they didn't know when she was born. "We think you're about six or seven," he'd said. "If I knew for sure, I would tell you."

After the builder man was done, she wound up with her very own bedroom, which was, as Ma'am liked to remind her, a major pain to have built. It had cost a lot of money, and they'd done it just for her. She had a dresser and a cot and an old TV that Mister had given her when Ma'am got a new one for their room. It only got a few channels, and the picture was terrible, but it was better than nothing. She was careful to keep the volume low so that Ma'am wouldn't have a reason to take it away from her. The TV was her only link to the outside world, and she learned a lot by watching the news and PBS. She had figured out how to read from *Sesame Street*, a secret she never shared with anyone else. Once she knew the sounds of the letters, it was easy to figure out the words in the books Jacob had given her, the ones left over from when he was a little kid. She hid them in one of the drawers in her dresser, unsure if Ma'am would allow her to keep them.

Mia went into the bathroom and washed her face and brushed her teeth, hurrying so that she'd be finished when Ma'am came down to tuck her in for the night. By the time she heard Ma'am's footsteps on the stairs, she had pulled the bookcase as far as she could, changed into her nightshirt, and climbed into her cot, pulling the sheet up to her chin.

"All set, Mia?" Ma'am's voice rang out from the other side of the doorway.

"Yes, Ma'am."

"Okay then." Ma'am pushed the bookcase until it was secure in the doorjamb, and the room went dark. A second later, the lock clicked shut, tucking her in for the night.

CHAPTER SIX

When Niki came down the stairs the next morning, Sharon was already at the kitchen table, coffee cup in hand, the newspaper spread out in front of her. She'd just finished eating a slice of cinnamon-raisin toast. Sharon acknowledged Niki's presence with a nod. "Good morning."

"Morning." Today Niki wore dark pants and a striped button-down shirt. On her feet were a pair of black flats. Not business professional, but definitely more conservative than yesterday. It was surprising how tiny Niki was without the bulk of her hooded sweatshirt. Her petite frame and trim waistline would be the dream of most women, and that wasn't the only difference Sharon noticed from the previous day. Niki's hair had been pulled off her face into a bun, bringing her high cheekbones, perfect skin, and big dark eyes into full view. The combination was stunning.

"You look great," Sharon said.

Niki pulled self-consciously at the front of her shirt. "I thought I'd apply for jobs today. I need to find work as soon as possible."

"Sounds like a good plan." Sharon nodded in the direction of the toaster. "If you want some cinnamon-raisin toast, help yourself."

"Thanks, I think I will."

They were, Sharon decided, diplomatically navigating around each other, each of them careful not to offend the other. After Niki had retired to her room the night before, Amy had called to see how the two of them were getting along, and she'd listened attentively before giving her mother a list of instructions. *Don't make too much of a fuss over her. Let her know in plain terms what you expect. Make her feel welcome, but don't smother her. Don't ask too many questions. She's liable to take off if she thinks you don't want her there.* Sharon felt conflicted about this string of directions. On the one hand, it was good to know. On the other, it was a little insulting. Everything Amy had mentioned she probably would have done anyway. But she guessed it was never a bad idea to have a reminder.

Sharon said, "There's coffee in the pot and orange juice in the fridge. Glasses and cups are in the upper cabinet to the left of the fridge."

Niki nodded and popped two pieces of bread in the toaster, then poured herself some juice while she waited. By the time she took a seat at the table, Sharon guessed enough time had passed to talk again. "So you're going to apply for jobs today?" she asked.

"That's the plan. I already called my old job and told them I quit because I moved and don't have transportation."

"Were they mad?" Sharon was curious. She'd never walked off a job in her life. There were times it had been tempting, but she'd always given two weeks' notice and stuck it out.

"I'm sure they will be." She grinned, revealing straight white teeth. "I left a voice mail."

Ah, voice mail. That made it much easier. "I would have loved that option when I was your age. So many things are easier now."

"Yep."

Sharon took a breath and mentally launched into business mode. If Niki was going to be living there, she needed to know what was expected of her. "I realized that yesterday we really didn't get a chance to talk." Niki's face clouded over, probably anticipating a lecture. Well, Sharon had no intention of going there. "We should probably exchange phone numbers, and I've got a house key for you too. That way you can come and go as you like."

Niki looked relieved. "Since we're talking, how much time do I have, and what are the rules?" She took a sip of her orange juice, her eyes still on Sharon.

"How much time do you have for what?"

"For staying here."

Sharon took in a sharp breath. Since the initial phone call with Amy, she'd rethought the whole situation. When she'd met Niki briefly at the mall, she'd judged her as the scary tough girl, the one who didn't take anything from anyone, and yes, there was something about her to back that up. She did, after all, opt to move out of the last house despite the woman's objections, so something had to have happened, and Sharon was willing to bet it involved the man who'd watched as Niki left the house. Spending even this short period of time with Niki made Sharon reconsider her original stance. Amy had been right. The girl had been through difficult times, and she deserved a chance to turn it around. "As long as we get along, you're welcome to stay for as long as you like," Sharon said.

"As long as I like," Niki repeated, as if she didn't quite believe it. "And what are your rules?"

"I can't really think of any offhand," she said, almost apologetically. "Just be a considerate guest. Don't leave wet towels on the floor, clean up after yourself—you know, all the commonsense stuff."

"And what's my curfew?" Niki asked with the practiced air of someone who'd gone through this many times before.

"Well, you're an adult, so you can keep your own schedule, as long as you don't disturb my sleep. If you're planning on staying out late, let me know ahead of time. If I hear someone come in at three in the morning, I'd like to know it's you and not some criminal breaking into the house." This was the same agreement Sharon had had with

Amy once she'd reached adulthood. It was borne of necessity more than anything else. Amy had been a good kid, and Sharon found she didn't have the energy to stay up late solely to police her. And, honestly? Some circumstances required late nights. When Amy had been a young college student living at home, she often got off work at eleven. If she and her coworkers went to an all-night breakfast restaurant afterward and got to talking, coming home at two or three o'clock wasn't that much of a stretch. "Does that work for you?"

"Sure."

They sat for a few more minutes, Niki eating and Sharon, pen in hand, working on a sudoku puzzle. After Niki finished, she picked up Sharon's plate and stacked it on her own, then rinsed them off in the sink and put them in the dishwasher. "So," she said, almost nonchalantly, "how much rent will you be charging me?"

Instead of answering the question, Sharon said, "Amy says you're saving up to get a car and a place of your own."

"That's the plan. It's taking me forever, though. I was living in an apartment with some other people right after I aged out of foster care, but I didn't have to come up with a lot of cash up front. I just moved in and paid them every month, so it didn't cost so much." She crossed the room and sat down at the table opposite of Sharon. "If I rent an apartment myself, I'll have to come up with a lot more money. I'm okay with getting a roommate and taking a bus to get around, but even with that I still need the first month's rent, or half the first month's rent if I'm splitting it with someone, and then there's the security deposit and furniture and buying all the cooking things." She gestured back toward the cabinets.

"It's a lot," Sharon said in a kind way. She thought back to when she was young. How had she gotten started going from nothing to moving out on her own? Thinking back, her parents had sold her one of their old cars for a pittance. It was a gift, really. Relatives who had cast-off furniture and housewares had also contributed to her cause, and she'd gotten the rest at Goodwill and from clearance sales at Kmart. In the ensuing years, she'd bought things as needed, and in later years she'd sometimes even bought things that weren't needed. Impulse purchases. Ruefully, she remembered the bread maker she'd used only a handful of times and the juicer she'd once vowed to use on a regular basis. She'd been able to get rid of the bread maker without an ounce of guilt, but for some reason she couldn't part with the juicer. It was only a matter of time, though. Looking back, she realized that she'd spent the first half of her life acquiring things and was now spending the second half getting rid of them.

Niki nodded. "You're right. It is a lot."

Sharon made a decision. "Let's not worry about rent for the moment. You can stay for free. You're in guest mode right now, and if that changes, I'll let you know."

"Wait." Niki seemed befuddled. "But you have to charge me something. I can't just live here and not pay."

"You can if I say so. It's my house, and I can do whatever I like," Sharon said. "As long as you're working toward a goal, I'm good with letting you stay here for free. If you start spending your money on stupid stuff like gambling or drugs, I'll rethink the whole thing."

Niki frowned. "I don't do drugs. Is that what you think of me?"

Sharon leaned forward, one palm flat on the table. Outside the window, behind Niki's head, she saw a small brown bird alight onto the bird feeder suction-cupped to the glass. "No, Niki, I don't think you do drugs, but the truth is that I don't know you and you don't know me, so I'm just putting it out there. I don't want someone living with me who's doing drugs or drinking to excess. It's not personal— it's just my policy. And who knows? You don't know me at all. I could be a drug addict. The only thing we both know for sure is that Amy has vouched for each of us. I'm thinking that means we're both okay."

Niki glanced around the room. "You're not a drug addict. No way you're a drug addict."

"You sound very sure."

"I'd be able to tell." She sounded confident. "You look clear-eyed and healthy. Your house is clean, and you're out of bed and facing the day already."

"I try to keep up with things." Sharon felt vaguely proud. "Still, for all you know, it could be a front. I might have a whole secret life."

"No." Niki shook her head, making her silver earrings sway. "You're definitely not a drug addict. I've seen lots of them. I would know."

CHAPTER SEVEN

The strip mall was two miles from Sharon's house. When Niki announced she'd be walking there, Sharon said, "Don't be silly. It's way too cold today. I can drive you."

Niki fidgeted, seeming to weigh both options. Finally, she said, "Are you sure?"

"Of course I'm sure. It's really not a problem. Besides, I have nothing better to do." Saying the words aloud took her by surprise. Did she really have nothing better to do? On one hand, Sharon's days were full. Depending on the season, she loved to be outdoors, either working in the yard or shoveling snow. She was never bored. The library and grocery store were frequent destinations, and her calendar was full of appointments: hair, dentist, routine medical checkups, lunches with friends, church on Sunday. Keeping her house clean and the laundry done were priorities for her, as she hated dirt and disorder. Taking care of all these small things meant she was always on the move: shaking the cat's food bowl to give it the appearance of fullness, wiping down counters, dusting the glass birds that had been her mother's prized knickknacks. She made a point not to sit down until after dinner, and only then to read a book or watch the news. The usual rewards for a productive day. Honestly, though, none of her activities were critical. All of it was unimportant compared to helping a young person find her way in the world.

As they got into the car, she asked Niki, "Do you have a driver's license?"

Niki pulled the seat belt across her body and connected the two parts with one sharp click. "Yep. Amy taught me to drive and then took me for my test. I passed on my first try." She turned toward Sharon, grinning. "I haven't driven much since then because I don't have a car, but it's good to have a driver's license for identification."

"You'll get a car eventually," Sharon said. "It all takes time." As she drove through her community, she pointed out landmarks to Niki —the library, the post office, the gas station.

They went a few more blocks and turned, and Niki pointed. "Amy's high school!"

"That's right."

Niki tapped on the glass. "She hated high school and skipped study hall and took summer classes so she could graduate a year early."

"You seem to know a lot about my daughter."

"We spent a lot of time together." Long pause. "She talked a lot about you too."

"Oh." Sharon raised her eyebrows. Amy hadn't told her much about Nikita, citing privacy issues, but apparently it hadn't worked the other way around. "All good things, I hope."

"All good," Niki assured her. "Not one bad thing."

Sharon pulled into the strip mall parking lot and surveyed the stores. A few upscale fashion boutiques, a jewelry store, a florist, a nutrition store, a gift shop, and a karate school. On one end stood a Walgreens. "Walgreens might be a good start," she suggested. "Every time I go in there, someone new is at the register." She pulled the car into a space close to the middle of the shopping center.

Niki shook her head. "Nah. Too corporate. I don't want to work for a big machine. Plus, they'd probably just tell me to apply online."

"Isn't that how most places operate nowadays? Seems like everything is online."

"Yeah, sort of, but I've found that with the smaller places they like to see you in person first, so I usually go in and make a case for myself. Then my application stands out." She unclipped her seat belt and turned to Sharon. "You sure you don't mind waiting?"

"Not at all. I have a book in my purse. Take all the time you need." She watched as Niki left the car and strode toward the storefronts, confidently heading into the florist shop.

In an effort to support local businesses, Sharon had been inside most of these stores at least once, but she'd found them mainly geared toward clientele with more disposable income than she'd have in her entire lifetime. Honestly, she had no idea how they stayed in business. She'd asked that very question of Amy once, and she'd replied, "There are any number of ways. Money laundering. Selling weapons out of the back room. Slave labor." The list of possibilities, she'd told her mother, was endless. Corruption was creative. If Sharon didn't know better, she'd have thought Amy was kidding. But she knew her daughter; Amy had a jaded view of the world, although she certainly wouldn't call it that. Her daughter saw it the other way around. She thought her mother viewed the world through a rose-colored lens. *Sharon-vision*, she called it. Sharon was, Amy once said, charmingly naïve to the ugly side of people. Not a compliment, but at least she'd called her charming.

Sharon got her book out of her purse but didn't open it, watching the door to the florist shop instead. When Niki came out, she had a grim expression, as if she'd gotten disappointing news, but it didn't slow her down. Decisively, she turned and went into the gift shop. She had no winter coat on, something Sharon had noticed when they were at home, but she hadn't questioned it. Based on what she'd seen of the girl's possessions, the only outerwear she owned was a hoodie. Sharon didn't think bringing up the subject was a good idea. At least not today. They were still finding their way with each other, but at some point, this lack would have to be addressed. Niki couldn't continue to go out in January without some kind of jacket. Besides being uncomfortable, it was also dangerous.

Niki wasn't in Nancy's Fancy Gifts for very long, something that wasn't surprising. Sharon would have guessed it wasn't her kind of place, since it was filled with collectible figurines, mirrors with gilded frames, and artistic wall hangings. On the lower end of the price scale was an assortment of greeting cards, but even those were at least ten dollars. Sharon knew this because when the place had first opened, she'd stopped in just to check it out. She'd immediately felt uncomfortable, something the sales clerk had seemed to pick up on, as she began hovering over her as if Sharon were a kid likely to break something. No, this wouldn't be the right job for Niki.

Within seconds of leaving that store, Niki confidently darted into the one next to it. She wasn't one to give up, that was for sure.

The sun was coming in through the windshield, keeping Sharon warm enough even without the engine running. She watched as Niki went from business to business, ending up at the nutrition store. When she didn't come out after fifteen minutes, Sharon cracked open her book and began to read.

She was so immersed in the story that it was a shock when Niki finally opened the door and got back into her seat. "Sorry it took so long," she said breathlessly, slamming the door shut. "But guess what?" Her voice was tinged with excitement.

Sharon glanced up to see Niki's eyes alight with delight. "What?"

"I got a job!" She held up a light-blue polo shirt with the words *Magnificent Nutrition* embroidered on the left side. "At the nutrition store. I can start tomorrow, he said. They just had a new employee ghost them, and so they needed someone right away."

"Congratulations!" Sharon said, giving her a fist bump. Thank God Amy had started that fist bump thing. Sharon had been stuck in high-five mode, which her daughter had informed her was, while technically not incorrect, not done much anymore, except in sports. "Tell me all about it."

On the way home, Niki filled her in. The store was not a franchise or a chain, and it had been open for three years. "It's owned by a husband-and-wife team. I talked to the husband. He's a nice old guy named Max. I'll get to meet his wife tomorrow. They only have two part-time employees and one who works thirty-five hours a week. That will be me. I'll get to run the juice bar. They have a little café in the back of the store, which is super cute, and all they serve is juice. He said I'll make some cash tips—not a lot, but it's still a nice extra."

"Cash is king," Sharon said.

"You've got that right." Niki smiled broadly, then reached up and removed the elastic from her bun, letting her hair fall to her shoulders. "I can't believe I got a job right away. I was kind of worried. I didn't want you to think I'm a slacker."

"I wouldn't have thought that." Sharon was touched that her opinion had worked its way into Niki's thinking. She realized again how wrong her first impression of the girl had been. As they pulled into the driveway, she asked, "So what time do you start tomorrow?"

"They open at nine, but he told me to come half an hour early for training."

Sharon paused on the driveway to wait for the garage door to open. "So eight thirty, then. I can drive you."

"Oh, you don't have to do that."

"I know I don't *have* to," Sharon said. "I want to. It makes me feel like I'm helping, so really you'll be doing me a favor. Besides, I have some errands to run in that direction anyway, so it's not a big deal."

"I really appreciate it." Her voice got smaller. "You and Amy are the best things that ever happened to me."

Sharon heard the emotion behind the words and was touched. Such a sad commentary on this girl's life that simple kindnesses were considered the best things that had ever happened to her, but Sharon felt fortunate to be able to play such a large role in another person's life. How often did that kind of opportunity come around? Not often enough. Or maybe she hadn't really been looking.

CHAPTER EIGHT

The next morning, Ma'am unlocked Mia's door early, reminding her to step lively. She clapped three times, and her voice was crisp. "No time to waste. The man is coming early to install the blinds." Mia knew what that meant. She had to finish her morning chores posthaste and eat quickly, then return to her bedroom until further notice.

Posthaste was a word Ma'am used a lot. The expression *until further notice* was another favorite. One time Jacob had mockingly repeated the phrase right to Ma'am's face, intoning "until further notice" in a whiny voice, and she'd slapped him so hard his ear had turned red. The slap had shocked both Jacob and Mia. Hitting was something reserved for Mia; Jacob got lectures or was grounded. Sometimes his mother took his phone away from him, but that was for the very worst offenses. Without his phone he was absolutely miserable, and his misery carried over to Mia. The slap that day had been unprecedented. Later he'd blamed Mia for it, saying, "If you'd gotten your chores done on time, she wouldn't have been in such a foul mood."

He was right, which made Mia feel awful. So much depended on her ability to do what Ma'am wanted in the correct time frame. The happiness of the entire household was determined by Ma'am's mood. Even Griswold seemed affected by it.

That morning, Mia hurriedly got dressed, washed her face, brushed her teeth, and went upstairs. She was greeted by Griswold, who excitedly nudged his nose up against her leg. Her first responsibility of the day was always to fill Griswold's food bowl and to give him fresh water. Next she would empty the dishwasher, if need be, or load it if there were dishes in the sink. This morning she avoided going by the window because two nights before Ma'am had pulled her out of bed to wash the larger cooking pots in the sink. Mia had worked hard to get them clean, but still got in trouble. It was her own fault, really, for not realizing that without the blinds she could be seen through the window. Ma'am had screamed when she saw Mia with her hands in the soapy water, scrubbing a soup pot. The scream had scared Mia so much that she'd peed a little. "Get away from that window, you stupid girl! What in the world do you think you're doing?" Ma'am had pulled her off the step stool and shook her so hard her teeth rattled and then angrily sent her off to bed. Later Ma'am had apologized, saying, "I'm sorry that it came to that, Mia. If you weren't always screwing up, I wouldn't have to be so hard on you."

Mia had nodded, not meeting her eyes. Ma'am continued. "Try using your head for once. I'm trying to teach you the proper way to do things, but it doesn't work if you don't listen."

When the pause was long enough to require a response, Mia had said, "I'm sorry."

Ma'am had nodded. "That's my girl."

The words had warmed Mia's heart. She wasn't part of the family, really, but she belonged to them. *That's my girl.*

After feeding the dog and emptying the dishwasher, she poured herself a bowl of cereal, careful not to drip the milk. She ate at the counter, while the rest of the family sat around the kitchen table. Mister took a last sip of his coffee and then silently went to gather up his phone and keys. She heard him shuffle through the coats in the hall closet, and then he appeared in the doorway wearing the jacket he wore to work, a pair of leather gloves in his hand. "Heading out now."

Ma'am didn't even look up. "Bye."

Jacob said, "See you later, Dad."

Mister said, "Have a good day, son. You too, Mia."

Mia liked it when he included her like that. She finished her cereal with a smile.

After tidying up the kitchen and getting permission to go to her room, Mia went back down the stairs, this time accompanied by Griswold. Normally he wasn't allowed in her room, but Ma'am made an exception this morning. "Otherwise he'll be underfoot during the installation."

Mia pulled the bookcase closed from inside her room, then settled back on her cot, patting the space next to her. Griswold jumped up, nestling perfectly along the length of her body. He was so warm and cozy. She stroked his fur and rubbed behind his ears. "Aren't you the sweetest, best dog?" she whispered. Griswold gave a soft snort as his tail thumped against the bed.

Mia was Griswold's favorite person in the family. Jacob said it was because she fed him, but Mia had another theory. It was because both of them were only noticed if they did something wrong.

Today was turning out to be one of the best days ever, second only to the time Mister had insisted she accompany them on a day trip to the state fair two summers ago. Ma'am had protested, but he was firm. "Can't she have a little fun, Suzette? If we run into anyone we know, we'll just say she's our niece, visiting for the week."

Ma'am had scoffed. "Our niece? She looks nothing like us! Besides, people are bound to ask how she's related, and what do I say then?" She folded her arms and defiantly raised her chin. "All my friends know I only have one brother, and he doesn't have any children. And your sister is way too old to have a child this young."

"Okay, then," he said impatiently. "We'll say she's the daughter of a cousin. Adopted from Central America." He winked at Mia, who felt her heart soar. It took everything she had to suppress a grin in return.

And so she was able to go to the state fair. She had to hold Ma'am's handbag the entire time, but it was worth it to experience all the sights and sounds. And to see so many people! Couples in love, families with a real mom and dad—the parents holding the hands of their small children or pushing toddlers in strollers. One dad hoisted a little boy onto his shoulders, saying, "Now you can see everything." Mia marveled at it all.

It had been hot that day, but she didn't mind. She could still taste the cream puff and fried cheese. The look on her face when she took her first bite of the cream puff had made Mister laugh with delight. They had walked through some of the animal barns too, and she had been overjoyed to see all the farm animals. Jacob had complained about the smell, which she'd silently agreed was pretty terrible.

Today, having the morning off, just her and Griswold, was nice too. When she heard the thump of work boots overhead, she knew the man had arrived to install the new blinds and her reprieve would soon be over. Ma'am's voice could be heard overhead, but she couldn't make out the words. The brisk, authoritative tone was one she was familiar with; clearly, Ma'am was giving the man instructions and letting him know she would not tolerate anything but his best effort. Ma'am expected nothing but the best.

Mia buried her face in the dog's soft fur. "Oh, Griswold. I love you so much."

In reply he whined, his tail thumping enthusiastically, and she knew that he was saying he loved her too.

CHAPTER NINE

Niki woke up early on her first day to work at Magnificent Nutrition. The transition from sleep to wakefulness came gradually and felt as peaceful as drifting on a cloud. She lay in bed for a minute, watching a slant of light come through the gap in the curtains and remembering where she was and how she'd gotten here. This had been Amy's room. Amy had slept in this very same bed, right here in the house she'd lived in with her mother. And now Niki was here, occupying the same space, living with the same woman. In a way, it was as if she'd stepped out of her life and into Amy's old life. The idea made her smile.

When Amy had been assigned as her advocate, she was the third one who'd taken on the job. The first one had quit when she'd had a baby. The second woman had bowed out after getting a job promotion. Her name was Angie. She'd apologized to Niki, saying the demands on her time were just too great. "It's not you, really," she'd said. Niki had just shrugged. People came and went pretty regularly in her life. She had come to expect nothing from other people. The fact that they'd done it at all had been phenomenal, considering it was a volunteer position, and Niki hadn't gone out of her way to show outward signs of appreciation.

The first two women had done a decent job looking out for her, but Amy had gone above and beyond. She'd taken Niki clothing shopping and bought her school supplies, attended parent-teacher conferences at her high school, and stood up for Niki when she'd been threatened with suspension for an incident in the school bathroom. An altercation that wasn't her fault. A group of girls had backed her up against a wall and held a pair of scissors to her neck. All of it came as a shock to Niki, because she had no idea why she'd been targeted. In short order, the leader of the bunch, a girl named True, started screaming that Niki had a lot of balls flirting with her boyfriend, a guy named Jace. When True threatened to kill her, Niki began to fight back. She ignored the scissors pressed against her throat, punched True in the arm, and kicked at another girl. When the girls backed off, she pushed through the group and managed to get out the door into the safety of the crowded hallway.

Once she made it to her next class, she vowed never to go to the bathroom during the school day again, and she sure as hell wasn't going to talk to Jace again either, not even to say hi. In her mind, the worst of it was over, but the next morning she was summoned to the vice principal's office and told she was being suspended for fighting. She tried to explain, but Mrs. Marzetti wouldn't listen, instead berating her as if the whole thing had been her fault. "I don't know what went on at your other schools, but we have zero tolerance for bullying at Central High," she said, pushing her glasses up the bridge of her nose. "Zero."

"They started it. They cornered me in the bathroom and held a pair of scissors to my throat," Niki said. "They threatened to kill me."

Mrs. Marzetti continued talking as if Niki had said nothing. Angrily, the older woman told her that one of the girls had a bruise the size of a tennis ball on her leg, and the other had a cut on her cheek. "You could have seriously injured them," she said indignantly.

"I didn't do anything to them. They attacked *me*. They threatened to kill *me*." The words hung in the air unacknowledged. Mrs. Marzetti told her to go to her locker and get her things. Her foster parents would be called to pick her up from school. Until then, she would sit in the entrance and wait.

Niki fought back tears of frustration as she left the room. This was a disaster. Her foster parents both worked full-time. Neither of them would come to get her until they were done with their shift. She'd be sitting for hours, and when they did show up, they'd be livid. They might even ask for her to be placed in a different home.

Crying, Niki made her way to her locker, fumbled her phone out of her backpack, and called Amy at work.

She'd barely gotten out the word *suspended* when Amy said, "Sit tight, Niki. I'll be right there." When Amy arrived a half hour later, Niki's heart swelled with gratitude at the sight of her advocate bursting through the door. Even better, as she began telling her what had happened, Amy was already irate on her behalf. By the time Niki finished the story, Amy was furious.

Amy stepped up to the counter where the two office ladies sat, silently tapping on their keyboards. "Excuse me," she said, her voice cutting through the quiet. "I need to see Mrs. Marzetti immediately."

They tried to give her the runaround, trotting out lines that sounded like total bull crap to Niki. *Mrs. Marzetti is busy. You should make an appointment—she could see you another day.* Amy leaned over the counter and said, "Another day won't work. I need to see her *now*." Her voice ratcheted up at the end of the sentence, startling Niki, who hadn't known Amy could sound like that.

The two women exchanged a look that made Niki wonder if they were going to call the security officer. Instead, one of them got on the phone and said something to Mrs. Marzetti in a hushed voice. When she hung up, she stood and said to Amy, "Mrs. Marzetti has a few minutes available. She can see you now." She pointed toward the hallway, and when Niki got up to follow, she said, "Not you, dear. This is just for the adults."

Amy beckoned to Niki. "This concerns her. She needs to be there."

Mrs. Marzetti's office was a different place now that Amy was there. Amy introduced herself as Niki's court-appointed special advocate. "I'm here because Niki's rights have been violated."

"How so?" Mrs. Marzetti frowned and tented her fingertips together.

"I believe that students in your care have a right to a safe environment, and when accused of a wrongdoing, they have the right to speak in their own defense. Niki has been deprived of both of these rights. As she's a foster child who's been through so much already, I find this especially egregious."

Especially egregious. Niki loved the expression and filed it away for future reference.

Mrs. Marzetti gave her the other girls' version of events and finished by saying that the school had zero tolerance for bullying. "Violence is not tolerated, and bullying is punished here."

Amy shot back, "I'm glad to hear that, because Niki has been bullied, and those girls are lying."

"They have injuries."

"Which they most likely inflicted upon themselves."

"And they back up each other's stories."

"As they would, of course. I don't know these girls, but I know Niki, and she is *not* a liar. I believe her version of events. She was attacked and threatened."

"We can go back and forth about this," Mrs. Marzetti said, "but I've made a decision and already filed the paperwork. My ruling stands."

Anyone else might have backed down or begged the vice principal to reconsider. Not Amy.

"Well then you'll have to unfile the paperwork," she said, "because here's what's going to happen. Niki will *not* be suspended. You'll be calling her foster parents and telling them it was a misunderstanding and she's not in trouble after all. Niki will be returning to her classes, and no further punishment will be given to her. And if there are any more of these mishaps, I expect a phone call from your office immediately, and I want Niki to be given the same consideration you give to the students that you favor."

Mrs. Marzetti began to object. "Wait a minute," she said indignantly.

Amy stood and talked right over her, the forward tilt of her shoulders establishing dominance. "No, you wait a minute. You should be ashamed of yourself, targeting a foster child who doesn't have a way to defend herself. I'm giving you an opportunity to make this right. If you're smart, you'll take it."

There was a stare-off between the two women. It probably only lasted a minute or so, but to Niki, it went on forever. Finally, Mrs. Marzetti sighed. "Niki, this time I'll let you off with a warning. I will call your foster parents to let them know. You may go back to class."

As Niki got up to leave, Mrs. Marzetti couldn't resist one final zinger. "True's parents are talking about calling their attorney."

Amy said, "*I* am an attorney. Please let them know I'd be happy to meet with their legal representative."

In the front office, Amy had handed one of the office ladies her business card, along with a request to have her number listed as Niki's first contact for emergencies.

Lying in Amy's old bedroom now, Niki thought back on this memory, and a slow grin crossed her face. Amy was a total badass, the boldest, best person she knew. Scrappy. Full of confidence and enthusiasm. Amy's mother, Sharon, wasn't much like her at all, which made her wonder what Amy's father had been like. "I never met the man," Amy had said when Niki asked about him. She said her mother had a one-night stand and opted to keep the baby. "I'm kind of glad she did," Amy said with a laugh. Her father never knew he even had a child, and Amy didn't seem to miss his presence or even wonder what had happened to him.

It was hard to look at a sixty-something woman and imagine her having casual sex and raising a baby alone, but then again, it was a lifetime ago.

Niki couldn't help but think that today, her first day on the job, was a new beginning in what could be a new life. Wanting to make a good impression, she put on her best pair of pants and the blue Magnificent Nutrition polo shirt, then pulled her hair up into a neat bun before going downstairs to get a bite to eat. After breakfast, Sharon drove her to the shopping center, dropping her off at the nutrition store and saying, "Call me when you're finished, and I'll swing by and pick you up."

Niki gathered her bag from the floor of the car. "Or I can just walk back. I mean, if it's too much trouble." She said it casually, her eyes downcast while she waited for Sharon's response.

"Don't be silly. There's no point in you being out in the cold walking through the slush when I can come get you in five minutes."

She and Sharon were just getting to know each other. Amy had told her that her mom was kind and easygoing, but Niki had learned that people had layers, and sometimes what lurked underneath the prettiness could be ugly and cruel. Of course Amy had known Sharon all her life, so presumably she'd encountered all sides of her personality, but people were often different with family members. Niki had learned that as a kid in foster care. Even the best families, the ones who clearly cared, couldn't help but favor their own flesh and blood when it really got down to it. This was different, though. Sharon was letting her stay in her home as a favor to Amy. She wasn't getting money for doing it, and she didn't seem to expect much from Niki. An open-ended stay as a guest. It seemed too good to be true, something that made her both grateful and suspicious. Good things didn't usually last for very long.

At least she didn't have to worry about some disgusting old guy pawing at her while she slept.

Getting a job so quickly seemed like a good sign. She was starting fresh. Things, she decided, might be different from now on. She knocked on the glass door, and when a woman came to let her in, she said, "Hi, I'm Niki. Max hired me yesterday?"

The woman, a tall blonde with frizzy hair, frowned. Her makeup was harsh-looking and garish under the bright store lights. She cleared her throat. "Yes. He hired you while I was out." The words hung in the air for one uncomfortable moment, and then she nodded. "I'm Max's wife, Dawn."

Niki had a talent for reading people's moods. *Taking the temperature of the room* was what Amy called it. From Dawn's body language and tone of voice, Niki surmised that Dawn clearly did not want her there. Mentally, Niki shrugged. Maybe Max hadn't gotten her approval, or maybe they couldn't really afford another employee. Either way, she wasn't about to give up before she even got started. She was here now and ready to work. "Max said you were in charge and would be training me?"

This seemed to soften things. Dawn said, "Have you worked in nutrition before?"

"No, but I'm eager to learn, and I promise you I will work hard. I think you'll find that I catch on quickly." Niki said the words with conviction, but to her they were like lines in a play. She did work hard, and she did catch on quickly, but it wasn't until Amy had coached her that she knew to say these things. Amy had said, "Employers need reassurance that you're the right person for the job. They also like it when you let them take the lead." *Let them take the lead.* A nice way of saying they wanted to be in charge, and the only thing they expected from employees was blind obedience. Well, Niki could play that game too. It was lame, but whatever.

"Good!" Dawn said. "I think you'll find there is much to learn, so you must pay attention to everything I say." She looked quite smug, as if ready to impart some earthshaking knowledge. "Let me show you around."

There wasn't much to the tour. The store was one big room, with the checkout counter and cash register off to the right side, and shelves of merchandise on either side. The juice counter was along the back wall, with a few café tables clustered in front of it.

Niki followed as the woman opened the refrigerator behind the juice bar, pointing out all the vegetables by name. "We got our celery, our beets, our carrots . . ." As she kept on, pointing out the ginger, apples, spinach, and on and on, Niki found herself nodding in agreement. When Dawn was done laboriously listing the contents of the fridge, she straightened up and said, rather sharply, "Don't you think you should be writing this down?"

Writing down the names of produce? Niki didn't speak the words that popped into her head. Instead, she said, "Yes, ma'am," and excused herself to get a notebook and pen out of her bag. An obedient employee, that's what she would be, even if it meant acting less than intelligent. That was the problem with these entry-level jobs. People assumed that if she was smarter she'd be doing something that required more mental acuity. Or at the very least she'd be attending college. They had no idea that she was in survival mode. Going to school wasn't an option and probably never would be, and just making it through the day was a priority.

As Dawn explained how things were done at the store, Niki realized that her job would be fairly straightforward. Washing and cutting produce was not difficult; knowing to wash her hands and use the provided gloves was common sense. Laminated cards behind the counter gave the directions for making each type of juice. Niki didn't need Dawn to demonstrate how to wipe off a counter, but she pretended to pay close attention. The cash register, which she would use only if Dawn or Max were not in the store, was very similar to the registers she'd used in other jobs, and wouldn't be a problem. "We prefer to handle all the transactions ourselves," Dawn said briskly. "You probably won't be at the register much, if at all." *In other words, keep your hands off our money.*

"Yes, ma'am." That was fine with her.

"When there are no customers at the juice bar, you'll be expected to clean, straighten, and stock shelves. If everything is in order, you can read up on all of our products. Customers will ask questions, and you'll need to be able to assist them in their selections." She waved at the shelves lining each side of the store, filled with plastic bottles of various vitamins, supplements, and powders. Labels above each area stated their purpose: *Energy! Weight Loss! Heart Health! Vitamins! Meal Replacements! Athletic Supplements!*

Dawn handed her two sheets of paper stapled together. "This is the employee handbook. Memorize everything on it, and put my number in your list of contacts. If you're ever going to be late, I need to know immediately. You can be written up for tardiness and fired for an unexcused absence. Here at Magnificent Nutrition, we value reliability."

Niki looked down at the dog-eared pages and said, "Of course. I think you'll find I'm very reliable."

Dawn presented another sheet of paper with a flourish. "And this is the Magnificent Nutrition employment agreement, which you'll need to sign. It says you agree to work for us a minimum of three months. It also lists all the reasons that give us the right to terminate employment. Also, here's a W-4 form. I'll need that filled out as well."

By the time the store opened, Niki had read the printouts and knew what was expected of her. It didn't take long to fill out and sign the other forms. None of this was as complicated as Dawn seemed to believe.

As the day progressed, Dawn hovered over her as she interacted with customers, watching carefully as Niki fed produce into the juicer and whispering directions to her every step of the way. It was her store, so Niki understood. She just hoped that with time Dawn would trust that she could do the job.

Max arrived in the afternoon shortly before Niki was to leave. He came in from the back, startling Niki, who was in the stockroom pulling merchandise to fill the empty gaps in the shelves. A trail of cold air followed him from outside. His face was ruddy from the cold. He nodded to her as he took off his hat and gloves, then shook off his coat, putting all of them in a locker off to one side. "So how was your first day?" he asked Niki.

"Fine, thanks," she said. "I'm learning a lot."

He nodded approvingly. "Glad to hear it."

Max walked past her into the store, and then she heard him greet his wife in a booming voice. "So how'd she do?"

Clearly, he was talking about her. Niki strained to listen to the response.

Dawn didn't even try to keep her voice down. "Not completely hopeless, but she's still on probation."

"I told you it would work out!" he said with fake cheer.

Dawn sighed heavily. "It hasn't worked out yet. One screwup and she's out the door."

CHAPTER TEN

When Niki made it through the first week of work without being fired, she considered it a triumph. Dawn never warmed up to her, but she did grudgingly admit that Niki was doing an acceptable job. Max was more friendly, but only when his wife wasn't around. Their lack of friendliness didn't bother her. She wasn't looking for a fan club, and she wasn't trying to build a career. She just needed to make money.

Money, money, money. Some people had far more than they could spend in a lifetime, so much that they could barely keep track of it. She wished they'd send some her way. She dreamed of winning the lottery or having some long-lost relative leave her a house and a vast fortune to go along with it. On really desperate days, she'd have settled for a windswept twenty-dollar bill landing at her feet.

She had no one to blame but herself. Amy had offered to pay for university classes or help her apply for scholarships, but she'd emphatically turned down both offers. She clearly remembered telling Amy, "Thanks, but no thanks." At that time, Niki was in the home stretch of her senior year of high school and mentally tired, exhausted really. She was ready to be done with classrooms and taking notes and memorizing random facts. Freedom was within reach, and she couldn't wait to have it in hand.

At eighteen, Niki was finished with people telling her what to do and giving her curfews. She was eager to get out into the world, to have her own place, to live life on her own terms.

She hadn't counted on it being so hard.

Right after high school, Niki had stayed on at her previous foster home for a few months, paying rent. Her foster mother, a grandmotherly type named Melinda, had said she could continue living there, but only for the summer because they would be moving that fall. The deadline had worried her initially, but by the end of August she'd met a group of young women who were renting a house and needed a roommate. They quickly worked out the details, and she was out the door and into their apartment on a day's notice. The place was a dump, and she had to share a bedroom, but their previous roommate had left a mattress for her to use, which was a plus. Rent was cheap, the house was on a bus route, and no one cared about her or her schedule. She came and went as she pleased.

Her roommates were so much fun initially. She reveled in the camaraderie, the sharing of food and liquor, the all-night gab sessions. They were nothing like the girls she'd known in high school. These young women lived for the moment. She found their stories about their families and coworkers hilarious and loved their relaxed attitudes. They were stoners, smoking so much pot that the apartment seemed perpetually hazy, as if in a dream. Even though she wasn't a smoker, it didn't bother her too much. What did bother her was the constant parade of men who came through the apartment. It wasn't uncommon to head into the bathroom first thing in the morning and be greeted by a strange guy with wet hair and a towel around his waist. Or no towel at all.

Even that wouldn't have been enough to make her move out. It was having someone steal $300 from her bag while she slept that did it. The bag had been on the floor right next to her mattress, so she'd thought it was safe for the night. *Ha!* Thinking about how long it took for her to make that money made her sick. So much time and effort for nothing.

She'd started seeing Evan about that time, and he said she could come and live with him and his friend. Evan was handsome, with dark curly hair and the kind of boyish grin she found hard to resist. He had a strong jaw and impressive biceps. Adding to the physical attraction was his magnetic personality and the way he spun tales of their life together. He was going to start a business, and they'd have plenty of money. He talked about trips they'd take and the presents he'd buy for her. Diamonds, cars, clothing. Anything her heart desired. She knew enough not to get her hopes up. She'd heard plenty of empty promises in her life.

It was easy to fall under his spell. He was charming in a twisted sort of way, throwing out compliments but then taking them back, always under the guise of a joke. One time he asked if she'd get in the trunk of his new car to check and see if the release lever worked. She agreed, but didn't think it was funny when he held the trunk closed. Still, Niki took it in stride. She went quiet and waited until he got worried and opened it himself. Then she pretended to be having a seizure, which freaked him out in a big way. Served him right. She could give it right back to him, and he seemed to like that about her. He had a good job and didn't smoke pot, being more of a beer drinker, which was really not a big deal most of the time, except he got mean when he drank too much, which was often enough. He started knocking her around, first grabbing her arm just a little too hard and giving her gentle but firm shoves. Weeks later when he started punching her, she packed her bags and found herself renting a room from a married couple she'd met through work.

That only lasted two weeks, because she woke up one night to find the husband leaning over her bed, one hand under the covers and sliding up her leg. Shocked, she sat up and asked, "What the hell's going on?"

"Nothing, nothing." He took a step back and held up his hands in surrender. "Just checking to see if you were okay. You said you felt sick, and we were worried." He scurried out of the room, gently closing the door shut behind him.

She'd never said she felt sick, but after he left the room she did feel nauseated, thinking about what might have happened if she hadn't woken up in time.

Niki didn't sleep the rest of the night. The next morning when she told his wife what had happened, she laughed dismissively and said, "He didn't mean nothing by it. I'll talk to him." She went over to the junk drawer in the kitchen and pulled out a brown rubber door stopper. "Next time you go to bed, wedge this under the door and you should be good."

Numbly, Niki walked away with the door stopper in her hand. Finding him in her room had been such a violation, and the fact that his wife downplayed it made her feel physically sick. She took the door stopper upstairs to her room and threw it under the bed, then packed up her things. One phone call to Amy, and within an hour Sharon was at the door to take her out of there. Niki knew that without Amy she'd have been without options. Reliable Amy. She couldn't imagine having a better friend or advocate.

Staying with Sharon was so easy, she almost wished that she was paying rent so she'd have a locked-in arrangement, something she could count on long term. Sharon's house was small, the smallest in the neighborhood, but it had three bedrooms and two bathrooms, which seemed a bit much for one old lady. In her younger idealistic days, she'd have imagined being adopted by Sharon and having the security of a permanent home. But she was beyond the age of adoption, and Sharon was too old to be her mother. Besides, Sharon already had a daughter.

After Niki had been living with Sharon about a week, her days began settling into a pattern. Sharon dropped her off in the morning and picked her up when her shift was over. When they arrived home, Sharon had dinner in the oven, always something hearty, with a vegetable or salad as a side dish. Over dinner, Niki told her about her day, spinning tales about customers and talking about Dawn and Max and the other employees, two high school girls whose work hours overlapped with hers only slightly. After they ate, Niki cleaned up the kitchen, something she'd insisted on from the first evening, and Sharon went into the living room to read. At that point, Niki usually excused herself to go upstairs, where she washed her work shirt out in the sink and hung it to dry above the bathtub. Dawn had promised another polo shirt was forthcoming when she was hired, but she hadn't mentioned it since, so Niki had her doubts. In the meantime, she counted it lucky that the shirt was polyester and dried quickly. Once that chore was over with, she went to her room, where she did yoga next to the bed and spent time on her phone, ignoring texts from her ex, Evan. *Baby, I miss you. I'm so sorry. It will never happen again. Please give me another chance.* She thought of blocking him and knew it might someday come to that, but the texts were tapering off in frequency, and some part of her liked that he wanted her back. It was never going to happen, but knowing it was completely up to her was empowering.

One night she found herself talking back to the texts. Evan wasn't known for being clever, so they were his usual.

I'm so sorry, Niki, it will never happen again.

"You got that right."

You gotta believe me, my life is nothing without you.

"Good, that's the way it should be." Saying the words aloud made her happy.

Please give me another chance.

"Been there, done that. You've used up all your chances."

Baby, I miss you.

"I'm not your baby."

After this last one, she shut the phone off and plugged it into the charger. Mentally, she felt as if she'd turned off Evan. "You have no power here," she said, setting the phone on the nightstand next to her bed.

When she heard a scrabbling at the door, she opened it to find the cat looking up at her with big green eyes. "Hey, Sarge. Come on in. What's happening?" She'd noticed that Sharon was in the habit of talking to the cat, and she found herself doing the same. Sarge wasn't a particularly cuddly cat, so when he came to visit her upstairs he always felt honored. Niki sat on the bed, and he hopped up next to her and allowed her to scratch under his chin, his purrs rumbling like a reliable engine. When Niki paused after a few minutes, he did a full-body stretch and then jumped down and went to the door, wanting to be let out. "See you later, Sarge," she said, closing the door behind him.

Glancing toward the window, she spotted movement in the Flemings' backyard. Quickly, she grabbed the binoculars she'd appropriated from the junk room and turned off the light in her bedroom. Raising the binoculars to her eyes, she adjusted the focus.

Except for the light over the back door, the yard was dark. The figure walking about wore a dark-colored hoodie and was holding something that lit up as she watched, shining a beam toward the ground. A flashlight. This had to be the teenage son Sharon had mentioned. *What is he doing?* Her eyes followed the movement of the light as he meandered around the yard, bending occasionally to pick something up. From the glow of the beam it was clear he was picking up dog poop, but why do it when it was pitch-black outside?

Niki was only idly curious about the family itself—it was the idea of a child being mistreated that had initially roused her interest. She'd noticed that Sharon made a point to drive past the Flemings' house after picking her up from her job, even though it wasn't the most direct route. On two occasions they'd spotted Mrs. Fleming, once in her car backing down the driveway, another time getting a package off her porch. There wasn't much that stood out, except for the woman's glossy red hair arranged in chic layers framing her face. A wealthy-suburban-lady cut. Very styled, in a color not seen in nature. She looked like a real high-maintenance type.

One other time they'd observed the teenage son as he walked

dispiritedly down the driveway, his hands in the pockets of his hooded sweatshirt, his jeans loose and sloppy. He was a portly kid, what her previous boyfriend Evan would have called a *heifer*. She'd corrected Evan once, saying that *heifer* only referred to a *female* cow, but he'd given her a withering glare that made her drop the subject before he got mad and became physical.

There was nothing about the Fleming family that indicated they had a foster daughter, so maybe what Sharon had photographed the other night had been a visitor after all. As she watched, Mrs. Fleming opened the back door to the house and screamed something that sounded like the boy's name followed by a continuous run of angry words impossible for Niki to make out. A little dog ran out between the woman's legs, and this seemed to aggravate her even more. Noticing the dog, the woman stepped out onto the porch and waved her arm in an aggressive manner. The shrill rise and fall of her voice cut right to Niki's core.

Niki tucked the binoculars under one arm and unlatched the window, then slid it up so she could hear better. A blast of cold air came through the screen, but it didn't matter. It was necessary if she wanted to hear more. She put the binoculars up to her face and scanned the yard.

Mrs. Fleming screamed, "Griswold, you get back here right now!" The little dog ran in circles, not responding to the command. "Jacob, stop what you're doing and grab that mutt!"

Jacob didn't even look up, but he waved his arm with the flashlight and yelled, "Ma, just go back in the house. I'll bring him in when I'm done."

The words were barely out of his mouth when she screamed back at him, "Don't you tell me what to do!" She looked up toward Sharon's house, and Niki stepped to the side of the window, even though she knew she couldn't be seen. "I want that dog in the house *now!*"

She was so angry that Niki anticipated a brawl right there in the snowy backyard, but instead Jacob ignored his mother, and she turned and went back into the house. The screen door banged shut, but the main door stayed open, the light from the house streaming out into the yard. A moment later she reappeared with a little girl, who she hastily pushed onto the porch. "Go get him," Mrs. Fleming ordered in a mean tone.

The girl trudged through the snow, calling out, "Griswold, come here, boy!" She wore jeans and an oversize sweatshirt that made her look even smaller than she was. Her hair was dark brown and cut into a short bob, just past her ears. At the sound of her voice, the dog stopped his crazed running and darted in a straight line right to her, joyfully leaping into her arms. She scooped him up and carried him back inside, where Mrs. Fleming stood impatiently waiting. Once the girl and the dog crossed the threshold, the door was slammed shut behind them. In the yard, the boy shook his head as he kept on searching.

The whole exchange lasted only a few minutes, and on the surface, it was really nothing. A dog got loose, a little girl was sent outside to round him up. Not a big deal. So why was Niki's heart pounding like it did during the suspenseful part of a thriller movie? Maybe it was because she could now confirm what Sharon had seen the previous week. There was definitely a little girl at the Flemings' house. Daughter? Niece? Foster child? Visitor? No way to know for sure. She didn't look like she was being abused either, unless you counted going outside for two minutes without a jacket.

But there was something off about the whole scenario. The child's clothes didn't quite fit her, and her hair looked like it had been chopped, rather than cut by someone who knew what they were doing. And why would Mrs. Fleming go out of her way to send the girl to get the family dog instead of doing it herself or waiting to let her son do it? By the dog's response, he clearly loved the little girl, so if she was a foster child, it was a good guess that she'd been living there for a while.

On the surface, the whole exchange appeared normal, but it still struck Niki as odd. Just odd. She wished she'd thought to take out her phone and get it on video.

Niki continued to spy until Jacob finished doing yard patrol and went back inside the house. She slid the window shut and latched the top before heading downstairs. She couldn't wait to tell Sharon what she'd just seen and that they finally had a name for the Flemings' son. Jacob.

CHAPTER ELEVEN

Sometimes Jacob wished his mother would die. Nothing too terrible, just a sudden heart attack or ruptured brain aneurysm—something fatal, but not terribly drawn out or painful. He imagined her collapsing and the rest of the family reacting to the sight: they'd cry in alarm and scramble to call 911. It would be best if it happened in the kitchen, he thought, where she could grab onto the counter on the way down, breaking her fall. That way there wouldn't be a lot of blood. Once the ambulance arrived, the paramedics would rush in and do what they could, but in the end, of course, it would be futile. "We're so sorry," they'd say, and he pictured himself mournfully nodding, sad but appreciative that they'd done their best.

Being motherless would bring him sympathy, and he'd be regretful that he and his mom never had much of a mother-son connection, but he wouldn't miss her, not for a minute. There was no point to her existence, as far as he could tell. The household was happier when she wasn't around. Even Griswold, who had a brain the size of a walnut, appeared nervous in her presence, his hindquarters trembling when she raised her voice.

Jacob tried to keep out of her way because just the sight of him provoked her. She either found things for him to do or criticized aspects of his personality and appearance. She said he had a bad attitude. His hair was too long. He needed to lose weight.

His weight was the most common complaint. The fact that he was fat made her insane, a symbol of her failure as a mother. She'd signed up for a family gym membership and was furious when he refused to go with her. She'd outlawed snack food of any kind and monitored anything he ate at home, forcing him to sneak around to buy junk food from the gas station on the corner. He was becoming a bit of a regular around there, stopping after school to buy bags of chips and sodas, which he surreptitiously hid in his backpack.

What his mother wanted was *the opposite of him*. She wanted a perfect son, an athlete with top grades, the type who competed on the debate team. His closet was filled with clothes she'd purchased—polo shirts and pleated khakis—none of which he would ever wear. When he was little she'd forced him to go to the barbershop on a regular basis, but when he hit his teen years he was able to physically resist, something that infuriated her. She'd given up on the idea of taking him to the barber, but he'd paid for it with weeks of her verbal abuse.

She was such a nutjob.

Occasionally, his dad would speak up in his defense. The last time had been when she'd hovered over him with a pair of scissors, threatening to cut his hair right there in the kitchen while he was trying to eat breakfast. His dad had looked up from his tablet and said, "Leave the kid alone. He's fine." This type of talk did not go over well with his mother, who could go off on an angry rant better than anyone he knew. At least it got her to put down the scissors and direct her ire at his father, allowing him to slip away.

After that, his dad had started taking him to the barber, but he let Jacob decide how he wanted his hair to be cut. Jacob liked it long, and not just because it made his mother crazy. Having his hair cut around his ears and off his neck made him feel exposed. Better to have a buffer.

His father said she'd always been moody, but she'd gotten worse after Olivia passed away. His sister, Olivia, had lived and died before he was even born, but he still thought about her from time to time. His mother never spoke of her, but his dad had told him the whole awful story. His dad had been out of town attending a medical conference. While he was away, Olivia, who was only five months old, had developed a fever, which his mother treated with infant acetaminophen. When the fever didn't break, she took the baby to the emergency room. Less than twenty-four hours later, Olivia was dead. His dad had rushed home from the conference as soon as he heard, but it was too late. The doctors said it was no one's fault. Sometimes, despite their best efforts, patients died. "When I heard it was meningitis, I had a bad feeling," his dad had said, shaking his head. Even years later, his eyes filled up with tears when he talked about Olivia. "When the baby died, your mother was destroyed. She blamed me, of course, for not being there." He'd sighed. "I'd hoped we'd get through it together, but it was never the same." Jacob got the impression that his dad blamed himself as well. "And when you were born, I thought it would help."

Sometimes Jacob wondered what it would have been like if Olivia had lived. Would she have been the golden child his mother had wanted? Would they have even bothered to have a second child? It added to the feeling that he was a disappointment to her.

The crazy thing was how much other people loved his mother. Teachers, neighbors, his friends. She could be charming when she wanted to be; too bad her own family never saw much of this side of her. During parent-teacher conferences, when discussing his terrible grades with his teachers, she was the epitome of the concerned, loving mother. He knew this because teachers often commented on it, one of them even telling him he was fortunate to have such a devoted, caring mom. *Ha ha!* If only they knew. The funny thing was how often this kind of comment surprised him when he should have been used to it by now. It had been going on his entire life.

When he was in grade school, she'd often volunteered in his classroom and accompanied the class on field trips. At school events she morphed into the perfect mom, calling him *sweetheart*, tousling his hair, telling cute stories about him to the other adults. Stories he didn't remember happening. It was confusing back then because he hadn't known it was just an act. He lost count of the times some other kid told him how lucky he was to have such a nice mother. Once one of the girls had told him that his mom was so beautiful: "Like a model." *Good grief.* What could he say to that? *That's just on the outside. You should see her cold, dead heart.* They'd never believe it. People were so easily fooled.

If only those same people could see her screaming about the dog getting loose in the yard. What did she expect when she stood there with the door open? She blamed Jacob because he hadn't cleaned the yard after school, but he'd just forgotten. It could have waited until the next day, but no, like a lunatic, she made him go out and pick up poop in the dark. And then she made Mia run out and get Griswold when Jacob had said he'd bring the dog in when he was finished. She couldn't even wait a few minutes. Everything was on her terms and her timeline. They were all prisoners to her whims.

Every member of the household knew that avoiding her was the best tactic for a peaceful existence. His dad traveled a lot for work, and Jacob suspected he added extra days onto his schedule to delay the inevitable return home. Jacob himself took refuge in his room and shut out his mother's harsh voice with the help of headphones. Mia, who had fewer options, had taken to hiding behind the couch. She thought Jacob didn't know this, but not much got past him. Mia played dumb, but she was smarter than his parents gave her credit for. They thought she could barely talk, which was laughable. When it was just the two of them, she talked plenty. She had a good vocabulary too. The little thing had somehow learned to read as well, but that was an unspoken secret known only by the two of them. That past summer he began giving her books he thought she might like, saying they were his when he was little when in fact he'd bought them at neighborhood yard sales.

It made her so happy. Seeing her face light up brightened his day a little bit too.

Mia was not mentally challenged, as his mother believed. There was nothing wrong with that kid's brain. Jacob could have corrected his mother, but he liked having an edge on her. Knowing something she didn't brought him immense satisfaction.

Living in this house was hell, but at least he could see a time when he'd be leaving for college. Poor Mia was doomed. She would be here forever.

CHAPTER TWELVE

The next afternoon, Niki was left alone in the store for the first time since she'd been hired. It had been a slow day, and after a trio of old ladies walked out of the store, she and Dawn were the only ones there. As Niki was cleaning up the juice station, Dawn approached and said, "I just need to run to the bank to make a deposit. I'll be back in fifteen minutes."

"Sounds good." Niki continued wiping the counter.

"So you'll need to cover the store while I'm gone." Dawn tapped a finger against the counter for emphasis.

"I understand. I will do my very best."

This wasn't the end of the conversation, however. As Dawn was heading out, she made a point to mention that she'd just replaced the cash register drawer. "So you should be all set if a customer comes in." Dawn met her eyes, waiting for a response, but Niki just nodded. She knew she was being tested. She'd encountered this kind of thing in foster homes and other jobs. Cookies and bags of chips conveniently left out. Money sitting unattended. Browsers left open to see if she'd use a device without permission.

People were always so quick to assume she would steal if given the chance. Well, she was a lot of things, and not all of them were good, but she was honest. She didn't take things that didn't belong to her, not ever. Sure, it had been tempting at times, but she had never succumbed. It was more a matter of practicality than integrity. Life as an honest person could be difficult, but life as a criminal always caught up to you. She knew friends and family members who resorted to stealing or writing bad checks to get money for drugs. No matter how careful they were, the story always had the same ending. It was very much, she thought, like circling a drain. You were going down at some point. You just didn't know when.

One of Niki's former CASAs, the woman before Amy, used to greet her by asking, "You keeping your nose clean, Niki?" Such a weird expression, like something from an old movie. Not to mention insulting. She wasn't a criminal—she was a foster kid, and not because she'd done something wrong. If anything, she went out of her way to play by the rules. Not that it was hard. People expected so little of her. Here at the store, for instance, they acted as if she needed constant supervision. Dawn had overemphasized the importance of handwashing and food sanitation, not knowing that Niki was fanatical about keeping herself and her surroundings clean. Fanatical bordering on obsessive. Niki found cleaning almost meditative. Wiping down counters, washing dishes, dusting. The act of transforming filth into cleanliness was satisfying on a soul level. Now that she was an adult and had control over her environment, she had definite preferences for how she wanted things.

Niki had finished cleaning the juice station and was stepping back to admire her work when the door opened and, to her surprise, in walked Suzette Fleming. The woman strode into the store, pulling off her leather gloves as she entered. She wore a knee-length tan suede coat that looked like it cost a fortune. Up close, her cherry-red hair looked even more striking, the blunt angles and layers so precise that she could have just walked out of a salon. Niki had told Sharon about seeing Mrs. Fleming, the dog, and the little girl the night before, so seeing Mrs. Fleming come into the store was a shock, as if she'd somehow conjured her up or inadvertently lured her into her personal sphere. The timing of her spying on this woman the previous evening and her sudden appearance at the store was unsettling. A wave of guilt came over her, a feeling that she was about to be confronted, so it was a relief when she came out from behind the counter and the woman showed no sign of recognition.

"Good afternoon," Niki said. "Welcome to Magnificent Nutrition. What can I help you find today?" This particular greeting had been scripted by Dawn, and Niki was required to say the words verbatim. It struck her as being a little bit pushy, but Niki didn't particularly mind. Usually people wanted to look around or asked about a particular product. Not this time, though.

Mrs. Fleming frowned as she shook off her coat and handed it to Niki. "Where is Dawn?"

"She just stepped out for a few minutes. I'd be happy to help you." Niki held the coat, not sure what to do with it. It was heavier than she would have expected; the material was soft and the lining expensive.

"No, no, no," Mrs. Fleming said, shaking her head. "I'm sorry, but that won't do. I have an understanding with Dawn. She's arranged to procure something specifically for me." Her voice was loud, and her stance, one hand on her hip, commanded respect.

"I can check the special orders in the stockroom," Niki said, carefully laying the coat across the counter next to the register. The store had limited shelf space, so they only carried the most popular products, but Dawn and Max would special order almost anything upon request. A few of their customers were weight lifters who bought protein powder in bulk. It was hard to believe the amount of money people spent on such things, but Niki wasn't about to question their judgment. These guys were enormous, all muscles, with shoulders that barely fit through the door. Niki hadn't noticed that any of the special orders had Mrs. Fleming's name on them, but she might have missed it. "If you give me a minute, I'll check and be right back."

Mrs. Fleming sighed impatiently. "Oh, honey, it won't be in the back. This is a private arrangement between Dawn and myself." She smiled as if Niki were a child who'd just said something nonsensical but oh-so-adorable. Mrs. Fleming leaned in toward Niki, so close that for a second she thought she was going to hug her. "Honey, here's what we're going to do. You're going to get on the phone and give Dawn a call and let her know I'm here waiting and don't have much time." She smiled, showing beautiful white teeth. "Okay, enough talking. Let's get started on that now."

Niki took in a long breath, considering. "She said she'd only be gone fifteen minutes, so I'm sure she'll be back any second."

"You really need to call her." Her voice was honey-coated, but her insistence made Niki uneasy. Dawn was a moody thing. Who knew what might irritate her? As if reading her mind, Mrs. Fleming added, "Believe me, she'll be glad. I'm one of her VIP clients."

This was the first time Niki had heard that there were VIP clients, but Mrs. Fleming spoke so authoritatively that she was willing to believe it. She'd been warned not to make any outgoing calls using the store phone; it was, in fact, a rule in the printout she'd been given. On the other hand, she did have Dawn's number in her list of contacts on her own phone. After vacillating for a second, she said, "I'll get my phone. It's in the back."

When she returned, Mrs. Fleming was standing in the same spot, peering into the mirror of a small compact. She snapped it shut and said, "What did she say?"

"I haven't called yet." Niki found Dawn's name and initiated the call, then held the phone up to her ear as she heard it ringing. "Hello, Dawn? I have a customer here to pick up a special order. Her name is . . . ?" Niki raised her eyebrows at Mrs. Fleming questioningly. She knew full well what the woman's name was, could even have recited her address if need be, but she couldn't let that piece of information slip. There was no good way to explain how she'd know such things.

Instead of answering, Mrs. Fleming lunged at Niki and impatiently grabbed the phone out of her hands. In a flash, she had it plastered to the side of her head. "Dawn, this is Suzette. We have a big,

big problem. Your idiot employee apparently doesn't know anything, so you need to get here immediately." She laughed brightly, as if making a joke. "Yes, yes, I know. I'm early, but then again I'm always early, so you should have known I'd be here. You know how cranky I get when I have to wait for my order." She chuckled at Dawn's response. "Okay then. I'll be here. Hurry! Buh-bye." She could have handed the phone back to Niki, but instead she walked over to the counter and set it next to her coat.

Niki felt a wellspring of exasperation build into full-fledged anger. She choked back the words she wanted to say and took a measured breath. She mentally went over her mantra: *You can't control other people, only yourself.* Nothing would be gained by unloading on this woman. She made a quick decision. She would contain her anger, pick up her phone, walk back to the juice counter, get back to work chopping up produce, and finish her shift. Dawn would be here any minute, and then *she* could deal with this red-haired bitch.

Niki went to get the phone, and from behind her Mrs. Fleming gloated. "Now that wasn't so hard, was it? You should have just listened to me in the first place instead of arguing. It's important to know your place, dear."

Up until that point Niki had felt in complete control, but now she'd been provoked beyond reason. Carefully, she turned around and said, "I do know my place. I was handling the situation in a professional manner. That phone is my personal property, and I did not appreciate having it grabbed out of my hands." The woman's face registered irritation at Niki's chastising tone, but she didn't respond. In fact, Mrs. Fleming made a point of not responding, pressing her lips together while defiantly raising her chin and looking away.

This wasn't good. If Mrs. Fleming had this attitude when Dawn returned, Niki might find herself in big trouble.

To defuse the situation, Niki asked a question. "Do you have children? We have a sale on kids' gummy multivitamins. They're berry-flavored, all natural, and sweetened with organic stevia leaf. Kids love them."

Mrs. Fleming didn't even look her way. "No, thank you."

"No, you don't have children, or no you aren't interested in the product?"

"I have a son who is seventeen. Far too old for gummy vitamins," she said with a sniff.

Niki sensed that in a minute this woman was going to become seriously angry, but she couldn't resist fishing a little more. Sharon had taken photos of a little girl, and she herself had seen the child in the Flemings' backyard. "So besides your son, there aren't any younger children in your household?"

"No. Not that it's any of your business." She gave Niki a steely glare. "Don't you have something to do? There's no reason for you to be talking to me." She made a point to snap open her handbag and rummage through the contents. Under her breath she muttered, "Impertinent."

Without a word, Niki went to the back of the store, where she turned her attention to inventorying the produce in the juice station mini fridge. Even from a distance she felt the tension in the store, so it was a relief when the front door opened and Dawn arrived.

"Hello, hello," Dawn called out cheerily, the words accompanying the chiming of the bell. "Sorry to keep you waiting. I came as quickly as I could."

Niki listened as the two women spoke in hushed tones, then watched as Dawn went into a locked cabinet behind the register counter and produced a small white paper bag, unlike the ones used in the store. Mrs. Fleming opened the bag and looked inside before tucking it into her handbag. She then produced a roll of bills and briskly placed them on the counter one at a time.

Dawn watched as the money was being laid out and nodded in approval. "We're all set, then. Thanks so much for stopping by, Mrs. Fleming."

"Just one more thing." Mrs. Fleming leaned in to whisper something, and both women glanced in Niki's direction.

There was a back-and-forth for another few minutes, and then Dawn called out, "Niki, could you please come here for a moment?"

Dutifully, Niki came out from behind the counter and joined the two women. "Yes?" She had a feeling she knew what was coming, so she held her head high and reminded herself that she'd done nothing wrong.

"Don't you think you owe Mrs. Fleming an apology?"

"Excuse me?"

"Don't play dumb, Niki. Mrs. Fleming told me you were very rude to her. We pride ourselves on excellent customer service here at Magnificent Nutrition, and the way you spoke to Mrs. Fleming earlier is not in accordance with our store policy. You need to apologize immediately."

She needed to apologize? Niki faced the two women, both of them looking at her with expectant smug expressions, and took a moment to swallow before speaking. "I'm sorry you weren't happy with the way I handled the situation, Mrs. Fleming. Next time, we can use your cell phone if you prefer." Niki noticed now that the stack of money on the counter behind Dawn was topped by a hundred-dollar bill.

Mrs. Fleming turned to Dawn. "See what I mean? She has an attitude."

"I don't have an attitude," Niki protested. "I was polite. Mrs. Fleming grabbed my phone out of my hand. I told her I didn't appreciate it."

"Niki!" Dawn said, shocked. "That is enough." She turned to Mrs. Fleming. "Believe me, I find this unacceptable. I am so sorry. This will be handled."

Mrs. Fleming frowned. "How? How will you handle this?" After a pause, she said, "Personally, I'd fire her for insubordination."

"Insubordination?" Niki said. "That's ridiculous. I wasn't insubordinate." She knew the definition of *insubordination*, and she hadn't crossed that line, not even close.

Dawn hesitated, but only for a second. "Niki, you're going to be written up for being rude to a customer. You need to leave now and go home and think about what happened here. We'll have a meeting tomorrow and discuss how this could have been handled better."

"You want me to leave *now*?" It was at least two hours before her shift was over.

"Yes, get your things and go. We'll talk tomorrow."

"Unbelievable." She said it quietly, her mouth aimed at the floor, but apparently not quietly enough.

"Niki," Dawn said, her voice a warning. "That's enough."

Wordlessly, Niki went into the back room, slipped on her hooded sweatshirt, grabbed her backpack, then returned, passing Mrs. Fleming and Dawn on her way to the store exit. Mrs. Fleming shot her a haughty look, and in return Niki gave her what Evan used to call her "death glare." Her throat seized up with the unfairness of the situation, but moments later, outside on the sidewalk, her anger abated when she came to the grim realization that it was too early to call Sharon to come pick her up. For one, she didn't think she could explain what had happened without crying. And she hated the idea of crying in front of Sharon. She knew none of this was her fault, really. Mrs. Fleming had been out of line, acting rude and superior. The woman had called her an idiot and grabbed her cell phone out of her hands. In a just world, Niki would have been in the right. But this wasn't a just world, and minimum-wage workers were expected to take whatever was dished out and never ever protest. That had been her mistake. She should have just said she was sorry and let it go, but some part of her couldn't stand being demeaned.

This inner strength was a fairly new development for her, and it didn't come easily. Her whole life she'd been a failure at sticking up for herself. It wasn't until she met Amy that she'd realized she had rights too.

And now she had to go home in defeat. She and Sharon were getting along so well, and Niki hated that she might think less of her because of this incident. The thought of disappointing Sharon was intolerable. Besides, Sharon had mentioned meeting a friend for lunch and had said that afterward the two of them were going to the mall to do some shopping. Two old ladies chatting over lunch and then walking around the mall. Who knew how long that might take? Sharon might not even be home yet.

Niki stepped off the curb and began the long walk to Sharon's house. A strong gust of wind smacked her in the face, and she reached back to pull her hood over her head. As she walked she leaned into the wind, blinking to hold in her emotions, but despite her best efforts, the tears came fast and hot, flowing down her cheeks. She wiped at her face with her sleeve and thought, *The hell with it.* She'd had a crappy day. She could cry if she wanted to. By the time she got to the edge of the parking lot, sobs overtook her with such force she was almost choking.

Niki kept walking, allowing herself to wallow in her own misery. The crying became part of the trek, her shoulders heaving as she kept her head down, one foot in front of the other, fighting the wind. The injustice of it was what really got to her. She could still see Dawn and Mrs. Fleming standing together, a united front against Niki. She couldn't keep working there, not if she wanted to hang on to her pride, but she couldn't quit either. Sharon would think she was a loser, and truthfully, she felt like a bit of a loser. She should have handled it differently. She should have let the whole thing slide. Yes, the woman had called her an idiot—so what? Customers were rude. It happened. This time, though, it had felt so personal.

She'd just have to start applying for other jobs right away and suck it up at Magnificent Nutrition in the meantime. She would take any job, any job at all, and quit as soon as she had something lined up for sure.

"I am not an idiot," she muttered aloud. At least the cold was motivating her to move quickly. Another fifteen minutes and she'd be home. With any luck, Sharon would still be out with her friend and she could pull herself together before dinnertime.

CHAPTER THIRTEEN

The sound of the key in the front door startled Sharon, who'd just gotten home and hung her coat on a hook inside the back hall. Her first thought was that it had to be Niki. Her second thought was that if it wasn't Niki, then it was someone breaking into the house, and she was in a world of trouble.

"Niki?" she yelled.

"Yeah, it's me."

So it was Niki, then. Of course it was. Who else? "You're home early today." Sharon slipped off her shoes and set them on the mat.

"Yeah, they let me leave before my shift was over."

Sharon called out, "I hope you didn't walk home. It's really windy out there."

"It wasn't too bad." And then a second later Niki added, "I'm going to take a nap before dinner, okay?"

"Sure." As Niki's footsteps echoed up the stairs, something nagged at Sharon. It wasn't that Niki was opting for a late-afternoon nap. It was, she thought, perfectly reasonable to want to rest, especially after a long walk home in the cold. So that wasn't the issue. It was the coming home early combined with the catch in Niki's voice as if she'd been crying. Sharon had a mother's intuition that told her something was wrong. Niki was early, which by itself meant nothing, but she was also sad. Something had happened. Maybe it had to do with her former boyfriend, the one Niki had only mentioned casually? *It didn't work out. He had a bad temper,* she'd said. *At times he was out of control.* It didn't take much for Sharon to read between the lines.

She went and stood at the bottom of the stairs, one hand on the newel post, and listened as Niki's footsteps crossed the ceiling above her head, ending with the creaking of the bed as she settled down to rest. Maybe she should go upstairs and talk to her? No, Niki was an adult, and Sharon didn't want to violate her privacy. Amy had been very clear about that: *Don't smother her. Don't ask too many questions.*

But there was a fine line between not asking and not caring. Caring about someone meant that sometimes you had to ask questions. Otherwise, how would you know?

As Sharon stood there wavering, the sound of crying reached her. Soft crying, probably not intended for her ears. She only heard it because of where she was standing. Crying was a deal-breaker in Sharon's mind. Hearing a child cry—even a grown-up child—couldn't be ignored. Not waiting another moment, she climbed up the steps, listening as she went. When she reached the top, the crying stopped, but she kept going, pausing outside Niki's door. It was slightly open. Pushing it the rest of the way, Sharon went in.

Niki was curled up on the bed, her body a comma against the bedspread. The blinds were still raised, making the scene bright, but a sense of gloom pervaded the room. Without a word, Sharon went to the closet and took out the spare blanket, then covered Niki, pulling the top edge around her shoulders and tucking the rest around her body. After she finished, she sat down on the edge of the bed and began to stroke Niki's hair.

Silently, Niki began to cry again, her shoulders hitching the way Amy's used to when she was fighting back tears. Unlike her mother,

Amy was tough, ready to take on anyone or anything. She rarely cried, and when she did, she tried to hold it back. Sharon, on the other hand, teared up during television Christmas movies and when reading, especially sad novels and touching greeting cards. She had a gift for crying, was a natural, in fact.

Even though they'd only known each other for a short time, Sharon felt a surprising tenderness for this girl. "I'm so sorry," she finally said, her words calm and measured. "Whatever it is, I'm sorry it happened. Just let it all out. It's okay."

Niki drew a great shuddering breath and seemed to calm down, so Sharon kept going, murmuring words of reassurance and stroking her hair. As horrible as it was for Niki to be so sad, it was nice for Sharon to feel useful, like she could make a difference.

A few minutes later, Sharon got up and went into Niki's bathroom, coming back with a box of tissues, which she set on the nightstand. She pulled one out and placed it in Niki's hand. In response, Niki sat up and blew her nose.

Sharon said, "Things will get better. They always do."

"Always?" Niki gave her a dubious look. Her eyes were red-rimmed and her face blotchy. Her hair, which had been pulled into a ponytail, was coming undone. She was a total mess.

"Well, sometimes it gets worse before it gets better," Sharon admitted, and Niki nodded like she had expected as much.

Grabbing another tissue, Niki dabbed her eyes. "What a crappy day."

"Would you like to talk about it?" Sharon asked hesitantly. "Sometimes it helps." She'd been worried about prying, so she was relieved when Niki nodded and started relating the story in bits and pieces, as if every word slightly pained her, but she was determined to get them out.

"Dawn told me to leave," Niki concluded. She wadded the tissue in her hand. "She said I was being written up and we'd have a meeting tomorrow to discuss it." Her voice was bitter and resigned.

"Do you think Mrs. Fleming recognized you at all?" Sharon asked.

Niki shook her head. "I don't think so. The light was off in my room when I was watching her last night. Plus, she doesn't seem like the type who notices other people."

Sharon nodded thoughtfully. "So what was in the white bag that Mrs. Fleming bought from Dawn?"

Niki tilted her head to one side, thinking, and finally said, "Oh, I don't know. I wasn't even thinking about that."

"Do you think it was something illegal?"

Niki's expression acknowledged the possibility. "Maybe. I mean, it wasn't with the special orders. And she paid for it with cash. A lot of cash. I noticed a hundred-dollar bill in the stack she left for Dawn."

Sharon pursed her lips in thought and said, "I think it's possible Dawn and Mrs. Fleming created a scene over your behavior as a distraction for whatever it was they were doing."

"Really?" Niki straightened up a little.

"Sure. A cash deal? Something's up. A transaction like that off the books? And she kept it in a locked cabinet?" Sharon felt indignant on Niki's behalf. "If Dawn is dealing drugs or shortchanging the IRS and it was found out, she'd be in a world of trouble. She could go to jail. Maybe Mrs. Fleming too. Dawn could lose the business. She probably didn't want you asking questions, so the two of them turned it around like you did something wrong—which, by the way, you didn't." She gave Niki's arm a motherly pat. "You handled it just fine. Better than I would have."

Niki grabbed another tissue and put it up to her nose. "I didn't even think of that. I was just so upset that she called me an idiot and grabbed my phone. And then she turned the whole thing around like *I* was the one at fault." She swallowed. "No one ever listens to me."

"I'm listening to you," Sharon said. "And I think you were completely in the right. I'm sorry you were treated that way. You didn't deserve it."

"Thank you." They sat in silence for a moment or two before Niki asked, "Do you think I should bring up what Mrs. Fleming was buying at the meeting tomorrow morning? Ask what was in the bag?"

Sharon said, "Oh, there's not going to be a meeting tomorrow."

"There's not?"

"I would hope not. Let me ask you one question: Do you want to keep working there?"

Niki sighed. "Well, no, but what else can I do? I don't have anything else lined up, and I can't sit around here all day. I figured I'd start filling out applications online and quit as soon as I got something else."

"It's up to you, but for what it's worth, I'd be glad to tell you what I think you should do."

"Tell me." Niki leaned forward, eagerness written on her face. Clearly she wanted some guidance.

"I would go in there tomorrow morning, give them their stupid polo shirt back, and quit."

"Just like that?"

Sharon nodded. "Just like that."

"With no notice at all?"

"Yep." Sharon watched the emotions play out on Niki's face. The uncertainty mixed with relief. She said, "I would think that taking a stand would be easy for you, Niki. You broke up with an abusive boyfriend and left that last house when it didn't go well. You quit your last job over the phone. I can tell that you're a strong person, and I think it's admirable. When I was your age, I was fairly spineless. It took a long time for me to give myself value."

"You won't mind that I'm unemployed and living in your house? You won't think I'm a quitter?"

"That's what you're worried about?" Sharon said in amazement and then chuckled. "Oh, honey, I don't care about that. You'll get something else soon enough. I have no doubt."

Niki took a minute to mull this over. "Okay then, I'll do it. I'll go in and quit tomorrow morning." She startled Sharon by leaning over and pulling her into a hug. "Thank you, thank you so much."

"For what? I didn't do anything."

"Thank you for listening to me and helping me." Niki pulled away, and Sharon saw that her eyes gleamed with fresh tears. "And for coming in and covering me up and being so nice."

"Not a big deal." Sharon shrugged. "I'm glad if it helped." She smoothed the front of her pants. "You deserve better than Magnificent Nutrition, Niki. I know you're feeling awful, but someday this will just be a funny story."

"You think so?"

"I know so." She stood up. "I think I'll go downstairs and start dinner. Don't worry about this anymore."

"Do you want help?"

Sharon smiled. "No, I've got this. Thanks." She crossed the room and stopped to look back when she reached the doorway. "You know I always hated that polo shirt."

"Me too."

"And they only gave you one. What was that all about?"

"I don't know." Niki looked down at the cheap polyester shirt. "They said they only had this one on hand and they'd ordered another one."

"You'd think it would have come in by now."

"Yeah."

"Well, the good news is that you'll never have to wear it again. Don't wash it before you give it back."

"I won't."

"I'll call you when dinner's ready. We're having spaghetti. You might want to keep that shirt on in case you accidentally drip some sauce down your front."

Niki nodded, her mouth stretching into a big smile. Sharon made her way down the stairs, her steps lighter than they'd been on the way up.

CHAPTER FOURTEEN

B y the time Ma'am came home, Mia had already set the table for the dinner she'd prepared earlier in the slow cooker. Chopping the carrots and onions had been the hard part. Jacob had helped her with the carrots, but he'd said she was on her own for the onions. "Cutting those things does a number on my eyes," he'd said before lumbering out of the room, his eyes cast down on his phone.

One time, a few months before, while chopping vegetables, Mia had wound up slicing her thumb. The cut had made a mess, and even though she'd held a paper towel to her hand, there had been blood everywhere, which got her in big trouble. Mister and Ma'am even got into a fight about it. Mister said Mia was too little to be using a sharp knife and that she shouldn't be using the stovetop either. Ma'am said he was being ridiculous, that the girl just needed to be more careful. Mister examined her hand and cleaned the wound, then put a Band-Aid on it. Every night after that he checked on it, peeling back the cover and asking her to bend her thumb, while his forehead furrowed with concern. When the cut had finally healed, Mia was a little sad that this was the end of having Mister check her thumb.

Ever since then, Mia could only use sharp knives on the days when Mister was out of town. Today was one of those days. She found that the rhythm of the house was different when Mister was gone, and she never knew what to expect. Sometimes Ma'am had all kinds of energy and wanted Mia to help her clean closets or wipe down all the baseboards; other times she stayed in bed and wanted Mia to bring her meals up to her room. The staying-in-bed days were good days for Mia because there was less to do. The bad part was that she had to listen carefully for Ma'am's bell and not keep her waiting.

This afternoon Ma'am came into the kitchen with a smile on her face. She still had her winter coat on, but she'd shed her boots and tucked her gloves into her pockets. "Oh, Mia," she said approvingly, "I could smell the beef roast as soon as I came in the front door." She lifted the lid and took a peek at the meal inside. "Not too bad," she said with a dip of her chin. "We'll make a cook out of you yet."

Mia said, "Yes, Ma'am." She'd just finished cleaning up the kitchen and now stood in front of Ma'am, her hands clasped together. When Ma'am left the kitchen to go to the front hall closet, Mia followed, awaiting her instructions. After Ma'am hung up her coat, she opened her handbag and took out a small white paper bag, then handed the handbag to Mia to be put away. Mia was about to do just that when Ma'am began to speak.

One hand on her hip, she said, "Oh, Mia, you have no idea how nice it is to come home after the day I had today. So much trouble! First I had to go to a board meeting, and that was aptly named, because believe me, I was bored. These ditsy women are planning a silent auction and don't have the foggiest idea of how to get organized. They talked and talked and talked and didn't get anywhere at all. Went round in circles. Of course, I knew how it all should go in the first minute, but I waited until they'd talked themselves into an argument, and then I stood up and took charge, giving each of them an assignment. You should have seen the look on Trina Meyer's face when I took over. She wasn't sure if she should thank me or strangle me." Ma'am let out a barky laugh, and Mia smiled. "And then I had lunch with Jana, and after that I ran some errands. Traffic was terrible. They have the interstate all torn up." She shook her head, the soft feathered layers bouncing as she did. "You're so lucky to be able to stay home."

"Yes, Ma'am."

"Oh, Mia, you're such a good girl. You know that, right?"

Mia nodded, her heart gladdened to be Ma'am's good girl.

"And you are so lucky to be here with us. When I think of how you were when we saved you, I can only guess what your life would have been like. Thinking about it makes me want to cry."

Mia hesitated, wanting to ask so many questions. Ma'am often referenced how she had saved Mia. She spoke as if Mia would remember everything that had happened, but Mia was just so little back then. Try as she might, she couldn't remember much about her life before she was part of the Fleming household. She had a faint memory of a woman singing to her. She could almost remember the sound of her voice, but not quite. There were other fleeting images that came to mind. Picking dandelions. The sensation of getting pushed on a swing, rising so high she might have been able to touch a cloud. But those images seemed like a dream or a wish. She might have been just imagining them. One time she'd asked Jacob about her life before she lived at their house. She'd asked him, "Where was I when I was saved?" She'd hoped for an answer, but Jacob just shook his head.

"Trust me," he said. "You're better off not knowing." He wouldn't say, but what he didn't realize was that she'd tricked him, because before that she wasn't sure if he knew anything at all. Knowing that he knew the story of how she came to live here was important because it meant that maybe, sometime in the future, Jacob might tell her more when he was in a better mood. She knew that she would ask again, and keep asking until he got tired of it and answered her question. And when he answered, she'd know it was the truth. Sometimes when she'd question him, he'd say, "You know I'd never lie to you, right, Mia?" And she agreed because he never had.

Ma'am, of course, was the one who constantly mentioned how

lucky Mia was to have ended up with them. From the way she spoke, it sounded like Mia had been in a dumpster or under a pile of leaves. Today, Ma'am's mood seemed warm and friendly, making Mia feel bold enough to ask a question, something she never did. She opened her mouth and started to say, "When I was saved—"

But Ma'am interrupted. "And then I had to deal with this new employee at the nutrition store." She let out a snort. "The things I have to put up with. This girl was unbelievable. The little snot had the audacity to talk back to me. The nerve! If I were Dawn, I would fire that girl. Imagine mouthing off to me, their best customer. How dare she!" She began to walk down the hall, the white paper bag dangling from her fingertips. Ten feet away, she turned around. "Mia! Try to keep up. The day is far from over, and there's so much still to be done."

Mia scrambled to catch up, Ma'am's handbag still dangling from her elbow. Ma'am would have a thing or two for her to do, but it wouldn't be as bad as usual. The white bag meant she'd be in a much better mood very soon. Before long, Ma'am would be lounging in her bathrobe, watching Netflix in bed, and then she'd forget all about Mia. Sometimes she even forgot to tuck Mia in for the night, and the door would be unlocked for the entire night. On those occasions, Mia had been too afraid to leave her room, but knowing she could walk around the house unmonitored was both scary and exciting. One of these days, she might actually try it.

CHAPTER FIFTEEN

The next morning Sharon drove Niki to work a little earlier than usual. Niki had said no to breakfast, saying she wasn't hungry.

"Let's just go and get it over with," Sharon said, holding up her car keys. "You'll feel better when it's done." For most of the ride they were silent.

"I'm not going to lie," Niki said as they turned into the parking lot. "I'm a little bit nervous." She glanced at Sharon, hoping for some reassuring words. They'd talked about her plan for quitting earlier at the house. Sharon was of the impression that this should be easy for Niki. She made some good points to back this notion: Niki had been the one to break off her relationship with Evan, she'd quit her last job without notice via voice mail, and she'd had no problem leaving the last place she'd lived after the incident with the husband. But—and this was a big *but*—the commonality among all three was that Niki had been pushed to her limit and had panicked, making decisions without really thinking about them. This time around it was different. She had time to mull over the sequence of events, and she felt as if she'd screwed up.

It might not be so easy to get another job, and how long would

Sharon let her live there if she was unemployed and not contributing financially? Even extreme kindness had its limits.

"It's okay to be nervous," Sharon said. "Have you changed your mind? Do you want to keep working there?"

"No." The word came out almost involuntarily. Niki did not want to work there—just the opposite, in fact. What she'd hoped for was to drop off her shirt and never set foot in Magnificent Nutrition again. The idea of quitting was appealing. It was the going inside and talking to Dawn that was the hard part. If she could, she'd do a drive-by quit, yelling "I'm done!" and tossing the shirt out the window as they drove past.

"It's okay to quit while being nervous. Either way gets the job done."

The parking lot was nearly empty. Sharon pulled into a space facing the storefronts. Through the glass, Niki saw both Max and Dawn inside the store. "Oh man, they're both here," she said, her heart sinking.

"Both?"

"Max and Dawn." Niki had never known a time when both of them were there when the store opened. She imagined it was planned, that they intended to tag team her with criticism, or maybe play good cop, bad cop. "I don't know if I can face them. Maybe I could call or text instead?"

"You could do that," Sharon said thoughtfully. "But don't you think it will feel good to face them and tell them why you're quitting? No one has the right to call you names and take your phone away from you. And for Dawn to take her side? That's just wrong. I would think speaking your truth would be empowering."

"I guess." Niki sighed, not moving a muscle.

"I know this feels like a big deal, but someday you'll look back and be glad you stood up for yourself. And very soon, something much better will come your way. Believe me, life turns around in an instant, usually when you don't see it coming. I've had it happen to me over and over again. One of the benefits of being old." Sharon smiled.

"Really?"

"Really. You want me to come in with you?"

"Would you?"

"Sure. I'll just stand by for moral support." Sharon shut off the engine, looped her purse over her shoulder, and opened the door. "Are you coming?"

"Yeah." Niki left her bag in the car and walked across the lot, the polo shirt slung over her arm.

Sharon entered the store first, holding the door open for Niki to follow. As Niki walked past, she whispered, "You can do this."

Niki had planned what she was going to say: *I can't continue working at a place that doesn't support their employees, so I am quitting. Yesterday was my last day.* The rest of the plan involved dropping the tomato-stained polo shirt on the counter and then turning around and leaving. Her plan was slightly complicated by the fact that Max was here, restocking a vitamin display on one side of the store, while Dawn was behind the counter giving her a steely-eyed look. It would be impossible to face them both at the same time, so she made the decision to give notice to Dawn. Niki drew a deep breath and walked over to the register, then set the shirt on the counter.

"What's this?" Dawn said sharply, looking at the shirt like it was roadkill.

Niki could almost feel Sharon's wave of support from behind her. *You can do this.*

She stood tall and said, "I can't continue working at a place that doesn't support their employees, so I am—"

"You gotta be kidding me," Dawn said, slamming her palm onto the counter. "You're quitting? After all the time we spent training you?"

Niki's heart pounded as she forced out the rest of the sentence. "So I am quitting."

Dawn yelled across the store, "Are you getting this, Max? The little bitch is walking out on us."

"Hey, hey, hey," Sharon protested, coming to Niki's side. "There's no need for name-calling. Let's try to be civil here. Niki could have just bailed on you, but instead she came to explain and return your shirt."

"And you bring your grandma to fight your fight for you?" Dawn came out from behind the counter, the stained shirt clutched in her fist. "You should be ashamed of yourself!"

From the other side of the store, Max weakly called out, "Now, Dawn."

Determined to finish, Niki said, "Yesterday was my last day."

Sharon said, "Let's go, Niki." She took her elbow and led her to the door.

Right before they left, Dawn yelled, "She signed a clause that said she promised to work for a minimum of three months. Did she mention that, Grandma? It's legally binding. We could sue her and win."

Niki had completely forgotten about having signed that agreement. Could it be legally binding? She looked to Sharon, who had a sudden fierce look on her face.

"I'm glad you mentioned legalities," Sharon said, her voice carrying across the room. "Because that's one of the main reasons I encouraged Niki to quit. I don't want my granddaughter working for a place where the owners are dealing drugs. I think the police would be very interested in hearing about your special orders for VIP customers."

Dawn's jaw dropped, and her face went pale. Sharon stood her ground, holding her glare for what seemed to be a really long time, then wordlessly she turned and went out the door, with Niki right behind her. Once they were inside the car, Niki said, "Well, that was a definite mic drop."

"Sure was!" Sharon said, starting up the engine. "Whatever that means."

"It's like . . ." Niki stopped to think. "It's like saying you got the last word. You showed her."

Sharon nodded. They sat for a moment, watching the store. Max had left the box of vitamins sitting on the floor and was now with Dawn behind the counter. From their vantage point, it looked like Max and Dawn were having an intense conversation.

Niki said, "Did you see her face when you mentioned drug dealing?"

"I surely did."

"Too bad we don't have any proof. I'd love to file a police report." As she spoke, Dawn picked up the receiver to the store phone and began punching buttons. Niki said, "Who do you think she's calling?"

"Suzette Fleming. They have to get their stories straight."

"You think?"

"Yes, I do. She's afraid, as well she should be." Sharon turned to Niki and gave her arm a gentle pat. "At least you don't have to worry about your three-month clause. They'll want no part of you after this."

"I hope you're right."

"I am right. You can count on it."

"Well," Niki said, "if they did sue me, they wouldn't get much out of it."

"That's the spirit." Sharon grinned and pulled out of her parking space. When they were almost to the turnoff that led into her neighborhood, she veered into the gas station on the corner. "This will just take a minute."

"I can pump if you want me to," Niki said, unclicking her seat belt.

"No, I've got it." Sharon pulled a ten-dollar bill out of her wallet and handed it to her. "Why don't you go in and get us some dough-nuts? Maybe four or so? Your pick. We can have a job-quitting cele-bration once we get home."

Oddly enough, Niki's appetite, which had been a dull void only fifteen minutes before, had suddenly returned, and now she felt her stomach twinge at the reference to doughnuts. Sharon seemed to have an innate sense for just how she was feeling. She took the money and went into the gas station, heading straight to the doughnut case. Through the front windows she saw Sharon talking to a woman at another pump. Sharon was an odd one to figure out. Friendly, but not too friendly. So quiet you'd think she could be easily pushed around, but Niki was getting the impression that there was a strength behind that pleasant facade. Sharon just didn't pull it out very often. Not like Amy, who was a *presence*. Amy drove assertively, and when she had the radio on, the music was loud. Sharon waved other drivers in front of her like she had all the time in the world, while Amy was impatient if the cars ahead of her took too long to move when the light turned green. "Take a look at that guy," Amy would say, pointing to a car in front of them. "Who gave that dipstick a license?"

If Amy had gone with her to Magnificent Nutrition that morning, she would have confronted Dawn right from the start, whereas Sharon didn't say anything until Dawn had insulted and threatened Niki.

Two different ways to be strong.

The doughnut display was half full with plenty of options, so Niki took a bag and with a piece of waxed paper chose two crullers, a Long John, and a jelly doughnut. Next to her, at the coffee stand, a woman in a gray wool coat and black high heels was pulling on a lever to fill a cup with cappuccino. When Niki got to the counter, she was greeted by an older man with a full head of wavy gray hair and a slight paunch. He was dressed in a red flannel shirt and jeans, a Northwoods look that Niki had noticed more of lately, so maybe it was coming back in style. This man didn't look like the kind of person who cared about style, though. He'd probably been dressing this way for sixty-five years. "Good morning, young lady," the man said, and his smile was so bright she couldn't help but smile back. "How many doughnuts you got lurking in that bag?"

"Four." She handed him the money, and he rang up the purchase and counted back her change.

"Here you are, miss. You have the best day ever, you hear?"

It was a cheesy line and one he probably said to every single customer, but even so, the positivity of it lifted her spirits. "I will." As she turned to leave, a sign posted by the door caught her eye.

HELP WANTED

Be part of the Village Mart team.

Good hourly pay, flexible hours.

Niki waited until after the other woman paid for her cappuccino, and then she backtracked to the counter. "I'd like to be part of your team," she said. "Do I apply online?"

"If you want," he said. "Or I can give you an application right this minute." He reached under the counter and handed one over. "If you're really interested, I can interview you now. My brother, Fred, is in the back room, and he can cover the register."

"I'm really interested," Niki said, glancing through the window. "Can I just run out and let my grandma know? It'll only take a minute."

"Take as much time as you need." He leaned back, crossing his arms and laughing. "I'm not going anywhere. I'll be right here."

CHAPTER SIXTEEN

L*ife turns around in an instant.* That's what Sharon had said, and Niki marveled at the truth of it. Within the span of two hours, she'd quit a job and then gained a better one. The Village Mart was owned by two brothers, Fred and Albert, both old guys who seemed afflicted with some kind of personality disorder that kept them in a perpetual good mood. Albert had smiled and cracked jokes during the interview, which put her at ease. After a few minutes, she forgot she was being interviewed and joked right back. She was hired on the spot.

The pay was a dollar an hour more than at Magnificent Nutrition, and the hours were better too: Wednesday through Sunday from nine a.m. to five p.m. She would never have to open or close—one of the brothers would always be with her. And best of all, the place was only a few blocks away from Sharon's, so she could walk to and from work.

The doughnuts she'd purchased turned out to be a celebratory new-job feast. "I knew you'd get something," Sharon said once they were home sitting at the kitchen table. She had her coffee cup in front of her and was now choosing a doughnut.

"I don't know about that." Niki took a sip of her orange juice. "But I'm feeling really good about this. It will be nice to have regular hours." Albert had given her the choice of the night shift or the day shift, and she hadn't hesitated in choosing day hours.

"You don't mind working weekends?"

Niki shrugged. "Nah. Every day is sort of the same for me. I'll work whenever they need me. I told them I could come in on my days off too if they needed someone." Albert had seemed particularly delighted to hear this. She took a sip of her orange juice. "Can I ask you a question?"

"Of course."

"When you were talking to Dawn, why did you say I was your granddaughter?"

Sharon smiled slowly. "Did that bother you?"

"No, I just wondered."

"Well, she assumed as much, so it seemed easier just to go with it. And then, after she called me your grandmother, I realized I kind of liked the idea. I'd be about the right age to be your grandma." She sighed. "Amy has made it very clear that she's not having kids, so I guess thinking of you as my granddaughter is a kind of wish fulfillment. I hope you don't mind."

"Mind?" Niki said, amazed. "I don't mind. I'd love to have you as a grandmother. I'd be *lucky* to have you as a grandmother." Sharon was far better than any of her own relatives. Even the nicest of them were unreliable, and all of them had so many problems. Dysfunction ruled—they had everything from addiction, to money problems, to the tendency to break the law. Sometimes she wondered how she'd come out okay, given her role models. Of course, she was still young. She had plenty of time to screw up.

"Good, because I ran into one of my neighbors at the gas station, and she'd noticed you and me coming and going in the car. When she asked who you were, I said you were my granddaughter and that you were living with me now." Sharon put her hands around her coffee mug. "It just slipped out. Funny how she just accepted it and didn't ask any more questions."

"I told Albert at the gas station that I was living with my grandma," Niki admitted. "It's too complicated to explain, and I didn't want to get into it." She'd learned long ago not to volunteer her foster-child status. People were either inappropriately curious, asking way too many questions, or else they reacted with pity. The pity was far worse. Niki didn't need people looking down on her, and she especially didn't want to be labeled as *the foster kid*.

Being placed in foster care hadn't been her fault. She and her mother had been doing just fine and could have gone on operating like that indefinitely. Yes, her mother was an addict, and often they were low on food or had to move because the rent wasn't paid, but she knew her mother loved her, and Niki always found ways to get them through each week. Single-handedly, she held them together. And then, when she was twelve, their stupid neighbor across the hall, Mrs. Washington, turned them in and suddenly they were being investigated. The woman at child protective services said that Niki shouldn't have to be the grown-up, that the system would help her mother get the help she needed, and the two of them would eventually be reunited. Instead, Niki was sent to live with strangers, and a few months later her mother overdosed and died. If Niki had been there, it would never have happened. She would have been able to stop it.

And then, all the friends and family members who'd drifted in and out of her life up until then drifted out permanently. Her father had been in prison the last she'd heard, but even if he wasn't, she barely knew him, and what she knew wasn't good. All the relatives had an opinion about what should happen to her, but no one wanted to be responsible for raising a child. The one uncle who said he would take her as long as he got the foster care money was ruled out due to his criminal past. At the time it had been a letdown, although in retrospect it was just as well.

"So that's it, then," Sharon said. "As far as the world is concerned, you're my granddaughter and I'm your grandmother."

"I'm still calling you Sharon, though, if that's okay."

"Fine with me."

Training at the Village Mart was a fun experience, something she could never have said about previous jobs. Albert and Fred were impressed by how quickly she caught on at the register and constantly complimented her on her interactions with customers. "Holy cow, she's on fire!" Fred said. "We better watch out, or Niki will be replacing both of us." He nudged his brother with his elbow.

"And that's a bad idea, why?" Albert answered, slapping the counter. Albert and Fred were the opposite of Dawn and Max, leaving Niki to wonder why some people were so miserable while others were naturally upbeat. The happiness of the two brothers was infectious. It shot off of them like moonbeams. Everyone who came into the gas station was affected by their congenial personalities. Customers always walked out with a smile on their faces. For the first time ever, she didn't mind going to work.

On her second day of work, she came back to Sharon's to find that a large box had been delivered while she was out, and it was addressed to her. "What's this?" she asked Sharon, who just shrugged.

"I guess you'll have to open it and see."

Inside was a winter jacket, gloves, scarf, and a hat, all gifts from Amy, who'd apparently been talking to her mother. Sharon had been fussing over Niki's lack of a coat for a while now, and she'd offered to take her to the store to shop for what she called *winter outerwear*. She'd made it clear that she would pay for it, saying it would be her pleasure. Niki had refused on principle. She was not a charity case, and she could tolerate the cold. Someday, when she felt like it, she'd buy a coat with her own money.

A gift, though, that was something different. Since Amy had gone to the trouble to pick all this out and have it shipped, it would be rude not to accept.

Niki pulled the coat out of the box and held it up against her front. It was a dark blue, almost black, and had just the right heft. Heavy enough to be warm but not so thick as to be bulky. It had a hood that lay flat against the back when not in use. She approved. The scarf was a maroon knit made up of one long loop, and the hat was a slouchy beret of the same color. The gloves were the same blue as the coat. She wasn't sure about the hat, preferring not to have anything over her hair, but everything else was just right.

She put on the coat, lifting her hair from underneath, and zipped up the front, then tried the gloves, which fit like they'd been custom-made for her.

"What do you think?" Sharon asked.

"Perfect," Niki said, splaying out her fingers to test the gloves.

"It looks good on you." She nodded approvingly. "Now I don't have to worry about you being cold. I always felt so terrible seeing you outside in just that hoodie, and now with you walking to work I was afraid you'd get sick."

She'd been worried about Niki being cold and getting sick? That was so sweet. Thinking about this made Niki feel like crying. She'd had some good foster parents, the kind who seemed to care about her, but she'd never gotten the sense that they *worried* about her. More like they wanted to do a good job. "You really are like a grandma," Niki said, and then she turned away, worried that if she saw Sharon's face she might start crying. "I think I'll text Amy and thank her."

Walking to work the next day was a better experience now that she had the appropriate outerwear. When she arrived at the gas station, Fred said, "Nice jacket."

"It's new," she volunteered. Fred and Albert had such a reas-suring presence that she found herself telling them things she wouldn't ordinarily reveal. "A present from a friend."

"Nice friend."

"You can say that." Niki had made a lot of friends over the years, but once she was no longer at the same school or job or foster home, they'd all seemed finished with her. People just didn't stay. Except for

Amy, which made her about the best friend she'd ever had. Unbe-knownst to Sharon, she texted Amy nearly every night. Sometimes it was just a brief exchange, but it was nice to shoot off a text knowing Amy was on the other end. Amy had been particularly impressed by how her mother had handled Dawn when Niki quit. Amy had replied, *I'm glad she has your back.* That made two of them.

Although it was only her third day working at the gas station, she was already comfortable with the routine, ringing up purchases, running outside to assist customers who were having trouble at the pump, and making sure the store was clean and orderly. At times, Albert told her to relax. "You're making me nervous. It's fine just to take a breather now and then. You'll notice we aren't killing ourselves."

The brothers knew their customers well, commenting on purchases or noting when someone drove a different car than they usually did. They knew a lot of their names, too, and made a point to introduce Niki to the regulars. "Niki just started earlier in the week, and she's already indispensable," Fred would say. "I don't know what we did without her."

The busy times were the best because the hours just went. At the nutrition store, the clock had moved at a sloth's pace. Here, the day flew. Even when customers didn't come inside, Fred or Albert had commentary about those filling up at the pump. And when no one else was around, they told her stories from their youth, the times they'd gotten in trouble at school, tales of growing up in the country, and the jobs they'd had before buying the gas station. So many stories and so interesting. They said she was a good listener, which wasn't hard because she enjoyed talking to them. They were funny and kind, a good combination.

After lunchtime there was a lull, but later in the afternoon it picked up again. That afternoon, Fred was stocking the beer cooler and she was behind the counter when Jacob Fleming walked in. He wore his usual sweatshirt with the hood up, his face obscured and head aimed downward, like he was attempting to be invisible.

Despite this, she recognized him right away. She felt the same jolt of familiarity that she'd had when his mother had come into the nutrition store. Until then, it had never occurred to her that she might encounter one of the Flemings at her new job, but now it hit home in a big way. This gas station had to be the closest one to their house, and they did have two cars that needed fuel. There was a real possibility that she might come face-to-face with Suzette Fleming again in the near future. Not a great thought, but she consoled herself with the fact that one of the brothers always worked with her, and they were nice about letting her leave her post to go to the bathroom or whatever. If the woman came in, she always had the option of slipping away and letting them handle the transaction.

Seeing Jacob not only reminded her of his mother, that vile woman, but it also put her in mind of the little girl she'd seen retrieving the dog from the yard. If Jacob came in on a regular basis, maybe she could establish a friendly connection with him and eventually get him to talk about the child. There was probably a reasonable explanation for why the little girl was staying with the family, but something nagged at her to find out for sure.

She watched as Jacob put his hood down, then skulked around the edges of the store, stopping in front of the snack section. After deliberating for a few minutes, he grabbed a big bag of chips, then went straight to the beverage cooler, opening the door and taking a can of Coke. Fred caught sight of him just as the cooler door closed. "Hello! Good to see you, Jacob."

"Thanks. Good to see you too." The words were a mumble, but the kid managed a slight smile. Even surly teenagers couldn't help but be affected by Fred's good cheer.

"Say hello to Niki, our new hire," Fred called out, gesturing with his thumb. "I think you'll find her to be an improvement over the other old codgers who work the day shift. Already she's making the place better."

Jacob loped up to the counter and set down his items. "Hi, Niki."

"Hey, Jacob, it's nice to meet you."

"Nice to meet you too." He fished some dollar bills out of his pocket while she rang up the purchases.

She counted out the change and dropped the coins into his palm. "Do you live around here?" she asked.

He nodded. "Over on Maple Avenue."

"I'm right behind you, over on Crescent Street," she said. "I moved in with my grandma not too long ago."

"I wish I could live with my grandma," he said, his face glum.

"Yeah, it's pretty sweet. Are your parents hard to live with?" A fishing expedition, but she had a feeling it was true, and the fact that he wasn't making a move to leave was a good sign. She had his attention.

"My mom is. My dad's okay. He's not around much, though." Jacob sighed.

"Tell me about it. Moms can be the worst," she said sympathetically, tucking a strand of hair behind her ear. "And at my house there was no escape. I'm an only child, so the focus was always on me. I always wanted a brother or sister. It would have been nice to have someone to talk to, but it never happened."

"Yeah, I'm an only child too."

"No other kids in the house?" She tried to sound nonchalant, even as she studied his face for a reaction. And there it was, a slight hesitation. Just for a moment, but she was sure of what she saw.

"Nah," he said finally, with a shrug. "Just me." He set his backpack on the counter and tucked his purchases inside. "Nice meeting you, Niki."

"Nice meeting you too. I hope to see you again soon."

He nodded and headed to the door, stopping to look back as he left. Niki gave him a smile and a small wave. She'd made a connection. He'd be back, she was sure of it. Then they could talk again. Eventually she'd get it out of him. Teenage boys didn't talk as much as girls, but she was gifted in listening and asking the right questions. Sometimes that was all it took.

Fred came and joined her behind the counter. "That was nice of you, making small talk with Jacob."

"Does he come in here a lot?"

Fred tilted his head, considering. "Depends on what you mean by a lot. Twice a week, maybe? Always to stock up on junk food. His mother doesn't allow it in the house, so we're his go-to place for salt and sugar. The first couple times he came here I could barely get him to make eye contact."

"You guys won him over." Niki said it as a statement.

"Wasn't easy. He's a shy one." Fred smiled. "And he's got something weighing on him, that's clear to see."

"Do his parents ever come in?"

Fred shook his head. "I've only seen him with his dad. Don't know the mom, but Jacob makes her sound like a prima donna, so I'm guessing she leaves the gas pumping to her husband." Niki had more questions, but at that moment, the door swung open and a petite blonde woman walked into the store. Fred went into greeting mode. "Mrs. Timmerman, looking lovely as always. How are you today?"

For now, Niki was content to let the subject of Jacob Fleming drop. There would be other opportunities.

CHAPTER SEVENTEEN

When Jacob got home, he was glad to see his mother's car wasn't in the garage. He hated the damn thing because it was an extension of her, a stupid, shiny car, a silver Audi designed to attract attention and admiration. She loved the Audi more than anything else in the world. Of course, she only loved it for three years, after which she traded it in for a *new* silver Audi. To Jacob, the replacement always looked almost exactly the same as the previous car, so he didn't see the point of it. His father felt the same way, and each time he tried to talk her into hanging on to her car for a few more years, but she always ignored him. "This year's model has better safety features," she'd say. Either that or she'd claim it got better mileage. It didn't really matter what she said—both Jacob and his dad knew the truth. It was all about status. Once his aunt had erroneously referred to his mom's car as an "Acura," and she'd stewed about it for a week. "As if I'd drive an Acura," she'd said, insulted.

The absence of the Audi meant that Jacob wouldn't be verbally assaulted with questions about his day as soon as he came through the door. This—along with the snacks in his backpack—put him in a good mood, and meeting Niki, the new employee at the gas station, had been a huge bonus to his day. Niki had been friendly and took an interest in him, and he thought it went beyond being nice to a customer. She'd just moved here, she'd said, and she lived on the street right behind him. Maybe she was looking for friends? She didn't look much older than him, but she worked the day shift, so presumably she didn't go to high school. Although that wasn't necessarily true. Jacob had a friend who'd gotten sick of being hassled all the time, so he'd quit going to his high school and now did online classes. It was possible that Niki was doing the same, or maybe she was homeschooling. Lots of kids were homeschooling now.

If it weren't for being home with his mother, Jacob could see himself doing online school. He couldn't do worse grade-wise, and it had to be better for his mental health. It would be nice not to have to deal with the deliberate jostling in the hallways and the insults about his weight in the locker room. The school bus was a particular nightmare. He'd explained to his parents that none of the other seniors rode the bus. His dad was sympathetic, but he didn't offer a solution. His mom told him walking would be good for him.

In high school he'd initially managed to stay under the radar, but his junior year the wind had shifted and he got targeted. One kid had pointed out his lack of a neck and chubby cheeks and called him "LEGO Head." The nickname had stuck, and now everyone, even the sophomores, knew him by that name. As nicknames went, it could have been worse, so he pretended to laugh it off. It still stung, even if he didn't show it. At times he found himself looking in the mirror and wishing he were someone different, someone who didn't have a big, fat head, sloping shoulders, and a pear-shaped body. It was bad enough being him, and now they had to torment him for it? If only they'd leave him alone. High school was a very specific type of hell. He knew one thing—once he got out, he was never setting foot in that building again. He would never go to class reunions, no matter how many years went by.

Arriving home, he hung his sweatshirt in the front hall closet and set his shoes on the mat. When Mia came out to see who'd arrived, he asked, "Where's Mom?"

Mia shook her head, apparently not knowing.

He tried again. "Did she say when she'll be back?"

"Not until later. She left you a note that said it might be late, and you're supposed to make me dinner. She said we're on our own."

Jacob set his backpack on the floor and unzipped the main compartment. "It's your lucky day, squirt. I bought us some chips." He'd really bought them for himself, but seeing her face light up made him wish the statement were true.

She followed him into the kitchen, where he gestured for her to take a seat at the table. Then he poured the can of Coke into two glasses, giving Mia the glass with the lesser amount. He dumped potato chips onto two napkins and slid one of them over to her before rolling down the top of the bag and tucking it back into his backpack. Mia picked up one chip and looked at it before popping it into her mouth, her legs swinging underneath the table. While she crunched, Jacob went and hid the crushed soda can underneath a layer of trash in the kitchen garbage can. He'd once tossed a can into the recycling bin, thinking his mother would never notice. He wasn't going to make that mistake again.

"This is good. Thank you, Jacob," Mia said. She was a funny thing, so grateful for anything that came her way.

"You're welcome."

"Did you get 'em at the gas station?"

Always with the questions. He tried to be patient with her, but sometimes it drove him crazy. He tried to keep in mind that if not for him, she wouldn't know anything about the outside world. She had that crappy TV in her room, but until Jacob's dad had bought an antenna at Best Buy, it hadn't shown anything but static. Even now the picture was terrible, but it was better than nothing. Inmates in prison had more entertainment options than poor little Mia. He nodded. "I got them at the Village Mart. There was a new girl working there. She was really friendly." He took a sip of Coke. "Really pretty too. Her name is Niki."

"Niki." Mia pronounced it like someone learning a new language. "What color is her hair?"

"Dark. Almost black."

"Like mine?"

"Like yours but longer. Past her shoulders. She has dark eyes like yours too." He grabbed some chips and crunched along with Mia. If his mother came in now she would kill him, but both he and Mia knew to clean up quickly if they heard the garage door go up. They were unspoken partners in crime in that regard. Neither of them wanted to invite her wrath.

"Did they have lots of potato chips?"

He nodded. "Lots of them. Doritos and Cheetos too." Doritos would have been his first choice, but he'd stopped buying them after he got in trouble for having Dorito dust on his shirt. He hadn't noticed it, but it didn't escape the watchful eyes of his mother. She noticed everything. Plain potato chips, he decided, were a safer bet.

"Did they have Hostess CupCakes?" Ever since Jacob's dad had once given her a Hostess CupCake, she was kind of obsessed with them.

"Yep. And all kinds of soda too. Bottles and cans. I didn't know if I should get Cherry Coke or regular, but I finally decided on regular."

"I like Sprite more than Coke."

"I know. Next time I'll get you a Sprite. And a Hostess CupCake too."

"Oh, would you, Jacob? That would be so cool!"

It took so little to make her happy; that was the good part about Mia. The bad part about Mia was having to keep her a secret. At first he'd found it difficult. So many times he'd almost slipped and mentioned her to a friend or a relative. One time he actually *did* say her name by mistake, and he had to make up a story about his little cousin coming to visit.

"Jacob?" Mia asked.

"What?" He belched to make her laugh, and it had the desired effect. Her giggles were like bubbles.

"Can I ask you a question?"

"You already did."

"Can I ask a *different* question?"

"Okay." He had an idea of where this was going, and it made him uneasy.

"Where did I live before I lived here?"

He exhaled. She deserved to know, and yet he'd been warned repeatedly not to tell. His mom had said they'd all go to jail if it got out. Of course, his mother never dreamed Mia would be the one doing the asking. Mia wasn't even like a person to her. More like a moving doll or a vacuum cleaner. "You lived in a different house. Not a very nice one."

"What was it like?"

Jacob thought back. He'd been almost fourteen at the time, old enough to remember exactly what he'd seen, but he also knew that having heard his mother's version of events related to his father over the years may have influenced his memory. She had a way of convincing people of different truths, ones that didn't jibe with reality. "It was old, and the roof was sagging. Inside there were bugs, and you were hungry and dirty."

"But, Jacob, didn't I have a mom and dad to take care of me?"

She was just a little kid, but sometimes she really did a number on his emotions. Something about her big brown eyes and the way she looked up to him twisted a knife in his gut. "No," he said sadly. "You didn't have anyone to take care of you. That's why we saved you and brought you here."

"So are my mom and dad dead?" Mia's gaze set upon him, patiently waiting.

"I don't know. Probably."

"But wasn't anyone with me?"

Jacob felt his frustration transform into irritation, and he snapped, "Enough with the questions! You know we're not supposed to talk about it. Stop being annoying."

Her head dropped, and he could no longer see her face. When she finally looked up, he saw tears glistening in her eyes. *Oh crap.* Now she was crying.

Softly she said, "But, Jacob, why aren't we supposed to talk about it?"

He sighed. "I don't know, Mia. Eat your chips." The mood in the room had changed; that's how much control his mother had. Even when she wasn't there, the idea of her loomed over them, putting a damper on things. Finally, he said, "There's nothing really to tell, Mia. All you have is us."

She sniffed and took another potato chip. Man, she was a slow eater, savoring each chip, while Jacob could have devoured the whole bag in one sitting if he let himself. Holding back from good food was not a strength for him. When something delicious was in front of him, he was frantic for it. When it was out of sight but available, it called to him. Mia took tiny, delicate, slow bites. Maybe that was why he had such a bulky body, while Mia was such a teeny thing.

Someday he'd tell Mia what he remembered about the time they found her, but today wasn't the day. She was too young and innocent, and her life before them was too ugly. All she had to know was that her former situation had been terrible, so Jacob and his mother had brought her home to live with them. He remembered how angry his father had been when they'd returned from a trip to Minneapolis for his grandfather's funeral and he'd discovered that they had somehow acquired a little girl somewhere in Wisconsin on the drive home.

It was clear-cut and simple. First they didn't have Mia, then they did. And the way they'd acquired her had almost seemed like fate. In fact, his mother said it had been fate—a second chance at having a little girl after losing baby Olivia.

About two hours after they'd found Mia and were back on the road again, his mother had stopped at Walmart for diapers and new clothing for her, while Jacob and Mia had waited in the car. That night they stayed at a hotel, and she cut the little girl's hair, which was so snarled and matted that a comb wouldn't go through it. Her next order of business was a bath. The water and the white washcloth turned a dingy brown, and when Mia came out she looked like a new child. Mia was silent the whole time, patting the water, allowing his mother to do what she wanted to her. Like a doll.

It turned out that Mia didn't need the diapers. She'd been wearing underpants soaked with urine when they found her, which made the car stink something awful, so they'd assumed she wasn't toilet trained, but it turned out that she knew how to use the toilet and could hold it until she had access to one. That first day she was silent the whole time, not crying, not making a noise, even when his mother yanked at her hair with the comb.

After that they fed her, and she ate as if she was famished. She ate so quickly that she threw up, and his mom made Jacob clean it up. After that they doled out the food in small quantities, which seemed to work better.

Jacob had been the one to carry Mia into the house when they returned home. She'd fallen asleep in the car. Once inside, he set her gently on the couch. Naturally, his father had lots of questions, and his mother gave him the abbreviated version, ending with, "And of course we had to take her out of there. What else could we do?" His mother made everything sound so black-and-white. She had two emotions, as far as Jacob could tell: she was either pleased that things were going her way or enraged that they weren't. Oh, she could disguise the *pleased* to make it seem like happiness or joy or pride. She could even fake laugh with the best of them. The rage was harder for her to camouflage, but she hid it by acting justifiably outraged or holding it in check. Holding back was a strategy for her. It made her feel superior when others became upset while she maintained a calm demeanor.

His dad said, "What about stopping at the closest police station? Did that thought ever occur to you?"

"The closest police station?" His mother looked amused. "We

were in the boonies, Matt. There was nothing out there. I was lucky to find the Walmart to get her some clothes."

Jacob remembered how furious his father had been when he heard that his mother planned to keep Mia. "You can't just keep another human being, Suzette," he'd said. "She's not a toy. She's a child. Somebody's child, and they have to be looking for her."

His mother gave him her coldest look, the kind guaranteed to plunge an emotional dagger. "Matt, just mind your own business."

That set him off in a big way, and he began ranting, telling her that this *was* his business, that it was his house and his family and that both of them could be convicted of felonies for kidnapping. He paced around the living room, making point after point, all of them valid, not that reason mattered where Jacob's mom was concerned. Through it all, Mia slept on the couch, her thumb in her mouth. If she could sleep through his parents fighting, Jacob decided, she could sleep through anything.

His father kept yelling, while his mother smiled as if she had the upper hand. She didn't do anything until he reached for the phone to call the police, and then she folded her arms and said, "Think carefully. Do you really want to do that? You know that I would be forced to tell them the real reason you decided not to practice medicine anymore. It would certainly make the news, and everyone would know. Or suppose I share the photos I have of you with your slutty girlfriend? Hmm? Or your perverted texts? What would your parents think of their golden boy once he's in handcuffs and thrown into prison for committing billing fraud?"

"You wouldn't." The blood drained out of his face.

"I would. Of course, I'd play it like you threatened to kill me if I ever told." She smiled at the thought. "And then everyone would know your true colors and comfort me in my grief."

He hesitated, the phone still in his hand. "You can't prove anything."

She laughed. "You're such an idiot, Matt. I have proof, copies of documents and screenshots of your texts with your lady friend. If you don't believe me, go ahead and call the police right now."

Looking stricken, he set down the phone. "So that's it, then. You'd turn in your own husband."

"Only if you force me to. Then I'd really have no choice." She ran her fingers through her layered hair. "Don't bother looking for the paperwork. It's locked up tight. And if anything happens to me, I've made arrangements to have the information made public." Her lips stretched into a mean smile. "But don't worry, darling, I'll visit you in prison. As for the little girl, if it comes up at all, I'll say she just showed up on our doorstep. Who's going to say anything different?"

They faced off, the tension so thick it made Jacob dizzy. Finally, his dad broke down. "I just don't understand, Suzette. Why? Why do you take such pleasure in being so mean and difficult? Why are you so unreasonable? It would be so easy not to be. Jacob and I don't deserve this. We have a good life. If only you would allow us to live in peace. I try to make you happy. What have we ever done to make you hate us so?" He suddenly looked older, defeated.

"Don't be ridiculous. I don't hate you. I just know what I want. I have a strong will, and that's a good thing. You admired that about me once, didn't you?"

His dad ignored the question but gestured to Mia with a nod of his head. "Okay, she can stay for tonight. But I'm going to do an online search. I'm sure someone is looking for her."

No one was looking for her, though. Nothing came up about a missing child from Wisconsin, and even when his dad widened the search, there weren't any missing girls fitting her description. Even though Mia was tiny, Jacob's dad estimated she was about three years old.

As the days and weeks went by, his father made multiple arguments against keeping her, but his objections weakened over time. Mia didn't say much at first, but sometimes she made sounds, and one of them, in response to being asked her name, sounded like "Mia," so that was what they called her. Every time she got sick his dad worried that she'd need a prescription, but that never happened. Mia almost never got sick, and when she did, it was just the sniffles. His mother said it was because she was safe in their home and didn't come into contact with other children. "She's away from all those nasty germs." She'd pat Mia on the head. "You are one lucky girl, you know that?"

At first his mother seemed to cherish Mia, calling her endearing nicknames, fussing over her, and dressing her up in cute little girls' clothing, but after six months or so, she appeared to tire of the whole thing. When she discovered Mia's eagerness to please, she put her to work doing chores around the house. With each passing month, Mia's work increased. She never complained, just did what was asked of her, always with good cheer and a smile on her face.

Years later Jacob read a story about Marie Antoinette traveling in her carriage with her entourage. When they'd paused at a poor village, she'd spotted a cute little boy and decided she wanted him, so she took him to live at the palace. In the story, Marie Antoinette had treated the child like a beloved pet, but she'd lost interest when she began to have children of her own. The similarities between the queen and his mother were uncanny. He knew that someday she'd tire of Mia, and then what? He shuddered at the thought.

Once he'd heard his parents arguing about what would happen when Mia got older. A week or so after Mia had come to stay with them, his dad had said, "What are you going to do when she gets old enough to ask questions? At some point she'll want to go outside and see the world. What then?"

His mother scoffed. "You worry for nothing. Mia barely talks, and she's content. She's happy here and does what she's told. She can't want what she doesn't know about."

"Well then what if someone else finds out she's here and wants to know where she came from? You can't explain away a human being, Suzette."

"Oh, Matt." She shook her head. "Now you're just dreaming up bad scenarios. You might as well ask, *What if a tornado wipes out the house? Or what if the roof caves in?* Life is uncertain, and anything could happen. Why dwell on the negative? You should try to be positive, like me."

"So you have no plans for her future? No idea of what you'll do when we're found out?"

"Who's going to tell?" His mom absentmindedly ran a finger over the beads of her necklace. "None of us, certainly. And Mia can't, so that's no problem."

"I can't believe you think this is fine and it will go on forever. You have your head in the clouds, Suzette. I'm not going to prison for kidnapping because you've lost your mind."

"No one is going to prison," she said dismissively. "If the worst happens, we can always drop Mia off back where we found her. No harm done. It's not like she can give details about our family. She doesn't even know where she is. She only knows a few words: *dog, yes, no, Mia*. How could they possibly trace her back to us?"

"She might know a lot more than that." His dad frowned. "Mia doesn't say much, but she listens. Who knows how much she comprehends?"

"Well, if you're that concerned, we can always give her the guinea pig treatment." His mom got up out of her chair and smoothed the front of her pants. "Or maybe you and your girlfriend can adopt her." She sauntered out of the room then, having gotten the last word.

Jacob, who'd been listening from the other room, had a tremor of anxiety at hearing his mother's words. She'd talked about his father having a girlfriend before, so that was nothing new, just one of her mean, untrue comments meant to rattle his dad, and Jacob too. It was the mention of *the guinea pig treatment* that made him gasp. He'd had a guinea pig when he was in third grade, a cute little fellow named Duffy. He was tan and white and lived in a cage in Jacob's room. Jacob had been endlessly fascinated by Duffy, watching him run on his wheel and taking him out to pet him.

His mother had not been as enamored of his guinea pig. She complained about the smell and the noises Duffy made. The sight of the wood shavings Duffy had kicked out of his cage onto the tabletop made her furious. Truthfully, Jacob didn't clean out the cage as often as he should have, but he was a kid. Besides, it was his room. If anyone had a problem with the mess or the noise, it should have been him.

One day he came home from school to find Duffy missing from his cage with the door slightly ajar. He frantically looked in the cage and then in his room, calling Duffy's name to no avail. Even though Jacob was a big boy, he began to cry. He went to his mother, who wasn't too alarmed, but she silently followed him into his room.

"See," Jacob said, stepping aside to let her see the cage. "He's not here. He was here this morning, and now he's gone."

"I see that." Her brow furrowed. "You must have left the cage door open. Was your bedroom door shut today?"

"No." Her comment about the cage door puzzled him. He was sure he'd closed the door and then secured it, but doubt sank in. Could he have forgotten?

He and his mother did a cursory search throughout the house, his mother actually getting on her hands and knees to look under the furniture. When his dad came home, he joined the hunt. "I don't think he could have gone too far," his dad said, focusing on the bedrooms upstairs. Finally, his father suggested leaving the cage on the floor with the door open. "Maybe he'll get hungry and come back."

"What a good idea," his mom said, nodding in approval.

That night, Jacob heard the sound of his parents arguing from behind their closed bedroom door. He couldn't make out what they were saying until he went into the hallway and caught his mother saying, "Well, maybe if you'd fixed the latch on the screen door, this wouldn't have happened."

"You'd have me believe a guinea pig went down the stairs and somehow pushed open the screen door and went *outside*?" His father sounded incredulous. "Tell me, Suzette, what really happened?"

"How should I know?" Jacob heard the scowl in her voice. "I helped Jacob look. He was so distraught. I felt so terrible for him."

Jacob never saw Duffy again. Eventually he and his father had cleaned out the cage and put it in the basement. He hadn't thought about Duffy in a long time, but hearing her talk about *the guinea pig treatment,* he felt all the pieces click together in his brain. How much she'd complained about Duffy. The cage door he was sure he'd secured. The fact that Duffy had mysteriously disappeared.

He'd always suspected his mother was capable of anything, and now he was sure it was true. He hoped that she'd given Duffy away rather than let him go loose outside. He wouldn't put it past her, though.

Now Mia interrupted his thoughts. "Jacob, what are you gonna make for dinner?"

"I don't know. What do you want?"

"A hot dog?"

Jacob knew there were hot dogs and buns in the freezer, in the bottom of the drawer underneath some other stuff. His mother probably didn't even remember they were there. "Okay, you got it. It's kind of early for supper, but if you want I could make it now. What do you think?"

"Yes, please."

"Your wish is my command, little one."

"Oh, Jacob, you're the best person in the world." She let out a small sigh, happy for now.

He couldn't help but smile. *The best person in the world?* It was a huge compliment, and he should have been pleased, but all he could think was that Mia knew only three people in total, so it wasn't much of a competition.

CHAPTER EIGHTEEN

Morgan had been missing for almost four years before they heard anything at all. It was a weekday evening in July, and they were doing the usual after-work activities. Edwin was at the stove cooking dinner, while Wendy sat at the kitchen counter with her tablet answering emails, when the police detective rang the doorbell.

Edwin turned from sautéing the vegetables to share a puzzled look with Wendy. "I'll get it," she said, sliding off her stool to go to the front door. She'd been expecting the in-person equivalent of spam, maybe a local kid raising funds for their sports team or a home security firm ready to give a sales pitch, so it was surprising to see Detective Moore standing on her front porch, a serious expression on his face.

"Mrs. Duran?" he said, and his apologetic tone made her heart sink.

"Yes?" Wendy found herself sucking in her breath as if she might need it later. "You have news about Morgan?" In an instant she heard the sound of her own heartbeat pounding in her ears. She clutched the side of the doorframe for support.

Instead of answering, he asked, "Is your husband home? I'd like to talk to you both."

She nodded. "Please come in." She left him standing on the front rug while she went to get Edwin.

Once they were all seated in the living room, Edwin took the lead. "You have news about our daughter?" He gave Wendy's hand a gentle squeeze. Never had she felt so grateful for his calming touch.

"I do." He had a leather-bound case in his hand, the size of a binder, something she hadn't noticed before, and he opened it now and rummaged inside.

Wendy couldn't stand waiting any longer. "She's dead, isn't she?" Saying the words aloud made her die a little inside, but she had to know.

"Ma'am, I don't know that." He pulled out something the size of a business card and got up to show to them. "Can you confirm that this is Morgan's driver's license?"

Edwin took it and held it in the palm of his hand, while Wendy moved closer to look on. It was clearly Morgan's driver's license—the one she'd been so happy to get at age seventeen. At the time Morgan had complained about the picture, but Wendy had thought she looked beautiful.

Edwin looked up. "Yes, this is our daughter's license."

"Was she in an accident?" Wendy asked.

"No." The detective shifted in his seat. "It was found during an investigation over in Ash County. A landlord there filed a police report regarding a conflict with a tenant. He said the tenants were overdue with the rent, and when he went to confront them, the man pulled out a handgun and took a shot at him. He missed, fortunately. By the time the sheriff's department went out to investigate, the tenants had left and the place was trashed. They found the license among the things left behind."

Ash County? Wendy processed the idea that her daughter had been in Wisconsin all along, that it was even possible she'd never left the state.

"Do you think she was held against her will?" Edwin asked a question that hadn't even occurred to Wendy.

"We don't have a lot of information, but it doesn't sound like it. The tenants were a young couple. It was a cash deal, and the landlord wasn't very helpful. Looking at the driver's license, he couldn't positively confirm the woman was Morgan, but he said it might have been. He couldn't give much in the way of a description of the guy, and he only knew his first name. Keith?" Detective Moore raised his eyebrows. "I believe that was the name of Morgan's boyfriend?"

So much to take in that Wendy felt as if she were being pummeled by words. Faintly she said, "Yes, his name was Keith."

"I have a copy of the police report, if you're interested."

Edwin said, "We'd like that, thank you."

"Thank you," Wendy repeated, but the words were hollow.

Could it really have been Morgan? Running out on a landlord and leaving a place trashed? Morgan and her brother had had a good upbringing. Wendy and Edwin had lived to make sure of that. How many times had Edwin said, "I just want our kids to be happy." Maybe they'd been too permissive? It was such a hard call.

Wendy didn't want to think her daughter would be living this kind of life, but the truth was she really didn't know.

Detective Moore met her eyes. She'd thought he was as young as Morgan, in his twenties, but the crinkles around his eyes and his look of compassion made her realize that he might be older. "Again, I'm sorry I don't have more information."

"Did the landlord know if the couple was married? Or did he know if they were employed?" Wendy asked.

He shook his head. "Once you read the report, you'll know everything I know. I came right over because I thought it was important to give you this update."

"Of course," Edwin said. "And we very much appreciate it." He glanced down at the license. "Can we keep this?"

"Absolutely." He returned his attention to the leather case and finally pulled out a few sheets of paper. "This is a copy of the police report. You can keep that as well."

Edwin reached over to take it. "Thank you."

Detective Moore said, "I'll leave you to it, then. If you have any other questions, feel free to call." He stood. "Not saying I'll know the answers, but if I can find out for you, I definitely will."

They followed him to the front door, thanking him again for coming out.

Detective Moore turned to say one last thing. "Just so you know, we haven't forgotten Morgan. I think about her all the time, in fact. We're just limited in what we can do, given the circumstances."

"We understand," Wendy said.

Edwin added, "We appreciate all your work on our behalf."

After the detective left, they sat back on the couch to read the report. It was brief and worded in a businesslike way. Despite the fact that there was a gun fired at the landlord, the report lacked drama. Just the facts. Wendy noted that the listed date of the altercation was only four days earlier. She wasn't familiar with the town, but a quick Google search showed it to be a two-hour drive from their house.

Once they finished reading, Edwin said, "So in theory she could have been only two hours away from us four days ago."

"In theory?" Wendy held up the driver's license. "I'd say it's more than a theory. You can't dispute that this is Morgan's."

Edwin had a pensive look on his face, what Wendy called his *thinking look*. She was one to rush to conclusions, while he preferred to mull over all the possibilities. Generally, his approach worked better, but it still drove her crazy.

He nodded. "The license is Morgan's, but we don't know that the woman in question was her. Someone could have found her license or taken it from her. Identity theft happens all the time. It even could be left over from a previous tenant."

"But the guy's name was Keith," Wendy argued. "That would be a major coincidence."

"True. But it could be a different Keith, or it might be the same Keith with a different woman."

They sat in silence for a moment until she asked quietly, "Why won't you let me hope?"

"Oh, darling." He pulled her into his arms. "I'm not trying to kill your hope. I'm trying to keep you from getting your heart broken."

"It's already broken." She rested her head on his shoulder. "I need this, Edwin. I can't tell you how much I need this."

"I know."

"I don't think you understand."

"I do understand. We just process things differently." He kissed the top of her head. "I've got a thought. Why don't we call the landlord and see what he can tell us?"

The landlord's name was Craig Hartley. A phone call made to the number on the report led to a recording. Edwin left a voice mail. "Hi, Mr. Hartley. This is Edwin Duran, and I'm interested in some information regarding your former tenants." He asked him to return his call as soon as possible, leaving both his cell phone number and Wendy's. After that they carried on with their evening, an uneasy feeling hovering over them.

At dinner, Wendy said, "What if he doesn't call back?"

"It's a little early to be worrying about that, don't you think?"

She tilted her head to one side. "It's not too early. It's been years. Every minute that goes by is too long to wait." She could tell by his silence that her point was made.

After they finished eating and cleaned up the dinner dishes, she made an announcement. "If we don't hear back by tomorrow morning, I'm taking the day off work and getting in my car and driving to that house. I want to talk to Craig Hartley in person. If I show him Morgan's photo, he might be able to confirm that it was her. And if it was her, I need to see where she was living four days ago."

"So you've already decided that the woman was Morgan?"

She nodded. "Yes. I've decided based on the driver's license and the guy's name being Keith. Besides that, I need to believe it was

Morgan. It's the first scrap of information we've gotten that points to the fact that she's still alive. I'm going. You can't talk me out of it."

"Well, if you're going, I'm going too. We'll do it together."

I t was midmorning when they arrived. Craig Hartley hadn't returned Edwin's call, so Wendy had tried again, leaving another message that morning, this time specifying that she thought the woman in question might be their daughter who'd been missing for several years. She thought that maybe he might be sympathetic to a mother's heartache, but she knew it was just as likely that he didn't care one way or the other. After all, the couple had skipped out on the rent and fired a gun at him.

The address for the house was listed as Quiet Creek Road, but the road transitioned from paving to gravel at some point, and the ride was bumpy. "Talk about being off the beaten path," Edwin murmured. When they got to where the road dead-ended, there was only one structure in sight, a house so ramshackle that Wendy couldn't imagine anyone living there.

"Do you think this is it?" she asked as he pulled the car over to the side of the road. She craned her head to look, but there wasn't an address posted anywhere.

"It has to be. This is the end of the line."

They got out of the car and stood, taking it in. The house, if you could call it that, was propped up on concrete cinders and built of weather-beaten gray wooden boards. If it had ever been painted or stained, there was no sign of it now. A small porch jutted off the front. The yard around the house was littered with trash—empty cans, scraps of paper and fabric, an old tire and other car parts—all of it moored in the mud. The roof, which sagged, was covered in something green and fuzzy. The whole thing wasn't even as big as their garage. "No one could live here," Wendy finally said.

"Let's check it out." Edwin took the lead, stepping onto the porch and peering through the dirty glass windows on either side of the door. "Can't see much."

Wendy grabbed the doorknob and found it turned easily. She gave it a push, and the door swung open with a creak. Edwin gave her an approving nod. Once inside, they waited for their eyes to adjust to the dim light. "I can't imagine that the power is on," he said. "Not if they didn't pay the rent."

"I don't think the place has power." Wendy rummaged through her purse and, upon finding her phone, turned on the flashlight app. The house was one big room, a perfect square of filth. The windows were streaked and grimy, and the floor was littered with piles and piles of garbage. At a glance, Wendy noticed empty yogurt containers, Hostess CupCake wrappers, and beer bottles. The only piece of furniture—a tattered mustard-colored couch—was pushed up against one wall. The overpowering pervasive smell could only be human excrement and urine. On one side of the room, a dented soup pot was on the floor, full of what looked like murky water. "Oh my word, the smell. How could anyone stand it?" She gingerly walked around the perimeter, looking for signs of Morgan. She'd envisioned coming across one of Morgan's possessions or something with her daughter's handwriting on it. Even a grocery list would have been encouraging, but it was clear there was nothing like that here. It was as if someone had emptied a month's worth of trash right on the floor of the house.

Edwin appeared stunned as well. "No electricity, no water, and I didn't see an outhouse. Maybe out back?"

Wendy shook her head. They could walk around the property before they left, but she sensed that it didn't matter. She did another walk around the house, wondering if sifting through all the garbage would yield any clues. Edwin must have had the same idea, because he came across a wire hanger and used it to poke through the refuse. Around the time she was ready to give up, Edwin had come to the same conclusion. "I hate to say it, Wendy, but there's nothing here."

"I'm not even sure this is the place," she answered. "It should be condemned. How could this be rented out?" Left unsaid, *who* would rent out such a place? Morgan could have come home at any time. Why would she have chosen to live in squalor instead?

"I don't know," he admitted. "You might be right and this isn't the place. If you want, we can drive down the road and check addresses again. Maybe someone will be home and can tell us where the Hartley place is."

On the porch, after they'd closed the door behind them, Wendy brushed off the front of her clothing, unable to shake the feeling of having walked through a large cobweb. At least outside the air was breathable.

When they were getting into their car, a white pickup truck pulled in behind them. They paused and waited until a beefy man wearing a baseball cap got out. He wore an untucked denim shirt, a shade lighter than his jeans, and a pair of cowboy boots. "Can I help you folks?" he called out as he approached.

"Are you Craig Hartley?" Edwin asked.

"I am." His eyes narrowed. "Who's asking?"

"I'm Edwin Duran, and this is my wife, Wendy. We left messages on your voice mail."

Craig Hartley gave them a hard look. "You're the folks is looking for your daughter. The one who went missing a few years back."

"That's right," Edwin said. "If you have a minute, we'd just like to ask you a few questions."

"I got a minute, but not much more than that." His tone was begrudging. "I'm a busy man."

"Thank you," Wendy said. "Do you know if the woman's name was Morgan?"

"Never heard her name. I only dealt with Keith."

Edwin asked, "What kind of car did they have? Did you get the license plate number?"

"A junker, and no, I didn't get the license plate number. I should have, I guess." He shrugged.

"Do you know where they were headed after here?"

"No, and frankly I don't care. I hope to never see them again."

Wendy reached into her purse and pulled out two photos. "This is our daughter, Morgan. Was she the woman who rented from you?" She handed the pictures to him, and he looked them over for a moment before shaking his head.

"Could be," he said, handing them back to her. "I barely saw the woman. I dealt with the man for the most part."

"What was he like?"

"Just your classic loser. A drug addict."

"You think he was on drugs?"

Craig made an exasperated snort. "Look, lady, I know you're missing your daughter and all, but if I were you, I'd hope to God that this couple had nothing to do with her. They were junkies is my take on it, okay? I found them squatting in my hunting shack, and they begged to be allowed to stay, so I rented it to them for fifty bucks a week. An act of charity, you might say. They paid for two weeks, and after that, nothing. They kept giving me all kinds of excuses, and I was a good guy, okay? I gave them weeks to get their act together. I finally had enough and was ready to kick them out, and then he got crazy and got out a gun and tried to kill me. When the cops came they were gone, and I found the place filled with crap. That's all I know. Now I'm left with the job of clearing out all the garbage they left behind. You try to do a good deed, and what happens? A bite in the butt, every time." He leaned over and spat in the dirt.

"I see." Wendy put the pictures back in her purse.

"I'm not sure you do," Craig said. "Now unless you're here to pay the rest of their rent, or to help me shovel out this house, I'm going to ask you to leave."

"Just another minute?" Wendy could hear the begging in her own voice. "Do you know any more about them? Did they have jobs or get visitors?"

"Lady, I don't know. They gave me some money. I let them stay. If I had it to do over again, I sure as hell would have told them to hit the road. That's what I get for being nice. Never again."

Edwin said, "When you're cleaning up, if you come across

anything that identifies them, paperwork or whatever, could you call us? Or tell the police?"

"Sure." He threw up his hands. "Why not? Now, if you'll excuse me." He left their side to cross the yard and go into the house.

"Thank you," Wendy called out after him.

They got into the car, not speaking until they were off the gravel and onto a paved road. *Back to civilization,* Wendy thought.

"Well, that was a waste of time," Edwin said. "We didn't get any definite answers."

"No, nothing definite," Wendy agreed. She thought about Craig Hartley's assertion that the couple were drug addicts. If it was Morgan, she was still alive but in desperate need of help. She felt a wave of sorrow wash over her. What a horrible, helpless feeling. She wouldn't wish this on anyone.

CHAPTER NINETEEN

When Niki left the Village Mart at six o'clock it was already dark, but she was only a few blocks from home, and there were sidewalks all the way there. The path was well illuminated by streetlights, so she never felt unsafe. Tonight the weather was frigid and windy, making her glad for her new warm clothing. Overhead, the night sky was crisp and clear, the moon a bright beacon against an indigo backdrop. She burrowed her face into the scarf and leaned slightly forward, taking hurrying steps. With her bag looped over one shoulder, she patted her right-hand pocket, double-checking for the pepper spray Sharon had given her. This was probably the most crime-free neighborhood she'd ever lived in, but it made her feel better to have it close at hand. You never knew.

Niki was halfway home when a car pulled up next to her and let out a short honk. She glanced over, not surprised to see Sharon driving. She'd noticed that Sharon had developed a tendency to *coincidentally* be out running errands right around the time Niki was due to walk home, and she would then stop to pick her up. Niki was tempted to tell her not to bother, that she was fine walking, but it was nice to have someone looking out for her.

Niki opened the passenger-side door and climbed in, setting her bag on the floor and clicking her seat belt.

Sharon waited until she was through and then proceeded on. "Did you have a good day?"

Niki noticed that she wasn't even pretending that the meetup was accidental anymore. "Pretty good. Guess who came in to buy snack food?"

"Who?"

"Jacob Fleming!"

"Really?" Sharon's voice had a slight tinge of incredulity. "Jacob Fleming. What are the odds?"

"Right?" Niki knew that Sharon would have the right reaction. "He's actually pretty nice. Fred introduced him to me, and we talked for a little bit."

"Did he tell you his mom tried to get some poor girl fired at the nutrition store?"

Niki laughed. "No, it didn't come up. I think we connected, though. Like on a personal level. I asked him where he lives, and he said Maple Avenue, and I said I live on the street right behind him. With my *grandma*." Both of them smiled at that. "We talked about families, and I mentioned I was an only child, and he said he was too. Then I said, 'No other kids in the house?' and I swear he hesitated. He said no, but you know how when someone pauses and you can tell by their expression they're about to tell a lie? I swear I saw it on his face."

Sharon took a turn onto Maple, and Niki knew that once again they were going past the Flemings' house. So many times they'd gone this route. It had never yielded any answers, but Sharon kept trying.

This time was different, though.

As they approached the Flemings' house, they could see that the garage door was up and a silver car was parked dead center in the middle of the garage. Mrs. Fleming was getting out of the driver's side; she must have just arrived home.

"There she is," Sharon said. "The Wicked Witch of Maple Avenue."

"Kind of weird that she parked right in the middle, don't you think? Where is her husband going to put his car?"

"Maybe he's out of town?" Sharon said as she pulled the car over to the curb. "Or maybe the car is getting serviced?"

"Out of town, I'd guess. I haven't seen him from my window for a day or two."

Sharon turned off the engine, and the headlights went dark. Mrs. Fleming was now opening the trunk of the car. "I'm going to go talk to her," she said. "I'm going to ask outright if she has a little girl living with her." Decisiveness crackled through her words.

"I'm not so sure that's a good idea," Niki blurted out.

"No, I'm doing it. I'm sick of watching and waiting. I'm just going to go and ask."

Niki felt a tightening in her chest. "She's not going to tell you anything, and she's a really mean lady."

Sharon shrugged. "I've dealt with mean ladies before. Trust me, they're all bark and no bite. Besides, what can she do to me?"

Niki watched as Sharon opened the door and trotted across the street to catch Mrs. Fleming before she went into the house. She heard her call out, "Excuse me!" and saw Mrs. Fleming pause and turn around.

Niki felt both fear and admiration as she watched Sharon jog up the driveway. An expression Evan liked came to mind. *Balls of steel.* Underneath her pleasant facade, Sharon had more nerve than most people, she'd give her that much. Niki craned her neck in order to see better and watched as the two women talked. The conversation didn't appear contentious, but it was hard to say from this distance. What could Sharon be saying that would justify asking about a stranger's family? Various ideas flitted through her head. Maybe Sharon was pretending to take a survey? Working for the US government as a census taker? In charge of the neighborhood watch? Niki couldn't even imagine. By the time Sharon came back to the car, the curiosity was killing Niki, especially since Sharon had a triumphant look on her face.

"Well?" she asked as Sharon climbed in and shut the door. "Did she tell you anything?"

"Oh, no. She wasn't going to budge at all. But she was pleasant. Guarded but pleasant."

Sharon started up the car and headed toward home. "I told her I just moved in down the street and that my two young grandchildren live with me. That one of the neighbors said she has a little girl the right age for them to play with, and I wanted to introduce myself so we could arrange a playdate. I said I wasn't sure if I had the right house, that I get forgetful sometimes. I totally played it like I was a ditsy old woman."

"I can't believe you came up with that. It's brilliant."

"I have my days," Sharon said with pride. "I gave her a made-up name and pointed down the road to show her my house. She wasn't even paying attention. I doubt she interacts with the neighbors, and she probably doesn't even know who lives on that end of the block. She seems kind of full of herself."

"Very full of herself," Niki said in agreement. "So what did she say when you asked if she has a little girl?"

"Oh, she denied it, of course. Said whoever told me that was misinformed. That she and her husband only have one child, a seventeen-year-old named Jacob. I apologized for the mix-up and asked if she could give me a referral for a dentist, since we are new to the area and all. She said no, that they aren't happy with their dentist and are looking for a new one themselves. So then I asked about pediatricians. I could tell she was getting aggravated, but she kept smiling. Finally, she cut me off and wished me luck. Said she couldn't talk anymore and had to get going."

Niki had been hoping for more. "Well, I give you credit for asking. You're braver than me."

The car turned down Crescent Street and proceeded onward. They were almost to the house now. Sharon turned into the driveway and pressed the button for the garage door opener. After a slight pause to wait for full clearance, she pulled the car inside. Once she'd shut off the engine, she said, "I still have to tell you the best part."

"Yeah? What's that?"

"Right as we were wrapping things up, the door to the house, the one inside the garage, opened up, and guess who was standing there?"

"A little girl?"

"Absolutely correct. This small girl opened the door and was standing there plain as day, her little face looking out. Mrs. Fleming yelled, 'Close the door!' and then she told me she had to go and rushed inside."

"And this happened right after she told you she doesn't have a little girl."

"Exactly. And I can tell you right now that it was not her son. I saw that child clear as day. It wasn't Jacob. This child was just a little peanut, maybe five or six, with dark hair cut in the most hideous bowl haircut. She popped her head out the garage door, and when Mrs. Fleming yelled she shut the door right away."

"So Mrs. Fleming lied," Niki mused. "I mean it was a complete lie, because if the kid was a foster child or was just visiting she would have mentioned it, wouldn't she?"

Sharon nodded. "I would think so. Most people would have said as much."

"But why would someone have a secret kid in their house?"

"There's no good reason that I can think of."

Niki thought about the news stories of people who'd been abducted and held prisoner for years. Did it ever happen in middle-class neighborhoods? Maybe. It's not as if people became more moral just because they had money. There were plenty of criminals and horrible people in all socioeconomic classes. "So should we call the police? Tell them what we know?"

Sharon said, "I feel like we have to do something, but maybe we should talk to Amy first?"

Niki agreed. "Amy will know what to do."

CHAPTER TWENTY

Mia knew she was in big trouble when she opened the garage door and Ma'am yelled at her, but she hadn't been punished yet, so she pushed the bad feeling away and thought about the fact that she and Jacob had a new secret. Thinking about it made her smile with delight.

A few days before, he'd come down to the basement after her bedtime and knocked lightly on the door before unlocking it and entering. She'd known it was Jacob before she set eyes on him because he was the only one who ever knocked.

Mia sat up in bed and squinted when he flipped on the light switch. "Jacob?"

"Sorry about that," he said, indicating the light. "Did I wake you?"

She shook her head. "No." Even if she had been asleep, she wouldn't have minded. Having Jacob come see her could make a whole day much better. It didn't happen often, but when it did he came bearing gifts: books, usually, or snacks. The last time it had been a word search book, brand new, and he'd given her a pen of her own to circle the words. This was the kind of book it was okay to write on, he'd told her.

Every time Jacob gave her a gift he cautioned her not to let his mom know. If Ma'am found out, he said, there would be hell to pay. Mia didn't know what that meant exactly, but she knew Ma'am well enough to know it would be very bad.

"Hey, squirt," he'd said that night a few days before. "Do you have a minute to do something really cool?" He held up a plastic bag.

Mia nodded eagerly, and he sat on the edge of her bed. "I'm going to ask you to do something, and it's going to sound kind of weird, but I think it's a good idea. I'll explain all about it, and then you can decide if you want to do it, okay?"

"Okay." She liked that he was giving her the choice, but she knew that if Jacob thought something was a good idea it probably was.

"See this?" He pulled a box out of the bag. "I bought it just for you, and I've already read the directions. It's a special kind of test." He opened the box and pulled out something plastic and held it in his hand. "This is a container that you spit into. Once it's full, I'll mail it to a special place, and they'll do tests on the spit, looking at something called DNA. The tests can tell us all kinds of things about the person who did the spitting. I'm hoping if you do this we can find out more about where you came from and if there are other people connected to you."

She was puzzled. "People connected to me? What does that mean, Jacob?"

He didn't answer for what seemed to be a long time, and then he said, "I don't think your mom and dad are alive, but you might have other relatives: aunts or uncles or cousins even. Maybe even grandparents. This test might tell us if you do."

Mia knew who all those people were from watching the television and from books, but she never thought she might have some of her own. "Do you really think so, Jacob? I might have a grandma?" Grandmas on TV were always so nice.

"It's possible. But look, Mia, the test might show nothing, so I don't want to get your hopes up, okay? We'd just be doing this to find out everything we can, understand?"

"I understand."

"If nothing comes up, I don't want you to cry about it. You still have us, right? So it's not like you've lost something."

She nodded. "Okay."

"Do you have any questions?"

"How does that work with my spit? How does it tell them about other people?" She wanted it to be true, but none of it made sense.

Jacob shook his head. "It's very complicated. Just trust me, it works. Do you trust me?"

"I trust you."

"You know I would never lie to you, right?"

"I know."

"So do you want to do it?"

"Yes," she said eagerly.

"You can't say anything to my mom and dad, though, you got it? If my mom found out, she might kill me. You don't want that, do you?"

"I won't say anything," she assured him.

Spitting into the tube was a big chore, but Jacob was patient with her. He talked her through it, telling her to take her time. The key, he said, was to let the saliva build up in her mouth for a while before spitting. At one point her mouth felt dry, and he let her take a break. She wasn't sure if she'd ever be able to get enough spit, but after a few minutes it was okay again. When her spit came all the way up to the line on the plastic container, Jacob gave her a fist bump. She watched as he took the wide part off the top of the tube and then screwed a cap on to seal it.

"It looks like a test tube," she said.

Jacob looked at her with surprise. "How do you know what a test tube is?"

Mia shrugged. "I just know."

"You're one smart little person."

She liked it when Jacob said nice things like that. As she watched, he put the test tube into a clear plastic bag and pulled off a strip of blue plastic along the top, then pressed it shut. Once that was done, he put the whole thing in a box and sealed it tight.

He said, "And that's all there is to it. I'll mail it in, and in a few weeks we'll get the results."

"The results?"

"A report that will tell us about your relatives."

"Will that come in the mail too?"

"No, I'll be able to see it online."

Mia nodded. She knew what online was. Jacob and his parents were always looking at their phones or other screens, but she wasn't allowed. They could find out all kinds of things online—what the weather was going to be like, what time the football game would be on, how long to bake chicken. Any question a person had could be answered by going online. Jacob let her look sometimes when no one else was around, and once he'd even taken a picture of her, but he was always the one holding the phone. Maybe someday she could do it too.

"So then you'll tell me what the report says?"

"Trust me, squirt, after I find out, you'll be the first to know."

CHAPTER TWENTY-ONE

"Mia!" Suzette bellowed as she came into the house. "Get over here right now!" She usually prided herself on having a lovely speaking voice—in fact, her college music teacher had complimented her on her dulcet tones—but this sentence came out in a guttural, excessively loud way. It infuriated her to hear her voice sounding so ugly when it was absolutely unnecessary. Why did her family drive her to this?

Mia sheepishly came out of the kitchen, her face showing that she knew she was in trouble and her body shaking with the knowledge of what was to come. *Good.* At least one person in this household understood when they'd violated the rules. Suzette was so tired of having to keep them all in check. It was exhausting.

"Yes, Ma'am?" Mia said quietly.

Suzette dropped her handbag and her shopping bags and grabbed Mia's arms so they were pinned to her sides. "What the hell was that all about?" When the girl didn't answer, she lowered her face so they were nose-to-nose. "Are you supposed to open an outside door? Ever?" She shook Mia so hard that the kid's teeth rattled.

"No, Ma'am."

"But you did it anyway, didn't you?"

"Yes, Ma'am."

"Why would you do that if you knew it wasn't allowed? Why?" She felt the anger build up inside her. She could snap this child's neck if she wanted to, but she held back. No one ever gave her credit for the times she could have acted out in anger. There were occasions when it was tempting. She could have ruined Matt's life and had him thrown in jail. She could have easily exposed Jacob for the clueless sloth he was, and as for Mia, no one would miss a child who didn't exist.

Not only did she not get credit for not tearing them down, she didn't get the accolades she deserved for doing the opposite. On a regular basis she talked up her husband and son, downplaying their many weaknesses and creating fictitious personality attributes they didn't have and never would.

She told stories of extravagant gifts Matt lavished on her, saying, "I tell him not to, but he insists! Says nothing is too good for his soul mate." The embellishments were justified by knowing that Matt would have given her these gifts had he only recognized how lucky he was to have her as his wife. She'd elevated him from a dolt to an enlightened husband, which was very kind on her part. In her spun tales, her husband wrote her love notes, which she quoted to the women in her social circles.

As for Jacob, she'd had to think long and hard about how to make him look good. His grades were atrocious, and he clearly wasn't an athlete. His taste in fashion was appalling, as were his manners. None of this was her fault. She tried to help him, she really did. The only option left was to depict him as a secret creative, an undercover genius, one who couldn't be bothered to conform to society's expectations. She was a one-woman public relations company in charge of making the Flemings the envy of everyone she came into contact with. And now Mia had done something so stupid it could destroy everything she'd worked so hard to build. She gave the girl another shake. "Answer me!"

"Sorry," she whimpered.

"Why, Mia? Why can't you listen?" So many times Mia was just a blank slate, her face giving not a clue as to what was going on in that damaged little brain of hers. This was one of those times, and it made Suzette furious. She shoved her against the wall, hoping for some kind of response, but Mia just trembled and shook her head. "Do you want the police to come and lock you up? Is that what you want?"

"No, Ma'am." The words came out in a whisper.

"That's what will happen, you know. You'll be thrown in a cold dark cell with no food or water, and there will be rats and bugs crawling all over you. Does that sound good to you?"

"No, Ma'am."

"Here we give you a nice home and keep you safe and warm. All I ask is for you to follow directions. It's not that hard, Mia, not that hard at all."

"Yes, Ma'am."

Suzette remembered a time when she'd thought Mia was a gift from the universe, an offering to help ease the loss of baby Olivia. *Ha!* She couldn't have been more wrong. Within a few months she'd realized that Mia lacked the spark that her daughter certainly would have had. Olivia would have been like Suzette, a charmer with a take-charge personality. This child had the personality of a dishcloth. She shook her again. "You need to learn, Mia. Start paying attention."

"Yes, Ma'am."

Jacob's lumbering footsteps came down the stairs as she finished correcting Mia. No doubt he was planning on defending the little minion, something he'd been doing lately. His interference was not appropriate. She would not allow a teenager, a mere child, to dictate how she should handle things in her own house. She still had Mia pinned against the wall when he came into view, and she didn't even bother turning her head to acknowledge his presence.

"Jeez, Mom, I could hear you all the way upstairs with my headphones on. What's wrong now?"

The sight of him, sloppy and fat in his oversize clothes, disgusted her. Even more off-putting was the insinuation that her raised voice was an overreaction. Did he think she wanted to come home to a problem that had to be addressed? No, she did not. How much nicer would it be if everyone did as they were told? The household would hum along like a well-oiled machine, and all would be right with the world. If they followed her rules, the house would be a damn utopia. It wasn't as if she asked for much.

Jacob came closer. "Mia, are you okay?"

So that was it. He didn't even care about her, but assumed that she was overreacting and that Mia was blameless. Essentially, he was choosing Mia over his own mother. What an insult, given all she'd done for him. In a surge of retaliation, she gave Mia a sudden push, knocking her to the floor. Mia went down hard, her head hitting the wall as she fell. Suzette was happy to see the shock on Jacob's face. She always knew how to get his attention. "Mia is fine," she said crisply. "We've reached an understanding, haven't we, Mia?"

Mia nodded as she slowly sat up. Jacob froze, his pudgy face showing his horror.

"And now, to drive the point home, Mia will be skipping dinner tonight—and so will you, Jacob, since you weren't keeping an eye on her." Judging from the look on his face, she'd picked the perfect punishment. Jacob was going to be crying in his room without his dinner, but it served him right. Where was he while Mia was exposing the family secret to some stranger in the garage? He needed to take some responsibility in all this. And it's not like skipping a meal would be a hardship for him. He had plenty of fat to burn.

"Okay, Mom. I'm sorry for not keeping an eye on Mia."

"That's better." She dusted off her hands. "Now go and tuck Mia in for the night, and I want you to spend the rest of the night in your room as well. You're both being punished."

"Yes, Mom."

Mia scrambled to her feet and followed Jacob to the basement stairs. Once they were out of sight, Suzette went into the kitchen to start off the evening. She could almost taste the glass of wine right now. There was an unopened bottle of Riesling chilling on the top shelf of the fridge. It would have been her first choice, but she really needed to polish off the merlot first. She didn't like to have a lot of open bottles of wine sitting around. So unseemly.

As she sat at the table, enjoying her first sips of merlot, her mind strayed to the old woman who'd boldly walked up her driveway uninvited. Such gall. She seemed harmless enough, but it was odd that she'd specifically asked about a little girl. It had to be a coincidence, but it was still unnerving.

This week was throwing all manner of grief her way. First Dawn from Magnificent Nutrition had called to say that her employee's grandmother had made threats about her special purchase, and now this. Suzette had heard the panic in Dawn's voice, but she wasn't worried. As far as Suzette was concerned, nothing could be traced back to her. She paid in cash and picked up an unmarked bag. Big deal. Even if she was caught with the pills, she could claim she had no idea what they were, that someone must have switched out her vitamins.

The old woman wasn't a worry either, just an annoyance. There was no way she could know about Mia. The child never left, and the windows on the first floor were always covered. No one knew she was there. Of course, then Mia had to open the door right at that moment, which was hideous timing. The woman hadn't seemed to notice. Luckily, she came off as a bit of a birdbrain, so no harm done. It couldn't happen again, though, and Suzette was sure it wouldn't. She'd driven the fear of God into Mia, and Jacob too. Or maybe it was *the fear of Suzette*. She laughed at her new turn of phrase.

It was times like this that she really missed her father. He'd been gone for nearly three years now. Three long years. So much time for her to be without the one person who knew her to the core, and approved wholeheartedly too. Her mother was still alive, but she was useless. She'd been a terrible mother when Suzette was growing up, and now, as an old woman, she was needy and difficult. Suzette was glad to let her brother, Cal, take charge in that area. He was, she was sure, scheming to take over her part of the inheritance. Such a greedy jerk, the way he acted like he cared about their mother, taking her to doctor's appointments and helping her with home repairs. He was so obviously trying to curry their mother's favor. Well, if he was going to squeeze her out of the family fortune, he might as well earn it.

Her father had always told her she was special, and he'd delighted in her every move. He'd say, "All you need to know about Suzette is that she's always right and she needs to be the center of attention." He said it with such affection that hearing those words made her glow. In his eyes, she *was* always right, and he was happy to have her be the center of his world. Throughout her childhood, he was her cheerleader. When other girls were mean to her, he told her they were jealous. If she didn't win a prize at school, he told her the officials were idiots. When friends turned their backs on her, he told her they'd be sorry someday. She was better off without them. Her father definitely had her best interests at heart.

Her mother was another story. She was always ready to knock Suzette down a few notches, telling her she was no better than anyone else and that she needed to learn how to compromise and get along with others. *As if.* Suzette had quickly learned to ignore all that defeatist blather. Her father's voice was the one she held on to.

Another bit of wisdom her dad had imparted? How to present herself to the world. He'd started off asking a question: "You want everyone to know you're the best, Suzette?"

She'd leaned in to listen, knowing even then how important this would be.

He'd continued. "There's only one way to make it clear to everyone else around you. First of all, you should know that your competition is not the smartest girl in the room, not the prettiest in the room, and certainly not the tallest, richest, or strongest. Your competition is the one who is the most confident. Confident people get what they want, and men are drawn to confident women like cats to catnip."

It was the best advice she'd ever gotten, and those had become her words to live by. At times she was tempted to share this knowl-edge with others—Jacob, for one, could certainly use a dose of confi-dence—but she always held back. Why should anyone else know this secret? It was intended for her, Daddy's princess, the most confident girl in the room and now the most confident woman in every room.

She took another sip of wine and smiled.

CHAPTER TWENTY-TWO

After Niki left a voice mail for Amy, she and Sharon ate dinner, still puzzling over the little girl Mrs. Fleming had adamantly denied lived in her house.

"Could she maybe be keeping her there for a good reason?" Sharon asked. "Like maybe she's hiding a friend and her daughter from an abusive spouse?" Thirty years before, Sharon had once done that herself for a work colleague. She'd forgotten all about it until just recently. Matilda was the woman's name. They'd worked together, but she barely knew her. Just to say hello to, basically. And then, one day, Matilda came to her door with her six-year-old son and a small suitcase and begged for a place to stay. "Just for a day or two," she said. "Until my mother arranges for our plane tickets home." Home was Nebraska, where she'd grown up. The husband knew all his wife's friends, but he didn't know Sharon, so her place was the perfect hiding spot. As soon as Matilda got word that the tickets were waiting for them at the airline counter, Sharon drove them both to the airport. That was pre-internet, so she never knew how the story ended. She hoped Matilda and her son went on to a happier life. The husband had sounded like a brute.

"Maybe." Niki sounded doubtful. "But there are other things that don't add up as well. I'll show you after we're done eating."

Once the dinner dishes were taken care of, both of them trooped up the stairs, the cat following right behind them. Niki grabbed a chair from the junk room and got Sharon situated before turning off the lights. "The last few days I've been watching every evening, and I've been noticing a pattern."

"A pattern?" Sarge jumped into her lap as if he wanted to be included, and without thought she began to pet him.

Niki looked through the binoculars for a minute before lowering them and putting them in Sharon's hands. "Yeah. All of the first-floor windows are always covered, even on the sides and the front. At least they were every time we drove past. The second floor seems to vary. Sometimes the blinds are up, sometimes they're down."

"Like normal people do," Sharon said, lifting the binoculars to her eyes. "Depending on if you're getting dressed or want more light in the room or whatever." She peered through the binoculars, not sure what she was looking at. The upstairs was dark, while the first floor had a few windows showing the glow of light behind the blinds.

Niki said, "I've never seen Jacob, so his bedroom must be in the front of the house, but the parents' room and their bathroom faces in our direction. There's another room, too, this side of the house off on the right. I think it's a home office. I've seen the dad, sometimes walking around in his boxers. He hasn't been around for a few days, at least not that I've seen."

"He walks around in just his boxers?"

"Just his boxers." She shook her head and laughed. "But he's nothing special, believe me. In case you were wondering."

"I really wasn't."

"And every night around eight o'clock, the lights go on in the basement, but only for a few minutes. Then they go off, but something else happens. Can you see what's happening with the basement window in the corner all the way on the left?"

Sharon moved her gaze to follow Niki's direction. "I can't really see it."

"Keep looking. It's hard to make out, but there's one part of the basement, one corner, where after the lights go out, I see a flickering of light. It's that way nearly every night."

Sharon kept her eyes on that side of the house, frustrated at not seeing anything. It was like that time in high school biology where all she could see were her eyelashes while the rest of the class was exclaiming over their view of paramecia. "I'm sorry, but I can't—" And suddenly, she could. Right in the lower corner of the house, she spotted a slight flickering of light. "I see it now. What is that? A candle?"

Niki said, "I think it's more likely to be someone looking at a laptop or watching TV in the dark."

"So they have a rec room in the basement?" She handed the binoculars back to Niki. "Do you think it's Jacob?"

"I don't know, but I have a theory. If you were keeping someone secret, where would you have them sleep?"

"In the basement," Sharon said, realization dawning.

"And say this little girl is being kept down there. It would make sense that she'd go to bed around eight, right? But tonight it's earlier. Why would that be? What happened today that's different from the past few days?"

Sharon's heart sank. "She got in trouble for opening the door when I was talking to Mrs. Fleming. Oh no, I hope I didn't make things worse."

"Don't beat yourself up over it. We're talking about a kid being held prisoner," Niki said. "I don't think it could get much worse."

They continued watching the house, even though not much happened. "What if one of us climbed the fence and looked through that window?" Sharon asked.

"I'm not against the idea," Niki said. "How high is the fence?"

"Six feet. I was appalled when they built it. It's hard not to take it personally when a neighbor builds a huge wall along the lot line.

There aren't even any spaces in between the boards. It's just a solid mass."

"So, wait," Niki said. "How long ago did they move in?"

"Five years ago or so? There was a lovely older couple who lived there before them. The Stoibers, Joyce and Bill. They'd raised their family there, and once the kids grew up it became too much to maintain. They retired to a condo in Florida."

"So the Flemings moved in and immediately built a wall?"

"Not immediately. They'd lived there maybe six months or so at that point. I stopped over once to introduce myself, but they weren't home and I never went back."

When Niki's phone rang, Sharon set down the binoculars while Niki went to answer it. Glancing at the screen, she said, "It's Amy." She put it on speakerphone.

Sharon was always amazed at how adept young people were with their cell phones. In the dark, hearing Amy's voice ring out, it was like she was in the room with them.

"Hey, Amy," Niki said. "Guess what your mom and I are doing right now?"

Amy generally hated when Sharon did this kind of thing, saying she had no time for guessing games, but apparently she was far more tolerant of Niki, because she chuckled and said, "Do tell."

"We're upstairs in your old bedroom, sitting in the dark, spying on the neighbors in back."

"The fence people?"

"The very same."

Sharon interjected. "The Flemings. Do you remember them?"

"Not really. I remember you talking about them building a fence, but I only knew the Stoibers."

Of course. The Flemings moved in long after Amy had moved out and created her own life apart from her mother and the family home.

Amy asked, "So why are you spying on them?"

Sharon let Niki fill her in, starting with the photo Sharon had taken the night of the super blood moon lunar eclipse and ending with how Sharon had gone up the driveway to ask Mrs. Fleming point-blank if she had any young children. After she was done laying it all out, Niki said, "So do you think we should call the police?"

"Hmm." Amy mulled it over, but only for a few seconds. "You haven't seen evidence of a crime, so it would be a tough call for the police. They'd probably investigate because they have to, but they might think of it as a nuisance complaint. A beef between neighbors. And the Flemings wouldn't have to let them search the house, so they wouldn't have anything concrete to go on."

"So we shouldn't call the police?" Sharon asked.

"I think you'd be better off contacting CPS—child protective services—and telling them what you just told me. This is really their area."

Niki said, "Do you think they'd take us seriously?"

"They have to—that's their job." Amy spoke to someone in the background, telling them it would be just a minute, and Sharon realized she was still at the office. "Tell you what," Amy said when she came back to the conversation. "Why don't you email me everything you know about the family and I'll see what I can dig up."

"We don't know much besides their names and where they live," Niki said.

"That's a good start," Amy said. "Send it and I'll see what I can do."

CHAPTER TWENTY-THREE

The next morning after Niki had left for work, Sharon had her phone in hand, finger poised above the screen ready to call child protective services, when the thing rang, startling her. Looking at the name on the screen, she was glad to see it was Amy.

"Amy!" she said. "It's so good to hear from you." She tapped the button to put it on speakerphone, the way Niki had taught her, and set it on the table in front of her. Niki was right—it was easier to talk this way.

"Hey, Mom, I only have a few minutes, but I wanted to let you know what I found out about the Flemings."

In the background Sharon heard faint noises, indicating Amy was once again calling from the office. No wonder she only had a few minutes. "Go ahead."

"Suzette Marie Fleming, maiden name Doucette, age forty-six. Born and raised in Minnesota, she graduated with honors from Loyola University, which is where I would guess she met her husband, Matthew John Fleming, age forty-seven. He got his undergrad at Loyola and then went to medical school at Northwestern."

"So he's a doctor?"

"*Was* a doctor. He was part of a practice in the Chicago area, then about six years ago he gave up practicing medicine and moved to Wisconsin, buying the house right behind yours, and got a job working for a company that sells medical equipment. He's a training specialist, travels around teaching staff how to use MRI machines, that kind of thing."

"Why would he give up being a doctor?" Sharon mused. "Too stressful?"

"Maybe," Amy said. "Or maybe he did something wrong or illegal and was caught. Sometimes if that happens the offender is given the option of quitting voluntarily rather than being charged with a crime. The house they had in Illinois was a mansion. Moving to your neighborhood was a definite step down for them. I find it hard to believe someone would give up a high-status job that required so many years of training unless something drastic happened."

"Wrong or illegal? Like what?"

"It could be anything. Sexually harassing staff, writing bad scripts, fraudulent insurance claims. You know, the usual." Amy, who had the killer instincts of an attorney, sounded downright cheerful.

"Oh." The idea of quitting a profession to avoid prosecution was foreign to Sharon's way of thinking, but it was just the kind of thing her daughter would pick up on. "What does his wife do for a living?"

"She worked in HR until their son was born and hasn't been employed since. Instead, she keeps busy being on the boards of several charitable organizations, most of them affiliated with big corporations."

"And their son?"

"Jacob Matthew Fleming, a senior in high school. He got his driver's license a year ago, but he hasn't had any moving violations as far as I can tell. His parents have had a few parking tickets, and his mom got one for going too slowly on the interstate. Otherwise, the family is clean. No complaints, no signs that they've broken any laws. Just your average middle-class Wisconsin family."

"With a very tall fence."

"Which they got a permit for," Amy reminded her. "Some people say good fences make good neighbors."

"So I've heard." Sharon tapped her fingernails against the table. "Anything else?"

"Nope, that's all I found."

If there were more out there, Amy would have found it. Sharon was sure of that. "Okay, thank you."

"Did you call CPS yet?"

"No, I was just about to when you called."

"So much for their clean record," Amy said, a grin in her voice. "Now that the neighbors are complaining."

"Do you think this is a bad idea?"

"No, not at all. If there is a child in danger, you're a hero. If you're mistaken, it's not a big deal. It's always better to err on the side of caution in a case like this."

Sharon knew Amy was right, but moments later, dialing the number for child protective services, she still felt like she was tattling on a neighbor with little evidence to back up her suspicions. It helped to be connected with Kenny, a thoughtful man who listened intently.

"Do you still have the photo you took that night?" Kenny asked.

"Yes, it's on my phone. It's not very clear, though, I'm sorry to say. It was dark, and I took it over the top of the fence."

"I'm sure you did the best you could." Kenny's tone was soothing. "Are you going to be home the rest of the morning?"

"I can be. Are you going to come out to my house?"

"Not me, but one of the staff members here. I'll tell you what— why don't you give me an hour or so, and I'll call you back to let you know when someone can come out and take a look at all the things you're telling me about."

Sharon exhaled in relief. "So you're for sure going to investigate?"

"We take every complaint seriously," Kenny assured her.

By the time Sharon hung up, a dark worry had lifted from her heart. Such a relief. She'd done all she could do for that little girl in the window. The authorities were involved now and would take care of everything.

CHAPTER TWENTY-FOUR

A t the end of the school day Jacob left the building and got on
the bus, but instead of taking it all the way home, he exited at
an earlier stop and began walking straight to the Village Mart. His
mother had done a good job terrorizing poor Mia the previous
evening, but what she hadn't known when she sent them off to their
rooms without dinner was that they'd already eaten. At that point,
little Mia had already polished off one and a half hot dogs, and Jacob
had eaten two hot dogs, plus the half she hadn't eaten. Added to that
were the chips and soda they'd had earlier, and both of them were
stuffed full. Neither of them minded going to their bedrooms for the
night either. Jacob would have been there anyway, and it was a
reprieve for Mia, who could settle in and watch TV undisturbed.

His mom prided herself on being so clever, when in fact she was a
total idiot.

After his mother had ordered them both to their rooms, he'd
taken Mia downstairs, and when they'd gotten out of earshot they'd
shared a smile, knowing they'd pulled one over on her. Before his
mother had arrived home and after they'd eaten, Mia had cleared the
table and wiped it down, and Jacob had washed the dishes by hand

and put them back in the cabinet. The hot dogs and buns that they hadn't eaten went back in the freezer, buried below the frozen vegetables and chicken nuggets. They had been careful not to leave a mess, and in the process, they'd left no evidence that they'd eaten dinner.

Mia's mood was only spoiled by her worry about being locked in. "I drank a lot of Coke," she said, although she really hadn't. "What if I have to go to the bathroom?"

Jacob knew what it was like to lie awake in bed and stress. "I'll tell you what," he said. "I'll close it, but I won't lock it. If you have to go to the bathroom, be really quiet and make sure to pull the door shut when you go back to your room afterward. And make sure you don't run the water or flush." His mother had nearly supernatural hearing at times.

"But in the morning . . . ," Mia said, her face mapped with worry, and Jacob knew she was imagining his mother coming across the unlocked door the next day. Then they'd both be in trouble.

"I'll make sure I'm the one who comes down in the morning," he promised.

"Will you?" The fear in her eyes melted away.

"I will. She'll never know."

"Thank you, Jacob."

"You're welcome."

"Jacob?" she said, sitting down on her cot. "Are you like my brother?"

What to say to that? She was as close to a sister as he'd ever had, and when he heard other kids talk about their siblings, they had the same kind of mixed feelings he had for Mia. She could be annoying, so much so that he found himself snapping at her, taking out the frustrations of the day by lashing out in her direction. Other times, the way she looked up to him warmed his heart. And of course, they both were in his mother's sights, so they shared a silent partnership in keeping her off their backs. "I guess so," he finally said. "Sort of like a brother."

"I thought so." She smiled, and his heart broke a little bit. Mia was so grateful for nothing, and it struck him once again how wrong it was for her to be here, closed up in their house. If it was up to his mother, Mia would never go outside, but his father said she needed the sunshine and fresh air. That human beings weren't made to be closed up all the time. So once in a great while Mia was allowed in the backyard during the day, but only when his mother was sure none of the neighbors were around, and even then it made her nervous. Jacob was pretty sure a six-foot-high fence provided the coverage they needed. His mom was paranoid by nature.

Mia occupied a very small world, and her days were filled with chores and more chores.

But if not with Jacob's family, where would she be? It could be far worse, according to his mother, and he'd seen it himself, so he knew it was true. When they'd first laid eyes on Mia, his mother had been driving on back roads on the way home from his grandfather's funeral. His mom was lost, having shut off the GPS because the voice annoyed her and she thought she knew better. His mother was a terrible driver to begin with, but she became a complete maniac when she was lost, pounding the steering wheel with her fist and swearing because she couldn't find any street signs. As if street signs would help on Wisconsin's endless country roads where everything looked the same.

Jacob had just been about to turn on the GPS and hit the "Home" setting when he'd glanced up to see something tiny moving right in the middle of the road. He'd screamed, "Mom, stop!" and grabbed the steering wheel, something that would have infuriated her under normal circumstances, but because she'd noticed the same thing he had, she was too busy slamming on the brakes to react to what he was doing. They stopped short of hitting the toddler girl, who was dressed only in sagging underpants, filthy socks, and stained pink pajamas patterned with cartoon cats. His mother threw the car into park and put on the four-way flashers, and then both of them got out and walked over to the little girl. Mia just stood there with her thumb in her mouth, regarding them with wide eyes. She didn't flinch or react at all, really. Her hair was thick and down to her shoulders, matted and greasy. Except for her big brown eyes, there was nothing cute about her.

His mother crouched down in front of her, examining her like a specimen. "Hi there," she said, actually sounding nice. "What's your name, sweetie?" Besides being dirty and smelling like pee, the little girl was silent and seemingly unfazed by how close she'd come to becoming roadkill. "Do you live around here?"

"Should we call 911?" Jacob asked, and when his mom nodded affirmatively, he got out his phone. But when he tried to make the call, he found out that there was no cell service. Not unexpected, since his mother had opted for the cheapest cell phone plan.

"It's because we're in the middle of nowhere," his mom said bitterly. "Like trying to call from the moon. It's impossible. Can't be done."

In his world history class, Jacob's teacher had actually played very clear recordings of audio transmissions from the moon for the class, but Jacob didn't think his mother would appreciate being contradicted at that moment. Or ever, really. He said, "Now what?"

His mom sighed. "Pick her up, and the two of you can sit in the back seat. We'll drive down the road and find out where she belongs."

It was one of the few times Jacob remembered his mother doing something decent with no thought for herself, but of course, when they eventually tracked down Mia's house, they were shocked at what they saw and afraid for their lives, so they got the hell out of there. Since they couldn't leave her there, the plan changed. And then they'd brought her home, and now Mia lived with them. Over the years there were times he was so angry with his mother, the way she taunted him about his weight and called him *useless*, that he was tempted to turn her in, tell the police about Mia and how his mother had kept this little girl in their house for three years. Getting arrested would serve her right. The only thing that held him back was that he'd googled and found out that his father was right. Kidnapping was a felony in Wisconsin. Most likely, both of his parents would be charged, and maybe he would be too. He was seventeen, close to being an adult. But even if they didn't charge him with a crime, without his parents, where would he live? With relatives out of state? And why should his dad go to prison? He was a good guy stuck in a bad situation.

So things stayed the same, and as the months went by, Mia had more questions, all of which she aimed at him. His parents thought she had a ten-word vocabulary, that's how quiet she was when they were around. It was a smart strategy, Jacob thought. His mother was threatened by those who thought for themselves, and she hated being talked back to. Mia had sensed this and kept up a nonthreatening facade.

All of these thoughts played through Jacob's mind on the walk home from school. He liked going to the Village Mart gas station, having the old guys greet him by name. There was a welcoming feel to the place. Now that they had the new hire, Niki, he was even more motivated to stop in. He didn't usually go two days in a row, but he wanted to see her again, and he also wanted to buy Mia some cupcakes and a Sprite.

When he pushed open the door, Niki looked up from behind the register and smiled right at him. When she said, "Hey, Jacob," it felt like coming home.

CHAPTER TWENTY-FIVE

Niki was the only one in the store when Jacob arrived. Albert was in the back helping to unload a truck. She had offered to be the one to carry the boxes into the storage room—it made sense, since she was strong and about a hundred years younger than Albert —but he'd waved away her offer. "Old guys like me need to keep moving," he'd said. "I'd rather wear out than rust out. You just stay inside where it's warm."

So she'd stayed behind the register, keeping an eye on the cars coming and going from the pumps. Only one guy came inside, and that was to buy cigarettes. He asked for Winston Lights, and when she turned to get them down from the shelf, he sheepishly said, "I vowed that if they ever got to be more than five dollars a pack, I'd quit, but that day came and went and here I am." He handed her a twenty, and she rang up the purchase and gave him change.

"It's a tough habit to break," she said sympathetically.

"Tell me about it." He stuffed the change in his pocket and told her to have a good day.

By the time Jacob walked in, Niki was glad for the diversion. She'd recognized him from a distance. There was something about the defeated way he walked, head down, face partially covered by the hood of his sweatshirt. He wore his bulky backpack slung over one shoulder.

When Niki greeted him by name, his face lit up. Niki knew that Sharon had planned to call child protective services that day to report the Flemings, but they wouldn't have started their investigation yet, she didn't think. As for Jacob, she'd planned to be friendly but not too friendly. Even though he appeared dejected, he wasn't necessarily blameless in whatever was going on in his house. He was a source of information and nothing else as far as she was concerned.

She watched as Jacob decisively opened the soda cooler, selecting a can of Sprite before darting back to the snack aisle. When he came to the counter, he plunked a package of cupcakes down and set the soda right next to it. "Hostess CupCakes," she said. "Good choice."

"They're not for me," Jacob said, seemingly embarrassed.

"Then they're an even better choice, because you're getting them for someone else."

"I guess." He set his backpack on the floor and leaned over to rummage in one of the pockets. When he straightened up he had a crisp ten-dollar bill, which he slid across the counter.

Niki scanned the can and the cupcakes. After putting the money in the register, she said, "For your girlfriend?"

"What?" His eyebrows rose.

"The cupcakes. You said they're not for you. Are they for your girlfriend?"

"I don't . . . I mean, I—" He shook his head, appearing flustered. "No. Just for a little kid I know."

"That's so nice of you!" Niki put the change in his hand. "I bet she'll love them!" She watched his face for a reaction.

Jacob nodded. "They're her favorite. It's kind of a surprise."

So now she'd established that they were for a little girl. Score one for Niki. She said, "So thoughtful. I notice that a lot of people don't think about anyone but themselves. I'm not sure why. Selfish, I guess. But it's not that hard to go out of your way for other people, you know? I mean, sometimes the smallest things can make a difference to someone. I know the whole Kindness Matters movement is sort of a cliché these days, but I still think it's true." Niki could hear herself rambling, but he wasn't moving and he seemed pleased, so she kept on. "You're a rare one, Jacob. Come back and let me know if she was happy to get them. I love hearing about this kind of thing." Inwardly she cringed, thinking how lame this sounded. *I love hearing about this kind of thing? What kind of thing would that be? Giving a kid some cupcakes?*

Despite her stupid-sounding attempt at conversation, it seemed to be meeting its mark. Jacob beamed like someone not used to getting compliments. "I will," he said. "I could come back tomorrow. I mean, if you're going to be working then."

Niki nodded. "I'm here Wednesday through Sunday from nine to five, so I'll definitely be working."

"Great." He put the cupcakes and soda in his backpack and pocketed the change.

"You can count on it. I'll be right here."

"It's nice to be able to count on something," Jacob said, and she sensed a wistfulness in his voice.

Niki nodded. "The world can be so random sometimes. It's good to know what to expect."

"Okay then. I guess I'll see you tomorrow." He hoisted the backpack over his shoulder and headed to the door.

"Bye, Jacob," she called out, and without turning around he held up a hand in farewell.

Niki kept her eyes on the wall of glass, watching as he walked past the first row of pumps, and frowning slightly when she saw two young guys approach him from the sidewalk. They called out to him in what appeared to be a friendly way, but she recognized the defensive hunch of his shoulders. These were not friends, and he was not happy to see them. Now the two of them stood directly in front of Jacob, blocking his way. She couldn't hear what they were saying, but

160

he seemed to be shrinking away from them. Niki had seen this kind of thing before, and she knew how it felt.

The door leading from the stockroom swung open, and she heard Albert's booming voice say, "Good to have that done. What did I miss?"

"Not much," Niki said, her gaze still on the three teenagers outside. "Just the usual at the pumps. And Jacob was in getting some snacks. He was buying Hostess CupCakes for a little kid he knows. Has he ever done that before? Buy something for someone else?"

"Not that I know of," Albert said, coming to stand next to her.

His words barely registered, because now the two boys were moving toward Jacob in a threatening way. One of them gave him a shove, making him stumble backward before he regained his balance. Without a pause, Niki said, "Back in a minute." She pushed past Albert and rushed outside, her heart racing. She approached the boys, calling out, "Hey, Jacob!"

All three stopped to look at her. Jacob appeared the most surprised. "Yeah?" he said.

She rushed up to his side and slipped her hand onto the crook of his elbow. "Good news! My boss said I can have off that night, so we can go out after all."

"Okay," Jacob said, a flicker of confusion on his face.

"I know I told you he said no, but I begged and told him it was important that we have that evening together, so he changed his mind. Good news, right?"

"Yeah."

"So it's a *date?*"

"Sure." Something in the way he said it made her think he was catching on. "Of course."

"Yay for us!" She leaned over and gave him a kiss on the cheek. "Don't forget. I went to a lot of trouble to work out my schedule."

"I won't forget," he promised, standing a little taller.

"Sorry for interrupting, guys," Niki said. "But girlfriends always come first."

"Sure, no problem," said the taller of the two. He exchanged a glance with his friend.

Then the second one said, "Catch you later, LEGO Head."

Jacob and Niki watched as the two boys sauntered off, heading in the opposite direction of Jacob's walk home. "Thanks," Jacob said, his cheeks flushing red. He seemed too embarrassed to meet her eyes.

"No worries. I have to get back to work," Niki said, hugging herself. Now that the exchange was over, she felt the chill of the wintry air.

"Okay, see you later."

She watched him walk off, then turned to dash back to the store. "Sorry about that," she said to Albert, coming through the door and taking her place behind the counter.

Albert still had his eye on the window, watching Jacob as he headed down the sidewalk. "Not a problem," he said gruffly.

"Is there something you wanted me to do?"

Instead of answering her question, Albert gave her an approving look and said, "I saw what you did there. That was nice, sticking up for Jacob."

Niki shrugged. "I've never liked bullies."

"No one does, but not everyone wants to get involved. The way you went to his defense was exceptional. I'd say that makes you a standout person, Niki Ramos."

Niki didn't feel like a standout person, but she took the compliment anyway. "Thanks."

CHAPTER TWENTY-SIX

Suzette felt like screaming. It was afternoon, almost time for Jacob to be coming home from school, when the doorbell went off—and kept going off. Ringing and ringing and ringing. She hadn't noticed when it first began, but at least ten minutes had passed by now. The ringing had a pattern. Two quick rings and then a very long pause, so long that each time she hoped it was over, only to have it ring again. She had a policy of not answering the door unless she was expecting someone, but this intruder—this woman—wouldn't get the hint. And it was definitely a woman standing alone on their front mat. Suzette had confirmed that by peering through the blinds.

The woman was well dressed by most standards, but Suzette had sized her up quickly, noting that the purse was a knockoff brand and her coat a nondescript navy peacoat that one could find at any department store. Could she be from one of the charities that Suzette was involved with? Not likely. She had the look of a real estate agent or a census taker. What a bother.

The doorbell rang twice more, and the noise of it was so grating that Suzette was ready to wring the woman's neck. Another quick glance out the window showed the woman standing calmly in front of the door like she had all the time in the world. Suzette went into the kitchen, where Mia was on her hands and knees washing the floor. The child was only halfway done. So ridiculous. Mia took forever to scrub floors, but she tended to do an exceptionally good job, so Suzette didn't like to hurry her. "Mia?" Suzette stood in the doorway, one hand on her hip.

The child paused in her work to glance up at her. "Ma'am?"

"You are to go downstairs *immediately*. Do not come back up until I call you. Do you understand me?"

Mia nodded, squeezing out the rag.

"Do it! Now!" It was infuriating to Suzette how she was forced to raise her voice. How difficult was it to follow orders?

Mia set the rag down next to the bucket, scrambled to her feet, and went to the basement door, pulling it shut behind her. When Suzette no longer heard the child's footsteps on the stair treads, she smoothed her hair and made her way to the front door. So much trouble to make the doorbell stop ringing. She'd take the woman's card and send her on her way.

When the door opened, the woman's face lit up as if in recognition. "Well, there you are," she said. "Suzette Fleming? I'm so glad I caught you at home." Her gray hair was clipped back on the sides, like she was a geriatric schoolgirl.

Her demeanor denoted a familiarity that made Suzette hesitate. Had they met at some point? Nothing about the woman seemed familiar. "Can I help you?"

She smiled. "I'm Franny Benson, a social worker from the county. I work for the Child Protection Unit. We've had a report from the neighborhood, and I'd love to ask you a few questions, if you have a minute." She held up an unimpressive photo ID.

Suzette let out an exasperated sigh. *Always with the questions. Is there no end to people wanting my opinion on happenings in the community?* "I'm afraid I'm not interested, but thank you and—" Suzette started to close the door, but the woman spoke out again.

"Wait! I understand you do a lot of work in the community serving on the boards of area charities?"

Suzette opened the door a little wider. "You know about my work?"

"Of course!"

"Really?" Suzette's lips slowly stretched into a smile. *She knows about my leadership on the boards.* And here Matt thought her work on the boards was just a waste of time. He'd said as much, saying that if she thought it was elevating her standing in the community she was dead wrong. "No one cares what a bunch of society women talk about sitting around a table in your so-called *meetings*," he'd said, putting air quotes around the last word. "The executives who are fawning over you only do it because you raise money for them."

Franny said, "If I could just come in for a few minutes, I'd love to talk to you."

"I can give you ten or fifteen minutes," Suzette said, relenting. She opened the door and ushered Franny inside, taking the woman's coat and hanging it in the front hall closet. "Right this way." Franny, her large handbag dangling from one hand, followed her into the living room. Suzette was justifiably proud of this room, with its tall curio cabinet filled with valuable Lladró figurines, and she made sure it was kept immaculate.

After they took their seats, Franny said, "What a lovely home you have."

"Thank you. We like it."

Franny rummaged through her bag and pulled out a small clipboard and pen. "I know you have limited time, so I'll keep this brief."

Suzette said, "I would appreciate it."

"How do you want to be known? Social activist? Humanitarian? Philanthropist?"

"You can use my name if you want. Suzette Fleming." She felt a surge of self-satisfaction. "And *humanitarian* comes closest to what I do, although I don't think of it that way. Just trying to do my bit."

"You're being modest, Ms. Fleming. If everyone took the time to work on behalf of charities, the world would be a better place."

"Thank you," she said, her gaze dropping to her folded hands. *Humanitarian.* She liked the sound of that word.

Franny's next set of questions had to do with Suzette's family. She jotted down the names and ages of her husband and son and inquired about Jacob's school. "So Jacob is your only child?"

"Yes," Suzette said, with a sweet shake of her head. "Jacob is a straight-A student with lots of friends. Our house is sort of the hub for local teenagers. They all congregate here—they're coming and going all the time. Many would say it seems chaotic, but I actually prefer it that way." She leaned forward. "I think it's best to keep an eye on them, don't you agree?"

"Oh, absolutely." Franny nodded.

"My husband and I are in perfect agreement when it comes to raising Jacob."

"I see. Do you have any other children living here? Maybe from a previous marriage or even just visiting?"

"No, not at all. It's just the three of us, and we love it that way. We're a very close-knit family. Jacob comes home from school and practically pours his soul out to me." She tapped her fingertips to her forehead. "The stories I could tell you! Just the usual teenage drama, but of course it seems serious to him. So I listen. It's important to be supportive."

"So important."

"You remember that age. There's always some crisis, and it's worse now with social media. Rumors fly, and gossip spreads like crazy. Not about Jacob, of course—he doesn't have to worry about such things—but he's like me, always looking out for the underdog. He's such a role model for other students. His father and I are quite proud of him."

"He sounds like a wonderful young man. So would it be fair to say that besides your son, there have been no other children in the house in the last week or two?"

"Besides his friends from high school?" Suzette frowned. "No. None at all."

"No younger children have been in your home?"

"Of course not. Did someone say there was?" This woman was getting on her nerves.

"I'm just following up on a report," Franny said. "Very routine. I'm visiting with several people in the neighborhood."

Was she imagining things? Something about the expectant way Franny looked at Suzette made her neck stiffen. It was almost as if this woman knew about Mia. But of course, that was impossible. More likely she was looking for families to do foster care. *As if.* Suzette let out a laugh. "I'm not interested in taking care of younger children. As you can imagine, my work keeps me pretty busy. You caught me at home today, but that's not usually the case. I'm almost always on the go. Now, did you have any more questions before I see you to the door?"

Franny blinked. "May I have a drink of water? I hate to ask, but I have a tickle in my throat. Just a sip or two would help."

"Certainly. Just a moment. I'll be right back." Suzette got up from her seat and walked out of the room. How tedious that she was now waiting on this woman, especially considering that she worked for the county, which meant that technically her taxes paid the woman's salary. Franny was essentially Suzette's employee. *Oh, why did I even allow her in the house? Live and learn. Never again.* Suzette walked around Mia's abandoned bucket and got a juice glass out of the cabinet, then went to fill it from the water dispenser on the door of the fridge. Two sips and she was showing this woman the door. When she turned around, she was startled to see Franny standing in the entryway to the kitchen. *The nerve.*

"What a lovely kitchen," she said with an air of nonchalance. "I'm guessing you updated it? The counters and cabinets all look brand new." She walked toward Suzette, running her hand along the countertop.

Suzette was done talking. "Here's your water."

Franny took the glass. "Thanks."

She didn't immediately take a drink, though. Suzette wanted to put the glass up to her lips and force her to drink. Instead, the woman just rambled on and on.

"I would love a kitchen like this." Her chin dropped down, and she took in the bucket on the floor. "Oh, I see I interrupted your housework. Is that why it took so long for you to come to the door?"

"Yes, I was right in the middle of scrubbing the floor," Suzette said.

"You don't have a cleaning lady?"

Suzette sighed. "I don't have any help at all. I do all of it, and that's the way I prefer it. When I do things, I know they're done right. Other people so often take shortcuts."

"I usually wear jeans when I do housework." Franny gave a half laugh. "I'm so clumsy, if I wore anything nice like you have on, I would probably ruin it."

"Yes, I'm very careful."

"You must be."

This exchange was making Suzette exhausted. "I don't want to be rude, but you really need to get going. I have an appointment, and I don't want to be late."

"Of course." Franny downed the water in one gulp. "Thank you for your time."

Suzette ushered her to the front hall, where she unceremoniously handed over the woman's coat. "Thanks for stopping in. Goodbye."

"Goodbye." Franny stuck out her hand, and Suzette reluctantly gave it a shake. "It was a pleasure to meet you."

"Likewise."

Suzette pulled the door open. "Oh, it feels like the temperature has dropped. You'll want to move quickly, I think." She pressed a hand against Franny's back and firmly guided her through the doorway. "Take care," she said, once the woman cleared the doorframe.

And good riddance.

CHAPTER TWENTY-SEVEN

Ever since Jacob had mailed in Mia's saliva sample, he'd logged onto the site nearly every day to check for the results. Getting the saliva sample without his parents finding out had been easy, and he knew Mia wouldn't say anything. Registering online had been simple as well. He'd needed a fake email address, which hadn't been hard to set up. He cracked himself up by putting in her name as Mia Mystique, and he gave her a fake birth date so she'd appear to be eighteen. He made sure it was on the privacy setting so that he could see other people's connections to Mia but they couldn't see details about her. All of this was done on the sly—easy enough, because once he was in his room his parents seemed to forget about him.

Luckily, he'd purchased the kit at a store, so the lab fees were covered by the cost of the box, and he didn't have to use a credit card. Otherwise, it never would have worked.

He was pretty proud of himself for having thought of this as a way to get more information about Mia. Jacob wanted to know about her background—partly for Mia, but also to contradict his mother, whose stance had always been that no one wanted her, that all she had was them. It seemed like a stupid assertion to Jacob. Just because

Mia wasn't on the missing children website didn't mean she wasn't wanted by someone.

Jacob knew his mother would have a meltdown if she knew what he'd done, but he didn't care. One good thing was that he'd felt a shifting of power lately. Maybe because he was now physically bigger than her, or maybe because he just didn't care anymore and she sensed that her grip on him was getting more tenuous. She was spending more time holed up in her room, while his father spent nights on the couch in his home office. His dad had even moved a lot of his clothes in there. Their little dysfunctional family unit was falling apart, which was both scary and exhilarating at the same time.

When his phone pinged to notify him that he'd received the email with the DNA results, he was in his room, having just finished getting dressed for school. A quick look at the time told him he had twenty minutes before the bus picked him up. If he had to skip breakfast, he would; he had a box of Pop-Tarts in his locker at school for just such an emergency.

Logging onto the site, he glanced over the home page, finally clicking on the *Ancestry* link. On that page, he was able to scroll down to something that said *DNA Relatives List*. Almost instantly, he saw a list topped by *Grandmother, Grandfather, Uncle*. The names next to them were *Wendy Duran, Edwin Duran*, and *Dylan Duran*. The words were a mental smackdown and made him gasp. *Holy crap, Mia has grandparents and an uncle?* He did some random clicking and came up with the percentages of shared DNA for each person. Jacob wasn't really sure how it worked, so he didn't know if 24.7 percent was the usual amount a person shared with their grandfather. He would have to do some googling later. Another page broke down her background, mostly European with 24 percent Puerto Rican.

The euphoric feeling of knowing he'd done it, that he'd singlehandedly figured out a way to find out more about Mia, turned into a sick feeling when he thought about what it meant. Now that he had this information, what would he do with it? He knew there was a way to reach out and message people on the site, but what would he say to them? And what if these were really bad people, like the guy who had shot at them? If that were the case, Mia would be better off staying with his family.

Another problem? The idea of his dad—who'd been against Mia staying with them from the start—having to go to prison sickened him. He had a feeling, though, that it might work out that way. His mother lied as easily as she breathed and was the more convincing of the two. What if Mia went off to these new people and his dad went to prison and Jacob was left alone with his mom? A horrifying thought. Still, he wanted to know more.

On a hunch, he logged into Facebook and did a search for the name Wendy Duran. A few came up, but the most likely candidate was an older woman who happened to live in Wisconsin. She hadn't posted much, but she also hadn't utilized the privacy setting, so Jacob could see everything. Old people were so dumb about social media, but this time it was to his advantage.

He clicked around until he noticed a family photo, the parents with a son and a daughter. Judging by their clothes, it wasn't recent. Wendy had written, "Family vacation. Dylan was fourteen, Morgan twelve."

Wendy Duran, who lived in Wisconsin, and had a son named Dylan.

This had to be the right family. He peered at the photo, trying to see if the daughter, Morgan, looked like Mia. She did, a little bit, but the likeness wasn't spot-on.

Now what? He wasn't going to do anything just yet. He needed time to think about this and decide the best way to go from here. But first he had to catch the school bus and get through his day.

CHAPTER TWENTY-EIGHT

Sharon had parked down the block, waiting and watching as Franny Benson left the Flemings' house. She'd liked the social worker well enough when they'd met earlier at her house, but she wanted to be absolutely positive that she'd follow through. Franny had an air of caring, so that was in her favor, but she didn't say much, so it was hard to get a read on her. She seemed most interested in the blurry photo, the one taken from over the fence. She'd stared at it for a long time and then asked Sharon to text it to her afterward. When Sharon had pleaded ignorance of how to do that, she'd graciously taken hold of the phone and sent it to herself. Afterward she'd wanted to go upstairs so she could see the vantage point from Niki's window, where she'd stood, first looking, then jotting down notes.

During Franny's entire visit, Sharon found herself babbling, trying to impress upon her that even though the evidence wasn't there, her instincts on this were strong. "I know I saw a little girl peeking out the garage door. I'd bet my life on it," she said.

Franny just nodded and kept writing. She appeared to believe Sharon, but her lack of response didn't give her much to go on.

"Will you go into their house and search?" Sharon asked.

"We'll do everything we can within the confines of the law. We have to work within the legal limits."

"I understand." Sharon didn't like it, but she understood. "Will you get back to me and tell me what you find out?"

"I'll be checking back with you, and you'll be getting a letter from my office letting you know your concern was screened in, which means the appropriate actions were taken. It's basically a confirmation that we followed up on your complaint."

"You do believe me, don't you?" Sharon had finally asked, wanting reassurance. Franny was kindly, but Sharon wanted more. A little outrage would go a long way.

"Why wouldn't I believe you?" Franny said, putting her notebook back in her bag. She followed Sharon downstairs and gathered up her coat and gloves, then shook Sharon's hand and said she'd be in touch.

It was only after she'd left that Sharon realized the woman hadn't actually given a straight answer to any of her questions. Franny had her reasons, Sharon was sure of this, but it still left her with an uneasy feeling.

Franny hadn't said for certain that she was going straight to the Flemings' house, but it was, Sharon thought, a safe bet. After she'd said goodbye to Franny, Sharon went to the front window to watch as the social worker's car moved down the street, and then she waited a few minutes before getting into her own vehicle. She wasn't following the social worker exactly, since Sharon drove around the opposite end of the block. Her rationale was simple: She lived in this neighborhood and often went down this street anyway. Who was to say that wasn't the case this time? And if she pulled over to the side of the road to look at her phone, well, that wasn't a crime, was it? It happened. Sometimes you needed to check your phone.

It was always a good idea to have a ready excuse. She'd been caught off guard a few times in her life and was now all the wiser.

When she drove past the Flemings' house, she spotted the social worker standing outside the front door, her back to the street. Sharon circled around one more time, then pulled over at the end of the block and shut off her engine. Franny had no idea what kind of car Sharon drove, so it was unlikely that she'd make the connection even if she spotted her. Franny's car, she noted, was parked curbside in front of the house. Minutes went by and nothing changed, and then suddenly, Franny stepped forward and was gone—inside the house, presumably, although at this angle Sharon couldn't actually see what had happened.

Fifteen minutes went by, and then, just when Sharon thought she couldn't stand the suspense, Franny came out of the house, made her way down the driveway, and got into her car. A minute later, Sharon saw the red flash of brake lights, and then the car was in motion, taking off down the street. Sharon felt disappointed. That was it? It was foolish, she knew, but some part of her had hoped to see Franny exit the house holding the hand of the little girl. Barring that, she'd have settled for a battalion of police cars converging on the house, officers swarming the place, search warrant in hand. The officers would search every nook and cranny until they found the child and saved her from whatever it was that was going on in there. This last idea was completely far-fetched, but Sharon liked it a lot, especially since she would come off as the hero in the story.

The observant neighbor who trusted her instincts and didn't give up—that was what the news media would call her.

It bothered her that the social worker's visit was so short and there was no discernible outcome. Watching the woman get into her car and drive away gave her a hopeless, let-down feeling. Could it be that the social worker had simply questioned Mr. or Mrs. Fleming, they'd denied having a little girl living with them, and now the case was closed?

That was the very question she asked Amy later that night during a phone chat. She and Niki had exchanged stories about their day after Niki had come home from work. Niki told her that Jacob had shopped at the Village Mart, buying what she believed to be cupcakes for the little girl, and Sharon had told Niki about the visit from the social worker. Now both of them sat at the kitchen table staring at the phone in front of them as if it were a Ouija board, capable of giving them answers.

Amy reiterated the question. "Are you asking if they'll just take the Flemings at their word?"

"Yes," Sharon said. "That's exactly what I want to know. Do you think the case is closed now?" She glanced up at Niki, who was leaning in to hear.

"Doubtful. I think when she told you they were going to do everything they could within the legal limits of the law, she was telling you that her hands are somewhat tied. Actually, I'm pretty impressed that she got into the house. She must be exceptional at her job."

Sharon knew Amy was right, but the whole process still made her impatient. She asked, "So if Franny did ask questions about a little child living at their house and Mrs. Fleming denied it, what then?"

"Well, she couldn't exactly accuse her of lying." Amy was on their side, but she still spoke from her place as an attorney, something Sharon found a little bit irritating.

"What's the whole point of her going to talk to them, then?"

"I'm guessing that the social worker took a non-adversarial approach in order to get invited into the house. People seldom let you in if they think they're in trouble, so she probably worded it as if it were a routine neighborhood call. Then once she was inside, she would be trying to get a sense of what the household was like, and she'd be looking for any signs of a child living there. She might have asked in an offhand way if they had a small child stay with them recently. As a social worker, she may be skilled in telling if people are lying. Once she's made the visit, decisions will be made as to how to proceed from that point. Just because you don't see anything happening doesn't mean nothing is happening. The local police might be informed, and they'll be keeping an eye on the house, watching to see when people come and go and if they have a child with them in the car. Your social worker may go and interview other neighbors and ask if they've seen anything suspicious. These are all things they can do within the limits of the law."

Within the limits of the law—there was that phrase again. "She did tell me to let her know if I saw anything else," Sharon admitted.

"Sometimes these things take time," Amy said. "The Flemings have rights too. And there is a possibility that you're wrong, you know."

"She's not wrong," Niki said, jumping in, and she proceeded to tell Amy about her encounter with Jacob. "I'm almost positive the cupcakes were for the little girl."

Amy chuckled. "I believe you, Nikita, but the cupcake argument won't hold up in court. Unless there's more to go on, CPS will have to proceed with caution."

"What if," Niki asked, sliding the phone closer to her side of the table, "we call the fire department one day when the whole family is gone and tell them we see smoke coming out of the house? Wouldn't they have to break in and search?"

Sharon was ready to applaud her out-of-the-box thinking, but Amy wasn't as enthused. "Falsely reporting a fire is against the law," she said firmly. "And they'll come down hard on the caller, especially if they can prove it was done willfully and maliciously."

"But how would they know?" Sharon asked. "We'll say we thought we saw smoke. People make mistakes." The cat rubbed against her ankles, and she reached down to pet him.

"Yes, people make mistakes, but what are the chances you saw smoke coming out of their house right after you reported the family to CPS?" Sharon could imagine Amy ruefully shaking her head.

"They'd make that connection?"

"Of course," Amy said. "And what if a real fire is called in while they're busy investigating a false report? Would you want to be responsible for someone else's death?"

Sharon sighed. "Of course not."

"Trust me, guys, I know your hearts are in the right place, but please don't do anything on impulse. I don't have time to fly to Wisconsin to bail you two out of jail."

Sharon said, "We're not going to jail." The idea was absurd.

"Promise me you won't do anything rash. You reported what you saw. Now sit back and let the experts do their jobs."

They ended the call with a promise to Amy that they wouldn't do anything rash. Afterward Sharon turned to Niki and said, "So I guess that's that. By the way, I thought your idea to call the fire department was brilliant."

Niki nodded thoughtfully. "I still think it's a good idea. I mean, I understand her point about taking firefighters away from a real fire, but what are the chances there would be a big fire right at that time?" They sat silently, considering the odds.

"We could still do it, but anonymously," Sharon suggested. Sarge mewed plaintively, and she patted her lap for him to come up. Once he'd jumped up and settled in, she rubbed behind his ears.

"Using what phone? Everything can be traced."

Sharon thought. "Is there a pay phone at the gas station?"

"No. I can't think of any pay phones around here."

"They still have them at the airport."

"And the bus station."

"Neither of which helps us. Both are too far away."

Niki tapped a finger on the table. "I do have one idea, a way for me to get a closer look at that basement window, but I'd need your help."

"Just say the word. I'll do it."

CHAPTER TWENTY-NINE

When Ma'am called Mia back upstairs to the kitchen, she was very angry. "What were you thinking, Mia, leaving your bucket in the middle of the floor like this?" Ma'am gave the bucket a little kick with the toe of her pointy shoe, and water sloshed over the top edge.

"Sorry, Ma'am," Mia said.

"*Sorry* doesn't cut it."

Mia didn't know what else to say, so she just nodded.

"Well, don't just stand there like an idiot. This floor won't clean itself. Get to work!"

Ma'am left the room, and Mia immediately got back to scrubbing, not even replacing the water, which had gotten cold in her absence. When Ma'am got in these kinds of moods, it infected the air, coloring everything in the house in a gray cast. Mia made a point to stay out of her way. After she was done with the floor, she began to dust, even though it wasn't dusting day. Griswold followed on her heels as if he felt the need to be next to a friendly presence. He was a smart dog.

When Jacob walked in the door after school, Ma'am pounced on him, berating him for coming home late, but Jacob was too smart for her. He said, "I remembered what you said about me needing more exercise, so I skipped the bus and walked home. I feel great. I might do it every day."

"Well, okay then." She sounded flustered. "But next time call if you're going to be late. I was worried sick."

"Okay, Mom, I will. I'm sorry I worried you." When Ma'am turned away, Jacob gave Mia a knowing wink. Ma'am went upstairs, and as soon as they heard the floorboards squeaking overhead, Jacob came over to Mia and whispered, "I got you a treat. I'm going to put it under your cot, okay?"

Mia bobbed her head up and down, barely able to stand her excitement. *A treat just for me!* Jacob really was like a big brother. After Jacob came back from the basement, he disappeared upstairs to his room, and Mia quickly ran out of things to do. For a few minutes she sat on the bottom step of the stairwell, giving Griswold some gentle petting. When a wave of tiredness came over her, she decided to lie down behind the couch for a little bit. The space between the couch and the wall made a cozy area just her size. She backed in feet-first until she wasn't sticking out at all, then closed her eyes to rest.

Mia didn't mean to fall asleep, but she did. The next thing she heard was Mister coming home from work, calling out, "Hello, I'm home." She came awake with a jolt and started to come out of her hiding spot, but then she realized that Ma'am was in the living room, sitting in a chair facing her way, waiting for Mister. Luckily, she didn't see Mia.

"I'm in here," Ma'am said.

Mia noticed that her voice was normal, so maybe she wasn't in such a bad mood anymore? She heard Mister set down his suitcase, followed by his footsteps as he entered the room, and the creak of the couch as he sat down.

"How was your day, dear?" Ma'am asked.

"It was a long one. My flight was delayed," Mister said. "I'm glad to be home."

"Ha!" Ma'am scoffed, and Mia tensed up.

Oh no. The question about his day had been a trap. She felt sorry for Mister, because she had an idea of how things were going to go.

"You think you had a long day? You have no idea. Wait until you hear what I had to deal with."

Mister was silent while Ma'am talked about a woman who had come to the door: "Pretending to be one of my fans." Instead, Ma'am said, the woman was just nosing around, asking questions about how many children were in the home. "Then she followed me into the kitchen and made a snide comment about Mia's wash bucket, saying something about my clothing, that it was too dressy for housecleaning. Not that it was any of her business!"

When Ma'am got wound up, words came out rapidly, slamming and bouncing against the walls, feeling like an angry assault. Even from behind the couch, Mia could sense her fury.

"Wait a minute," Mister said, interrupting. "She asked how many children we have?"

Ma'am hated being interrupted, and her cold tone reflected this. "Yes, Matt. Among other things. She wanted to know my opinion of Jacob's school. Don't they do surveys or have focus groups for this kind of thing? You'd think they'd have a more efficient way of gauging all of this than going door to door. And since when is it my responsibility to keep them informed? They obviously have no idea how busy I am."

"And she was a social worker who works for the county?" His words came slowly, reminding Mia of how Jacob sounded when he explained things to her.

"I told you all this already, Matt. Try to keep up."

"Suzette, listen to me." Mia could tell he had shifted his weight on the couch. "What if she knows about Mia and is investigating? What if someone found out she's living here and notified them?"

"It was a *routine* visit, Matt. She was visiting everyone in the neighborhood." Mia could picture Ma'am frowning and folding her arms across her chest, the way she did when displeased.

"Of course she would say that," Mister said. "You have to be the stupidest person on the planet, Suzette, letting a social worker into the house."

"I'm stupid? You're saying I'm stupid?" Behind the couch Mia shifted uncomfortably. She felt the need to visit the bathroom, but there was no way she was coming out of her hiding spot now.

"In this case, yes."

Out of nowhere, Ma'am screamed so loudly that Mia shook. No words came out—it was just an angry, frustrated cry, frightening in its intensity. It went on for so long that Mia covered her ears with her hands.

When it stopped, Mister said, "Are you finished acting like a child, Suzette?"

Mia heard Ma'am leap out of the chair. She shouted, "I don't have to listen to this!" The next thing she heard was Ma'am storming out of the room and up the stairs, with Mister following behind her, still making his point about the social worker.

Mia shimmied out of her hiding spot and went straight to the bathroom. She did her business with a sigh. Once she'd washed her hands and dried them, she peeked out through the open door. The coast was clear. Now she just had to find something to do so she'd look busy when Ma'am came back downstairs.

J acob had his headphones on and was deep into a game when he heard his mother scream. He paused and uncovered his ears to listen. *Now what?* It didn't sound like she was hurt; the pitch was more furious than pained. After she stopped screaming, she stormed up the stairs, his father following behind her and calling her name. Another argument. It was like a battlefield around his house half the time. His father was making a point about letting someone into the house, and then he said something about Mia. It struck Jacob as ironic that little Mia, the sweetest, least threatening person ever, had the power to drive fear into his parents' hearts.

Of course it wasn't really *her* making them afraid, but the idea that they'd get into trouble because of her. Sometimes his father would go months without bringing up the subject, and even Jacob would forget that Mia's existence in their home wasn't legally sanctioned. If no one brought it up, it almost felt like she'd been adopted. Or *saved from a horrible life*, as his mother put it. But then something would happen to spook his dad, and he'd bring it up to his mom, and they'd have an all-out fight with name-calling and accusations. Each of them threatened to put the other in jail, or to out their bad deeds to his grandparents, something Jacob found funny. As old as they were, they still didn't want their parents to know that they'd done something wrong. So stupid. The approval of his mother and father meant nothing to him right now. By the time he was in his forties, he would be too busy living his life to care about their opinions.

He heard his dad shout, "Would you just use your head for once, Suzette? Have you ever heard of social workers making routine calls before?"

"Of course I've heard of them making routine calls." She was always so defensive. "That's what they do, Matt." You could never tell her anything.

Jacob got to his feet and opened the door to eavesdrop.

"I'm telling you, it sounds like someone knows about Mia and reported us."

His mother scoffed. "Oh, Matt, stop being so dramatic. No one knows about Mia. How could they?"

His dad wasn't going to give up. "Think for a minute! Has anyone seen her? Maybe through a window? Have you mentioned her in conversation? Was she in any photos that you posted on Facebook, maybe in the background?"

"The windows are covered, and she hasn't gone outside in months."

Jacob made his way down the hallway to his parents' bedroom. The door was ajar.

"How about pictures on Facebook?"

"I never post photos from home," his mom said imperiously. "That is my professional account. I only put up images taken during events and meetings."

"I have a bad feeling about this."

When they fought, Jacob always sympathized with his dad. His mother had a tendency to dismiss his father's concerns, belittling him at every turn. The irony was that his dad was so much smarter than she was.

"Oh, Matt, let it go. If the woman comes back, I won't let her in. You're making a big deal out of nothing."

Jacob gave the door a gentle push so it swung open. His mother was sitting on the edge of the bed, inspecting her fingernails. His dad stood over her. Jacob cleared his throat, and both of them turned to look.

His mom said, "Jacob, darling, this isn't a good time."

Jacob said, "Someone did see Mia."

"What?" His dad snapped to attention. "What did you say?"

"Someone did see Mia. A woman."

"When was this, son?"

"Yesterday, while you were gone. Mom was in the garage talking to a neighbor, and Mia opened the door to look. Mom made a big deal out of it. She sent both of us to our rooms without any dinner."

His dad gave his mother an accusatory look. "You weren't going to tell me about this?"

"It was nothing. Jacob is blowing it out of proportion." His mother stood. "Some busybody from down the street came up to talk to me when I was unloading the trunk of the Audi. We talked for a minute, and then I got rid of her." She shrugged.

"Did she see Mia?"

"I don't know how she could have. It was only for a second, and then I let Mia know she should close the door."

His father said, "If it was no big deal, why did you send the kids to their rooms without dinner?"

"For not listening, of course." She could twist things any way she wanted. "Mia was told to never open an outside door, and Jacob should have been keeping an eye on her. They both know the rules, and I needed to enforce them. Consistency is essential when disciplining children, Matt. You'd know that if you spent a little more time around here instead of gallivanting around the country doing whatever it is you do." She waved a hand in his direction.

"And what did the busybody down the street come to talk to you about?"

His mother sighed dramatically to show that she was weary of his questioning. "She and her grandchildren just moved to the neighborhood. She wanted to know if we had any young children so she could arrange a playdate. I said we only had a teenage son and sent her on her way. Honestly, Matt, I'm getting a headache. I think we're done talking here." She turned and went into the bathroom, shutting the door firmly behind her.

His father went and stood with his nose to the door. "You don't see the connection, Suzette? Someone comes and asks if we have young children, and then a social worker comes snooping around right after that? Something's up. You're living in a fool's paradise if you think we can just go on like this forever. It's time to come clean about Mia."

"Get away from the door, Matt," Suzette called out. "We're done talking. Let it go."

CHAPTER THIRTY

That evening, Ma'am had Jacob tuck Mia in for the night since she was going to be retiring to her room for the evening. "I have an awful headache and don't want to be disturbed," she said, but both Mia and Jacob noticed the bottle of wine she had in her hand as she trooped back up the stairs. She hadn't said a word to Mister, who was sprawled on the couch, watching TV, the remote control balanced on his stomach. Anyone wandering into their house right now would never guess that a major battle had just taken place.

That's how it was sometimes. The calm after the storm.

Jacob walked Mia down the stairs, not speaking until they reached her corner of the basement. "Remember, I left a treat under your cot," he said. "It's in a plastic bag. Leave the wrappers and can inside the bag when you're done, and I'll come get them first thing in the morning."

"Thank you, Jacob."

"I'll leave this unlocked," he said, gesturing to the latch. "So you can brush your teeth after you eat. Mom is going to be kind of out of it, so I don't think we have to worry, but be careful anyway."

Mia nodded. They both knew the firestorm that would erupt if

Ma'am ever caught Jacob sneaking her treats and leaving her door unlocked. The wine made it unlikely that she'd be coming downstairs, but it was best to be careful.

She sat cross-legged on her cot. "Jacob? Why did Mister think the lady was asking about me?"

"You heard that, huh?" He was impressed. Not much got past Mia.

She nodded earnestly.

"You don't need to worry about anything," Jacob said, hoping his words were reassuring. "We'll watch out for you and make sure no one takes you away."

"But why would someone take me away? Where would I go?"

"Look, Mia." He crouched down to her height. "Usually when people save a child, they make it official and file paperwork and talk to a judge, stuff like that. We skipped over that part because you were in such a bad place that it was an emergency. We *had* to take you out of the situation right away and bring you here."

"But couldn't you talk to a judge now and explain?" She made it sound so simple.

He took in a deep breath. *How to explain?* "No, because we'd get in trouble for not doing it right away. It's very complicated, but you don't need to worry about it. Just eat your treat. Tomorrow things will be back to normal around here. You know how Mom gets." He stood up, satisfied that he'd covered all her concerns.

"But if the lady comes back . . ."

"She won't, and if she does, Mom won't let her in."

"Okay." She seemed satisfied.

"Good night, Mia."

"Good night, Jacob."

He swung the door shut and waited, hearing her squeal of delight when she discovered the Hostess CupCakes and the Sprite.

"Thank you, Jacob," she called out.

"You're welcome, squirt." He hoped she wouldn't eat all of it at once and get sick. He almost went back to caution her against overeating, then decided against it. Mia wasn't like him. He had no control over his cravings for food, whereas she was self-regulating and would stop when she was full. She was smart like that. Not only that, but she totally had his mother's number. Not everyone could navigate the Suzette waters like Mia did.

For a little kid, she sure had life figured out.

CHAPTER THIRTY-ONE

They pulled on their winter gear—coats, hats, scarves—Sharon even opting for winter boots, while Niki preferred the nimbleness of her sneakers. Getting her feet wet was less important than being able to scale the fence quickly and quietly.

"You sure about this?" Sharon asked, getting the step stool out of the closet. It was the folding variety, the kind that reminded Niki of a small ladder. Sharon had grabbed a length of rope earlier from the garage, and now she looped it around the handle of the step stool, making a secure knot.

"Sure." Niki pulled on her gloves. "What's the worst that can happen? If they see me, I'll run like hell." She was not as confident as she let on. Suzette Fleming was one scary woman, and she wouldn't put it past her to call the police and have her charged with trespassing. Of course, that could only happen if she caught her, and Niki wasn't planning on getting caught. It was a simple plan. She'd shimmy over the fence, cross the yard, look in the window, take a few pictures, and be back again before anyone could even notice.

The social worker needed something concrete, some *proof*, and photos were proof. How they got the proof might be problematic, but maybe not, especially since there was a child at stake. It was easier to ask for forgiveness than it was to get permission.

It was the perfect night for a reconnaissance mission. Niki hadn't spotted Jacob's dad for several days, so he was probably out of town. Jacob wouldn't be looking in that direction, since his room was on the opposite side of the house. His mother wouldn't be a problem either, as it was too early for her to be upstairs. Niki made sure to pick a time when all the rooms facing the backyard were dark. No lights, no people. Just the mystery of a flickering light coming from a basement window.

The weather was perfect too. Snow was coming down in a powdery mist, the breeze strong enough that any footprints she made would be long gone by morning.

Niki tied the scarf over the lower half of her face and pulled the hood over her head. From head to toe, only her eyes were visible. She doubted if the Flemings had a security camera in the back of the house. Even if there was a camera, it would probably be focused on the entry points of the house, while she would be approaching from the corner of the yard. Logistically, she was unlikely to be spotted, but it was still a risk. Keeping herself covered up ensured she would be unidentifiable on film.

They exited through Sharon's back patio door. When Niki glanced back, she saw Sarge watching as they trooped through the snow to the back of the lot. "The cat probably wonders what we're doing," she said.

"*I'm* wondering what we're doing." Sharon laughed quietly, the step stool tucked under her arm, the length of rope dragging in the snow. When they got to the back of the lot line, she unfolded it and positioned it right in front of the fence. "Are you nervous?"

Niki shook her head. "No. This will only take a few minutes, and if it works, we'll have more to go on."

"As long as you're not caught."

"That won't be a problem. I'm sneaky like a ninja."

Sharon had been sufficiently encouraging when they'd first

discussed Niki doing this. She'd said she was for it in theory, but worried in practice. She didn't want Niki to get hurt or in trouble. Now if Amy were here, she wouldn't have allowed Niki to climb over the fence to spy on the neighbors. As tough as Amy was, she was still an attorney and, by association, a classic rule follower. She talked about procedure and due process and making sure bases were covered. Niki could tell that Sharon was a little more wishy-washy. She preferred going about things the right way, but the maternal side of her overruled it this time. She had a mother's concern for both the unknown child and for Niki. She'd justified the trespassing by saying, "I've had kids cross through my yard before. Not saying I love it, but it's not a big deal." Of course, no one had had to scale a six-foot fence to get to her property.

Niki patted her pocket, making sure she had her phone, then took a tentative step onto the step stool. Sharon held it firm, whispering, "I'm not sure it's high enough."

"Watch me." Niki stood on the top step and glanced at the Flemings' house to see if it was still dark and quiet. Once that was confirmed, she grabbed the top of the fence and swung a leg over. Two horizontal crosspieces held the fence slats together on the other side. They were sturdy two-by-fours, the higher one positioned in a good place for her to rest her toe as she shimmied over the top. In a second, she'd scaled the fence and dropped to the ground on the Flemings' yard. "Go ahead," she said quietly. Just as planned, Sharon lifted the folded step stool and slid it over the top of the fence. Niki pulled it down, set it in place, and opened it so it would be ready for the trip back.

Quietly, she crossed the yard along the fence line, aware of every noise: a dog barking in a neighboring yard, the slight whistle of the wind, the sound of a car off in the distance. Snow came down in a powdery mist, blowing in such a way it was hard to know if it was snowing or simply blowing around. She made her way carefully, aware that every step made a footprint that betrayed her presence, but she was reassured that soon the shifting snow would cover her tracks.

The small light in the basement window was what drew her, like a moth to a flame. Close up it became apparent that this light was dimmer than she'd thought. In fact, it was amazing that she'd spotted it from her bedroom window. When she got to the house, she was disappointed to see that the basement window was made of glass block. Eight perfect squares, four on the top row, four beneath them. Solid, wavy, and impenetrable. The source of the light was stronger at this distance, but she couldn't see what caused it or who was inside. She curled her fingers into a fist, thinking she might knock on the glass, then decided against it. What would that accomplish? Most likely she'd just scare the child, and the noise might possibly alert other family members.

No, this had been a waste of time. She turned and went back the way she'd come, staying close to the side fence until she reached the place where she'd left the step stool. Tossing the rope over the top, she whispered to Sharon, "Get ready, I'm coming over." She waited until the rope was taut before stepping up. Coming over the fence from this side was far easier. She had the crosspiece to step on and was able to swing both legs over with ease, then a quick drop to the ground and she was done. Sharon pulled on the rope, hand over hand, until the step stool was level with the top of the fence, and then Niki stood on tiptoe to reach up and grab the handle. With a little maneuvering, they were able to get it over the top and back down on their side.

"Did you get pictures?" Sharon asked.

Niki shook her head. "Nothing to take a picture of. The basement windows are glass block."

"Oh, too bad," Sharon said, disappointed. "Well, at least you get credit for trying."

They trudged silently back to the house, where Sarge waited for them behind the patio door, one paw up against the glass. It almost looked like he was waving.

CHAPTER THIRTY-TWO

Suzette paced slowly in the dark, a glass of wine in hand. Here in the comfort of her own bedroom, with all the lights off, she could drink and not be judged. She'd taken to leaving a glass and a corkscrew in the bathroom cabinet back behind her row of facial cleansers. Having them close by was ideal for those evenings when she needed alone time, something that happened more frequently when Matt was home. Tonight she was in a foul mood. Obviously Matt's fault. Always Matt. The one member of the family she couldn't keep in line. She could handle the boy, and Mia was a piece of cake. She could keep them in check through sheer will and stern looks.

Matt, though, was another story. It was clear he thought he was the smarter of the two of them, and then he'd actually *berated* her. *The nerve.* She took a slug of wine, emptying the glass, then poured herself another one. Her eyes had fully adjusted now, and even in the dark she could pour like a master sommelier. *Take that, Matt.* The bottle, which had been about two-thirds full, was getting low, and she found herself wishing she'd brought another bottle upstairs as well.

She sat down in the wing chair near the window and crossed her legs, still thinking about Matt's tirade. Even through the warm alcohol buzz, she could hear his derisive words: *You're living in a fool's paradise if you think we can just go on like this forever. It's time to come clean about Mia.*

Time to come clean? What was he thinking—that they'd walk into a police station with Mia and say they'd found a lost child? He was out of his mind. If the social worker had come because they were being investigated, it wasn't an issue any longer. Per usual, Suzette had handled the situation with finesse. And even if the social worker wanted to return, Suzette had an answer for that. She just wouldn't let her into the house, and that's all there was to it. No warrant, no entrance. Problem solved.

It was her house, dammit, and she made the rules.

She turned her attention to the window, wondering if anyone had thought to let Griswold out. Mia seemed particularly attentive to the dog's needs, so it was likely to have been already taken care of. Funny how the two least intelligent beings in the household had bonded. Those two could have come from the same litter, the way they'd connected, kindred spirits, each one motivated by food and praise. Like primitive soul mates. It was easier for Mia and Griswold, Suzette decided. All their needs were taken care of by others. Not a worry in the world.

Must be nice.

She'd emptied her glass and was getting up to pour herself another when something in the yard caught her eye. It was dark outside, but not pitch-black. There was a partial moon overhead, and the neighbors to one side had their back porch light on. And the streetlights beyond provided some illumination through the row of houses. Still, it wasn't easy to figure out what she was seeing. She got out of the chair and went right to the window.

Movement. Someone was in her yard, walking along the side fence. She narrowed her eyes. Jacob? No, the person was slimmer and moved more nimbly. It wasn't Matt either, as far as she could tell. Her heart quickened. She wondered if she should yell down to Matt and let him know someone was outside. Or should she call the police? The person came closer as Suzette watched, and then they were so near to the back of the house that she didn't see them anymore. Were they going to break in? Her cell phone, she suddenly remembered, was on the kitchen counter charging. She could yell down the stairs to Matt, but she really hated that idea. After so much wine she'd be certain to slur her words, and wouldn't he love that?

Let him deal with a burglar breaking into the house. She hoped there was a struggle and that Matt wound up on the wrong end of a knife. That would teach him to talk disparagingly to her.

The intruder came into view once again, walking to the back of the property along the fence line, then climbing up over the fence so quickly that it was like watching a gymnast do a routine. A second later, something bulky rose up over the fence and was pulled over the top and out of sight. A ladder? It had to have been.

Why would someone be in their yard? She downed the last bit in her wineglass, then left the room and went down the hall, passing Jacob's room. She saw the light under his door, but it was completely quiet. Doing his homework, she hoped, but more likely playing a game. *Oh well, not my problem.* She continued on, heading down the stairs. After leaving her wineglass in the kitchen sink, she went into the living room to confront Matt, who was watching a crime show on television. *Typical.* "Did you know someone was just in our backyard? I saw them from the bedroom window."

He kept his eyes on the screen. "It was probably Jacob letting the dog out. Or maybe you just imagined it."

Maybe she just imagined it? A reference to her drinking. *Rude.* "Wrong," she said. "Jacob is in his room, so it wasn't him. I definitely saw someone walking through our yard, and then they climbed the back fence to leave."

"Huh," he said. "I haven't heard anything. It was probably some kid. One of Jacob's friends from school screwing around." He yawned.

"Jacob doesn't have any friends."

"Now you're just being mean. So unnecessary, Suzette."

She swore he did this kind of thing to make her crazy. "Someone climbing a six-foot fence and walking around on our property doesn't bother you? They could be casing the house to break in later."

"Doubtful." He picked up the remote and began flipping through the channels. "If you're really worried, we can keep the outdoor lights on all night."

"I keep telling you we need a security system."

"Yes, and I told you that if you want a security system, you should make some calls and get some estimates. I can't do everything, Suzette."

When he started in with this kind of unproductive, antagonistic talk, she found it best just to walk away. There wasn't enough time in the world to get baited with this nonsense. Besides, the wine was making her head swim, and she needed some silence to think this through. Jacob had been in his room, so he wasn't going to be any help.

Obviously she was once again on her own. She went to the front hall closet and put on her winter boots, then pulled on her coat and gloves before getting a small flashlight from the junk drawer in the kitchen. In the back of the house, she flipped on the back porch light before going outside.

The severe cold caught her off guard, nipping at her cheeks and whipping her hair. Her breath fogged out in the wintry air. The cold slapped away the warm buzz of the wine. Being outside in this weather irritated her. This was a job for Matt or Jacob, but Matt wasn't willing to help her, and Jacob probably wouldn't do it correctly. *Useless. They are both useless.*

She walked to the back fence where she'd seen the ladder being retrieved, but there was nothing there, not even tracks in the snow. The powdery dusting of snow whipping around was obscuring the evidence. She shone the flashlight's beam onto the fence slats, scanning for places where the wood may have been nicked, but didn't see anything out of the ordinary. She turned and retraced the intruder's steps, walking along the fence line, the flashlight leading the way.

As she got closer to the house, she saw impressions in the snow that may or may not have been footprints. They weren't clearly defined, and with each passing minute there was less to see. She got to the house and looked up at her window. This had been a blind spot from her angle upstairs in the bedroom, the place where the person had paused before turning around. Her attention was drawn to the basement window, the one leading to Mia's room. The little brat was watching TV down there, which wasn't particularly shocking. Suzette didn't care what she did at night, as long as she was rested enough to get her chores done.

The alarming part was a fleeting thought that whoever was in the yard had focused on that window because they'd suspected Mia was down there. Thank goodness the window was glass block.

When she got inside, wet and frustrated, emotions began to build. She was indignant that someone had trespassed on their property, irritated at Matt's refusal to take her concerns seriously, and aggravated at having to go outside in the freezing cold to investigate. The more she thought about it, the angrier she became.

Suzette shook off her snow-covered coat and gloves and dropped them on the mat by the back door. Next she stepped out of her boots, then went down the basement stairs to fetch Mia. Someone had to clean up the wet clothes, and it wasn't going to be her.

When she got to the far end of the basement, she was puzzled to discover that the lock on Mia's bookcase had never been secured. Jacob had obviously screwed up. Pulling the bookcase toward her revealed Mia sitting cross-legged on her cot watching TV and eating something that looked like a cupcake. Mia's shock at the sight of Ma'am's face was priceless. She lowered the cupcake to her side, as if that would help.

"Mia?" Suzette said sternly. "What do you have in your hand?"

Mia raised her left hand, showing it was empty.

"The *other* hand." Suzette hated the way her voice sounded, so coarse and raw. She absolutely hated it. Why was she always put in the role of the ogre? She didn't want to have to enforce the rules, but someone had to. From the outside her life looked like a dream, but in reality it was actually very trying. Sometimes thinking about everything she had to keep track of gave her a raging headache.

Mia raised the other hand, the one holding a cupcake wrapped in a napkin.

"Are you supposed to be eating in your room?"

Mia shook her head.

"Answer me, dammit! Use your words!" Suzette knew she was just on the verge of losing it, something that infuriated her. She prided herself on being in control and wasn't going to let a disobedient child take that from her. She drew in a sharp breath and through gritted teeth said, "I'll ask you one more time. Are you supposed to be eating in your room?"

Mia's eyes welled up with tears. "No, Ma'am."

"So you knew you weren't supposed to be eating in your room, but you did it anyway. Is that right?"

Mia started to nod, but then forced out a "Yes, Ma'am."

"Why, Mia, why would you do that when you know it's not allowed?" Suzette wanted to grab hold of her shoulders and shake her until she was limp, but admirably she held back. "Why?"

Her chin dropped down, and she mumbled, "Don't know."

"Do you think I'm stupid? Did you think I wouldn't find out?"

"No, Ma'am."

"Give it to me." Suzette held out her hand, and Mia gave her the cupcake. "Well, what do you know. A Hostess CupCake. Did you get this from Jacob?"

Mia hesitated, and now tears streamed down her face.

"Answer me! Did you get this from Jacob?"

"Yes, Ma'am."

"Come with me." Grabbing Mia's arm, she pulled her off the bed, then dragged her up the stairs. On the first floor, she paused at the bottom of the stairs leading to the second floor and screamed, "Jacob, get down here right now!" then continued on to the living room, pulling Mia along with her. She was ready to give Matt a good talking-to, and this time she wasn't going to let him brush her aside.

CHAPTER THIRTY-THREE

Jacob had his headphones on and was, for once, deep into doing his homework. His English teacher had assigned the class personal essays, with an emphasis on the *personal*. Mrs. Rathman had suggested a few topics: detailing what defined them as individuals, writing about an event that changed their life, or telling a tale of overcoming a hardship. Jacob was at a loss to come up with any of these things, so his essay was completely fictitious, the story of the time spent fishing with Great-Uncle Stevie and all the wisdom the older man had imparted to him shortly before his unexpected death from a heart attack right after they'd returned the boat to the rental place. Since he wasn't constrained by the truth, Jacob was able to really get into it, embellishing the story with emotive details sure to bring a tear to Mrs. Rathman's eyes. If his test grades weren't going to be a selling point, he might as well write a killer essay.

He was interrupted when the door swung open and he saw Mia standing in the hallway, a hesitant expression on her face. Taking off his headphones, he said, "Yes?"

"Ma'am wants you to come downstairs." From the way she said it, he knew he wasn't being summoned for something good. And because his mother had sent Mia, it was likely she had tried yelling for him but he hadn't heard her, which meant she was already infuriated. Anyone not responding to her demands made her crazy.

"Am I in trouble?" he asked.

She nodded.

"What for?"

"The cupcake. I'm sorry, Jacob." Her lower lip trembled in a way that made him both sympathetic to Mia and angry with his mother.

"Don't worry about it, Mia. It's not your fault. I'll take the blame."

Mia went ahead and led him downstairs and into the living room, where his father sat on the couch, his legs stretched out on the coffee table. His mother, meanwhile, stood in front of the picture window, a cupcake in her hand. Her posture was relaxed, but she had the crazy-eyed look Jacob had come to dread.

"Mia said you wanted me?" he asked casually, taking a seat next to his father. Mia, not knowing where to go, stood near the doorway.

"What, pray tell, is this, Jacob?" She held the cupcake up in a smug way that indicated he was busted.

Jacob tilted his head to one side. Having his dad next to him gave him a shot of courage. "Looks like a Hostess CupCake to me, Mom, but I have a feeling you already knew that."

"Disrespectful," she seethed, throwing the cupcake at him. The cupcake hit his knee and skidded across the coffee table, landing on the floor. "How dare you give this to Mia? How dare you! You know the rules in the house. There is absolutely *no eating in the bedrooms.* Ever. And another rule? We eat only during mealtimes. No snacking. Do you understand?"

Jacob nodded. "I know those are the rules."

"And yet you chose to ignore them."

"I wasn't ignoring them. I just thought I'd make an exception this one time and let Mia have a cupcake."

"An *exception?* There are no exceptions." Her voice was harsh and loud. "What you've done is unforgiveable. It's bad enough that you've blatantly disregarded my rules, but to involve Mia, who will now think she doesn't have to listen to me? Inexcusable!"

His father swung his legs off the coffee table and sat up, resting his elbows on his knees. "Suzette, I think you're making too big a deal out of this. Jacob was just trying to do something nice."

Out of the corner of Jacob's eye he saw Mia, trembling where she stood. Jacob said, "You're acting like I killed someone, Mom. It's just a cupcake. I'm overweight, but Mia isn't. Why shouldn't she have a treat now and then?"

His mother was clearly enraged, but instead of exploding, she drew it in and spoke slowly and deliberately. "I will not listen to this any longer. All of you are being put on notice. Jacob, I don't want to find any trace of cupcake here or in Mia's room. If I find even a crumb, I'm putting your phone down the garbage disposal. I'm going up to my room, and I don't want to be disturbed for the rest of the night." She stormed out of the room. A few minutes later, they heard her rummaging in the refrigerator. They all knew what that meant. Another bottle of wine for her exile in the bedroom.

Once they heard her go upstairs, his father turned to Jacob and said, "Is it me, or is she getting worse?"

"Hard to say," Jacob answered. "Maybe worse?" It was difficult to gauge. She was so inconsistent mood-wise, and yet her rages did seem to be happening more frequently.

"Do you know where she's getting her pills these days?"

"Not a clue."

His dad said, "Mia, I need to talk to Jacob for a little bit, so why don't you go on downstairs to your room? And make sure you brush your teeth, okay?"

She nodded and was gone.

His dad pinched the bridge of his nose and sighed. "Jacob, we need to talk."

"Okay," Jacob said. They so seldom had time to talk one-on-one that it occurred to Jacob that this might be a good time to tell his dad about Mia's DNA results. He'd let his father go first, and then they could discuss Mia's relatives.

"First of all, I want to apologize that you had to grow up in such a dysfunctional family. You're almost eighteen now, and I know there haven't been too many good years. I could say I tried my best, but looking back, I'm not sure it was my best. I fell short in so many ways, and I'm really sorry for that."

"Don't be sorry. You're really a great dad."

His father held his hand up. "I appreciate it, but I'm not looking for compliments. I've made a lot of mistakes. You might already know that I had to quit the medical practice because one of the administrators discovered I had committed a crime. Well, multiple crimes, actually. Billing fraud involving Medicare. I did it because I wasn't bringing in enough revenue, and I was afraid of losing my job. A woman who worked for me helped. You may have heard your mother mention her." He raised his eyebrows. "This other woman, her name was Jayne. We were *involved*—something I'm not proud of, seeing as we were each married to other people at the time. Both of us were fired, and in exchange for not getting the police involved, I agreed to give up my license to practice medicine. I haven't seen or talked to Jayne in years. It was a shameful, terrible thing, and I regret every minute of it."

This was pretty close to what Jacob had heard his mother talking about over the years, but it was different hearing his father admit it. Sadder. "Everyone makes mistakes."

His dad shook his head. "This was a really big mistake, and it was compounded by your mother, who frequently reminds me of what I've done, and uses that knowledge to do whatever she wants to do. I should have never let her blackmail me into keeping Mia here. If you want to know the truth, I'm disgusted with myself. I've decided that after you graduate from high school, I'm coming clean."

"Coming clean?"

"I can't live like this anymore. I'm going to the police and admitting everything. I talked to an attorney friend and threw our scenario at him—hypothetically speaking, of course—and he thinks that there's a good chance that the statute of limitations on the billing fraud might be in my favor. If that's the case, I wouldn't be prosecuted. But there's still the issue of Mia. You were a minor when she was brought into the house, but your mother still might try to pull you into this, and you might get charged as well. I think, though, that if both of us have the same story, we might be able to distance ourselves from the kidnapping charge. My hope is that even if I get dragged into this mess, you'll be spared."

"But *we* didn't mean to kidnap Mia."

"I know." His dad sighed. "I'm thinking that our story will be that your mother just came home with her one day and said she was her cousin's daughter, adopted from Central America. The story we heard was that Mia was staying with us while the cousin was undergoing treatment for cancer. A family favor that wound up lasting far longer than we originally anticipated. Do you think that's a story you'd feel comfortable repeating?"

Jacob nodded. "If it would help."

"It would help a lot. There would still be a criminal charge, but if it went well, your mother would be the only one charged. It's a long shot, and likely I'll be implicated, but at least you'd be spared. I've talked to your grandmother and your uncle Cal and said we might be having some family issues in the future that would leave you on your own. They agreed that they would be there for you."

"Okay." Jacob frowned.

His dad clapped a hand on his shoulder. "This won't happen for a while, so we'll have time to get our stories straight. It's important that we're consistent on the details. But we'll work on it, okay?"

"Sure, Dad." Jacob realized this wasn't the right time to tell his dad about Mia's DNA test results. If the authorities found out that someone in the household had put in for a test like that, it would contradict the story his dad had concocted explaining Mia's presence. He was starting to regret having done it at all.

"I love you, Jacob. We'll get through this."

"I love you too." His mind spun. Right now no one else knew about the DNA test. "But what will happen to Mia if we follow your plan?"

"I'm not sure." His dad sighed again, and now Jacob noticed how worn down he looked, as if he hadn't had a good night's sleep in a very long time. "She'd become a ward of the state initially, I would think, and if they can't find her family, she'll probably go into foster care."

"So she might go to strangers?" Jacob imagined Mia's fear at being sent away, and his heart sank. Her life now wasn't a great one, but at least it was familiar.

"I know, it would be difficult for her, but think of it this way— she'll be able to go to school and interact with kids her own age. Have a somewhat normal life."

"And she won't have to do chores every day."

His dad nodded. "I'll clean up the cupcake mess in here. Why don't you go down and check on Mia and make sure there are no crumbs in her room. When your mother sobers up, we don't want her getting started again."

CHAPTER THIRTY-FOUR

J acob took the handheld vacuum down to Mia's room and found her sitting on her bed, eyes wide. "I'm sorry, Jacob. I'm so, so sorry."

"You don't need to be sorry. You didn't do anything wrong."

"But the cupcake . . ."

"Mia, it's not a big deal. Mom just made it a big deal. A lot of kids I know have snacks all the time, even in their rooms, and their parents don't even know or care."

"Really?" She sat up straighter.

"Yes, really."

"So other families are different?"

She knew so little of the world. Jacob found it both sad and amusing. If she could remember where she came from, she'd see how different things could be. The day they'd picked her up, filthy and smelling terrible, they'd taken her in their car and his mother had driven down the road, going in the direction from which Mia had come. They didn't see any houses until they reached a rundown wreck of a shack right where the road came to a complete stop. "I guess this is it," his mom had said, pulling the car over to the side and putting it into park. She'd turned off the engine and got out of the car, but Jacob, sitting in the back seat with the little girl on his lap, hadn't moved a muscle. His mother couldn't be serious. This couldn't be someone's house. "Jacob!" she'd barked. "Get a move on. I don't have all day."

They crossed the trash-strewn front yard and went up to the door, his mother taking the lead and Jacob carrying the child, who was now sucking her thumb. "Hello! Is anyone home?" his mother called out cheerily, as if they were making a social visit, dropping off soup for a sick neighbor or bringing flowers to someone with a death in the family. When she knocked on the door, the long groan it made when it swung open reminded Jacob of a haunted house.

"I don't think anyone lives here," Jacob said.

But his mother was already entering the place and gesturing for Jacob to follow. Once they were inside, their eyes took a minute to adjust to the light. "Hello? Is anyone home?" his mom called out, her voice echoing. Inside, it was one big boxlike room, the inside walls made of plywood. There were windows on each side, but all of them were grimy. The place was stinky, like someone had taken a crap in the corner and left it there. A plastic garbage can in the corner was overflowing, with litter on the floor surrounding it. Big black bugs scuttled around the trash. A sagging couch along the wall held a mound of what looked like dirty laundry. "Look," his mother said, toeing something on the floor. She picked it up, holding it with pinched fingertips. Miniature dirty pink pants decorated with cartoon cats. "This matches the little girl's top." A sign they were in the right place. She dropped the pants back onto the floor.

Jacob set the little girl down, and she toddled over to the couch, patting the pile of clothing. With a start, Jacob realized there was a person underneath that pile of clothing. He could only see what looked like the back of a head, but it appeared to be a woman. He pointed, and his mother saw it too.

"Hello!" she called out loudly. "We've returned your child." She gave Jacob's arm a shove. "Go wake her up."

Reluctantly, Jacob went over to the couch, standing over the little girl. Close up he could see that the woman was covered with multiple tattered blankets. The little girl laid her head against the woman's back in a show of affection. "Excuse me," he said, and when the woman didn't budge, he gently moved the blankets away from her face. What he saw horrified him. The woman's face was mottled in color, like something in a horror movie. The part of her arm that was exposed was discolored as well, and when he went to give it a push, it was firm. Too firm. The temperature of her skin was all wrong too. Not cold, exactly, but cooler than that of a human being who was alive. His voice came out as a loud whisper. "She's dead."

"Oh, for God's sakes," his mom said, like this was a major inconvenience. She came over to see for herself, and he could tell by the way her brow furrowed that she was coming to the same conclusion.

"Do you think it's her mother?"

"Looks like it." She sighed. "I guess we can't just leave her here with a dead woman. Pick her up, Jacob, and we'll drop her off at a neighbor's house."

Jacob lifted the toddler up, propping her against his hip, still reeling from what he'd seen. They'd just come from his grandfather's funeral, but seeing Grandpa in an open casket was less awful than seeing the woman on the couch. The sight was burned into his brain, along with the smell of the place, and the feeling that bugs were crawling over his skin. Holding the little girl against his body with her smell of pee added to the sensation of being dirty. What a place. How horrifying to think that the dead woman was probably this little girl's mother and that they lived here.

They were on the porch heading down the steps when a man suddenly rounded the corner from the back of the house. He was a massive guy, wearing a sweat-stained tank top and mud-splattered jeans, a gun in one hand swinging at his side. He lurched as he walked, as if struggling to keep his body upright. He didn't see them until Jacob's mother said, "Hello? Does this little girl belong to you?"

Jacob knew the exact moment the dark-haired man registered

their presence because his eyes locked onto them and he reared back, the arm holding the gun swinging upward and aiming right at them. "What you doing?" he asked angrily.

His mom froze in place, raised her arms in surrender, and said, "Hold on a minute. We found this child walking down the road and are just bringing her home."

The man muttered a string of the very worst profanity, all of it directed at Jacob's mother. Some of them were words Jacob had *thought* of in regard to his mother, but he never would have said them aloud.

Finally, the man blurted out, "Did Hartley send you? You can just tell him . . ." This was followed by another barrage of profanities, all curse words aimed at Hartley, whoever that was.

"We'll just leave now," his mother said, and she nodded at Jacob, an indication to put the little girl down, but Jacob's arms were locked around the child, who now rested her dirty head against his shoulder.

"Damn right you'll leave now," he said with a growl, and that's when he began shooting at them. *Bang, bang, bang!* The noise echoed in Jacob's head, accompanied by the man's growling laughter.

His mother screamed for him to get in the car, and she didn't have to say it twice. Jacob's heart had never pounded so hard. He felt like he was having a heart attack. Clutching the little girl even closer to him, he got into the back seat of the car as fast as he could. His mother ran around to the other side of the car, got into the front seat, and started the engine. To Jacob it felt like it all went in slow motion.

There was no room to turn around, so she drove the car in reverse, and all the while the man followed slowly, walking down the middle of the road, the gun still aimed at them. "Hurry, hurry, hurry!" Jacob yelled.

"What do you think I'm doing?" she responded, her voice frantic. When they got a fair distance away, she did a Y-turn, then gunned it, the tires squealing. It was only when they could no longer see him in their rearview mirror that she said, "Did you get hit, Jacob?"

"No, I'm okay. What about you?" His mother was fine too, and so was the little girl.

They were an hour away from that squalid place before they remembered they'd planned on leaving her at a neighbor's. By that time, she was asleep. Before he knew it, his mother had shopped for clothing, checked into a hotel, and given the little girl a bath. When she finally tucked Mia into bed, she went right to sleep, her thumb in her mouth. Jacob remembered his mom standing over her and saying, "Olivia used to sleep sucking her thumb like that." Her comment stood out because his mother had never mentioned Olivia to him before. "It's like I'm getting a second chance." Some switch had been flipped, but Jacob couldn't make sense of it.

His father was the one who'd pointed out that a trip to the police station would have been the obvious course of action, given that they'd discovered a body, been shot at, and acquired a child who didn't belong to them. His mother had scoffed and said it was easy for him to come up with solutions. Who knew what he'd actually have done if he had been in that situation?

It was hard to believe that Mia, the girl with the big brown eyes sitting on the cot in front of him, was the toddler girl from that day. It seemed like she'd always belonged to them.

Coming out of his thoughts, he realized she was still waiting for a response to her question about families being different.

He told her, "Every family is different, but mine is pretty messed up compared to most of them. Now move." He gestured for her to get off the bed, and she got up and stood in the doorway. He got to work, pulling the plastic bag he'd given her out from under the cot, and then he turned on the vacuum cleaner and ran it over the bed. Afterward, he turned his attention to the floor. He didn't see any crumbs, but he vacuumed anyway just to be sure.

"I didn't make a mess," she said after he'd finished. "I was careful."

"I see that. Good job." He opened the plastic bag and saw that the cupcake wrapper was inside. "Where's the soda can?"

She went over to the dresser and opened a drawer, then brought out the can and handed it to him. "I didn't drink all of it."

"Do you want to finish it off?"

"No, I had enough."

"Suit yourself," he said, downing the rest and topping it off with a large burp just to make her laugh. He put the can in the plastic bag. "You know I'll have to lock the door tonight, so if you have to wash up or go to the bathroom, do it now."

"I'm okay," she said. "I did all that already."

"All right then. Good night, Mia."

"Good night, Jacob. Can I ask just one more thing?"

"Sure, if it's quick."

"Did you find out about the spit test? Did it tell you where I come from, I mean?"

He wasn't ready to tell her what he'd found. "I got some news, but it's kind of confusing, and I'm still figuring out what it means. When I know more, I'll let you know."

"Okay. Thank you, Jacob."

"Sweet dreams, Mia. See you tomorrow." And with that, he swung the bookcase closed and secured the lock.

CHAPTER THIRTY-FIVE

For more than two years, Edwin watched as Wendy kept Morgan's driver's license like a talisman, periodically taking it out of her jewelry box to turn it over in her hand, studying her daughter's face as if doing so would bring her back. Occasionally, she'd call to check in with Detective Moore. When she related their conversations to Edwin later, she always said, "He's so nice, always apologizing for not knowing anything." Edwin wanted to tell her to stop calling, but he knew it was a compulsion with her, a maternal need to do *something*, anything. He understood and listened.

When her phone rang one Saturday morning, she didn't even hear it because she'd just stepped out of the shower and was drying her hair. Edwin answered and came into the bathroom to find her. "Detective Moore called," he told her. "He has some information about the site where they found Morgan's driver's license, and he's coming over to discuss it with us."

"When?"

"He said he's about ten minutes away."

"What kind of information?"

Edwin had an idea, but it was a horrible, awful thought, and he wasn't going to say it in case he was wrong. "I don't know, Wendy. You now know as much as I do. I guess we'll just have to wait for him and find out."

He was the one who greeted Detective Moore at the door and showed him into the living room. Wendy got up to shake the detective's hand, and Edwin noticed how the man grasped his wife's hand while giving her a long, kindly look. The obvious compassion took his breath away and made him think this wasn't going to be good news.

Wendy said, "Can I get you something to drink, Detective? I know you're on duty, but we have soda, water, juice?"

"No thank you, ma'am. I won't be here long."

With all the pleasantries out of the way, Detective Moore took a seat across from where they sat on the couch and began to speak. "This may be bad news, and if so, I'm so sorry to be the one to tell you this. I've gotten a call from the sheriff's department in Ash County. The house where Morgan's driver's license was found was torn down, and yesterday, when they were leveling the property, they found human remains buried behind where the structure had been."

"What kind of human remains?" Wendy asked, the very question that had come to Edwin's mind as well.

"The official forensic report hasn't come back yet, but the medical examiner said it's a female and estimates an age of mid to late twenties. They believe from the state of the remains that the time of death was more than two years ago, but they'll know more later."

Now Edwin knew what it meant to be speechless. He had questions but couldn't seem to summon them into speech. His mouth was unable to form the words.

Who knew that when they had some definite news, Wendy would rise up and be the strong one? Her voice was calm and steady. "What can we do to help determine if it's our daughter or not?"

Detective Moore looked relieved that she'd broached the question. "Since the driver's license was found there, they'd like to make a comparison to Morgan's dental records, if you're comfortable with that."

"Of course, anything we can do to help."

Edwin echoed her words. "Anything to help." He felt as if he were outside his body watching this whole awful scene unfold in front of him.

Wendy asked, "Wouldn't DNA be a better indicator?"

"They can do a definitive ID from dental records, and I believe it may be faster as well. Regardless, that's what they asked for."

Wendy nodded. "How did the death occur?"

He shook his head. "I'm sure that will be in the official report, but as of right now, they don't know the cause of death."

"I see." Wendy reached over and took Edwin's hand. "Was there anything with the body that might give us more information? Clothing or jewelry?"

Detective Moore shook his head. "There wasn't much to go on. They found the remains fully clothed, jeans and a T-shirt, socks but no shoes. She was wrapped in multiple blankets and covered with a large piece of plastic. They didn't find any jewelry."

The remains. Edwin felt faint. All these years he'd been telling Wendy not to be too hopeful, but now he realized he'd been saying it for his own benefit. Even as he'd told his wife to be prepared for the worst, he'd wanted to be proved wrong. Part of him always thought Morgan would come home someday. That she'd hit rock bottom and come back to their loving arms, worse for the wear, but still, with their help, she would get treatment and they'd have their daughter back. The nightmare would be over.

Wendy's voice broke into his thoughts. "How do we go about getting the dental records over to the authorities in Ash County?"

"Here's my card." Detective Moore handed it to her, and even though Edwin knew she already had his card, she politely accepted it. "You can either get the physical records and drop them off at the station, or if they're digital, just have the dentist send them to me. No worries. I'll take it from there."

It took an enormous effort, but Edwin managed to say, "Thank you, Detective."

"I wish it was good news, but you know, this might not even be Morgan. We just need more information."

Wendy got up to see Detective Moore to the door, while Edwin sat, head in his hands, still processing the news. Out in the entryway, he heard Wendy thank him for coming and the detective again apologize for being the bearer of what could be bad news. "I'll get back to you as soon as I know something," he said.

After Wendy closed the front door, she returned and sat next to him. "You okay?" she asked, giving his arm a light squeeze.

"That was not the news I was hoping for." He sat up and met her gaze.

"I know, but we really don't know anything yet."

She held her palm against the side of his face, and the gesture unmoored him, cutting loose the emotion he'd been trying to keep in check. Despite his best efforts, he let out a sob, and then it all came out at once. He cried like he had when he was a little boy, his body convulsing, a trail of tears streaming down his face. He found himself saying, "I'm sorry, I'm so sorry," not even sure why he was apologizing.

Wendy stroked his back in small circles of comfort, while making soothing noises. Eventually she got up and returned with a box of tissues. He blew his nose, the loud honking a contrast to his well-spring of grief.

"I don't know what's wrong with me," he said.

"There's nothing wrong with you. You've lost a child. Your reaction is completely normal."

"You seem to be handling this a lot better than me."

"I've had my moments all along. Times when I was sure she was dead. I've cried before, and I will again. But right now, I'm empty and I feel like I need to know. If it's her, then we'll know. It's not that I want it to be her, but this not knowing is eating me up."

"I can't stand the thought that something terrible happened to her." He could only think that the young woman was murdered or had accidentally overdosed. "I'm her father. If I can't protect my own daughter, what good am I?"

"She left of her own accord. We tried everything we could to find her. It's not your fault. You couldn't have protected her—you weren't there."

"I know that intellectually, but emotionally, the failure eats at me." He wiped his eyes with the back of his hand. "I wouldn't wish this feeling on my worst enemy."

"I know." She continued rubbing his back. "This is hell on earth. Sometimes I wake up in the morning and I think, *How can this be my life? This is the kind of thing that happens to other people, not us.*"

They were both silent for a minute, and then he said, "And if it *is* her, what do we do? Have a funeral now, not even knowing what happened?"

Wendy leaned into him. "One step at a time. Let's just see what the dental records say first before we ask any more questions."

"You're right." Letting her take the lead felt good. She'd lifted part of the emotional load from him, and he willingly let her. The only way they'd get through this was together.

"I think Dr. Meek has Saturday hours. I'll call about the dental records. If I explain why we need them, I'm sure they'll get to it right away."

CHAPTER THIRTY-SIX

Suzette rolled over in bed and opened her eyes to see that the room was filled with sunlight. Through lidded eyes, she noticed that the blinds were still halfway raised. How was it that she'd neglected to lower them?

A glance at her phone showed her it was already midafternoon. She groaned. Having always prided herself on keeping things under control, this was a definite misstep. The pills mixed with the wine were to blame. The combination was too much for her system.

She thought back to the events of the night before, and it all came flooding back to her—the intruder in their yard, Matt's dismissal of her concerns, and Jacob conspiring against her by letting Mia eat a cupcake in her room. Her own family was flouting her rules. No wonder she'd retreated to the comfort of her room and the warmth of the wine. It was completely understandable, but she also knew it couldn't happen too often. Once in a great while, overdoing it could be written off as a fluke; more often than that pointed to a problem. She had to be careful not to give Matt any ammunition against her. She wouldn't put it past him to commit her to rehab. Anything to get her out of the way.

Well, luckily, she was wise to him.

As she sat up, the pounding in her head intensified. Her mouth felt like it was filled with dust. Slowly she made her way to the bathroom. Once there, she downed two ibuprofen, then brushed her teeth. Her hands gripping the edge of the sink, she leaned forward and looked into the mirror, horrified by her own reflection. She hadn't washed her face the night before, and the area surrounding her eyes was smeared with eyeliner and mascara. Her skin was blotchy and her hair messy. Not bed-head cute, but horror-show messy. *Ugh.* Seeing herself looking like this was even worse than feeling sick. *Pull it together, Suzette. You're better than this.*

The warm water of the shower helped, and shampooing her hair made her feel more like herself again. By the time she stepped out of the shower and wrapped a towel around herself, she was happier with the mirror.

After she applied her makeup and put the finishing touches on her hair, she took a step back and smiled. *There you are.* Restored to her rightful appearance. The fairest of them all. Or at least, the fairest among her social circle. It's not like she could compete with twenty-year-olds, but then again, why would she want to? At this stage in the game, she was the epitome of elegant sophistication.

Suzette slipped on her bathrobe, tightened the belt, and strode into the bedroom. As she was about to make a turn into her walk-in closet, the window caught her attention. There was nothing out there now, but she knew what she'd seen the night before. Someone lurking around in the dark in her yard, without *her* permission. The idea made her blood simmer.

She scanned the fence line and the house behind it. It was a small home, shaped like a child's drawing of a house, with none of the charming details found throughout the rest of the neighborhood. It didn't fit into the area, but that had never bothered her since it was tucked away behind her house. Having no interest in the neighbors, she didn't know who lived there, but it might be time to pay them a visit and ask if they'd seen anything the night before. Matt had brushed away her concerns as if she'd been ridiculous, but she had a feeling this neighbor might be sufficiently alarmed that someone was using their yard to get to the Flemings' yard. Maybe they'd even have some information for Suzette—video footage from a security camera, or an idea of who the intruder might be. She might just crack this case yet. Wouldn't that put Matt in his place?

By the time she went downstairs, her mood had lifted. A cup of coffee and a piece of toast helped settle her stomach and quell her headache. Mia was busy dusting in the living room. Suzette noticed with approval that she'd cleaned up the breakfast dishes and wiped down the counters.

Suzette poured herself another coffee and thought through how she would spend the next few hours. If she left right before Jacob was due to arrive home from school, she could avoid him, and if her absence extended beyond dinnertime, she could dispense with cooking dinner. Scheduling it that way would also ensure she wasn't home when Matt walked through the door. Timing was everything. She'd text a few of her professional friends and see if anyone wanted to meet for drinks and dinner. Or drinks and appetizers. It was all the same to her. Get a few women together and add some alcohol, and it was a recipe for a fun evening. Women often gave up their secrets once the liquor had loosened their lips, something that delighted Suzette, who loved having information that gave her the upper hand. If she came home around her usual bedtime, she could sail past whoever was still awake and go straight to her room.

She sent out a few texts, and while waiting for responses, she wrote a note for Jacob and Matt. *Everyone is on their own for dinner tonight! I'm meeting some board members for a planning dinner.* She wrote *Suzette/Mom* underneath and drew a heart alongside her signature to show that she didn't hold a grudge.

Her first stop would entail speaking with the neighbor who lived in the starter house behind her. After that little conversation, she'd do some retail therapy. The local strip mall had a jewelry store that wasn't half bad and a boutique that hadn't seen the benefit of her

Visa card in a while. Killing time there would be easy. After an hour or so, she'd certainly have heard back from at least one of the women. One in particular, a single woman in her fifties, was a sure thing. This woman, a dowdy Suzette-wannabe named Mary, constantly vied for her attention at board meetings and had been angling for them to get together for months now. Up until now Suzette had ignored her pathetic hints, but today she was willing to throw Mary a bone with some one-on-one time. It would be her good deed for the day.

Suzette gathered up her purse and put on her coat before remembering she needed to give Mia some instructions. "Mia!" she called out, and right on cue, the little mischief-maker made her appearance, the dust cloth still in her hand, her eyes wide with anticipation. Suzette crouched down to Mia's level and faced her nose-to-nose. "I'm going to be out of the house until late tonight, do you understand?"

"Yes, Ma'am."

"While I'm gone, I'm going to need you to do some laundry. Do all the towels in my bathroom, and do not forget the washcloth in the shower stall this time. Got it?"

"Yes, Ma'am."

"After you've done that, do the sheets on both my bed and Jacob's. Jacob can put his own back on, but you'll have to make up the bed in my room."

She nodded vigorously.

Suzette approved of the way Mia always aimed to please. If only some of that would rub off on Jacob. She said, "So to recap, you'll need to do the towels from my bathroom, the sheets from my bed *and* from Jacob's, then put my bed back together again. After that, you can have the rest of the night off. Jacob should be home any minute. He'll give you something for dinner and take care of bedtime. Do you understand?"

"Yes, Ma'am." Her little head bobbed up and down.

Suzette stood up, hoping Mia would remember the directions. Usually she did, with minor exceptions like neglecting to include the washcloth in the load of towels, or the time she forgot to return the cleaning supplies back to the closet. "That's a good girl. I'll see you tonight."

What a difference a few hours made. Now that Suzette felt like herself again and had a plan for the rest of the day, her outlook had brightened considerably. Behind the wheel of her Audi, she was her best self. A fabulous woman in a luxury car sure to attract the envy of onlookers. She drove around the block until she found the house directly behind her own. From this angle, it looked even more drab. *Nothing to recommend here.* She pulled up in front and wondered what could make it look better. *Shutters?* She tilted her head to one side. No, nothing would improve the shedlike appearance of this house. A total tear-down. She got out of the car, slung her purse over her shoulder, and headed up the front walkway.

Suzette had already rehearsed the speech in her head. She'd start with an introduction. The homeowner would already know of her house, and maybe she'd even know Suzette's name. She had so many contacts, and it always surprised her how interconnected people could be—one look at Facebook and the truth of that was apparent. After some small talk, she'd inform them that her yard had been compromised the night before by what could only be someone planning to commit a crime. They were going to be so grateful for the information.

She stood up straight and rang the doorbell. A moment later, she thought she heard the shuffling of someone inside. She pressed the button again and this time was rewarded with the opening of the door and an older woman opening the screen door just wide enough to talk.

"Yes?"

"Hi, I'm Suzette Fleming. I live right behind—" She stopped, processing the woman's face, which not only looked familiar, but now also changed from a pleasant countenance to an expression of shock, as if she recognized Suzette as well. "Have we met?"

"I'm sorry, you caught me at a bad time," the woman said, starting to close the door, but before she could Suzette had grabbed the edge of the door and stuck her foot in the opening. She remembered now, and the memory raised her ire. The woman in front of her was the busybody with the frumpy hair and nondescript clothing who'd claimed to live down the block, the one who'd asked if she had a little girl.

"You!" Suzette said, her voice loud. "You were the one who wanted to know if I had a little girl." She felt her body start to tremble with fury.

"I'm sorry, but you need to go." The woman tried to close the door, but Suzette was blocking it now.

"I'm not going anywhere until you explain to me what's going on." Suzette stepped over the threshold and pushed the door open, shoving the woman backward. "Why are you stalking me?" She was in the front entryway now, facing off with her. At such close range it was apparent that she was just a little mouse of a woman. One Suzette could easily intimidate.

"Get out of my house. Now." The woman looked shocked at her boldness.

Suzette laughed. "Not until you tell me what your problem is with me and my family."

"You're crazy. You need to leave now. I'm going to call the police." The woman was trying to keep her voice steady, like she was in charge, but Suzette detected fear and knew she had the upper hand.

Suzette said, "Go ahead and call the police. Then you can explain why you've been nosing around, climbing over my fence, trespassing on my property, looking in my windows." The woman's eyes widened, making Suzette think she was onto something. "That's right," she said smugly. "Last night. In my yard. I know it was you, and I have it on film as well." She leaned toward her and watched as the woman shrank back. "What do you have to say to that?"

"I believe you are mistaken, and I think you should go."

"I'm not mistaken," Suzette insisted.

"You need to leave right this minute."

"Explain yourself!"

The woman turned on her heel and walked away from her, the very thing Suzette hated. She was up for almost anything: drama, tears, anger. But she couldn't stand being ignored. From down the hall, the woman said, "In a minute I'll have the police on the phone, and you'll be charged with unlawful entry."

Suzette wasn't that well versed in small crimes and misdemeanors, but "unlawful entry" sounded like an actual thing. She yelled back, "I'm leaving, but don't think I'm going to forget about this. The police will be reviewing the video footage, and once they confirm it's you, they'll be taking you away in handcuffs." She slammed the door on her way out and strode angrily down the walkway to her car. The nerve of the woman to talk to her that way.

After she'd gotten into her car and buckled her seat belt, Suzette took a quick look at her phone, smiling when she saw there was a new text. Mary had messaged back saying she'd love to meet for drinks and dinner, and she'd suggested a new restaurant across town. *They have small plates!* Along with a smiley face and some random food emojis. As if small plates were some new, exciting concept. Poor, sad Mary had so little in her life. Suzette confirmed the place and texted back with a time.

Tonight would certainly be the highlight of Mary's year. Suzette was glad she was the one who could give her this thrill.

CHAPTER THIRTY-SEVEN

When Sharon realized that Suzette wasn't going to budge, she left her standing in the front hall and went to retrieve her phone from the kitchen counter. It was a relief when Suzette yelled that she was leaving, but the encounter still left Sharon shaking. After she heard the door close, she returned to the front of the house and peered through the gap in the living room drapes, watching Suzette in her car. From what she could tell, Suzette was sitting there, calm as could be, boldly looking at her phone. Was she talking to the police? It didn't look like it, but it was hard to say.

Sharon still had her eyes on the car as Suzette pulled away from the curb and drove away at a leisurely pace. Apparently Sharon's threat of calling the police hadn't worried her at all. Was that because she had nothing to hide, or was the woman completely lacking in remorse?

Letting the drapes drop, she turned her attention to her phone, quickly dialing Amy's number. As usual, it went to voice mail, so Sharon frantically filled her in on what had happened and asked her to call back as soon as possible. "It's urgent," she said.

Ten minutes later, Amy called back, opening the conversation by saying, "Have you completely lost your mind?"

"In my defense—" Sharon started to say, but Amy wasn't going to let her go there.

"I thought you'd be a good influence on Niki. I never imagined you two would dream up some half-baked plan and you'd get her in trouble." From there, Amy went on to talk about how Sharon had done the complete opposite of what Amy had advised. "Didn't I tell you to sit tight and let the experts do their jobs? Didn't you promise me you wouldn't do anything rash? You agreed with everything I said, so I'm not sure how all this happened." From the exasperation in her voice, a person would have thought she was the parent and Sharon was the kid.

"I'm willing to concede that we might have made a few mistakes . . ."

"A few mistakes?" Amy whooped with laughter. "Talk about an understatement."

"We can't go back, though, so what's your advice for what I should do now? Do I call the police and tell them she forced her way into my house? Or should I call the social worker and let her know everything that has happened?"

"How about doing both?"

"Yes, but if we tell the whole story, won't we get into trouble for going into her yard?"

"You might, but that's a relatively minor offense."

"I wouldn't care if it were just me, but I don't want Niki to get into trouble."

Amy sighed. "This sounds like something you should have thought of *before* you had Niki climb a fence and spy on the neighbor."

"What if I just call the social worker and explain? Do you think she can help me navigate the situation legally?"

"Oh, Mom."

"What?"

"It's not her job to help you get out of trouble. I can't believe you even asked that."

Sharon could picture her daughter shaking her head disapprovingly. She took a breath and said, "Help me out here, Amy. I just don't know what to do."

"Mom, I have a meeting in ten minutes," she said abruptly.

"So you have nine minutes to talk me through this?"

"No, I have zero minutes. I always take a few minutes before a meeting to go over my notes, and I really should be doing that right now."

So why didn't she wait until after the meeting to call me back? Sometimes Amy was a puzzle. "Well, thanks anyhow. I'll figure something out."

"I'm sure you will. Oh, and, Mom?"

"Yes?"

"Going forward, don't open the door for strangers."

Amy wrapped up the conversation by saying they'd talk later in the day. Sharon thanked her for calling, even as she felt as if the discussion hadn't been helpful at all. When it came right down to it, her only option was to file a police report saying that Suzette had forced her way into her house and threatened her, but she had no proof that the incident had actually happened. There also was a risk in doing so, since Suzette could bring up the fact that Niki had been in their yard peering into their windows the night before. She'd claimed to have video footage, something Sharon thought dubious, but she'd made the accusation with such conviction that it did leave her wondering.

No, she decided. She wasn't going to call the police. Let Suzette make the first move, if there was going to be one. There was one person she wanted to talk to, though. Picking up her phone, she called Niki and left a quick voice mail. Thirty seconds later, her phone rang.

"What's up?" Niki asked cheerfully.

"Can you talk?"

"Sure, there's no one in the store, and Albert said it was okay. Funny thing you called—I just saw Suzette Fleming drive by. She's a terrible driver. Barely paused at the stop sign."

"She's the reason I'm calling."

When Sharon finished telling the whole story, Niki was irate on her behalf. "She *pushed* her way into the house?" Niki said. "Now that takes balls."

"I was really afraid," Sharon admitted.

"Well, of course you were," Niki said, her tone protective. "Anyone would be."

"At one point she got aggressive, and I honestly thought she was going to hit me."

"That *bitch!*" Niki exhaled in disgust.

"She wouldn't leave until I went to get my phone and told her I was going to call the police."

"Did you call them?"

"No, I didn't want to start something." Sharon knew Niki would understand the meaning behind the words.

"So are you okay now?"

"If I'm going to be completely honest, I'm still a little shaken up."

"Yeah, I bet. Just a minute, okay?"

"Certainly."

Sharon could hear Niki's voice in the background. When she returned, she said, "It's slow here, so Albert said I could go home early. I'm getting my coat right now."

"I can pick you up." The offer was half-hearted but sincere.

"No, keep the doors locked and stay inside. I'll be there in ten minutes."

A wave of relief washed over Sharon. "Thank you, Niki."

CHAPTER THIRTY-EIGHT

Sharon had hot tea ready when Niki got home, so after she took off her coat and boots, they both sat down at the kitchen table. After Sharon was done relating the full story of the confrontation with Suzette, Niki made a decision. "I'm going to go over there right now."

"No, you don't want to do that."

"Yes, I do. Just listen a minute." Niki had an argument ready. "It's a fair guess that Mrs. Fleming is gone, and I saw the school bus go by, so Jacob should be home by now. I think he really likes me. I bet I can get him to tell me what the deal is with the little girl. And if I can get in the house, maybe I'll even see her and get a photo."

Sharon shook her head, and Niki knew she was thinking about Amy's warning.

"Oh, honey, I can't let you do that. We're already in trouble. She says she has video footage . . ."

Niki scoffed. "She doesn't have video footage. You said she seemed surprised to see you, right? That she seemed nice at first, but then she recognized you, and that's when she got mean."

"Yes, that's exactly what happened."

"And she thought it was you climbing over the fence?"

Again, Sharon nodded. "That's right."

"She's got nothin'." Niki waved a hand dismissively. "She saw something in her backyard, or maybe she noticed my tracks in the snow, but she certainly doesn't have video footage, or she'd already have reported it to the police. She came over to ask if you'd seen anything, and then when she recognized you, she knew something was up. She only lashed out at you because she's scared. We're onto her and she knows it." She wrapped her hands around the warm mug.

Sharon leaned over and gave her arm a motherly squeeze. "It's nice that you want to see this thing through, but you can't go over there. I can't let you take a chance like that." She sighed. "No, I'm thinking we need to pull back. Amy said to let the experts handle it, and I think that was good advice. I should have listened to her in the first place."

"You're afraid Amy is going to get mad."

"That's part of it," Sharon admitted. "She's already mad. And I don't want her to get even madder. But she does have a point. We need to let the social worker handle this. We're probably just making things worse."

"Maybe it can't get any worse." Niki took a sip of her tea. "You wouldn't believe the horror stories I've heard. Knowing what I know, I can't stand by and do nothing. Give me ten minutes with Jacob and he'll crack like an egg. A simple conversation, that's all I'm saying. What could go wrong?"

"And what if Mrs. Fleming answers the door? She'll recognize you from the nutrition store."

"But she doesn't know I'm connected to you," Niki pointed out. "If she comes to the door, I'll say that I came to apologize for my behavior. I know her type. I'll ask for her forgiveness. Really lay it on thick. Believe me, it will totally make her day."

"Oh, Niki." Worry crossed Sharon's face, but she didn't say no.

"I've got this. And if it comes up with Amy, I'll tell her it was my idea and you advised against it."

Niki didn't waste any time after that. She pulled the elastic off of her ponytail and combed through her hair with her fingers before putting on her outerwear and heading for the door. Sharon offered to drive her, and Niki responded, "Don't be ridiculous. It's just around the block."

As Niki made her way down the front walk, Sharon called out, "Be careful!" Niki gave a wave in return.

When she got to the Flemings' house, Niki hesitated for a second and stared at the house from the street. There was nothing menacing about the place. The windows on the first floor were covered, but even that didn't look suspicious. Some people liked privacy. The driveway and front walk were neatly shoveled, and the garage door was lowered. No one passing by would guess there was anything out of the ordinary going on here. Which made it even more imperative to see this thing through. Gathering up her courage, she strode up the driveway and turned onto the L-shaped front walk until she was on the front porch. She gave the doorbell button a push and slipped off her gloves, tucking them into her coat pockets.

A long time passed before the door opened, but when it did, Jacob was the one who answered, his face peering around the edge of the door as if afraid of what he might find there. When he recognized her, his expression changed to guardedly happy. "Niki?"

"Hey, Jacob!" She kept her tone light, as if they were old friends who'd unexpectedly run into each other. "I *thought* this was your house. Do you have a few minutes?"

He sucked in a breath and glanced back over his shoulder. "Sure. What's up?"

"Someone dropped a twenty-dollar bill at the Village Mart, and no one's come back to claim it. I thought of you right away and wanted to check to see if you're missing any money."

His eyes narrowed in thought. "I don't think so."

Niki unzipped her coat. Quickly shaking it off, she slung it over one arm. She leaned toward him so that their noses almost met. "Well," she said in what she hoped was a seductive way, "as long as I'm here, how about a tour of the house? I'd love to see inside the world of Jacob Fleming."

"You want to come in?"

"Yeah, just for a few minutes. I won't stay long, I promise."

"Umm . . ." From the look on his face, it was clear he wanted to let her in, but something was holding him back.

"Are your folks home? I can come at another time." She tossed her hair over her shoulder and gave a flirtatious laugh. "Although I'm here right now. Ready and waiting."

Jacob shook his head. "No, my parents aren't home." He turned to look behind him. "It's just me." He held up a finger. "Can you wait just a minute? Don't leave." He closed the door to narrow the gap, but he didn't shut it all the way.

Niki felt the cold but kept her coat off, certain she'd be going inside soon. She had counted on Jacob Fleming being like most guys. She suspected she was right.

When he returned a few minutes later, he opened the door wide, grinning. "Come on in."

Inside, she wiped her feet on the front rug, a wool rectangle patterned with fleur-de-lis. "I like your house," she said, looking around.

"It's not mine," he said. "And you don't have to be nice. My mom picked out everything, and her taste sucks."

"She won't mind that I'm here?"

He shook his head. "She's gone until later tonight."

Niki laughed and placed a hand on his arm. Without his usual hoodie he looked less bulky, but the gray T-shirt with the biohazard symbol he wore wasn't all that flattering either. His hair fell over his forehead and curled around his ears. Jacob had the appearance of someone who was trying to hide in plain sight, but in this instance his expression said he was glad she was there. "I want to see all of it," she said.

He walked her through each room, and she made positive comments as they went along. In the laundry room, she spotted a little dog curled up on a dog bed. "Hi, puppy," she said.

"That's Griswold."

"Can I pet him?" When Jacob nodded, she bent down and stroked his head. "Such a good boy," she cooed. "Aren't you a sweet thing." When she finished, they continued on, ending up in the kitchen. "Everything is spotless," she marveled, running a finger over the island counter. "It even smells clean." She grinned at him. "Like a hospital."

"My mom is mentally ill that way. She's a big fan of those bleach wipes." He placed his hand on the counter next to her own. "And if anything is ever dirty or out of place, she has a complete meltdown. Usually she blames me, even if it's not my fault."

"Wow, how terrible for you." She set her hand over his. "I can sympathize."

"Your grandmother is crazy too?"

"No, she's okay. I've encountered other crazies, though. I have no idea why people have to be that way."

"Me either."

He leaned in as if to kiss her, and she squeezed his hand and turned her head. "I want to see the upstairs."

Jacob led the way, nervously talking as he went. "Don't be surprised if my room is a mess. I kind of like it that way. It's the one place I can be myself. If it was up to my mom, it would be empty except for the furniture." He opened a door on the left and said, "My dad's office." Niki noticed a bedroom pillow and a folded blanket on the sofa opposite the desk and had an idea of what that was all about. On the same side of the hallway, they passed a bathroom and a room Jacob called his mother's room. He opened the door to reveal a bedroom filled with white furniture with gold trim.

"What do you call this style of furniture?" she asked.

"French provincial," Jacob said, drawing out the words theatrically. "My mother has a thing for anything French. She thinks it's the ultimate in class." He pulled a face. "She'd like the whole house to look like Versailles. Luckily, my dad thinks it's tacky." He pointed at a door opposite. "Moving on."

Across from his mother's bedroom was a guest room. Niki made a point to walk in and look around, scanning the room for traces of a little girl. She opened the closet doors to find it empty except for a few lonely hangers. An upper shelf held folded blankets and an extra pillow. On the floor sat two boxes, both of them marked *Christmas*. She turned to Jacob. "You really have an empty room that sits here except for when you have guests?"

"Oh, yeah. And here's the best part. We've never had overnight guests."

"Never?"

"Not once," he said, his hand making the shape of a zero. "And not in my old house either. No one's allowed to stay over. My mom just likes the idea of having a guest bedroom."

"Huh." Niki closed the closet doors. "Must be nice."

"Not really." He beckoned with one finger. "One more room to see. Mine." He grabbed her hand and pulled her down the hall. She was struck by how bold he'd become in such a short period of time. It didn't take much to encourage a guy who'd never had encouragement. He walked through the door first, kicking a pile of clothing to one side and sweeping an arm across the room. "This is it."

Niki walked to the middle of the room and pretended to look around. A bulletin board on one wall displayed a ribbon for winning an elementary school talent show, a certificate for completing a wood-working course, and two photos of beautiful girls lounging on the beach in bikinis. She recognized one of them as being a Victoria's Secret model in her younger days. "Friends of yours?" she said, pointing.

"Yeah."

He had a framed band poster of a group she'd never heard of, but otherwise the walls were bare. The bed was unmade, and his desk was completely covered with clutter. She sat on the edge of the bed. "I said I wanted to see your inner sanctum, and I guess this is it."

"This is it," he repeated, eagerly crossing the room to join her. He reminded her of a jowly dog trying to hold back while anticipating a treat. He sat so close to her that their thighs touched. When he reached over and rested his arm along her backside, she resisted the urge to pull away.

"You know, Jacob, it was the craziest thing, but when we first met, I felt a connection between us." She turned to meet his eyes and saw the hope behind them. She felt guilty for leading him on, but she justified it, knowing she wouldn't let it go too far.

"Oh my God. I felt that way too. I never thought you would, though." He blinked and, as if overcome, cast his eyes downward.

"I'm not saying it's a romantic feeling," she continued. "But I'm getting something from you. A vibe. I feel like you need a friend, someone to confide in."

"I have friends," he said quietly, moving his right foot to kick a pair of boxer briefs under the bed. "So you feel sorry for me?"

"No, that's not it." Niki spoke slowly, leaning into him. "But I do want to know what's weighing so heavily on you. I can tell that something is bothering you. You always look like you have a secret you don't want to keep."

"I do?"

She nodded and smiled. "And I know what that's like, to be involved in something you know is wrong, maybe even illegal, but it's not your fault and you can't see your way clear. You'll feel better if you tell me about it. No judging, I promise."

"I don't know what you're talking about. I don't do drugs, if that's where you're going with this."

"No, I would never think that."

"Okay," he said grudgingly. "Not saying I haven't tried things—"

"I know, I know. I'm sorry. That's not what I meant." She rested her hands on her knees and looked away. "I'm getting a feeling that it's something with your family. You're an only child?"

"Yes."

"So no other kids live here?"

"Just me."

She caught the defensiveness. "It's hard when there are no other kids in the house."

Jacob looked at her and blinked. "I'm used to it."

"So who did you buy the Hostess CupCakes for? That was so nice of you."

"Just a kid I know. Her name is Mia. She likes cupcakes."

Her name is Mia. "How do you know her?"

Instead of answering he leaned in, ever so slowly, and she had a sinking feeling he was coming in for a kiss. Quickly she darted in and gave him a peck on the cheek, then stood up and smiled provocatively. Jacob seemed a little dazed. "I'll race you down the stairs!" She took off running, knowing that in a second he'd be right on her heels and that she had to stay ahead. By the time she reached the bottom of the stairs she heard his thundering footsteps behind her, but she kept going to the closed door he'd indicated led to the basement. Without hesitating, she opened it and flipped on the light switch.

"Wait!" he called out, his arm reaching, but she didn't wait.

Instead she went down, two stairs at a time, her feet clattering on the hard surface. Getting to the bottom of the stairs, she rounded the corner to see one large open room with a door on the far right. For a basement, it was nice enough. The cement walls had been finished with drywall, and the floor was some kind of vinyl planking. What was unusual was how empty it was, devoid of furniture, lacking storage boxes. No photos or artwork on the walls. The only thing that broke up the stretch of white walls was one large bookcase on the far end and three glass block windows, two on one side of the room and one on the opposite side.

"Niki, wait!" Jacob yelled. He was downstairs now, looking at her like she'd lost her mind.

"Sorry, Jacob! I wanted to see everything," she said, her arms outstretched, turning in a free-spirited way. "All of it."

"There's nothing to see," he said, sounding annoyed.

"Really? Well what about this?" Niki strode over to the door and ceremoniously pulled it open. She'd been expecting to find a child, or at least a space where a child was staying, so it was puzzling to find a small bathroom—toilet, shower, and pedestal sink with an oval mirror above it. She walked in and scanned the room. Not much to it, but it was spotless.

Jacob came to her side. "It's just the downstairs bathroom," he said. "My mom doesn't like anyone down here." His tone was stern. "Time to go upstairs." He grabbed her elbow and steered her away from there.

Once they'd returned to the first floor, Niki gave an excuse for having to leave. "My grandma is expecting me at home." She apologized for going down to the basement. "I should have checked with you first before I went downstairs. That wasn't cool."

"It's okay," he said.

"I've got a thought," she said. "Why don't we exchange numbers?"

He nodded, getting out his phone, then dialed the number she gave him.

When it rang, she held it up. "Got it. Thanks. I'll add you to my contacts." She hurried into her coat and gave him a quick hug before she went out the door. "See you later, Jacob."

"Later." His voice was tinged with disappointment.

"I want you to know that I'm here for you, Jacob. Seriously, if I can ever help you in any way, let me know."

Her offer made him smile. "I'll keep that in mind."

As she walked down the driveway, she hugged her arms around her, pleased with her discoveries. The glass block window that had fronted the flickering light was missing. The place it should have been was somewhere behind the bookcase. The other curious thing? On the pedestal sink in the bathroom stood a plastic cup holding a child-size toothbrush.

Little Mia was downstairs somewhere behind the wall.

CHAPTER THIRTY-NINE

Suzette raised a finger as the waiter came by. "Another martini, please." It was the only thing that could save the evening. By the third one, she no longer minded looking at the photos of Mary's infant grandson, and by the fifth, she actually saw Mary haloed in a rosy glow.

When Mary said, "Wow, you can really put them away," Suzette took it as an overdue compliment.

They sat and drank long after the dinner plates were cleared away, ignoring the server's suggestion that they take their drinks and head over to the bar. Mary drank herbal tea, something that made Suzette cringe on her behalf. The woman might as well wear an ID badge identifying herself as a senior citizen. Generously, Suzette pretended to approve.

Mary dipped her tea bag into the cup and said, "I find this helps me sleep at night."

"Whatever it takes," Suzette said warmly, lifting her martini glass.

For the last hour, Suzette had let Mary carry the conversation. She smiled and nodded at what seemed to be appropriate moments, but her mind was far away, drifting uncomfortably to what she was beginning to think of as the Mia problem. First the social worker and then the neighbor, digging into her personal business, asking if there were young children in her household. The neighbor, that frowsy nobody, had even asked specifically about a little girl. *Busybody*. Suzette had dismissed Matt's assertion that the social worker was there for a reason and that reason was Mia, but now, with a sinking feeling, she realized he was right. Not that she'd ever admit it.

Well, if Mia's presence was a problem, there was only one thing to do about it, and that was to take Mia out of the equation. Should the social worker come again, she'd find nothing out of the ordinary. Yes, she'd have to take care of the problem, and do it right away. There was no time to waste.

Once Mia was gone, the household would have to readjust in a big way. Suzette would most likely have to hire a cleaning lady, something she wasn't looking forward to, but the house wasn't going to clean itself. She hoped Jacob and Matt wouldn't make a fuss about this change. She would have a good defense for her actions. Matt had long said they couldn't keep the child, so she only needed to retort that she'd finally taken his advice.

She remembered back when she'd returned the guinea pig to the pet store. The clerk behind the counter hadn't wanted to take it back, so she'd just scooped the little beast out of the shoebox, left it sitting on the counter, and walked out. No minimum-wage employee with ear gauges was going to tell her what to do.

Of course, Jacob had been crestfallen when he discovered the empty cage, but he'd gotten over it soon enough. Mia could go back to where she came from, none the worse for wear. If anything, she was in far better shape than when they'd found her. She supposed Jacob would "miss" her, but it was always something with him, and it wasn't as if Mia could stay with them forever. Truthfully, she was starting to regret bringing her home in the first place.

Despite her pounding headache the next morning, Suzette got out of bed and started her day, taking a quick shower and getting dressed. Some pills for the pain, an extra tablet to lift her mood, and she was off to a good start. After a cup or two of coffee, she'd be ready to carry out her plan.

Once downstairs, she was glad to discover that she was the first one out of bed. Suzette headed down the basement stairs, unlatched the bookcase and swung it open, then flipped on the light switch. "Wake up, sleepyhead. Time to start your day!"

Mia sat up and groggily rubbed her eyes. "Yes, Ma'am."

"Hurry. Wash up and get dressed. I'll have breakfast for you when you come upstairs." Suzette was feeling lighter as she climbed the stairs. Today she'd be fixing a problem.

By the time Jacob and Matt came downstairs, Mia was already at the counter eating her oatmeal. Suzette had folded in a liberal amount of brown sugar and topped it with a smiley face made of raisins. She'd set it down along with a glass of milk and said, "Here you go, Miss Mia. Enjoy!" Mia had smiled and dug her spoon right into the bowl.

Such a good girl.

Jacob regarded his mother suspiciously when he came into the kitchen. "You're up early," he said.

She shrugged. "Just woke up and decided to start my day." She smiled in a friendly way. Jacob might be a bit of a mess now, but someday he'd get a growth spurt and shed some of that baby fat. In time, too, he might be more willing to let her choose his clothes. With an improved appearance would come a better attitude and maybe a dose of confidence, all of which would make him ready for public viewing. He was her son, her only child. She wasn't going to give up on him yet. Suzette was a big believer in second chances and keeping her options open.

"Okay." Jacob walked past and went to the pantry closet, getting out a box of Cheerios. At the counter, he poured the cereal into a bowl and sliced a banana over the top. With a glance, he noticed Mia's breakfast. "Hey, squirt. Where'd you get the oatmeal?"

"I made it," Suzette said. "Would you like some?"

Jacob squinted in confusion. "No thanks."

Matt poured himself a cup of coffee, and the family ate and drank in silence. Mia took forever to finish her oatmeal; she was still working on it when the guys headed out the door together. Matt had offered to drop Jacob off at school on his way to work so he wouldn't have to take the bus.

To show there was no ill will between them, Suzette fluttered her fingers in a friendly wave and called out, "Goodbye! Have a good day!"

After they left, she pulled up a stool and sat next to Mia. "Today's a very special day," she said. "We're going for a ride in the car, and I'm going to show you where you lived when you were a baby. Would you like that, Mia?"

Mia's eyes got wide and she nodded, a spoonful of oatmeal still in her mouth. Her reaction was a tad unsettling. The child followed directions well enough, but Suzette doubted her intellectual capability went much beyond that. In this case, Mia would have had to understand the concept of doing something now in connection with what had happened in the past. The idea was clearly too abstract for someone as simpleminded as Mia. Most likely she was responding to Suzette's tone of joyous anticipation.

"It'll be fun," Suzette promised. "You'll see."

While Mia finished eating, Suzette went downstairs and retrieved a pillow and blanket from Mia's room, then set about putting everything in place so her plan would go smoothly.

Later, when Mia became so groggy that she dropped gracefully to the floor, Suzette wrapped her in the blanket and carried her out to the car.

CHAPTER FORTY

J acob had bolted out of his first-hour class after telling Mrs. Taylor he felt like he was going to be sick. He actually did feel ill, but it had more to do with the sinking feeling that something was off at home than any physical ailment. His mom's early start to the day was unusual in and of itself. Adding that to her superficially cheery manner and the fact that she'd made oatmeal for Mia—well, it was weird. Weird enough to raise alarms.

Even his dad had commented on it on the drive to school, saying, "Looks like your mother will be starting one of her new careers soon." She hadn't done anything like that in a long time, but years before she'd gone through different phases, deciding on new life paths and setting lofty goals for herself. His mother was full of good ideas, but none of them stuck. And all of them began with an uncharacteristically good mood and a large dose of optimism. Just like that morning.

This time felt different, though. Something was up, and Jacob thought it concerned Mia. He wasn't sure exactly what was going on, but he knew he didn't like it. He left school without permission and headed home. The walk was dreary, the winter day gray and the sidewalks lined with slush. He was warm enough in his jacket layered over his hoodie. Jacob never wore a hat, but after a few blocks he pulled his hood up because his ears were cold.

Turning onto his street, he saw his mother backing down the driveway. If she spotted him, he was in trouble, but the car went in the other direction, stopping for a long time at the stop sign before driving on. His father said she was an overly cautious driver, but Jacob thought she was just terrible at it. Slow and inattentive. The fact that she was leaving the house this early was highly suspicious. She rarely had appointments at this time of day.

After walking up his driveway, he punched the code into the garage door opener. Mia might have some insights into what was going on, and if not, he would search his mother's bedroom for clues and then call his dad.

Inside the house, he didn't waste any time. "Mia? Mia?" He walked through the first floor, checking every room and looking behind the couch, but he couldn't find her. Frowning, he went upstairs and called her name, the empty rooms echoing his voice back to him. A frantic feeling gnawed at his throat, and he went back down the steps, now yelling. "Mia! This isn't funny. Come out now!"

His last stop was the basement, where there was no place to hide. He crossed the room, glanced into the empty bathroom, and went right to the bookcase, releasing the latch. It swung open easily, and his heart sank when he saw she was gone, and so was her pillow and the top blanket. *Where the hell is Mia? What has Mom done?*

In his heart he knew she'd taken Mia somewhere, but just to be thorough, he checked the house again. Methodically he went from room to room, looking in every closet and opening the cabinets where Mia might fit. When he finished, he got out his phone and called his dad. When voice mail kicked in, he left a message, careful not to say anything that might incriminate them in the future. "Dad? I came home from school sick, and Mom's not here. She took the package from the basement, the one Griswold likes so much? I'm really worried. Call me." His father might be in a meeting or driving somewhere. Sometimes he didn't check his phone for an hour or two.

Jacob looked at the tracking app on his phone and saw that his mother was on the move. He tried calling her phone, and per usual, she didn't answer. She had probably turned the ringer off at one point and forgot to turn it back on. His mom was the least tech-savvy person he knew. She thought she was current because she could text and knew about emojis.

Where could she be going? The usual places people took their kids—the dentist, the hair salon, clothes shopping—didn't apply here. If Mia had gotten injured, he could see a trip to a hospital or walk-in clinic, but that didn't fit with what he saw on the tracking app. Besides, whatever his mother was doing seemed premeditated.

Out of habit, Jacob opened the refrigerator door and looked in, one foot jiggling nervously. For once, nothing looked good. He shut the door and sat at the counter, looking at the tracker on his phone again. His mom had now turned onto the interstate. His grandmother in Minnesota lived in that direction, but they hadn't gone to see her in years. He frowned, trying to figure it out. His mother would never take Mia on a visit. Besides, she had nothing good to say about his grandma or his uncle, both of whom lived in the same area.

So it probably wasn't to visit his relatives, especially not with Mia along for the ride.

A stray thought suddenly hit him, and the awfulness of it made him drop his head into his hands. *No.* She wouldn't be taking Mia back to where they found her, would she? Could his mother even find the place? And even if she found it, would the scary guy still be there waiting for his kid after all this time? *No.* The shack was a cesspool, and that dude had to be long gone. Mia had no memory of any of this and would be so frightened. Even his mother wouldn't be that heartless. Or would she be?

He mulled it over some more. His mother wouldn't kill Mia. At least he didn't think so. It would be too messy and hard to cover up, but he wouldn't put it past her to abandon a child. He could envision his mother stopping in front of a local police station and telling Mia to get out, then driving away.

All of these thoughts horrified him. He called his mother again. "Mom, come home right now. Whatever you're doing, it's a bad plan! Come home and we'll figure out another way." He clicked off, sure that he had probably made it worse. His mother hated being told what to do.

Oh, why didn't he have a car? So many of the other kids at school had cars, either their own or one they could use. Meanwhile, he was the loser, the outcast who took the bus. His mind sorted through everyone he knew. Was there *anyone* who would lend him a car so he could follow his mother?

Only one person came to mind, and he barely knew her, but just the day before she had said, "Seriously, if I can ever help you in any way, let me know."

He got on his coat and headed for the gas station.

CHAPTER FORTY-ONE

Luckily, when Jacob arrived Niki was behind the counter and there weren't any customers in the store. Fred was stocking the beer cooler, in sight, but out of hearing range.

Jacob was out of breath when he came barreling through the door, and he made it clear that he needed to talk to her. In three minutes, he divulged all the information she'd unsuccessfully tried to wheedle out of him the day before. His voice was frantic as he explained that the little girl who lived with them, Mia, was missing, that his mother had taken her. From what she could tell, he wanted her to lend him a car so he could follow them and make sure nothing bad had happened to the little girl. Every new piece of information he imparted led to her asking more questions; it seemed to frustrate him that she wasn't grasping the urgency of the situation.

"I just need your car," he said, leaning forward, his hand flat on the counter. "That's all there is to it. If you let me borrow it, I promise I'll fill the tank, or pay you whatever you want. I haven't got time to explain it all."

She held up a hand, traffic-cop style, and told him to hold on a minute. "I know you're in a big hurry, but I need a little more information from you."

She asked a series of questions and was astounded by the answers. When he was done spilling the family secrets, Niki recapped. "So your mother just *took* a little girl three years ago and she's been in your house ever since, and no one knows about this besides you and your parents?"

Jacob nodded. "Yeah, I know it sounds bad, but it wasn't up to me. You don't know my mom. She was blackmailing my dad into keeping Mia because—"

Niki's hand went up again. "I don't really care about that part. You know we should call the police, right? This was kidnapping and God knows what else."

He looked down. "But I don't want my dad to get into trouble."

"Oh, Jacob, it's too late for that," Niki said. "All of you are in a world of trouble. There's no getting around it. This is a terrible, terrible thing."

When he looked up, he had tears in his eyes. "I don't care about me. Right now, I'm just afraid for Mia. This could go really bad for her. My mom is crazy. I don't know what she's gonna do."

"Are you willing to talk to the police?" Niki asked.

"Sure, but I can't right now. There's no time." His voice was getting louder. "They'll want to investigate and ask all these questions, and all of that will take forever, and something terrible could happen to Mia in the meantime."

"This really seems like something the authorities should handle."

"They won't be able to find her." Jacob's voice came out in a hoarse cry. "But I will."

Fred came forward. "Jacob? What's going on?"

"He wants to borrow my car," Niki explained. "His mom drove off in the car with a little girl named Mia." She and Jacob exchanged a look. "A relative of theirs. Jacob's afraid something is going to happen to Mia."

"What would happen?" Fred said, his head tilted to one side.

"My mom is . . . kind of unhinged. And a terrible driver. I've been tracking her on my phone, and I know where they are. I just need to stop her and make sure Mia is safe."

"If you want to leave work, Niki, you can," Fred said. "Jacob here looks too distraught to drive himself."

Niki said, "I don't actually own a car. I walk to work."

Jacob said, "You made me go through all that and you don't even have a car?" It came out as an accusatory wail.

Fred nodded regretfully. "I'd drive you myself, but I have a delivery coming in soon and I have to be here to sign for it."

Jacob threw up his hands in frustration. "I don't know what to do. I really need to find Mia."

Fred reached under the counter and pulled out a ring of keys. "Tell you what—my Camry is in the back. You can use it as long as Niki drives. I'll need it back by six at the latest."

Niki froze, while Jacob said, "Thank you, thank you! I can pay you when I get back."

"No need for payment. Just replace the gas." Fred turned to her and said, "This okay with you, Niki?"

Niki couldn't believe what had just transpired. Fred and his brother, Albert, had to have the kindest hearts of any men she'd ever met. *Who just lent someone their car?* "Yeah, it's okay," she said.

"We better get going," Jacob said. "There's not much time."

CHAPTER FORTY-TWO

As soon as Wendy opened the door and saw Detective Moore standing there, hat in his hands and an apologetic look in his eyes, she knew it wouldn't be good news.

"Good evening, Mrs. Duran." He nodded. "Is your husband home too?"

Without a word, she let him in and went to get Edwin.

When all three of them were seated in the living room, he broke the news. "I'm so sorry to tell you this, but I heard from the medical examiner, and Morgan's dental records were a match."

Wendy drew in a sharp breath, his words hitting her as if she'd been physically smacked. She put her hand to her mouth and made a conscious effort to breathe. She wanted to ask questions, but she didn't think she could bear to hear the answers. Part of her wanted Detective Moore to go, to leave them in peace, but another part was grateful for his presence and compassion. She glanced over at her husband, whose face had grown pale.

Edwin said, "It's a positive identification, then? The remains they found are definitely Morgan?"

Detective Moore sat forward. "Yes, sir."

His use of the word *sir* was what struck her. Before, she'd guessed him to be about the age of her own children, and now she knew this to be true. He was just a kid himself, Wendy realized. A young man doing his job, probably wishing that giving bad news wasn't part of his workday. She blurted out, "What was the cause of death?"

"That's still pending. I was told it didn't look like a homicide, but it's too early to say for sure."

"So it may be drug-related?" Edwin asked.

"Possibly. We'll know more later. You'll be contacted when the investigation is finished. They'll want to know how you want to handle the transportation."

"Transportation?" Wendy asked, not understanding.

"For the funeral," Edwin said gently. He turned to the detective. "Isn't that right?"

"Yes, sir."

The funeral. What a horrible thought. But of course that was what people would expect, a service to bring closure. She looked at the family photo hanging above the fireplace. She'd thought that someday when she and Edwin had passed away, this picture would remain for Morgan and Dylan and their families. Something to be passed down from generation to generation, a moment in time of the four of them. She'd never dreamed that one of her children would die first. How was that fair? How was that even possible? A lump formed in her throat.

Detective Moore said, "Again, I'm so sorry. There is another piece of news as well."

She sat up. "Yes?"

"The medical examiner confirmed that Morgan had given birth at some point."

"Morgan had a baby?" Wendy asked.

"Yes, ma'am."

"But how can they know that?" Edwin asked. "It's been so long. I'm assuming we're talking about skeletal remains?"

Detective Moore looked uncomfortable. "Yes, sir. I was told that the medical examiner can tell by looking at the pelvic bone. If a woman has given birth, there are a series of pockmarks along the inside of the bone."

"So it's for certain?" Wendy asked. "Without a doubt?"

"Yes."

Which meant they had a grandchild and hadn't even known it. She looked to Edwin, who said, "Any news on where Keith and the baby might be?"

"No, sir." Detective Moore suddenly looked as if he himself was about to cry.

Wendy had a sudden thought. "But there must have been a birth certificate."

"That would be correct, assuming the paperwork was filed," Detective Moore said.

Wendy listened as Edwin and Detective Moore talked about what was involved with tracking down a birth certificate. As sympathetic as the police department was, she got the impression that pursuing the location of the child wasn't a huge priority. Detective Moore said, "Of course this is an ongoing investigation, and every effort is being made to find the man who'd been living there. Even if it was an accident, the fact that the death wasn't reported and was hidden is a crime in and of itself."

Wendy mulled this over. She knew that without Keith's full name or at the very least a photo it would be difficult to find him. Morgan was dead, and her baby was out there somewhere. Would they ever get answers to what had happened to them?

The detective asked if they had any other questions, and when they said no, he stood up to leave. At the door he turned and said, "When we get the full report, I'll be in touch."

After the door closed behind him, Wendy leaned against the wall and forced out a sigh. "So that's it, then," she said, her eyes welling with tears. For years she'd monitored the website, answered comments, and searched online for clues. She'd visited that horrible seedy bar, begging people for information. She'd wished for Morgan to come home, and she'd prayed for her daughter's safety. Her prayers had been especially heartfelt and frequent, in the hope that they'd carry more weight. All this activity had kept her busy, but it hadn't brought Morgan home, and now she was gone forever.

Edwin wrapped his arms around her, a circle of warmth and love. He held her close, and she closed her eyes, listening to his ragged breathing, and a minute or two later, the quiet sounds of his sobbing. Edwin wasn't one who cried, hadn't even cried at his own father's funeral, but the finality of knowing his child was gone forever had broken him.

She said, "We have to find the baby." Even as she said the words, the futility of it hit her full force. They hadn't been able to find Morgan. How would they locate a child they knew nothing about?

CHAPTER FORTY-THREE

"Where are we going?" Niki asked as she adjusted the seat and mirrors. She was still in awe of Fred's generosity, especially now that she was sitting in his car. It wasn't new, but the interior was spotless, and it even smelled clean. If it weren't for the assorted change in the cup holder, it could be a vehicle on a dealership lot. If this were her car, she sure wouldn't be lending it to a teenager.

Jacob stared at his phone. "We'll need to take I-94 north, but as we get closer it veers off to the west."

"I'm hoping you're going to walk me through this?" Even though she'd had her driver's license for months now, she hadn't done much driving. Amy had told her it would become second nature, but without access to a car, she hadn't had the opportunity to get to that point. Right now, she still needed complete focus to drive safely.

"I'm good with directions. By the way, I really appreciate this."

"I know." She buckled her seat belt and started up the engine. When she heard Jacob's buckle click, she moved forward, pulling the car out of the parking lot.

He was surprisingly good at directing her, which eased her mind somewhat. In minutes they were on the interstate heading out of town.

"You have an app to track her phone?" Niki asked.

"Yeah. She could track me too if she wanted to, but she'd have to check the app."

"She doesn't?"

"No."

"Because she trusts you?"

He forced out a harsh laugh. "No. She doesn't trust anyone. And she doesn't bother to keep track of me because what would be the point? It clearly wouldn't benefit her, and she's all about her. She doesn't give a crap about me." He laughed bitterly. "Plus, she probably doesn't even remember that she has the app. My mother is not what you'd call tech-savvy."

His voice rang with disdain; there was obviously no love there. Niki knew there were parents who didn't love their children and that the reverse was true as well, but her own mother had loved her beyond measure, and it went both ways. The fact that her mom had been addicted to drugs and alcohol was a tragedy, but she'd never doubted her mother's love. How awful to be part of the Fleming family. On the surface they had it all, but underneath it sounded like there was no respect or affection, much less love.

"How long are we going to be on this stretch of road?" she asked, keeping her eyes ahead. Luckily, traffic was light.

"A long time. Another forty miles or so."

"Can you do me a favor? Go into my bag and get my phone. I need to call my grandma and let her know what's going on."

He unzipped her bag and found her phone. She talked him through finding the contacts, told him to click on Sharon's name, and had him put it on speakerphone. When Sharon answered, Niki explained the situation. Sharon was astounded to hear her neighbors had kept a little girl in their house for three years. Once she got over the shock of the news, she made it clear she wasn't enthused about

Jacob's plan of action. "I really think you should have called the police," she said, echoing Niki's initial instincts.

"I hear you," Niki said, keeping her eyes on the road. "That was my first thought too."

Jacob broke in, "The police wouldn't understand, and explaining it all would have taken too long. And now that my mom's driven out of the county, they would have said it was beyond their jurisdiction."

"Don't you think they would put out an AMBER Alert?" Sharon asked.

"Nah," Jacob said. "We don't even know if Mia is her real name, and we don't have a last name or a picture of her or anything. They couldn't have issued an alert. They don't have enough information."

He sounded so sure, as if he'd thought this through. Niki wondered where he'd gotten his facts. The internet? *Law & Order*?

He added, "I think we can catch up to her, and once we have her exact location, we can call the police then."

"What's the license plate number on your mom's car?" Sharon asked.

A good question, Niki thought.

"I don't know," Jacob answered. "When we catch up to her, we can call and give it to you then. Or maybe the police can look it up?"

"The two of you chasing after her sounds like it could be dangerous. Why don't you come on back and we'll talk this over?"

"No," Jacob said firmly, not even waiting for Niki to weigh in. "I need to be the one to do this. She's my mom, and I know how she thinks. We have to keep going. Mia's probably scared, but she knows me, so I have to be the one to find her."

"Well, be careful," Sharon said, her voice coming out overly loud. Niki could tell Sharon still wasn't convinced. "And call me with updates. I'm going to put a call out to Franny Benson. She'll know what to do. She'll probably want the police to be involved, and she might want to talk to you first, so make sure to answer your phone, okay? Even if you don't know the number."

"Will do," Niki said. After they'd ended the call, she asked Jacob, "You seem pretty sure we'll be able to catch up to her."

"I'm not *completely* sure," he said. "But I saw her leave the house, and it was right before I went to the gas station. Plus, if you ever saw my mom drive, you'd understand. She drives really slow, like excruciatingly slow. One time she even got a ticket for it, which made her furious." He glanced down at his phone. "She stops a lot too."

"Why does she stop?"

"It's kind of a weird compulsion with her. She'll stop at rest stops and fast-food places and go inside to touch up her makeup and check her hair, and then while she's there she'll corner some poor person. She can't stand her own company, always has to be interacting with other people. She likes to make small talk with strangers. Asking for directions, or about the weather or road conditions. The topic isn't important. What's important is having people look at her. She likes to wave her hands around, and a lot of times they comment on her nails or her jewelry. She has a lot of rings, and usually people notice and compliment her."

"Really?" Niki asked in amazement.

"Oh yeah, I told you she's crazy," Jacob said. "And we can probably catch up because she gets lost a lot, sometimes even with the GPS, because she doesn't always believe the directions and thinks she knows better."

"She doesn't believe the directions?"

"Just thinks they're wrong. You wouldn't believe the level of craziness we're talking about. And now she's trying to find a place from memory from three years ago, and that time we were totally lost. Not only that, but that house might not even be there anymore. It was barely standing when I saw it."

"So you're pretty sure she's going back to the place you found Mia?" In her peripheral vision, she saw him vigorously nod his head.

"Sure, that's how her mind works."

"You sound pretty certain."

"I've lived with her long enough to know. If something doesn't work out, she just tries to undo it. She's cycled through more friends than most people ever have in a lifetime. Everyone loves her at first, and some of them still love her after she's dropped them. They can never figure out what they did wrong. My mom can take offense at anything. Someone just looks at her the wrong way or doesn't laugh at her jokes the way she wants them to, and she's so done with them. Sometimes these women call and apologize over and over again, or send notes or gifts. She totally loves it, but none of it makes a difference. Once she makes up her mind that someone is out, they're out of her life for good. There's no going back. I told you, she's insane."

"So what did Mia do wrong?"

"Mia? She couldn't do anything wrong if she tried. She's such a good little thing, not a mean bone in her body."

"No, I mean, why would your mom want to take her back?"

"Oh, that." Jacob sighed. "It's because this woman from the county stopped in and was asking questions, and then some neighbor lady was snooping around. I'm thinking it freaked her out and she wants Mia out of our house so she doesn't get into trouble. If Mia's not there, it's like it never happened."

A woman from the county. A neighbor lady was snooping around. Niki's mind spun with the realization that she and Sharon had been the ones responsible for this little girl's fate. They may well have started something terrible. *But it wasn't our fault,* she thought defensively. Neither she nor Sharon would ever harm a child. They'd been trying to save the little girl. They couldn't help it that Suzette Fleming was deranged. Only a very sick person would snatch a child and keep her as a servant in her home for three years. Poor little thing. With a renewed sense of urgency, Niki veered out of her lane, passing a Buick going less than the speed limit. Suddenly, finding Mia as quickly as possible was more important than her qualms about expressway driving.

"That's more like it," Jacob said in approval. "Keep going like that and we'll be caught up in no time."

Jacob couldn't believe how freeing it was to confess to Niki. In one day, Mia had gone from being a family secret to becoming someone he could talk about, and that made Mia seem like a full-fledged person. Niki had so many questions. "I know you said your mom blackmailed your dad into keeping Mia a secret, but why did you not tell anyone? You seem like you care about Mia, and you knew it was wrong . . ." She gave him a side-eye before returning her gaze to the road. The day was gray, but traffic was light, so at least that was in their favor.

"I thought about turning my mom in, maybe making an anonymous tip, or dropping Mia off at a police station, but she's so little and she would have been afraid."

"You don't think she was afraid sleeping downstairs in the basement by herself?" For the first time, Niki's voice sounded judgmental.

"You don't understand," he said. "This is my family we're talking about. I know the whole thing is weird, but when you're right in the middle of it, it seems normal. Mia was always happy. I mean, it would be different if she'd been crying or miserable, but she always has a smile on her face."

"Maybe because she doesn't know any better?"

"Maybe," Jacob admitted. "But honestly, it wasn't up to me. I was a kid too."

"Yeah. But you knew it wasn't right."

"Yeah, I did know it wasn't right, but I kept waiting for one of them to do something. And you know what? We checked the missing children websites, and no one was looking for her. The house she came from was horrible. I wouldn't want my worst enemy to have to live there." This was only partly true. Jacob's worst enemy was a kid named Liam Johnson. Liam had the locker adjacent to his and would randomly slam Jacob's locker door against him when he went to switch out his books. One time he pushed it so hard Jacob thought he might have broken his arm. The impact left a huge bruise that lasted for weeks, a reminder of Liam's cruelty. From then on, Jacob just carried all his books in his backpack and didn't use his locker at all. And he avoided Liam Johnson as much as possible.

Thinking back on Liam Johnson made him sure that some people were just terrible human beings, without redemption. Such random meanness, and for what? Jacob had never done anything to him. Liam Johnson deserved to live in that awful shack, but he couldn't think of anyone else who did.

"You're making excuses."

"Maybe," he said, "but in a way, we saved Mia from a horrible life. And think about this—if my parents went to jail, I'd have no one, and I'd wind up in foster care or get shipped off to live with relatives I barely know. And there was a chance I would be charged as well. So all of us would be screwed. My mother got us into an impossible situation."

"Foster care isn't the end of the world," Niki said. "And you know what? It's not always about you, Jacob. There's a little girl involved. I don't care if she was in a horrible situation. You had other options, then and later. You could have called the police." They drove without speaking for fifteen minutes or so, the only noise occurring when Niki tried to find good music on the radio. She went from static to country music to talk radio and back again before finally giving up.

CHAPTER FORTY-FOUR

Suzette sighed heavily. Driving had never been her strong suit, and it was definitely not how she wanted to spend her time. In an ideal world, she would have been wealthy enough to have a full-time driver at the ready, but that was never going to happen as long as she was married to Matt. So, here she was, wasting a good chunk of the morning driving across Wisconsin. The problem was that being at the wheel for more than a few minutes made her tired and antsy. And then there were the navigational challenges. Back in the days of road maps, she'd found them to be as comprehensible as hieroglyphics. Even with GPS there were difficulties. Road construction, unclear directions, turnoffs that weren't labeled—all of which made her doubt she was going the right way.

The only thing she remembered about the location where they'd found Mia was that it was somewhere just north of Harlow, Wisconsin. She and Jacob had been driving home from her mother's house, and she'd gotten off the expressway in search of a place to eat. A billboard had claimed a family restaurant was just five miles off the interstate, so she'd exited and followed the signs, but they'd never found it. She drove and drove, thinking it would be around the next curve.

Instead, they'd become hopelessly lost, driving for miles over bumpy country roads, past farm fields and meadows, not another car in sight. Basically a nightmare.

Even though three years had passed, she was fairly certain she'd know it on sight. The trick was finding it. If she couldn't find it, she could go straight to her alternate plan and leave Mia at a police station in the vicinity. She had the girl wrapped in a cozy blanket already. Sleeping like a princess under a spell. Suzette could imagine carrying her up to a doorway and leaving her outside. It wasn't that cold out. Someone would find her soon enough, and even if it took a while, Mia was tough. She'd be fine. So it was a good plan. *Unless . . .* And here she paused to think about what could possibly go wrong. Unless they had cameras outside and she could be spotted. Somehow she doubted that a police station in the boonies would be so sophisticated as to have security cameras outside, but it was possible, and she didn't want to take any chances. She had to find the house. That's all there was to it.

Suzette had been driving about an hour and a half when her stomach rumbled with hunger, and she realized that all she'd had that morning was a piece of toast. *Damn.* She didn't function well on an empty stomach, and today, of all days, she had to be on top of her game. There was no getting around it—she'd have to make a quick stop.

She thought back to how she'd dosed Mia's oatmeal with crushed sleeping pills. Her math had been spot-on—she'd calculated the amount she needed for herself and adjusted for the weight difference. Whenever Suzette took the full amount, she'd fall into a sleep coma that lasted anywhere from four hours to a whole night. Sometimes she woke up confused that it was morning. Based on this, she thought that Mia wasn't likely to stir until they arrived at their destination, and maybe not even then. Suzette had been lucky, too, that the weather had cooperated for this trip. It was warm for this time of year. Well, maybe not warm, but above freezing anyway, and the sun was melting the snowbanks. And as long as she didn't make any sudden turns, there shouldn't be any problems with Mia shifting from her spot.

She drove for a while, scanning the roadside, dismayed at not seeing an exit sign for miles. Finally, a billboard promised that the next exit would have a gas station and a family diner. She'd really been hoping for a fast-food drive-through so she wouldn't have to leave the car unattended, but she was out of options. Hopefully, she could pick up something quick to go.

When she drove off the interstate, she veered onto the ramp, happy she could see the diner ahead. The parking lot was crushed gravel, while the building, rounded steel with large windows, sat on a concrete pad. An actual diner, she mused, like something out of a 1950s movie. She got out of the car, her handbag handle looped over her bent arm, and walked toward the door, only pausing to press the key fob to lock the car door. Once inside, she swiftly took it all in: a revolving pie case by the front register, a long curved counter with one customer, and a row of booths along the outside windows. All but one booth was vacant, and that one was occupied by two old women sipping coffee. A hanging arrow pointed to the restrooms, something that sounded good at the moment. She bypassed a waitress carrying a tray of food and made a quick stop in the ladies' room. After she washed her hands, she checked her hair and face to confirm her appearance was public-ready.

Back in the diner, she went up to the register, waiting to be acknowledged. The waitress she'd seen only minutes earlier was nowhere in sight. She tapped her toe impatiently. Behind her a man's voice said, "You don't have to wait. Just take a seat."

Suzette turned to see who had spoken. It was the guy at the counter, a burly man in his fifties wearing a tan workman's jacket and a worn denim baseball hat.

He did a double take. "Well aren't you a breath of fresh air." His voice was admiring. "Not from around here, are you?"

"No," she said, pulling her handbag close. "Just passing through."

"Take a seat," he said, indicating the stool next to him. "Liz will be right out. She's brewing some more coffee." He jerked his chin toward a swinging aluminum door.

"No, thank you," she said primly. "I just need something to go."

"Suit yourself."

She recognized the hurt in his voice and knew it was from being rebuffed. Right around the time she graduated from college she'd noticed that she had this sort of indefinable effect on people. A magnetic appeal. Charisma. People were drawn to her and wanted to be her friend. At first she'd allowed it and had a big group of hangers-on following her every move. Soon enough, though, she'd learned to be discriminating. It was exhausting keeping that many admirers in line. But now she found she missed those days. Jacob and Matt's attentions fell way short of the desired amount, and her friends from her charitable boards weren't able to keep up.

Suzette slid onto the stool next to the working man. "Hi, I'm Suzette." She watched as he perked up, lifting his coffee cup as if toasting her.

"Hi, Suzette. Nice to meet you. I'm Craig."

He held out his hand, and she shook it with a smile. His hand was big and warm. "Nice to meet you, Craig. Maybe you can help me get some food and a coffee to go? Something quick, maybe a Danish or some toast?"

A slow smile crossed his face. Men always liked to help. "Sure thing." He cupped his hands around his mouth. "Liz! Hungry lady out here needs you ASAP." He turned to Suzette. "She'll be out in a sec," he said confidently.

A few moments later, a woman pushed through the door, a pot of coffee in one hand. "Cripes, Craig. Do you have to yell?"

He jabbed a thumb in Suzette's direction. "It's an emergency. This pretty lady needs something quick to go."

Liz turned and set the coffeepot on the burner. "What can I get for you?"

"A coffee with cream, and something easy to eat as I drive. Do you have a Danish or maybe some toast?"

Before she could answer, Craig jumped in. "Why don't you have the cook make her a breakfast sandwich, Liz?"

Suzette frowned. "Oh, that's not really necessary . . ."

Craig sat up straight. "Well, they don't have Danish here, and toast just doesn't seem like enough. A lady like you deserves something a little more special. He can do it quick, can't he, Liz?"

Liz nodded. "Just a few minutes. Probably not much longer than it takes to make toast."

"Well, okay then." Suzette was about to ask what was in the sandwich, but Liz had already left to put the order in, so instead she made small talk with Craig, pretending to be interested in his job in construction. When he finished his tiresome droning about work sites and finally asked about her line of work, she said, "I used to be a model in my younger days, but now I run a charity for children with disabilities."

"A model, huh? I'm not surprised," Craig said. "I'd pegged you for a model when you walked in the door. Something about you." He shook his head. "A real elegance."

"Oh, that's so kind of you to say." She rested her hand on his elbow, but only briefly so it was something special, like experiencing the brush of a butterfly's wings as it flew past. "But that was so long ago." She put a hand to her chest.

"It couldn't be that long ago," he said. "You don't have a line on your face."

As she did with every interaction with a man, she imagined what it would be like to be Craig's girlfriend or wife. After a minute she decided that while the initial adulation might be nice, the tedium of the conversation would quickly wear thin. And as vile as Matt had treated her lately, at least his educational level and professional standing gave her the right kind of status in the community. What must it be like to attend social functions with construction workers and their spouses? Inwardly, she shuddered at the thought. No, she decided, Craig qualified as more of a counter dalliance—a few minutes of conversation that would leave him wanting more. Years from now he'd still be thinking of the redhead named Suzette, the former model, who'd smiled at him one morning at the diner. He'd remember the brief touch of her fingers on his arm and be wondering, *What if?* "Oh bless you," she said. "What a nice compliment."

"And now you run a charity for kids?" He took a sip of his coffee, his eyes never leaving her face. "You're practically a damn saint."

"I believe in giving back." Suzette looked at the aluminum door and wished it would swing her way. What could be taking so long? "When I leave this world, I like to think it will be a better place for my having been in it."

"Oh, that's nice." He nodded in approval and began talking about his sister, a certified nursing assistant who worked at a nursing home. *Ugh.* As if that were in the same league as running a charity for disabled children. Suzette feigned interest but was relieved when Liz finally returned with a carryout cup and a white paper bag, folded and stapled at the top.

Liz set everything down on the counter in front of Suzette, along with a bill. Craig snatched up the piece of paper and said, "This is on me."

"Well, aren't you nice." Suzette stood up, taking the bag and cup. "Thank you. Have a good day." She left the diner without looking back. Once in the car, she set the coffee in her cup holder and opened the bag, glad to see it contained napkins along with the sandwich. Picking the pieces of bacon off the top, she took a bite and sighed with approval. A fried egg and cheddar cheese on a flaky biscuit. Craig had been right. This was far better than toast. She ate half of it before starting up the car. She could nibble on the rest while she drove.

CHAPTER FORTY-FIVE

Jacob noticed how intensely Niki concentrated—her hands only leaving the wheel to briefly play around with the radio, which she did for a minute or so before giving up. Otherwise, she kept her eyes on the road, not saying a word. Every now and then she frowned. He said, "Are you mad at me?"

She kept her gaze forward. "No. Why do you ask?"

"You're just being awfully quiet." He didn't comment on the real reason he thought she might be angry with him. He'd sensed how horrified she'd been to learn he'd played a role in keeping Mia at their house. Her reaction was understandable. There's no way someone from outside the family could understand the power his mother had over him and his dad. Her moods affected all of them, dictating their behavior. She created scenarios, lies and situations, that couldn't be undone. Over and over again she insisted on her version of events. Even when he knew she was wrong, her spinning caused him to doubt himself. "I just thought you might be mad . . ." He looked down at his phone.

"I'm not mad. I'm quiet because I'm not used to being on the interstate." Niki sighed. "If you want to know the truth, I'm not used to driving at all. I have my license, but I don't have a car, and I haven't driven all that much. Going this fast is very stressful for me."

"Oh." That made sense. "Well, I'm sorry you're stressed. Do you want me to drive?" He hadn't driven all that much either, but speed didn't bother him.

"No, but thanks. I'll be fine."

"I know when we find Mia we'll have to go to the police, and she's going to be taken away. I'm really going to miss her," Jacob admitted. Mia was the only one who greeted him with a smile. It took so little to make her happy. She was grateful for the smallest things. Mia not only loved him, but she loved him even though she had no reason to do so. Mia was love.

"Well, since she doesn't have any relatives, she'll go to foster care. She's still little. Maybe someone will adopt her."

"But she does have relatives," Jacob said, the words coming out without thought.

Niki said, "What relatives? You said she wasn't on the missing children's website."

"She wasn't." He took a deep breath, knowing he was going to tell her everything. All along he'd wanted to tell someone, but there'd been no one he could tell. "I did a DNA test on her recently. You know, the kind where you spit into a tube and mail it back in."

"And what were the results?"

"She has grandparents and an uncle. Their names were there and everything. I looked them up on Facebook. The grandma was the only one with a Facebook account, and she looked nice. She's an accountant."

"So they're probably good people."

"I guess," he said. Something in her voice made him squirm with guilt. "I only just found this out."

"Does Mia know?"

"She knows I did the test. She doesn't know about the Durans. I told her I was still trying to figure out the results."

"The Durans. That's the name of her people?"

"Yes. The grandma is Wendy Duran." *Her people*. Mia had people. Such an odd concept.

They continued on in silence for the next two hours, interrupted only by a phone call from Niki's grandma saying she'd left a voice mail for the social worker and would call back when she knew more. "You be careful, Niki," she said, and Jacob could hear the love in her voice. "I don't want anything to happen to you."

"We're being careful," Niki assured her. "I'll let you know if anything happens."

"This whole thing is making me nervous. I feel like the police should be called."

Niki said, "Can you wait a little bit? Once we catch up to her, we'll know more. Right now we're not sure of anything."

Niki's grandma agreed to wait, but Jacob could tell she was conflicted. About a half hour after the phone call, Jacob noticed something new on his tracking app. "She's not moving anymore. It looks like she got off the expressway and then stopped."

Niki said, "Do you think she found the house and is leaving Mia there?"

He shook his head. "I'm pretty sure that's not the right location. It doesn't seem far enough. She probably just stopped somewhere to get some food or go to the bathroom or something." He hoped he was right. If Mia was strapped into the back seat, he could only imagine how frightened she might be. His mother would have given her a story to explain the drive, something fantastical, like they were going to visit an amusement park or off to ride a pony. Lies came easy to her. But Mia was not as gullible as his mother thought, and Jacob suspected she'd eventually see through it and then get worried about being so far away from home. He kept his eyes on the phone. "I'll let you know when she starts moving again."

"At least this gives us a chance to catch up." She punched the accelerator and was now fifteen miles over the speed limit, something Jacob appreciated given how much expressway driving scared her. They'd been gaining on his mother all along. Now they had a chance to actually catch her. Now that they were so close, he knew there would be a confrontation. Mentally, he went over what he would say. He'd tell his mother that it was over, that the police knew now, that she wasn't in charge anymore. Jacob would insist on taking Mia back with them. His mother would be furious, and who knew what she'd do? Whatever way she chose to lash out, he could take it.

He had to. Mia was depending on him.

Twenty minutes later, he noticed his mom was on the move again, and he told Niki, "She's on the road now, heading north." Just as he'd thought, her stop had been little more than a brief pause on the way there. He knew this because she didn't turn back to go home but continued on course.

"How much farther?"

"Not too much," he said. "Another twenty-five or thirty miles, maybe?"

Niki pushed her hair back behind her ear and sped up to the car in front of her, then veered around it before returning to her lane.

Jacob grabbed the dashboard. "What the hell, Niki?"

"You want me to catch up with her? I'm going to catch up with her."

"Yeah, but it doesn't help if we get in an accident or get stopped for a speeding ticket. We want the police involved, but not until we get there."

A fine mist came out of nowhere, turning into a drizzly rain that covered the windshield. Niki said, "Jacob, could you figure out the windshield wipers for me?" Her voice was tight.

"On it." He leaned over and twisted the end knob of the lever until the wipers swept back and forth at the right pace.

"Thanks."

He returned to his phone. "She just got off the expressway and is on a highway. I'll let you know when it's time to exit."

Niki nodded, her concentration on the road ahead. "So what are we going to do when we see her? Just follow her?"

"Play it by ear, I guess."

They continued in silence as Jacob watched them close the gap. His mother was going more slowly now, driving on country roads that were probably not clearly marked. His best guess was that his mother had *thought* she'd found the right exit and was now driving around, looking for the house or any landmarks she remembered being near the house. He could imagine her frustration at not seeing anything familiar. He shook his head. *She is hopelessly lost.*

When they got to the exit, Niki made a turn to the right, accelerating and coming to a quick halt at the stop sign at the end of the ramp. "How far?" she asked.

"Almost there. Maybe a few minutes." He continued to direct her, past a gas station and down a country lane. On either side, farm fields lay bare, gray and wet, waiting for spring. Small clumps of snow dotted the ditches on either side. The lane ended in a *T*, and Jacob said, "Take a right here."

They'd been following the road for a few minutes when Niki said, "Are you sure we're going the right way?"

She'd just finished the sentence when Jacob spotted his mother's car pulled over to the side of the road. "That's it," he said. "The silver Audi, parked on the right." The lights were still on, and the exhaust coming out of the tailpipe indicated that the engine was still running. His mother was either making a phone call or looking at her GPS. She was so stupid. "Pull up behind her."

When the car came to a halt, Jacob said, "Wait here. I'll go talk to her and get Mia." He leaped out and strode over to the driver's side of the Audi. He'd expected to see Mia strapped in the back seat, but except for his mother in the front, the car was empty. A feeling of horror filled him. What had his mother done this time? He stood next to her window while his mother, oblivious to his presence, looked at the GPS on her phone. The GPS on her dashboard was on as well. Her wiper blades whipped back and forth, sending a fine mist when they came his way. For a split second he stood and processed the scene. If Mia wasn't with her, where was his mother trying to go? And even more importantly, where was Mia?

He rapped on the glass, startling her. Her head jerked upward. Upon recognizing him, a range of emotions flitted across her face in the space of seconds. He knew them all, having seen them many times before—confusion, annoyance, and finally what looked like the beginning of rage. She rolled down the window. "Jacob, what are you doing here?" She said each word as if they began with a capital letter.

"Mom, where's Mia?"

She glanced back to see the car parked behind her. "You need to leave right now and go home. Your father and I will deal with you later. You are in big trouble, mister."

"Mom, I'm not going anywhere." His hand was on the wet roof of her car, and he leaned in. "You need to tell me where Mia is."

"She's at home, of course." She spat out the words. "Have you been following me?"

"Mia isn't at home. You took her somewhere. Where is she?" Fear clawed at him. "Is she alive?"

She reached through the window opening and pushed him away. "How dare you! You hacked into my phone, didn't you? You hacked into my phone and tracked me! You little shit."

True to form, when she got really angry, her ladylike facade slipped away and she couldn't help but resort to profanity. So many times the shock of her verbal attacks had made Jacob and his father let things go in order to walk away in peace, but Jacob wasn't going to allow her to deflect this time. "You need to tell me where she is or I'm calling the police. Tell me now."

Her eyes flashed with rage. "You have a lot of nerve." She rolled the window up.

Jacob pounded his fist against the glass and yelled, "Just tell me! Is she okay?"

His mother revved the engine, and then realizing it was still in park, she shifted into drive. She gave him a slight finger wave of derision as she drove off.

"Don't go. Wait! We can talk about this." Jacob jumped back as she swerved toward him and bounced back onto the road. In that moment, he got a nose full of exhaust fumes. He ran back to where Niki was parked and climbed into the car. "Go, go, go!" He frantically pointed to the windshield. "We have to follow her. She's done something to Mia."

CHAPTER FORTY-SIX

"What do you mean she's done something to Mia?" Niki asked as she stepped on the gas. "Did she hurt her?" She took in a sharp breath, envisioning the child tied up in the back seat, bruised and bleeding.

"I don't know what she did to her. She's not there!"

Not there? Niki pursed her lips as she watched the taillights of the silver car in the distance. Mrs. Fleming was driving like a maniac, way too fast for such slippery roads, and now, making things worse, her car had veered across the center line. Niki gripped the steering wheel. "Mia wasn't in the car?"

"No."

"Then why are we still chasing her?" Ahead, the silver Audi took a left onto a side road, and Niki followed suit. They drove past a run-down barn with a sagging roof. One lone cow stood out in the rain in the adjacent field.

"Because we have to find out what she did to Mia!"

"And how is chasing after her going to do that?"

"We can catch up to her and then cut her off," Jacob said, his voice fraught with emotion. "Make it so she has to stop. And then I'll make her tell me."

"Oh, Jacob, no." Niki relaxed her foot on the accelerator. She'd been on board to save a little girl. She'd borrowed a car and faced her fear of driving on the interstate and driven for hours with Jacob, who was nearly a stranger. But she wasn't going to get into a high-speed chase that could only end in an accident, not under any circumstances, but especially not in a borrowed car. This was the time to hand things over to the police. "Too dangerous."

"But . . . !" He held the phone close to her face. "She's heading down to a dead end. About a mile down."

"So it's a dead end. What's the difference?"

"Because she'll have to stop. All we have to do is follow her and box her in. Trust me, she's gonna get pissed off and yell, but she won't do anything to damage her car. She loves that thing."

"Jacob," Niki said, sighing. She didn't lack sympathy for his predicament. She recognized the panicky tone that came when things didn't work out the way you wanted them to. She'd been there herself. But it felt like the end of the line. "Sometimes you have to know when to call it quits."

"Please, Niki, please." He sounded on the verge of tears. "Just go. I know I can get her to tell us where Mia is. We've come this far." He put his hands together. "Just another ten minutes. I'm begging you. I wouldn't ask if it wasn't important."

Oh no, now he was getting to her. One last look at his impassioned face sealed it. She shook her head even as her foot hit the gas pedal. This felt like a mistake, but he'd made a good point. They'd come this far. "Ten more minutes," she said begrudgingly. "Then we're turning around and going back."

He exhaled loudly. "Thank you."

Fred's car had a surprising amount of pick-up. She zoomed down the curving road, not seeing the silver Audi anymore, but there weren't any side roads either, so it was a safe bet Suzette Fleming was just ahead. The rain was only a mist at the moment. The wipers swept it away before it barely landed.

She kept up the pace, but carefully now because she was aware of the bends in the narrow two-lane road, slick from the rain. In the cup holder, her phone went off, but both of them ignored it.

"Just a little more," Jacob said, his eyes flicking from his phone to the windshield. The road now crested above the farm fields that sloped down on either side. They passed a large retention pond, its surface as smooth as glass. Next to it a large wheeled irrigation machine waited for the day it would be needed. "Not too much farther."

As he spoke, Niki spotted red brake lights at the end of lane. At the same time, Jacob cried out, "There she is! Now turn the car sideways so she can't get past us."

Niki eased on the brakes and turned into the left lane. She went forward and then reversed, and repeated the maneuver in an attempt to turn the car, while Jacob powered down the window and stuck his head out to get a better look. Looking back at Niki, he said, "Stop the car. I'm getting out."

He got out of the car and ran the forty feet to where his mother's car was jerking back and forth, obviously trying to make a U-turn. He could see now that the dead end was defined by a fieldstone wall running along the end of the road. A metal sign, peppered with what looked like bullet holes, sat atop a metal pole, with the words *Private property. Keep out.*

As Jacob got closer to the car, he had a clear view of his mother's face, contorted in anger. She was so very angry. The kind of fury that at home would be directed at him in the form of screaming and insults, and might get Mia slapped. "Mom!" he shouted as he got closer. Sometimes she could be distracted and pulled out of a bad mood. Today it was doubtful, but he had to try. "Let's talk about this!"

He was right outside her window, but she didn't even turn her head to acknowledge his presence. Ignoring him, as if he wasn't even there. The ultimate insult. She went back and forth, driving just a few feet in each direction, like a teenager who'd just gotten her learner's permit and wasn't quite sure how it was done. He walked alongside the car as she went, saying, "You might as well stop and talk to me. You're not going anywhere until you tell me where Mia is!"

Too late he remembered that no one gave his mother ultimatums. She managed to get the front wheels aimed back toward the open road, and she gunned it, the car lurching forward. Jacob jumped back as she drove off, and he watched helplessly as she headed straight for Niki's car. "Mom, stop!" he yelled.

CHAPTER FORTY-SEVEN

Niki saw the Audi heading right at her and tried to back up, but she only managed a few feet. She felt her heart pound in her chest and watched as the Audi hurtled her way. The car barreled at her with unnerving speed, while also seeming to move in slow motion. Her mind filled with regret. *I should have followed my instincts and turned around to go home when I had the chance.*

She saw Suzette's fierce expression and braced for an impact that never came. Just before they would have collided, the Audi made a sudden turn, barely missing the front bumper of Fred's car and leaving the edge of the road, the passenger side of the silver car so low that for a moment Niki thought it might flip over. Craning her head, she watched as Suzette lost control of the car, driving completely off the pavement. The car headed down the embankment at an abrupt angle, bouncing and shimmying as it went, hitting the edge of the irrigation equipment and slamming into the water. As the front of the vehicle plunged into the retention pond, nose down, Niki clearly heard Jacob wail, "Mom!" as he began to run toward his mother.

She got out of the car and followed him, the soles of her shoes slapping against the wet pavement. He headed down the small hill and she followed, slowing her pace when he narrowly missed taking a tumble before righting himself. "Mom, Mom, I'm coming!" he screamed, his voice infused with an emotion she hadn't heard before. Niki thought of all the foster kids she'd met, and how even the ones who'd suffered horrible abuse at the hands of their parents seemed to miss them, as if the love from a child to a parent was a given, even when it wasn't reciprocated.

With tentative steps, she half slid her way down to the car, careful not to lose her balance. Ahead of her, Jacob had splashed his way toward the driver's side door and was yanking unsuccessfully on the handle. "Unlock the door, Mom!" he screamed. The car was angled in such a way that the back tires were barely wet, while the front tires and the lower part of the door were completely submerged.

Niki called out, "I don't think the door will open when it's in water like that!"

"It has to open. Her airbag went off, and she doesn't look good. We have to get her out!"

"I'll see if Fred has something in the trunk we can use to break the window." She clambered up to the road, breathless in her need to hurry. When she got to the car, she retrieved the keys and popped open the trunk. Fred's trunk was as neat as the rest of the car, and empty too. She pulled at the trunk lining, and it came up on one side. Peeling it back, she saw a thin board covering most of the storage compartment. Off to the right was a smaller board with a cut-out handle. Frantically she pulled at this one, finding a folded-up jack underneath.

After getting it out, she hurried back to the crash site and made her way down the hill. Jacob walked briskly toward the bank, and she waded into the freezing water to meet him halfway. She grimaced as the cold soaked through her shoes and jeans to her skin. *How is he able to bear standing in this water?* Without saying a word, he took the jack from her outstretched hand and returned to the window.

"Mom," he said. "You need to move back. I'm going to break the window." His mother must have said something that sounded like an objection, because he replied, "There is no place around here to get a tow truck, Mom. We're in the middle of nowhere."

Niki splashed her way back to the shore to call 911.

CHAPTER FORTY-EIGHT

Mia's head felt fuzzy and her body heavy. For a long time, she drifted in and out, aware of the buzz of a vibration and the sound of music. She had no sense of where she was and couldn't manage to open her eyes.

Her arms were pinned to her side, but her head rested on something soft and cushy. She couldn't overcome her sleepiness, so she gave in to it.

She dreamed. It was a troubling nightmare of being chased by monsters. She ran through the house trying to get away from them, but they were everywhere: behind furniture, popping out of closets, hiding around corners. On one go-round, she saw Ma'am sitting at the kitchen table calmly drinking her coffee. She went to ask for her help, but then Ma'am turned into a monster too, her face morphing into something truly horrible, a shiny mask with yellow pointy teeth and dark menacing eyes. Her manicured nails became claws that skewered Mia's arms and shook her so hard her teeth rattled, after which Monster-Ma'am tossed her across the room. She threw her so hard that the back of Mia's head knocked against the wall. It was the force of hitting the wall that woke her up, she thought.

For a few minutes she was confused, not able to make sense of her surroundings.

She opened her eyes and saw only the darkest dark. She was wrapped up in some kind of fabric that held her arms to her sides. She felt a hard edge against her back, but nothing made sense. Was she still in the bad dream? She wiggled and squirmed and was finally able to get her arms free. Feeling around her, she could tell she was in a tight, enclosed space, but she couldn't make sense of it. At the same time, she felt something wet down below and was horrified to realize that she had peed her pants.

Oh, she was going to be in so much trouble for this.

Ma'am hated crying, saying it was for weaklings, so Mia had learned to hold back, no matter what. Even when she was most afraid or sad she'd never shed a tear, but this time she couldn't help herself. She was so scared that the tears came. Above the sound of the music, she heard voices echoing around her, yelling things she couldn't understand. The voices sounded close and far away at the same time, but one of the voices, a man's, sounded upset and angry. Mister had once watched a movie where a woman was buried in a box under-ground by a bad man. The woman in the box almost ran out of air before being saved at the very last minute. Mia thought that this was what had happened to her. It was dark and cold, and she was trapped. It was the only thing that made sense. Was the angry man whose voice she heard the one who'd buried her?

The other voice, a woman's, sounded nicer, but Mia didn't know her. Sometimes Ma'am acted nice and a second later got mean. It would be risky to call out for help, but if she didn't, she might be trapped forever.

"Hello?" Her voice was raspy and weak. Her mouth was dry. She swallowed and tried again. "Help. Please, help." It took all her effort, and for what? Her words were trapped by the space around her.

Would someone find her in time? If they didn't, she would die. Of course, she was going to get punished when they saw she'd peed herself. That was for babies. Mia was way too old to have an accident.

Maybe they wouldn't notice the wet spot.

The thought of dying under the dirt made her chest squeeze so tight she couldn't breathe. Fear pushed out the tears, and she let loose, crying and crying. Her face was wet, and her nose was running, and she was chilly and miserable. Finally, not caring anymore, she let out a wail and then a sob. From there, she couldn't seem to help herself. One sob led to another.

Mia had never felt so hopeless and miserable. She hoped that dying wouldn't hurt too much.

CHAPTER FORTY-NINE

Niki was almost to the shore when she heard a thin cry. She stopped to listen. There it was again. She cocked her head to one side. *Is it coming from the car?* She splashed back through the freezing water, ignoring Jacob, who was arguing with his mother, and instead focusing on the back of the Audi. Someone was definitely crying. Placing both hands on the top of the trunk, she leaned in. "Hello?"

The crying softened to a dull sobbing, loud enough so Niki knew there was a child in the trunk. "Mia, is that you?" No answer, just the sound of more muffled weeping, the breathless sobs of someone crying too hard to talk. *It has to be Mia. Who else could it be?* Niki yelled to Jacob. "Mia's here! She's in the trunk."

"What!" He was at her side in an instant. "Mia, are you in there?"

"Jacob?" The voice was so heartbreakingly small and tentative that for a moment Niki forgot how cold she was.

"Yeah, Mia, it's me, Jacob."

"Jacob, I'm scared."

"I know. It's okay. We're going to get you out of there." He sloshed back to the window and shouted, "Mom, Mia's in the trunk? You've got to be kidding me! You need to open it right now! What? Well, then you need to find it." He glanced back at Niki. "She can't find her key fob." He went back to his mother. "Is it in your bag, Mom? Can you look in the bag?"

While he was dealing with his mother, Niki leaned down and spoke loudly. "Mia, I'm a friend of Jacob's. My name is Niki. Are you hurt?"

There was a slight pause. "Niki from the gas station?"

"Yes, that's me. Niki from the gas station. Are you hurt?"

"I don't think so. But I'm scared. It's so dark. I don't know where I am."

"I know you're scared, honey, but just listen to me. You're inside the trunk of a car. That's why it's dark. If you follow the sound of my voice and feel around on this side, you might find a handle or latch that will open the trunk, and I'll be able to get you out."

"A handle?"

"Yes. Right near here." Niki spoke louder. "Can you follow the sound of my voice and see if you can find it? It will feel like something you can pull on."

"I don't know." Mia's voice was shaky. "I'm sorry, Niki. I'm really sorry, but I don't know where you are."

Niki knocked on the top of the trunk. "How about now?" She heard a knock from inside the trunk in response.

Mia's voice came through. "Over here?"

"Good girl! You're in the right spot. Now feel all over and see if you can find the handle."

"I think I found it." Her voice rose with excitement.

"Good girl! Now pull on it and see—" The trunk lid popped open to reveal a little girl tangled up in a blanket, her hair mussed and face red and blotchy. "Mia? Honey, are you okay?"

Mia blinked in the sunlight. "Are you Niki?"

"Yes, I am. I'm Jacob's friend. Come on out and I'll take you to my car where it's warm. Okay?" Mia nodded, and Niki scooped her up into her arms and carried her from the car.

CHAPTER FIFTY

W hen Niki made it back to Fred's car, she set Mia in the front seat, covered her with the blanket, and started up the engine to get the heater going. Then she turned to the wide-eyed child and said, "How are you feeling, Mia? Does anything hurt?"

Mia shook her head. She was oddly quiet, given the circumstances. In shock, maybe? She tried again. "That had to be scary being locked in the trunk."

"I was afraid." Mia's lower lip trembled.

"Well, you're safe now." Niki spoke soothingly. "I'm going to be on the phone calling for help. Will you be okay for a minute or two?"

"Yes." She craned her head to look back at the Audi still sitting in the pond. "Is Jacob going to come here?"

"Probably in a few minutes. We'll just wait for him."

Niki was relieved when her call went through, but it took a lot of explaining to make the operator understand that not only had there been a car accident, but she was also reporting a crime. "A kidnapping?" the operator said. "Was the child reported as abducted?"

"No." Niki looked at Mia's sweet, dazed expression. "It's a long story. I'd be happy to tell the police when they get here. The main thing is we'll need an ambulance and the police and a tow truck."

Niki stayed on the line while the operator coordinated the response. She smiled down at Mia, who was watching her with rapt attention. "You okay?"

Mia nodded. "Jacob says you're pretty."

"That's nice of him."

"And he says you have hair and eyes the color of mine."

"That's true."

Mia tilted her head and gave Niki an appraising look. "Sometimes Jacob buys me things from the gas station."

"I know. Hostess CupCakes, right?" Slowly, Mia's mouth stretched into a smile, warming Niki's heart. She couldn't help but notice that despite her bedraggled appearance and terrible haircut, Mia really was a beautiful little girl. *Oh, sweetheart, how could you be lost for so long and have no one looking for you?*

As if Jacob had heard them talking about him, the back door of the car opened and he jumped inside, setting the jack next to him on the seat. "Oh man, I'm cold. I had to get out of the water. I couldn't stand it any longer." The words came out through a chattering of teeth. "She won't let me break the window. She's yelling that we need to call 911."

"Already done," Niki said, showing him the phone. The car was really warm now, the blowing air dry and hot. She angled the vents to better reach the back seat.

Mia turned to look at Jacob. "Is Ma'am mad at me?"

Shivering, Jacob said, "Mia, you're not in trouble. She is. Don't worry about it."

Mia pushed the blanket over the seat. "You can have this, Jacob. I'm warm now."

"You sure?"

"I'm sure.

He pulled it toward him, accepting it gratefully. "Thanks, squirt."

Fifteen minutes later, just as the operator had predicted, they saw the revolving red lights of emergency vehicles approaching. Niki got out of the car to greet them. "I'm the one who called 911," she said to the first deputy to get out of the car. She felt like she was living someone else's life, someone who took charge and knew what to do. Adulting at its most extreme. The deputies introduced themselves, and then another sheriff's office car arrived, followed by an ambulance and a tow truck.

The deputies had so many questions, all of which she answered first from standing alongside Fred's car and later in the back of the ambulance. She handed her car keys to a deputy sheriff who promised the car would be moved to the parking lot of the sheriff's office.

Shortly after the emergency responders arrived, she, Mia, and Jacob were transported by a deputy sheriff to a medical clinic to be examined for exposure to the cold. The problem of Jacob's mother being trapped in the car in the pond was left for others to solve.

Once they arrived at the medical clinic, Mia clung to Jacob until he said, "It's okay, Mia. These are nice people. They want to help us." Still she hesitated, gesturing for Jacob to lean over so she could whisper something in his ear. He answered aloud, "You can tell them anything you want. Answer all their questions. You won't get into any trouble. I promise. No one is going to get mad. I promise you, Mia. You know I wouldn't lie to you, right?"

Reluctantly, she allowed one of the nurses to take her hand and lead her away, although she did look back at Jacob and Niki as she was led down the hall. After that, Jacob and Niki were separated and taken to their own examining rooms. After the doctor had checked her out, saying she was fine, a nurse brought Niki gray sweatpants and white socks to replace her wet clothing, and Niki gratefully pulled them on.

In the lull after the examination, Niki called Sharon, who answered, "Niki! Thank God! Why didn't you answer your messages?" Her voice rang with real concern.

Niki said, "I'm sorry, but so much has happened. I guess I wasn't paying attention." She filled Sharon in, and then Sharon told her what had happened on her end.

"I've been talking to Franny Benson, and she called the police. They came out to the house and questioned me, but I didn't have much to tell them."

"They need to call the Ash County Sheriff's Office," Niki said. "They're the ones who responded to the 911 call. They're handling things here."

"Ash County Sheriff's Office," Sharon repeated, and Niki knew she was writing it down. "Where are you right now?"

"I'm at the Friendly Care Walk-In Clinic on Main Street," Niki said, looking around. She was in the tiniest of rooms, the size of a health room in an elementary school. A hand sanitizer dispenser was positioned next to a sink and opposite a small desk with a computer. She was sitting on the examination table, even though there was an upholstered chair nearby. She was clearly in a room intended for children because the mural on one wall featured bears in tutus. "But I don't think I'll be here much longer. The deputy said we're going to be driven back to the sheriff's office for more questioning."

"Listen, Niki. I talked to Amy, and she said not to tell them anything until you have a lawyer present. Even though you weren't involved in abducting the little girl, it's best to cover your bases. Ask for an attorney."

"I think it's too late for that. I already answered all kinds of questions."

Sharon sighed. "Oh, Niki. I wish you'd called me first."

"I wish that too," Niki answered. Really, what she wished for was that Sharon could be at her side right now. At that moment there was nothing she wanted more. Suddenly, she was flooded with emotion. She'd been strong in dealing with law enforcement and the medical team, but now the feelings bottled up inside her spilled forward: gratitude for Sharon's caring ways, relief at having found Mia in the trunk, worry for how things would go from here. *How could anyone think I might be involved?*

"It is what it is," Sharon said matter-of-factly. "We can't go back and undo it."

"I'm so sorry I didn't call you," Niki said, her voice emotional. "What if Jacob's mom says I knew about this or something? She could say anything. I could be in big trouble."

"Oh, honey, let's look on the bright side. You found the little girl. You're a hero! And we contacted Franny before any of this happened, so she'll vouch for you and so will I. Amy is just doing what she always does—making sure there are no loopholes. We'll get through this."

We'll get through this. That line tugged at Niki's heart. She wasn't alone anymore. "Thanks, Sharon."

CHAPTER FIFTY-ONE

Everyone was so nice to Mia that she found it confusing. At the clinic the nurse and doctor were so kind, saying she was a brave girl. The nurse said Mia could call her Jenny. She was a smiling woman with dark curly hair pulled up into a ponytail. She gave Mia clean pants that were too long. After Mia put them on, Jenny said, "I'm sorry, Mia, but we don't have any your size. I think I can make these work, though." She knelt down on the floor and rolled up the bottoms until they were just the right length. Jenny looked up and smiled. "Better?" Her smile was so friendly that Mia felt like crying for some reason. All she could do was nod. Then Jenny put Mia's wet underwear and jeans in a plastic bag and set them aside. She didn't even say anything about Mia peeing in her pants.

The doctor, a tall man with glasses, looked inside her mouth and ears, and did some other tests to check to see if her heart was healthy and if her lungs were doing a good job of breathing. He measured how tall she was and had her stand on a scale to see how much she weighed. None of it hurt at all. Then he asked how old she was, and when she said she didn't know because she didn't know when her birthday was, he and Jenny looked at each other and got strangely quiet. Mia thought she had messed up, but he just said, "However old you are, I think you're just perfect." He gave her a big smile and then asked if he could shake her hand, because she was his favorite patient so far this month. When he finished, Jenny said that Mia was in wonderful health and was the best-behaved little girl she'd ever seen.

Then a nice lady deputy came and said she wanted to talk to Mia, so they went to a room in back. One of the nurses came in and brought Mia a sandwich and a juice box, and the nice deputy, whose name was Amanda, sat with her. Mia could hear sounds outside the room—phones ringing and doors opening and closing—but Amanda didn't seem to notice. She was in her uniform, but she must have had the day off, because she didn't work at all, just watched Mia eat, and then, when she was done, she got out some coloring paper and crayons and asked if Mia wanted to draw some pictures.

Mia wasn't used to drawing pictures, but Amanda was so nice that she didn't want to make her mad, so she picked up a crayon and began to draw some trees. Amanda told her she could use more than one crayon—in fact, she could use any colors she wanted and could even switch off whenever she felt like it. Mia was glad she told her this, because she hadn't been sure of the rules.

Amanda started coloring too, and then she asked some questions in a really nice way. Mia tried hard to think of the right way to answer. She knew that if she said the wrong thing Amanda might get mad, so she was careful.

Amanda said, "Mia is such a lovely name. What's your last name?"

Mia shrugged. She knew that Jacob's last name was Fleming and so was Ma'am's and Mister's. She saw it on the envelopes that came in the mail. Once she'd thought her last name might be Fleming too, but Jacob had told her that wasn't true. She had a last name, he said. They just didn't know what it was.

"You don't know what it is, or you don't want to tell me?"

Mia thought carefully. Jacob had told her it was safe to answer all questions here, and Amanda did seem nice. "I don't know."

"That's okay. Sometimes we don't know things."

Mia let out a sigh of relief. Jacob was right. Amanda was not going to get mad at her. "I know Jacob's last name. It's Fleming."

"Jacob. Is he the boy who came in with you?"

Mia nodded. "Jacob is nice to me."

"Do you and Jacob live in the same house? With his mom and dad?"

"Yes."

"Does anyone else live in the house?"

"No."

Without looking up from her paper, Amanda said, "So, Mia, I think I'm going to draw a picture of the house where I live. Do you want to draw a picture of your house?"

Mia glanced her way, trying to assess the situation. She wasn't sure how to answer. It was clear Amanda wanted Mia to say yes. The problem was that Mia couldn't draw the house because she didn't really know what Jacob's house looked like from the outside. She had only seen the front from the car when they had gone to the state fair, and that had been a long time ago and she didn't really remember. She'd gone out the back door into the yard several times, but even then she hadn't stopped to look at the house because she was too busy noticing the trees and the sky and the way Griswold jumped around in the grass. *Griswold.* She had been gone a long time. He was going to miss her and wonder where she was. Thinking about this made her sad. Mia had already cried once today, and she was not going to do it again, so she blinked back tears and looked away from Amanda.

Amanda said, "It's okay. You don't have to draw your house. It was just an idea."

Mia nodded. "Okay."

"What would you like to draw?"

"Can I draw Griswold?"

"Sure. What's a Griswold?"

Mia found herself smiling. "Griswold is a dog. Jacob says he loves me best."

"Of course you can draw Griswold. I would love to see what he looks like."

Mia selected a brown crayon to match Griswold's fur.

They colored for a long time. Amanda loved her picture of Griswold, and she also loved the one Mia drew of her room in the basement. She wanted to hear all about the bookcase and how Mia's room was a special secret. Then Mia started to feel better about telling Amanda things, so she drew a picture of Ma'am and Mister and Jacob together. Ma'am's hair color was not quite the right color of red, but the rest of it was very good. She even did Jacob's shaggy hair. "Where are you in this picture?" Amanda asked.

"I'm not in the picture. It was a Tuesday, so I was scrubbing the shower stall. I always get it really clean," she said proudly.

"I see. Did you have different chores every day?"

Mia nodded. "And sometimes I did extra so Ma'am would be happy."

Amanda asked a lot of questions about Mia's chores. Mia told her about the time they went to the state fair and that sometimes she got to go outside in the backyard, but not that much because someone could see her and they'd send her away, which would be very scary. She leaned across the table and whispered, "Sometimes Ma'am gets really mad, so please don't tell her I was talking about things."

"I won't tell her." Amanda smiled. "What does Ma'am do when she gets mad?"

"Sometimes she doesn't do anything." The times she did nothing were terrible because Ma'am just got a look on her face that made Mia shudder. The look told Mia that something inside of Ma'am was building up to something awful, and she never knew what it was or when it was coming out. The times Ma'am reacted right away were terrifying but easier. "Sometimes she hits and yells and pushes. Sometimes she just yells. One time she threw plates at Mister and they broke into lots of pieces and made a big mess and all of us had to clean it up."

"That sounds frightening," Amanda said. "So you really haven't left the house in a long time, then?"

"Today I did." Mia looked around. "Do you know when I can go home? I have to feed Griswold." She didn't say how much she missed him. That was a private thing.

Instead of answering her question, Amanda said, "It's hard sometimes to meet new people and go new places, but we're having a nice time right now, aren't we?" When Mia nodded, she added, "So sometimes change is a good thing. Try not to be afraid of change, Mia, okay? There are lots of people who want to help you."

Mia said, "Okay," even though Amanda wasn't making sense. Mia didn't know lots of people, so who were these people, and how could they want to help her? And help her do what? It was confusing and overwhelming being out of the house, and she didn't think she liked change. But she was a good girl, and if Amanda told her not to be afraid, she would try her best.

They colored, and then Amanda tried to get Mia to play dolls with her, but Mia didn't know the rules of dolls, so it was hard to know what to do. When another lady knocked on the door, Amanda excused herself and got up to talk to her. They spoke so quietly that Mia couldn't hear what they said. When Amanda came back to the table, she said, "Mia, this lady is a social worker. She works with kids when they have problems. Her name is Franny Benson."

Franny Benson crouched down so that she could look right in Mia's eyes. "Hi, Mia. It's nice to meet you."

Mia noticed her long gray hair pulled up on the sides and her dark eyes fringed with long lashes. Franny Benson had crinkles around her eyes and a big smile. Her teeth were slightly crooked, and her earrings were tiny silver monkeys that looked like they were hanging by one arm off her earlobes. She looked like a television grandma. On the TV shows Mia watched, grandmothers were always nice. "Hi," she said shyly.

Franny Benson took a seat at the table. "You can call me Franny if you want." She looked at Mia's pictures and thought they were so good. "You did a wonderful job," she said, making Mia beam with pride. She asked Mia to identify the people in the picture and also asked some of the same questions Amanda had asked, but it was easier for Mia to talk this time. Franny didn't seem like she was trying to get Mia to say things. It seemed like she asked because she cared. When Mia was done, Franny said, "I'll tell you what, Mia. Amanda has to go back to work, and I bet you're tired of being here too."

Mia nodded.

Franny continued. "I'll be the one taking care of you now, and I'd like to take you somewhere where you will be safe. We'll be driving in my car. I have snacks in my car, and we can listen to music. You can ask me any questions you want, and I promise I'll tell you the truth. How does that sound?"

"Why can't I go home?"

"The people you were living with—the Flemings—they aren't going to be there, and you can't stay alone." Franny shook her head sadly. "I know this is difficult for you, but it can't be helped. Kids can't stay by themselves. The law says you have to be with a grown-up."

"I stay alone lots of times."

"I know, but you really weren't supposed to be alone." She gave Mia a small smile. "They have a law that says so. It's to make sure kids are safe."

"Jacob could stay with me."

"Oh, honey, Jacob's not a grown-up just yet, and he won't be there either."

"But where will he be?" Her voice came out louder than she'd intended. Everything was changing so fast.

"I don't know. Someone else is going to find a safe place for him to be while we get this all sorted out."

Mia felt wet tears falling down her cheeks. She couldn't hold them back, but at least she wasn't making any noise. "I don't want to go somewhere else."

"I know. It's not easy, is it?" Franny got out her phone. "Just give me a minute, Mia. I need to make a phone call. I think I know someone who can help." She got up and went out into the hallway to talk.

While she was gone, Amanda gave Mia a Kleenex. "Everything's going to be fine, Mia. You'll see."

When Franny came back into the room, she placed the phone on the table in front of Mia. "There's someone who'd like to talk to you, Mia."

"Mia?" It was Jacob's voice coming out of the phone.

"Jacob!"

"Hey, squirt! I have to go meet with my uncle, so I'm not going to be home for a while. Franny Benson is a real nice lady, and you need to go with her right now. She said you can stop for something to eat, and you can even get Sprite if you want."

She looked up to see both Amanda and Franny studying her with kindly expressions. "But what about Griswold? Someone has to feed him."

"Niki has my house key, and she's going to take care of Griswold while I'm gone, so you don't need to worry about him."

"But, Jacob"—here she stopped due to a catch in her voice —"what about your mom and dad?"

"They want you to go with Franny too," he said. "They're not going to be going home for a long time." There was a pause, and then he said, "Everything is going to be okay, Mia. Just go with Franny. Have I ever lied to you before?"

"No."

"You're going to be fine, Mia. You'll see. It's all going to work out."

"Okay. If you say so." After Jacob said goodbye and Mia said goodbye back to him, she turned to Franny and said, "I'm ready to go now."

CHAPTER FIFTY-TWO

By the time Uncle Cal arrived, Jacob had unburdened his soul to the deputies. Off the record and voluntarily, of course, because he was still a minor. It felt so good to finally tell the story, his way. And when the social worker, Franny Benson, called him right after that, he readily agreed to talk to Mia and reassure her that it was fine to go with Franny in her car. After their conversation was over, he was sad to realize that he might never see Mia again.

Three hours later, he and Uncle Cal were at a different location, this time the police station near his own house, to answer even more questions. His father met them in the hallway, along with an attorney. Jacob had never been so happy to see someone in his entire life. He gave his dad a big hug. When they pulled apart, his dad said, "You have nothing to worry about, Jacob. I'll take care of everything." Then he turned to Uncle Cal and shook his hand. "I can't tell you how grateful I am that you're doing this for us. Thanks, Cal."

"Of course," Uncle Cal said. "That's what family's for."

Since his grandfather died, they hadn't visited with his grandmother or uncle, and they rarely even spoke to them on the phone. His mom had said this was because they'd been critical of Jacob, making fun of his weight and mocking his poor grades. "No one talks about my son that way!" she'd said indignantly. Now Jacob was pretty sure none of it was true. Cal seemed like a good guy. And he definitely understood how Suzette's mind worked.

Instead of judging Jacob for not divulging Mia's imprisonment sooner, Cal had been sympathetic. "Suzette always did have a way of boxing a person in. Don't beat yourself up, Jacob. You were a kid yourself."

Now at the police station, he and Uncle Cal sat outside on a bench while his dad and the attorney spoke to the police. They had a long time to talk. Uncle Cal said, "Your dad told me on the phone that both he and your mom will probably be charged and go to prison. I hope that's not the case, but if it is, I want you to know you're not alone. You can come and live with me if you want, or if you want to finish out your high school year, your grandma has offered to come down and stay with you until then. She can either move into your house or rent an apartment for the two of you for a few months." He gave Jacob's arm a pat. "We'll get it worked out."

After two hours, an officer came to where they were sitting and asked them to follow him into the room where his father had been taken for questioning. When Cal and Jacob took a seat at the table, Jacob's dad said, "The detectives have some questions for you, son, and I want you to answer them as truthfully as you can."

Jacob said, "Sure, Dad." His eyes shifted from the two detectives to his father and then to the attorney. Everyone seemed so relaxed. Maybe his dad wasn't in trouble after all.

Almost as if he'd heard his thoughts, his dad said, "We've been able to reach an agreement, and part of that agreement is that you are not being charged for any crimes, so you don't need to worry about that, okay? I've got it all worked out."

So that meant his dad had taken responsibility for everything. Jacob felt his eyes cloud up, and he quickly blinked back tears. He nodded to show he understood.

The detectives' questions had to do with how Mia had been

found in the first place. Jacob described the drive down from his grandmother's house into Wisconsin. Detail after detail poured out as they asked more and more questions. Jacob answered as best he could, trying to keep it to just the facts, the way they kept reminding him to do.

When all was said and done, the older detective thanked Jacob for his cooperation and said he was free to go home with his uncle. "Someone from social services will be in touch," he said. "Normally there would be a process to make sure that you, as a minor, would have a relative designated to stay with you, but since you'll be eighteen in two weeks, my guess is that an informal agreement will be sufficient."

Uncle Cal spoke up. "I promise you that either his grandmother or I will be with Jacob for the rest of the school year. Or longer, if that's what he wants."

"That's a great comfort to me," his dad said. "Thank you, Cal."

"But what about Mia?" Jacob asked.

The detective met his gaze. "Mia is in good hands. She's being well cared for by social services, and we're going to do everything we can to see if she has any relatives. If we can't find any family members—"

"But she does have family!" Jacob said. "Grandparents and an uncle. I can tell you their names."

CHAPTER FIFTY-THREE

The next day, Amy let herself into the house and walked into the kitchen while Niki and Sharon were still eating breakfast. "Amy!" Sharon said, getting up to greet her. "Why didn't you tell me you were coming home? We would have picked you up from the airport."

Amy held up a hand. "Don't even start with me," she said. "Both of you are on my list."

"What list?" Niki asked. Fred had given her the day off, so she was still in pajama bottoms and a T-shirt, a stark contrast to Amy's wool coat and dress pants.

"Would you like some coffee?" Sharon got up to get a mug out of the cabinet.

Amy ignored both questions. "I thought that if the two of you were living together it would be a good thing." She pointed at her mother. "I thought you'd like having some company in the house." Turning, she gestured to Niki. "And I thought *you* could benefit from living with an older person who would be a steadying influence. Did I ever dream that the two of you would spur each other on and get into legal trouble? No, I did not. And yes, I'll take that coffee." She took off her coat and slung it over the back of a chair, then sat down opposite Niki. "With a splash of cream, please."

Sharon got the mug of coffee ready and put it in front of Amy. "Having Niki here has been a godsend, both for me and for a little girl named Mia, who is now freed from years of servitude. Don't be mad. You did a good thing, Amy, putting us together." She reached around from behind and gave her a hug, resting her cheek on her daughter's head.

Niki watched them, her smile broadening. Sharon had called her a godsend, and clearly she meant it. Even Sarge seemed to be excited to have her around, coming upstairs every evening and meowing at her closed door to be let in for a visit. For once she was in someone else's house and didn't feel like an outsider.

Yesterday Sharon had driven to Harlow with the social worker, Franny Benson, to pick Niki up from the sheriff's office. Niki had been so happy to see her that without thinking she'd rushed into her arms, and Sharon had hugged her in return. The deputies had taken Sharon's statement, and Franny's too, and then Franny had left the sheriff's office to see to Mia. Before Sharon's arrival, the deputies had seemed skeptical of Niki's story. One of them, a husky man with a silver-gray buzz cut, had asked, more than once, "So you're saying that before today, you had no knowledge that this little girl had been kidnapped and was being held illegally in your neighbor's house?" And then he insinuated that since she and Jacob were good friends, she had to have been involved, or at least had some knowledge that a crime had been committed. She told him that she barely knew Jacob, but she could tell he didn't quite believe that either. He said, "So you took the day off of work, borrowed a car from your employer, and drove all this way to help out someone you barely know?" Put that way, it did sound unlikely. The whole while she was being questioned Niki was afraid she was going to be arrested, but that ended once the two older women arrived.

After Franny and Sharon gave their statements, Sharon took it a step further, saying, "You can't imagine how proud I am of Niki. Both of us were suspicious that something was going on at the Flemings' house, but she was the one who wouldn't let it go. I'm sure many people would have just looked the other way, but not my Niki. Who knows what would have happened to that little girl if not for her? I don't know if your department gives out awards to citizens, but if you do, she definitely qualifies."

Not my Niki.

Maybe she imagined the shift in the deputy's attitude toward her, but she didn't think so. Before Sharon arrived, they appeared to consider Niki a possible suspect; by the time Sharon was done talking her up, Niki was a hero. Of course, it helped that both Jacob and his father had absolved her of any responsibility regarding Mia, but she didn't know about that until much later.

They'd driven home then in Fred's car, Sharon at the wheel, Niki in the passenger seat. Along the way, Niki had called Fred, who said not to rush, that he'd get a ride home from his brother. After that she'd called Amy, who seemed floored at the news of everything that had transpired. She hadn't said much. That was yesterday. Today Amy had found her voice.

She said, "You're not getting off that easy, Mom. You're the adult here. I hold you responsible." Her tone was gruff, but her expression had softened, and she leaned back into her mother's embrace.

Sharon gave her a final pat and then took her place at the table. "Did you come all this way to yell at me?"

"No, I came because you said the local authorities asked you to give a statement downtown this afternoon. I figured you could use an attorney."

Niki said, "They said it's just a formality. That it would be the same questions we answered yesterday."

"You still should have an attorney present."

Sharon took a sip of her coffee. "Criminal law isn't really your area of expertise, though."

"You're right, but they don't know that. Besides, I know enough to keep the two of you from getting into even more trouble."

"That's one advantage of having a daughter who's an attorney," Sharon said. Amy's demeanor softened then, and they settled into an easy back-and-forth, talking about Amy's flight from Boston and how long she could stay. Just one night, as it turned out, much to Sharon's disappointment. "You can't stay even a little longer? Another day, maybe?"

"Twenty minutes ago you didn't know I'd be here at all. Now you're complaining that I'm not staying longer?"

Niki sat back and took in their back-and-forth banter. At first glance they were a study in contrasts, the older lady with her sensible shoes versus the uptown attorney. Their personalities were just as different, and yet the connection and love between them was undeniable.

They were talking about the weather now, how it was unseasonably warm for this time of year. Sharon said she hoped that all the melting wouldn't lead to flooding. Through all of their talk, Niki found her mind wandering to the events of the day before. When there was a pause in the discussion, she blurted out, "How do you become a social worker?"

Sharon lowered her coffee mug and smiled. Through the window behind her, Niki noticed a little brown bird land on the bird feeder.

Amy said, "You start by getting a degree in social work. Are you thinking that's something you'd like to do?"

"Yes. Or at least I know that I want to do some kind of work with foster kids." To fill the silence, she said, "I think I'd be good at it."

Sharon spoke up. "I think you'd be great with foster kids."

"I'd have to agree with that," Amy said.

The idea of taking university classes was so foreign to Niki it was almost unfathomable, and yet the idea filled her with such excitement and hope. "How long does it take to get a degree like that?"

Amy said, "A bachelor's degree is a four-year degree, but it's not unusual for it to take a little longer. Another semester or two sometimes."

"Oh. Four years." At minimum, and with another year, five. Her heart sank. So long to have to go to classes and write papers and study. Even longer to actually get to the point of working as a social worker, so she could make a difference and help kids like Mia. "I'll be twenty-two or twenty-three by then," she said. So much time would have passed between now and then. How would she support herself and pay for tuition for four or five years? Could someone like her even get a student loan? She didn't know anyone who ever had.

Sharon laughed. "You'll be that age no matter what you do. Wouldn't you rather be a twenty-three-year-old social worker than still be working at a job you don't find fulfilling?"

"Sure. It's just . . . a lot." And if she had to go to school part time, it would take even longer. She'd be ancient by the time she finished.

"A lot?" Amy asked, her voice cutting right through her hesitation. "A lot of what?"

"A lot of time. A lot of money," she said dispiritedly. Without intending it, her shoulders slumped in defeat, and she turned her attention to the nearly empty juice glass in front of her. She raised it to her lips and took the last sip.

"Are you thinking it sounds overwhelming?" Sharon asked. "Almost undoable?"

Niki nodded, wondering at how Sharon often seemed to know what was on her mind.

"It doesn't have to be. You have us to help guide you through it." She turned to Amy. "Right?"

"Of course," Amy said. "I've made the offer before, and it still stands. I'll pay your tuition as long as you get good grades. Not a loan. A gift. Just because I have the money and you deserve it."

"If you don't mind attending the state university, you can keep living here and commute every day," Sharon said. "I like having you around."

Niki didn't have a name for whatever it was she was feeling at that moment. She nodded, her eyes brimming with tears. Amy reached over and gave her forearm a gentle squeeze. "You're not alone, Niki. We'll help you every step of the way."

"There's no turning back. You're stuck with us now," Sharon added cheerfully. "And we would be honored to help."

For the first time since her mom died, Niki felt like she was part of a family. She looked from Sharon to Amy, her throat choking with happiness, and could only manage to speak two words. "Thank you."

CHAPTER FIFTY-FOUR

A few months after getting confirmation of Morgan's death, the Durans got another visit from Detective Moore. Just like before, Wendy ushered him into the living room, where he sat opposite her and Edwin. "Yes?" she prompted. "You have something to tell us?" The anticipation was something palpable, a tremor under her skin.

"Yes, I do. Actually, I have two things to tell you. The first is that Morgan's boyfriend, Keith, is dead."

"How?" Wendy's voice was almost a whisper. "How did it happen?"

"An altercation in a bar last week," Detective Moore said. "After he was asked to leave a bar, Keith became belligerent and pulled out a gun. The owner of the business happened to keep a pistol behind the bar. He shot him in self-defense, and Keith died at the scene."

She said, "I see."

"Keith's full name was Keith William Caswell."

Edwin asked, "How did they link him to Morgan?"

"Mr. Caswell had an old department store credit card that belonged to Morgan in his wallet. One of the detectives did some legwork and contacted our department. They also searched for Keith's next of kin and discovered his mother is dead and his father is in prison."

Sounds about right. Wendy needed a moment to let the information sink in, and then another thought occurred to her. "But what about the baby?"

"That's the second thing I came to tell you," Detective Moore said. "Unrelated to Mr. Caswell's death, there was another development. We've found your granddaughter."

We've found your granddaughter. The words took Wendy's breath away.

Detective Moore explained that the police didn't actually *find* her as much as she was presented to them, but the end result was the same. They had a granddaughter, a little girl named Mia. Edwin had a million questions, but Wendy only had one. "When can we see her?"

They would have gotten in their car and gone for her that day, but there were legalities to take care of—DNA confirmation and other paperwork—but Detective Moore promised it would be fast-tracked because this was an extreme case.

Wendy counted down the days until she could hold that little girl in her arms.

The first time Edwin and Wendy met Mia, they weren't sure what to expect. The story of her last three years was incredible and horrific. How did a child deal with that kind of trauma? By that point, she'd been in a temporary foster placement, and the social worker had suggested they visit at least once or twice before they took her home. Her caution had made Wendy think that maybe Mia wouldn't be receptive to them, but when they went into the house, the foster mom took them to where Mia was watching a Disney movie with two other children, little girls about her age. After the foster mom introduced them, Wendy crouched down to make contact, and she was surprised when Mia immediately asked, "Have you come to take me home?" She had bright eyes, chestnut-colored hair, and looked so much like

Morgan when she was a little girl that Wendy wanted both to rejoice and cry.

They didn't take Mia home that day, but they did a few days later. Wendy couldn't believe that all of Mia's worldly possessions fit into one small plastic grocery bag. That was soon rectified after they went shopping for new clothes and toys. She soon found out that Mia was easily pleased, but also afraid of making them angry. If Wendy or Edwin went in to give her a hug, Mia would flinch as if expecting to get hit. It was heartbreaking.

The social worker told them that there might be a honeymoon period, followed by a period of acting out. "Mia has gone through a tremendous trauma," she said. "It's like she's had poison poured into her for three years, and it has to come out in order for her to heal. Unfortunately, it will come out in your direction."

Mia experienced nightmares of being trapped, and she also had crying fits and was unable to explain why she was so upset, but so far she hadn't done or said anything Wendy found to be too extreme. For the most part, she was a happy kid. She was seeing a therapist, a kind woman named Michelle, who was going to help them navigate whatever came next.

One child couldn't replace another, but Wendy found that having Mia softened the raw grief of losing Morgan. Mia had quickly taken to her uncle, Dylan, equating him with Jacob, but they hadn't introduced her to any of the other relatives yet, wanting her to adjust gradually. They also decided to have her homeschool for the time being. Wendy took a leave of absence from work and didn't miss it at all.

Mia never talked about the abuse she'd suffered at the Flemings' house, but she spoke in general terms of how nice Jacob had been to her and how much Griswold had loved her. "He gave me kisses every day," she said.

Wendy was concerned that Mia was repressing the bad memories, but Michelle said not to worry about it. "Give her time. She'll let you know when she wants to talk."

When Jacob had called on their landline five months after they'd brought Mia home, Wendy had been startled to hear from him. Then she remembered that their number could be found in an online search. She got the impression Jacob had expected her to tell him off or hang up. He stammered as he explained who he was, and he apologized for bothering her, going on for so long that she finally asked, "Can you please tell me why you're calling?" She said it politely, of course, but she wasn't about to hand the phone over to Mia. When he explained what he had in mind, Wendy stalled, saying she wanted to discuss it with Mia's therapist first and would get back to him. She and Edwin were in the therapist's office when Michelle said, "Mia, I'm wondering what you would think about seeing Jacob again. How would you feel about that?"

Mia perked up in her seat, her gaze turned toward the door. "Is Jacob here?" Her voice was bright with excitement.

"No," Michelle said, keeping her tone neutral. "But he would like to see you sometime in the next few weeks. It's up to you, though." They discussed Jacob coming to the house with his uncle, just for a short visit. "Your grandparents would be with you the whole time, and you can end the visit anytime you want. Everything is staying the same. It would be just a short visit. You wouldn't be going anywhere with Jacob."

To Wendy's surprise, Mia was overjoyed at the thought of seeing him again. The therapist had told them privately that it might provide some closure, but that they should stay with her every second and cut the visit short if she found it too distressing.

Now the day for the visit had arrived, and so far, Mia seemed excited to see Jacob again. She made her bed first thing and arranged her stuffed animals neatly on her dresser. "Wait until Jacob sees my room!" she exclaimed. "Grandma, can I show him the whole house?"

"Of course," Wendy said. "Whatever you want." She'd talked to Jacob a few more times by then, and she felt better about the visit. Jacob seemed sincerely concerned about Mia and wanted to see for himself how she was doing. He also wanted permission to give Mia a gift. Of course, Wendy said yes.

So much had led up to this day. Wendy hoped her instincts were correct. She prayed they were correct. Her little granddaughter had been through enough.

CHAPTER FIFTY-FIVE

They arrived right on time, thanks to Uncle Cal's meticulous planning. Jacob had let his uncle drive, nervous about Mia's reaction upon seeing him again. Her grandmother had said that Mia was excited at the prospect of his visit, but a nagging thought troubled him. Even though he and Mia had spent three years together and had been as close as any two kids could be, the dynamics had been wrong. She wasn't a sibling or a guest or even a foster child. Mia had been a prisoner, and now, having been reunited with her family, she had to see the difference between a loving family and a place to stay. A place where she was treated like a servant and trapped in a hidden room in the basement. So much had been stolen from her, and he worried that seeing him might trigger bad memories or feelings of anger. He wouldn't blame her, and maybe, if she lashed out at him, he'd even deserve it. Still, he worried.

His therapist had pointed out that he had been a victim too, something that alleviated his guilt somewhat. Moving to Minnesota and changing schools had helped as well. Instead of being LEGO Head, he was the new kid in a high school that was intrigued by new kids. A fresh start. He'd made two friends and had plans to attend the university in the Twin Cities next year. His grandmother and uncle were good to him, so loving that at first it made him suspicious. Jacob found he had trouble letting his guard down. He hadn't realized how well his mother had trained him over the years until he tried to shake off everything she'd imprinted on him. His grandmother had apologized for all Jacob had gone through. "Your mother was selfish from little on. I used to wonder if it was my fault, but I raised Cal exactly the same way and he turned out fine." She'd shrugged, sadness in her eyes. "I'm sorry I wasn't there for you, Jacob. I tried many times, but she shut me out."

Jacob had visited his father in prison twice so far, but he hadn't had the nerve to visit his mother just yet. She was furious at him, that much he could count on. On the advice of his therapist, he wrote her a long letter, but she never wrote back, even though he'd included a sheet of paper and a self-addressed envelope. No one could say he hadn't tried. He'd made the effort. Now it was on her.

They pulled up to the curb in front of the Duran residence. It was a cheery-looking older home, a two-story bungalow with a big porch and red and yellow tulips on either side of the stairs leading to the front door. A recent rain had freshened the lawn, bringing out the green in the grass. Uncle Cal said, "This is it." He turned off the engine and gave Jacob a smile. "It's going to be fine, Jacob. You don't need to worry."

"I know." He tried to sound confident.

When Mia's grandmother answered the door, Jacob said, "Mrs. Duran? I'm Jacob, and this is my uncle, Cal."

"Call me Wendy." She opened the screen door, beckoning them inside. They hadn't even passed the threshold when Mia came bounding down the stairs. "Jacob!" she called out joyfully, and then she came to a stop when she saw that he held a leash with Griswold at the other end, straining to reach her. She dropped to her knees and held out her arms. "Griswold!" Jacob let go of the leash, and Griswold jumped into Mia's arms, licking her face and whining happily. If a dog could smile, Griswold was doing just that, matching the smile on Mia's face.

Jacob had seen a hundred online videos of dogs reunited with their owners, but he'd never seen anything that matched the joy between Mia and Griswold.

Jacob knelt down next to her. "Hey, squirt, what do you think of your gift?"

"My gift?" She had her arms wrapped around Griswold, but her little face peered around him to look at Jacob, who just pointed at the dog. She squealed. "Griswold is my gift? I get to keep him?"

"Yes, he's yours now. I'm going off to college next fall, so I won't be around. He needs someone to take care of him."

Mia looked up at her grandparents. "Can I keep him, Grandma and Grandpa? He's a very good dog. He won't be any trouble at all."

Edwin said, "Of course you can keep him, Mia. Jacob checked with us ahead of time. We wanted it to be a surprise."

Cal and Jacob stayed for about two hours. Mia gave them a tour of the house, claiming everything as her own. "This is my kitchen, and my backyard, and my laundry room . . ." Griswold stayed right by her heels the entire time, bounding along next to her as if not wanting her out of his sight for even an instant.

Wendy served snacks, and they made small talk in the living room. Jacob told Mia about his new school, and she chattered away about her room and going shopping with her grandmother.

Later, when they were out in the yard watching Mia throw a tennis ball to Griswold, Jacob said to Wendy, "I appreciate you letting me see her again. She looks great. So happy."

"Mia wanted to see you too. I think it was important to her." Wendy exhaled. "I don't know if this is something we'll do again, though." She waited for his reaction.

Jacob nodded. "I understand." He took a deep breath. "I feel like it's important that I tell you I feel terrible that I didn't speak up sooner about my mother keeping Mia at our house. I knew it was wrong. A million times I wanted to tell someone, but then I chickened out. I am so, so sorry."

Wendy nodded and said, "I appreciate your apology, Jacob."

"Sometimes I lie awake at night worrying about her, and I think about all the times I could have stood up to my mom and didn't."

"I'm going to be honest with you, Jacob. If you had called three months ago, I would have hung up on you. Mia's therapist has been helping all of us deal with our anger and loss. Working with her has given me a new perspective. You were a victim too. It helps knowing you had a role in saving Mia. And my husband and I appreciate that you submitted her DNA."

"It was something, anyway." He swallowed. "I could have done it sooner."

"There's no point in beating yourself up over it. We can't go back. Mia is happy and safe now. Everyone deserves a fresh start, don't you think?"

"I sure hope so," he said. Then he added, "Thank you."

When it was time for them to go, Mia gave Jacob a big hug. "You never were my brother, were you?"

"No," he said sadly. "I would have been lucky to have you as a sister, but you were never a Fleming, lucky for you. You belong here with your grandma and grandpa, Mia Duran."

She patted the top of the dog's head. "Thank you for my gift."

Jacob smiled down at her. "Griswold was really yours all along, Mia. He always did love you best."

ACKNOWLEDGMENTS

Many thanks to my early readers for their thoughtful comments and excellent catches. Kay Ehlers, Charlie McQuestion, Michelle San Juan, and Barbara Taylor Sissel—you're the best!

Once again, copyeditor Jessica Fogleman served as both my editor and educator. She has a brilliant mind for details, and every time we work together I'm grateful for her insights. Jessica, I've learned so much from you over the years and was thrilled we could work together again. Per usual, any remaining errors are mine, since I was the source of the trouble to begin with.

A big thank you to early readers MaryAnn Schaefer and Ann Marie McKeon Gruszkowski for catching consistency mistakes. I'm honored that you read the story so carefully and saved me from embarrassment.

Scores of gratitude to Kathi Cauley for taking the time to answer my many questions regarding child protective services. My fictional social worker knew the rules but went a little off script, which happens sometimes in novels. I take the blame for any digressions.

I want to thank my review team (Karen's Cool Kids) for reading this book ahead of time and helping to get the word out. Their encouragement and honest reviews mean so much to me. I feel lucky to have them in my corner.

To my McQuestion home team—Greg, Charlie, Rachel, Maria, Jack, and Boo—I love you all. You keep me sane and happy.

And finally, a shout-out to my readers. You are the reason I write novels. Your support and reviews keep me going, and I hope to never let you down. From the bottom of my heart, thank you.

Made in the USA
Monee, IL
02 January 2022

f3b6738b-23b1-467b-bef1-330178c914baR01